She was halfway down the slope when Huiva screamed. She had learned to react fast. Reining in, Elva snatched loose the gun at her waist. "What is it?"

Huiva cowered on his mount. One hand pointed skyward.

It came down swiftly, quiet in its shimmer of drive fields, a cigar shape which gleamed. Elva holstered her pistol again and took forth her binoculars. An emblem was on the armored prow, a gauntleted hand grasping a planetary orb. Nothing she had ever heard of. But—

Her heart thumped, so loudly that she could almost not hear the Alfavala's squeals of terror. "A spaceship," she breathed. "A spaceship, do you know that word? Like the ships my ancestors came in, long ago...Oh, bother! A big aircraft, Huiva. Come on!"

She whipped her hailu back into gallop. The first spaceship to arrive at Vaynamo in, in, how long? More than a hundred years. And it was landing here! At her own Tervola!

The vessel grounded just beyond the village. Housings opened and auxiliary aircraft darted forth, to hover and swoop. The people, running toward the marvel, surged back as hatches gaped, gangways extruded, armored cars beetled down to the ground.

Elva had not yet reached the village when the strangers opened fire.

Look for these other TOR books by Poul Anderson

Poul Anderson
CONFLICT

TOR

A TOM DOHERTY ASSOCIATES BOOK

CONFLICT

Copyright © 1983 by Poul Anderson

Acknowledgments: The stories published herein were first published and are copyright as follows:
"Time Lag," *The Magazine of Fantasy and Science Fiction,* copyright © 1961 by Mercury Press, Inc.
"High Treason," *Impulse,* copyright © 1966 by Impulse
"Alien Enemy," *Analog,* copyright © 1968 by Davis Publications, Inc.
"The Pugilist," *Fantasy and Science Fiction,* copyright © 1973 by Mercury Press Inc.
"I Tell You It's True," *Nova 2,* copyright © 1972 by Walker and Co.
"Kings Who Die," *Worlds of If,* copyright © 1963 by Digest Productions Corp.
Reprinted in *The 8th Annual of the Year's Best SF,* published by Simon & Schuster, © 1963 by Judith Merril
"A Man to My Wounding," *Ellery Queen's Mystery Magazine,* copyright © 1959 by Davis Publications, Inc.
"Among Thieves," *Astounding Science Fiction,* copyright © 1957 by Street and Smith Publications, Inc.
"Details," *Worlds of If,* copyright © 1956 by Digest Productions Corporation.
"Turning Point," *Worlds of If,* copyright © 1963 by Digest Production Corporation.

A TOR Book

Published by Tom Doherty Associates, 8-10 West 36 Street, New York, N.Y. 10018

Cover art by Kevin Eugene Johnson

First TOR printing: August 1983
Second printing: July 1984

ISBN: 0-812-53088-8
CAN. ED.: 0-812-53089-6

Printed in the United States of America

CONTENTS

TIME LAG

522 Anno Coloniae Conditae:

Elva was on her way back, within sight of home, when the raid came.

For nineteen thirty-hour days, riding in high forests where sunlight slanted through leaves, across ridges where grass and the first red lampflowers rippled under springtime winds, sleeping by night beneath the sky or in the hut of some woodsdweller—once, even, in a nest of Alfavala, where the wild little folk twittered in the dark and their eyes glowed at her— she had been gone. Her original departure was reluctant. Her husband of two years, her child of one, the lake and fields and chimney smoke at dusk which were now hers also, these were still too marvelous to leave.

But the Freeholder of Tervola had duties as well as rights. Once each season, he or his representative must ride circuit. Up into the mountains, through woods and deep dales, across the Lakeland as far as

7

The Troll and then following the Swiftsmoke River south again, the route ran which Karlavi's fathers had traveled for nearly two centuries. Whether on hailu back in spring, summer, through the scarlet and gold of fall, or by motorsled when snow had covered all trails, the Freeholder went out into his lands. Isolated farm clans, forest rangers on patrol duty, hunters and trappers and timber cruisers, brought their disputes to him as magistrate, their troubles to him as leader. Even the flitting Alfavala had learned to wait by the paths, the sick and injured trusting he could heal them, those with more complex problems struggling to put them into human words.

This year, however, Karlavi and his bailiffs were much preoccupied with a new dam across the Oulu. The old one had broken last spring, after a winter of unusually heavy snowfall, and 2000 hectares of bottom land were drowned. The engineers at Yuvaskula, the only city on Vaynamo, had developed a new construction process well adapted to such situations. Karlavi wanted to use this.

"But blast it all," he said, "I'll need every skilled man I have, including myself. The job has got to be finished before the ground dries, so the ferroplast can bond with the soil. And you know what the labor shortage is like around here."

"Who will ride circuit, then?" asked Elva.

"That's what I don't know." Karlavi ran a hand through his straight brown hair. He was a typical Vaynamoan, tall, light-complexioned, with high cheekbones and oblique blue eyes. He wore the working clothes usual to the Tervola district, leather breeches, mukluks, a mackinaw in the tartan of his family. There was nothing romantic about his appearance. Nevertheless, Elva's heart turned over when he looked at her. Even after two years.

He got out his pipe and tamped it with nervous motions. "Somebody must," he said. "Somebody with enough technical education to use a medikit and discuss people's difficulties intelligently. And with authority. We're more tradition-minded hereabouts than they are at Ruuyalka, dear. Our people wouldn't accept the judgment of just anyone. How could a servant or tenant dare settle an argument between two pioneers? It must be me, or a bailiff, or—" His voice trailed off.

Elva caught the implication. "No!" she exclaimed. "I can't! I mean . . . that is—"

"You're my wife," said Karlavi slowly. "That alone gives you the right, by well-established custom. Especially since you're the daughter of the Magnate of Ruuyalka. Almost equivalent to me in prestige, even if you do come from the other end of the continent, where they're fishers and marine farmers instead of woodsfolk." His grin flashed. "I doubt if you've yet learned what awful snobs the free yeomen of Tervola are."

"But Hauki, I can't leave him."

"Hauki will be spoiled rotten in your absence, by an adoring nanny and a villageful of tenant wives. Otherwise he'll do fine." Karlavi dismissed the thought of their son with a wry gesture. "I'm the one who'll get lonesome. Abominably so."

"Oh, darling," said Elva, utterly melted.

A few days later she rode forth.

And it had been an experience to remember. The easy, rocking motion of the six-legged hailu, the mindless leisure of kilometer after kilometer—where the body, though, skin and muscle and blood and all ancient instinct, gained an aliveness such as she had never before felt—the silence of mountains with sunlit ice on their shoulders, then birdsong in the woods and a river brawling; the rough warm hospitality when she stayed overnight with some pioneer, the eldritch welcome at the Alfa nest—she was now glad she had encountered those things, and she hoped to know them again, often.

There had been no danger. The last violence between humans on Vaynamo (apart from occasional fist fights, caused mostly by sheer exuberance and rarely doing any harm) lay a hundred years in the past. As for storms, landslides, flood, wild animals, she had the unobtrusive attendance of Huiva and a dozen other "tame" Alfavala. Even these, the intellectual pick of their species, who had chosen to serve man in a doglike fashion rather than keep to the forests, could only speak a few words and handle the simplest tools. But their long ears, flat nostrils, feathery antennae, every fine green hair on every small body, were always aquiver. This was their planet, they had evolved here, and they were more animal than rational beings. Their senses and reflexes kept her safer than an armored aircraft might.

All the same, the absence of Karlavi and Hauki grew sharper each day. When finally she came to the edge of cleared land, high on the slopes of Hornback Fell, and saw Tervola below, a blindness that stung descended momentarily on her eyes.

Huiva guided his hailu alongside her. He pointed down the mountain with his tail. "Home," he chattered. "Food tonight. Snug bed."

"Yes." Elva blinked hard. *What sort of crybaby am I, anyhow?* she asked herself, half in anger. *I'm the Magnate's daughter and the Freeholder's wife, I have a University degree and a pistol-shooting medal, as a girl I sailed through hurricanes and skindove into grottos where fangfish laired, as a woman I brought a son into the world . . . I will not bawl!*

"Yes," she said. "Let's hurry."

She thumped heels on the hailu's ribs and started downhill at a gallop. Her long yellow hair was braided, but a lock of it broke loose, fluttering behind her. Hoofs rang on stone. Ahead stretched grainfields and pastures, still wet from winter but their shy green deepening toward summer hues, on down to the great metallic sheet of Lake Rovaniemi and then across the valley to the opposite horizon, where the High Mikkela reared into a sky as tall and blue as itself. Down by the lake clustered the village, the dear red tile of roofs, the curve of a processing plant, a road lined with trees leading to the Freeholder's mansion. There, old hand-hewn timbers glowed with sun; the many windows flung the light dazzlingly back to her.

She was halfway down the slope when Huiva screamed. She had learned to react fast. Thinly scattered across all Vaynamo, men could easily die from the unforseen. Reining in, Elva snatched loose the gun at her waist. "What is it?"

Huiva cowered on his mount. One hand pointed skyward.

At first Elva could not understand. An aircraft descending above the lake . . . what was so odd about that? How else did Huiva expect the inhabitants of settlements hundreds of kilometers apart to visit each other?—And then she registered the shape. And then, realizing the distance, she knew the size of the thing.

It came down swiftly, quiet in its shimmer of drive fields, a cigar shape which gleamed. Elva holstered her pistol again and took forth her binoculars. Now she could see how the sleekness was interrupted with turrets and boat housings, cargo locks, viewports. An emblem was on the armored prow, a gauntleted hand grasping a planetary orb. Nothing she had ever heard of. But—

Her heart thumped, so loudly that she could almost not hear the Alfavala's squeals of terror. "A spaceship," she breathed. "A spaceship, do you know that word? Like the ships my ancestors came in, long ago. . . . Oh, bother! A big aircraft, Huiva. Come on!"

She whipped her hailu back into gallop. The first spaceship to arrive at Vaynamo in, in, how long? More than a hundred years. And it was landing here! At her own Tervola!

The vessel grounded just beyond the village. Its enormous mass settled deeply into the plowland. Housings opened and auxiliary aircraft darted forth, to hover and swoop. They were of a curious design,

larger and blunter than the fliers built on Vaynamo.
The people, running toward the marvel, surged back
as hatches gaped, gangways extruded, armored cars
beetled down to the ground.

Elva had not yet reached the village when the
strangers opened fire.

There were no hostile ships, not even an orbital
fortress. To depart, the seven craft from Chertkoi simply made rendezvous beyond the atmosphere, held a
short gleeful conference by radio, and accelerated
outward. Captain Bors Golyev, commanding the flotilla,
stood on the bridge of the *Askol* and watched the
others. The light of the yellow sun lay incandescent on
their flanks. Beyond reached blackness and the many
stars.

His gaze wandered off among constellations which
the parallax of fifteen light-years had not much altered.
The galaxy was so big, he thought, so unimaginably
enormous. . . . Sedes Regis was an L scrawled across
heaven. Tradition claimed Old Sol lay in that direction,
a thousand parsecs away. But no one on Chertkoi was
certain any longer. Golyev shrugged. Who cared?

"Gravitational field suitable for agoric drive, sir,"
intoned the pilot.

Golyev looked in the sternward screen. The planet
called Vaynamo had dwindled, but remained a vivid
shield, barred with cloud and blazoned with continents,
the overall color a cool blue-green. He thought of
ocherous Chertkoi, and the other planets of its system,
which were not even habitable. Vaynamo was the
most beautiful color he had ever seen. The two small
moons were also visible, like drops of liquid gold.

Automatically, his astronaut's eye checked the claims
of the instruments. Was Vaynamo really far enough
away for the ships to go safely into agoric? Not quite,
he thought—no, wait, he'd forgotten that the planet
had a five percent greater diameter than Chertkoi.
"Very good," he said, and gave the necessary orders to

his subordinate captains. A deep hum filled air and metal and bones. There was a momentary sense of falling, as the agoratron went into action. And then the stars began to change color and crawl weirdly across the visual field.

"All's well, sir," said the pilot. The chief engineer confirmed it over the intercom.

"Very good," repeated Golyev. He yawned and stretched elaborately. "I'm tired! That was quite a little fight we had at that last village, and I've gotten no sleep since. I'll be in my cabin. Call me if anything seems amiss."

"Yes, sir." The pilot smothered a knowing leer.

Golyev walked down the corridor, his feet slamming its metal under internal pseudogravity. Once or twice he met a crewman and accepted a salute as casually as it was given. The men of the Interplanetary Corporation didn't need to stand on ceremony. They were tried spacemen and fighters, every one of them. If they chose to wear sloppy uniforms, to lounge about off duty cracking jokes or cracking a bottle, to treat their officers as friends rather than tyrants — so much the better. This wasn't the nicenelly Surface Transport Corporation, or the spit-and-polish chemical Synthesis Trust, but IP, explorer and conqueror. The ship was clean and the guns were ready. What more did you want?

Pravoyats, the captain's batman, stood outside the cabin door. He nursed a scratched cheek and a black eye. One hand rested broodingly on his sidearm. "Trouble?" inquired Golyev.

"Trouble ain't the word, sir."

"You didn't hurt her, did you?" asked Golyev sharply.

"No, sir, I heard your orders all right. Never laid a finger on her in anger. But she sure did on me. Finally I wrassled her down and gave her a whiff of sleepy gas. She'd'a torn the cabin apart otherwise. She's prob'ly come out of it by now, but I'd rather not go in again to see, captain."

Golyev laughed. He was a big man, looming over Pravoyats, who was no midget. Otherwise he was a normal patron-class Chertkoian, powerfully built, with comparatively short legs and strutting gait, his features dark, snubnosed, bearded, carrying more than his share of old scars. He wore a plain green tunic, pants tucked into soft boots, gun at hip, his only sign of rank a crimson star at his throat. "I'll take care of all that from here on," he said.

"Yes, sir." Despite his wounds, the batman looked a shade envious. "Uh, you want the prod? I tell you, she's a troublemaker."

"No."

"Electric shocks don't leave any scars, captain."

"I know. But on your way, Pravoyats." Golyev opened the door, went through, and closed it behind him again.

The girl had been seated on his bunk. She stood up with a gasp. A looker, for certain. The Vaynamoan women generally seemed handsome; this one was beautiful, tall and slim, delicate face and straight nose lightly dusted with freckles. But her mouth was wide and strong, her skin suntanned, and she wore a coarse, colorful riding habit. Her exoticism was the most exciting thing: yellow hair, slant blue eyes, who'd ever heard of the like?

The tranquilizing after-effects of the gas—or else plain nervous exhaustion—kept her from attacking him. She backed against the wall and shivered. Her misery touched Golyev a little. He'd seen unhappiness elsewhere, on Imfan and Novagal and Chertkoi itself, and hadn't been bothered thereby. People who were too weak to defend themselves must expect to be made booty of. It was different, though, when someone as good-looking as this was so woebegone.

He paused on the opposite side of his desk from her, gave a soft salute, and smiled. "What's your name, my dear?"

She drew a shaken breath. After trying several times,

she managed to speak. "I didn't think . . . anyone . . . understood my language."

"A few of us do. The hypnopede, you know." Evidently she did not know. He thought a short, dry lecture might soothe her. "An invention made a few decades ago on our planet. Suppose another person and I have no language in common. We can be given a drug to accelerate our nervous systems, and then the machine flashes images on a screen and analyzes the sounds uttered by the other person. What it hears is transferred to me and impressed on the speech center of my brain, electronically. As the vocabulary grows, a computer in the machine figures out the structure of the whole language—semantics, grammar, and so on—and orders my own learning accordingly. That way, a few short, daily sessions make me fluent."

She touched her lips with a tongue that seemed equally parched. "I heard once . . . of some experiments at the University," she whispered. "They never got far. No reason for such a machine. Only one language on Vaynamo."

"And on Chertkoi. But we've already subjugated two other planets, one of 'em divided into hundreds of language groups. And we expect there'll be others." Golyev opened a drawer, took out a bottle and two glasses. "Care for brandy?"

He poured. "I'm Bors Golyev, an astronautical executive of the Interplanetary Corporation, commanding this scout force," he said. "Who are you?"

She didn't answer. He reached a glass toward her. "Come, now," he said, "I'm not such a bad fellow. Here, drink. To our better acquaintance."

With a convulsive movement, she struck the glass from his hand. It bounced on the floor. "Almighty Creator! No!" she yelled. "You murdered my husband!"

She stumbled to a chair, fell down in it, rested head in arms on the desk and began to weep. The spilled brandy crept across the floor toward her.

Golyev groaned. Why did he always get cases like

this? Glebs Narov, now, had clapped hands on the jolliest tawny wench you could imagine, when they conquered Marsya on Imfan: delighted to be liberated from her own drab culture.

Well, he could kick this female back down among the other prisoners. But he didn't want to. He seated himself across from her, lit a cigar out of the box on his desk, and held his own glass to the light. Ruby smoldered within.

"I'm sorry," he said. "How was I to know? What's done is done. There wouldn't have been so many casualties if they'd been sensible and given up. We shot a few to prove we meant business, but then called on the rest over a loudspeaker, to yield. They didn't. For that matter, you were riding a six-legged animal out of the fields, I'm told. You came busting right *into* the fight. Why didn't you ride the other way and hide out till we left?"

"My husband was there," she said after a silence. When she raised her face, he saw it gone cold and stiff. "And our child."

"Oh? Uh, maybe we picked up the kid, at least. If you'd like to go see—"

"No," she said, toneless and yet somehow with a dim returning pride. "I got Hauki away. I rode straight to the mansion and got him. Then one of your fire-guns hit the roof and the house began to burn. I told Huiva to take the baby—never mind where. I said I'd follow if I could. But Karlavi was out there, fighting. I went back to the barricade. He had been killed just a few seconds before. His face was all bloody. Then your cars broke through the barricade and someone caught me. But you don't have Hauki. Or Karlavi!"

As if drained by the effort of speech, she slumped and stared into a corner, empty-eyed.

"Well," said Golyev, not quite comfortably, "your people had been warned." She didn't seem to hear him. "You never got the message? But it was telecast over your whole planet. After our first non-secret landing. That was several days ago. Were you out in the woods or something? — Yes, we scouted telescopically, and made clandestine landings, and caught a few citizens to interrogate. But when we understood the situation, more or less, we landed openly in, uh, your city. Yuvaskula, is that the name? We seized it without too much damage, captured some officials of the planetary government, claimed the planet for IP and called on all citizens to cooperate. But they wouldn't! Why, one ambush alone cost us fifty good men. What could we do? We had to teach a lesson. We announced we'd punish a few random villages. That's more humane than bombarding from space with cobalt missiles. Isn't it? But I suppose your people didn't really believe us, the way they came swarming when we landed. Trying to parley with us first, and then trying to resist us with hunting rifles! What would you expect to happen?"

His voice seemed to fall into an echoless well.

He loosened his collar, which felt a trifle tight, took a deep drag on his cigar and refilled his glass. "Of course, I don't expect you to see our side of it at once," he said reasonably. "You've been jogging along, isolated, for centuries, haven't you? Hardly a spaceship has touched at your planet since it was first colonized. You have none of your own, except a couple of interplanetary boats which hardly ever get used. That's what your President told me, and I believe him. Why should you go outsystem? You have everything you can use, right on your own world. The nearest sun to yours with an oxygen atmosphere planet is three parsecs off. Even with a very high-powered agoratron, you'd need ten years to get there, another decade to get back. A whole generation! Sure, the time-contraction effect would keep you young — ship's time for the voyage would only be a few weeks, or less — but all your friends would be middle-aged when you came home. Believe me, it's lonely being a spaceman."

He drank. A pleasant burning went down his throat.

"No wonder men spread so slowly into space, and each colony is so isolated," he said. "Chertkoi is a mere name in your archives. And yet it's only fifteen light-years from Vaynamo. You can see our sun on any clear night. A reddish one. You call it Gamma Navarchi. Fifteen little light-years, and yet there's been no contact between our two planets for four centuries or more!

"So why now? Well, that's a long story. Let's just say Chertkoi isn't as friendly a world as Vaynamo. You'll see that for yourself. We, our ancestors, we came up the hard way, we had to struggle for everything. And now there are four billion of us! That was the census figure when I left. It'll probably be five billion when I get home. We have to have more resources. Our economy is grinding to a halt. And we can't afford economic dislocation. Not on as thin a margin as Chertkoi allows us. First we went back to the other planets of our system and worked them as much as practicable. Then we started re-exploring the nearer stars. So far we've found two useful planets. Yours is the third. You know what your population is? Ten million, your President claimed. Ten million people for a whole world of forests, plains, hills, oceans . . . why, your least continent has more natural resources than all Chertkoi. And you've stabilized at that population. You don't want more people!"

Golyev struck the desk with a thumb. "If you think ten million stagnant agriculturists have a right to monopolize all that room and wealth, when four billion Chertkoians live on the verge of starvation," he said indignantly, "you can think again."

She stirred. Not looking at him, her tone small and very distant, she said, "It's our planet, to do with as we please. If you want to breed like maggots, you must take the consequences."

Anger flushed the last sympathy from Golyev. He ground out his cigar in the ashwell and tossed off his brandy. "Never mind moralizing," he said. "I'm no martyr. I became a spaceman because it's fun."

He got up and walked around the desk to her.

538 A.C.C.:

When she couldn't stand the apartment any more, Elva went out on the balcony and looked across Dirzh until that view became unendurable in its turn.

From this height, the city had a certain grandeur. On every side it stretched horizonward, immense gray blocks among which rose an occasional spire shining with steel and glass. Eastward at the very edge of vision it ended before some mine pits, whose scaffolding and chimneys did not entirely cage off a glimpse of primordial painted desert. Between the buildings went a network of elevated trafficways, some carrying robofreight, others pullulating with gray-clad clients on foot. Overhead, against a purple-black sky and the planet's single huge moon, nearly full tonight, flitted the firefly aircars of executives, engineers, military techs, and others in the patron class. A few stars were visible, but the fever-flash of neon drowned most of them. Even by full red-tinged daylight, Elva could never see all the way downward. A fog of dust, smoke, fumes and vapors hid the bottom of the artificial mountains. She could only imagine the underground, caves and tunnels where workers of the lowest category were bred to spend their lives tending machines, and where a criminal class slunk about in armed packs.

It was rarely warm on Chertkoi, summer or winter. As the night wind gusted, Elva drew more tightly around her a mantle of genuine fur from Novagal. Bors wasn't stingy about clothes or jewels. But then, he liked to take her out in public places, where she could be admired and he envied. For the first few months she had refused to leave the apartment. He hadn't made an issue of it, only waited. In the end she gave in. Nowadays she looked forward eagerly to such times; they took her away from these walls. But of late there had been no celebrations. Bors was working too hard.

The moon Drogoi climbed higher, reddened by the hidden sun and the lower atmosphere of the city. At the zenith it would be pale copper. Once Elva had fancied the markings on it formed a death's head. They didn't really; that had just been her horror of everything Chertkoian. But she had never shaken off the impression.

She hunted among the constellations, knowing that if she found Vaynamo's sun it would hurt, but unable to stop. The air was too thick tonight, though, with an odor of acid and rotten eggs. She remembered riding out along Lake Rovaniemi, soon after her marriage. Karlavi was along: no one else, for you didn't need a bodyguard on Vaynamo. The two moons climbed fast. Their light made a trembling double bridge on the water. Trees rustled, the air smelled green, something sang with a liquid plangency, far off among moon-dappled shadows.

"But that's beautiful!" she whispered. "Yonder songbird. We haven't anything like it in Ruuyalka."

Karlavi chuckled. "No bird at all. The Alfavala name—well, who can pronounce that? We humans say 'yanno.' A little pseudomammal, a terrible pest. Roots up tubers. For a while we thought we'd have to wipe out the species."

"But they sing so sweetly."

"True. Also, the Alfavala would be hurt. Insofar as they have anything like a religion, the yanno seems to be part of it, locally. Important to them somehow, at least." Unspoken was the law under which she and he had both been raised: The green dwarfs are barely where man was two or three million years ago on Old Earth, but they are the real natives of Vaynamo, and if we share their planet, we're bound to respect them and help them.

Once Elva had tried to explain the idea to Bors

Golyev. He couldn't understand at all. If the abos occupied land men might use, why not hunt them off it? They'd make good, crafty game, wouldn't they?

"Can anything be done about the yanno?" she asked Karlavi.

"For several generations, we fooled around with electric fences and so on. But just a few years ago, I consulted Paaska Ecological Institute and found they'd developed a wholly new approach to such problems. They can now tailor a dominant mutant gene which produces a strong distaste for Vitamin C. I suppose you know Vitamin C isn't part of native biochemistry, but occurs only in plants of Terrestrial origin. We released the mutants to breed, and every season there are fewer yanno that'll touch our crops. In another five years there'll be too few to matter."

"And they'll still sing for us." She edged her hailu closer to his. Their knees touched. He leaned over and kissed her.

Elva shivered. *I'd better go in,* she thought.

The light switched on automatically as she re-entered the living room. At least artificial illumination on Chertkoi was like home. Dwelling under different suns had not yet changed human eyes. Though in other respects, man's colonies had drifted far apart indeed. . . . The apartment had three cramped rooms, which was considered luxurious. When five billion people, more every day, grubbed their living from a planet as bleak as this, even the wealthy must do without things that were the natural right of the poorest Vaynamoan — spaciousness, trees, grass beneath bare feet, your own house and an open sky. Of course, Chertkoi had very sophisticated amusements to offer in exchange, everything from multisensory films to live combats.

Belgoya pattered in from her offside cubicle. Elva wondered if the maidservant ever slept. "Does the mistress wish anything, please?"

"No." Elva sat down. She ought to be used to the gravity by now, she thought. How long had she been here? A year, more or less. She hadn't kept track of time, especially when they used an unfamiliar calendar. Denser than Vaynamo, Chertkoi exerted a ten percent greater surface pull; but that wasn't enough to matter, when you were in good physical condition. Yet she was always tired.

"No, I don't want anything." She leaned back on the couch and rubbed her eyes. The haze outside had made them sting.

"A cup of stim, perhaps, if the mistress please?" The girl bowed some more, absurdly doll-like in her uniform.

"No!" Elva shouted. "Go away!"

"I beg your pardon. I am a worm. I implore your magnanimity." Terrified, the maid crawled backward out of the room on her belly.

Elva lit a cigaret. She hadn't smoked on Vaynamo, but since coming here she'd take it up, become a chainsmoker like most Chertkoians who could afford it. You needed something to do with your hands. The servility of clients toward patrons no longer shocked her, but rather made her think of them as faintly slimy. To be sure, one could see the reasons. Belgoya, for instance, could be fired any time and sent back to the street level. Down there were a million eager applicants for her position. Elva forgot her and reached after the teleshow dials. Something must be on, loud and full of action, something to watch, something to do with her evening.

The door opened. Elva turned about, tense with expectation. So Bors was home. And alone. If he'd brought a friend along, she would have had to go into the sleeping cubicle and merely listen. Upper-class Chertkoians didn't like women intruding on their conversation. But Bors alone meant she would have someone to talk to.

He came in, his tread showing he was also tired. He skimmed his hat into a corner and dropped his cloak on the floor. Belgoya crept forth to pick them up. As he sat down, she was there with a drink and a cigar.

Elva waited. She knew his moods. When the blunt, bearded face had lost some of its hardness, she donned a smile and stretched herself along the couch, leaning on one elbow. "You've been working yourself to death," she scolded.

He sighed. "Yeh. But the end's in view. Another week, and all the damn paperwork will be cleared up."

"You hope. One of your bureaucrats will probably invent nineteen more forms to fill out in quadruplicate."

"Probably."

"We never had that trouble at home. The planetary government was only a coordinating body with strictly limited powers. Why won't you people even consider establishing something similar?"

"You know the reasons. Five billion of them. You've got room to be an individual on Vaynamo." Golyev finished his drink and held the glass out for a refill. "By all chaos! I'm tempted to desert when we get there."

Elva lifted her brows. "That's a thought," she purred.

"Oh, you know it's impossible," he said, returning to his usual humorlessness. "Quite apart from the fact I'd be one enemy alien on an entire planet—"

"Not necessarily."

"—All right, even if I got naturalized (and who wants to become a clodhopper?) I'd have only thirty years till the Third Expedition came. I don't want to be a client in my old age. Or worse, see my children made clients."

Elva lit a second cigaret from the stub of the first. She drew in the smoke hard enough to hollow her cheeks.

But it's fine to launch the Second Expedition and make clients of others, she thought. *The First, that captured me and a thousand more. (What's become of them? How many are dead, how many found useless and sent lobotomized to the mines, how many are still being pumped dry of information?) . . . that was a mere scouting trip. The Second will have fifty warships, and try to force surrender. At the very least, it will flatten all possible defenses, destroy all imaginable war potential, bring back a whole herd of slaves. And then the Third, a thousand ships or more, will bring the final conquest, the garrisons, the overseers and entrepreneurs and colonists. But that won't be for forty-five years or better from tonight. A man on Vaynamo . . . Hauki . . . a man who survives the coming of the Second Expedition will have thirty-odd years left in which to be free. But will he dare have children?*

"I'll settle down there after the Third Expedition, I think," Golyev admitted. "From what I saw of the planet last time, I believe I'd like it. And the opportunities are unlimited. A whole world waiting to be properly developed!"

"I could show you a great many chances you'd otherwise overlook," insinuated Elva.

Golyev shifted position. "Let's not go into that again," he said. "You know I can't take you along."

"You're the fleet commander, aren't you?"

"Yes, I will be, but curse it, can't you understand? The IP is not like any other corporation. We use men who think and act on their own, not planet-hugging morons like what's-her-name—" he jerked a thumb at Belgoya, who lowered her eyes meekly and continued mixing him a third drink. "Men of patron status, younger sons of executives and engineers. The officers can't have special privileges. It'd ruin morale."

Elva fluttered her lashes. "Not that much. Really."

"My oldest boy's promised to take care of you. He's not such a bad fellow as you seem to think. You only have to go along with his whims. I'll see you again, in thirty years."

"When I'm gray and wrinkled. Why not kick me out in the street and be done?"

"You know why," he said ferociously. "You're the first woman I could ever talk to. No, I'm not bored with you! But—"

"If you really cared for me—"

"What kind of idiot do you take me for? I know you're planning to sneak away to your own people, once we've landed."

Elva tossed her head, haughtily. "Well! If you believe that of me, there's nothing more to say."

"Aw, now, sweetling, don't take that attitude." He reached out a hand to lay on her arm. She withdrew to the far end of the couch. He looked baffled.

"Another thing," he argued. "If you care about your planet at all, as I suppose you do, even if you've now seen what a bunch of petrified mudsuckers they are . . . remember, what we'll have to do there won't be pretty."

"First you call me a traitor," she flared, "and now you say I'm gutless!"

"Hoy, wait a minute—"

"Go on, beat me. I can't stop you. You're brave enough for that."

"I never—"

In the end, he yielded.

553 A.C.C.:

The missile which landed on Yuvaskula had a ten-kilometer radius of total destruction. Thus most of the city went up in one radioactive fire-gout. In a way, the thought of men and women and little children with pet kittens, incinerated, made a trifle less pain in Elva than knowing the Old Town was gone: the cabin raised by the first men to land on Vaynamo, the ancient church of St. Yarvi with its stained-glass windows and gilded belltower, the Museum of Art where she went as a girl on entranced visits, the University where she studied and where she met Karlavi—*I'm a true daughter of Vaynamo*, she thought with remorse. *Whatever is traditional, full of memories, whatever has been looked at and been done by all the generations before me, I hold dear. The Chertkoians don't care. They haven't any past worth remembering.*

Flames painted the northern sky red, even at this distance, as she walked among the plastishelters of the advanced base. She had flown within a hundred kilometers, using an aircar borrowed from the flagship, then landed to avoid possible missiles and hitched a ride here on a supply truck. The Chertkoian enlisted men aboard had been delighted until she showed them her pass, signed by Commander Golyev himself. Then they became cringingly respectful.

The pass was only supposed to let her move freely about in the rear areas, and she'd had enough trouble wheedling it from Bors. But no one thereafter looked closely at it. She herself was so unused to the concept of war that she didn't stop to wonder at such lax security measures. Had she done so, she would have realized Chertkoi had never developed anything better, never having faced an enemy of comparable strength. Vaynamo certainly wasn't, even though the planet was proving a hardshelled opponent, with every farmhouse a potential arsenal and every forest road a possible death trap. Guerrilla fighters hindered the movements of an invader with armor, atomic artillery, complete control of air and space; they could not stop him.

Elva drew her dark mantle more tightly about her and crouched under a gun emplacement. A sentry went by, his helmet square against the beloved familiar face of a moon, his rifle aslant across the stars. She didn't want needless questioning. For a moment the distant blaze sprang higher, unrestful ruddy light touched her, she was afraid she had been observed. But the man continued his round.

From the air she had seen that the fire was mostly a burning forest, kindled from Yuvaskula. Those wooden houses not blown apart by the missile stood unharmed in the whitest glow. Some process must have been developed at one of the research institutes, for indurating timber, since she left. . . . How Bors would laugh if she told him. An industry which turned out a bare minimum of vehicles, farm machinery, tools, chemicals; a science which developed fireproofing techniques and traced out ecological chains; a population which deliberately held itself static, so as to preserve its old customs and laws — presuming to make war on Chertkoi!

Even so, he was too experienced a fighter to dismiss any foe as weak without careful examination. He had been excited enough about one thing to mention it to Elva — a prisoner taken in a skirmish near Yuvaskula, when he still hoped to capture the city intact: an officer, who cracked just enough under interrogation to indicate he knew something important. But Golyev couldn't wait around for the inquisitors to finish their work. He must go out the very next day to oversee the battle for Lempo Machine Tool Works, and Elva knew he wouldn't return soon. The plant had been constructed underground as an economy measure, and to preserve the green parkscape above. Now its concrete warrens proved highly defensible, and were being bitterly contested. The Chertkoians meant to seize it, so they could be sure of demolishing everything. They would not leave Vaynamo any nucleus of industry. After all, the planet would have thirty-odd years to recover and rearm itself against the Third Expedition.

Left alone by Bors, Elva took an aircar and slipped off to the advanced base.

She recognized the plastishelter she wanted by its Intelligence insignia. The guard outside aimed a rifle at her. "Halt!" His boyish voice cracked over with nervousness. More than one sentry had been found in the morning with his throat cut.

"It's all right," she told him. "I'm to see the prisoner Ivalo."

"The gooze officer?" He flashed a pencil-thin beam across her face. "But you're a — uh — "

"A Vaynamoan myself. Of course. There are a few of us along, you know. Prisoners taken last time, who've enlisted in your cause as guides and spies. You must have heard of me. I'm Elva, Commander Golyev's lady."

"Oh. Yes, mistress. Sure I have."

"Here's my pass."

He squinted at it uneasily. "But, uh, may I ask what, uh, what *you* figure to do? I've got strict orders—"

Elva gave him her most confidential smile. "My own patron had the idea. The prisoner is withholding valuable information. He has been treated roughly, but resisted. Now, all at once, we'll take the pressure off. An attractive woman of his own race . . . "

"I get it. Maybe he will crack. I dunno, though, mistress. These slant-eyed towheads are mean animals —begging your pardon! Go right on in. Holler if he gets rough or, or anything."

The door was unlocked for her. Elva went on through, into a hemicylindrical room so low that she must stoop. A lighting tube switched on, showing a pallet laid across the floor.

Captain Ivalo was gray at the temples, but still tough and supple. His face had gone haggard, sunken eyes and a stubble of beard; his garments were torn and filthy. When he looked up, coming awake, he was too exhausted to show much surprise. "What now?" he said in dull Chertkoian. "What are you going to try next?"

Elva answered in Vaynamoan (oh, God, it was a year and a half, her own time, nearly seventeen years cosmic time, since she had uttered a word to anyone from her planet): "Be quiet. I beg you. We mustn't be suspected."

He sat up. "Who are you?" he snapped. His own Vaynamoan accent was faintly pedantic; he must be a teacher or scientist in that peacetime life which now seemed so distant. "A collaborator? I understand there are some. Every barrel must hold a few rotten apples, I suppose."

She sat down on the floor near him, hugged her knees and stared at the curving wall. "I don't know what to call myself," she said tonelessly. "I'm with them, yes. But they captured me the last time."

He whistled, a soft note. One hand reached out, not altogether steady, and stopped short of touching her. "I was young then," he said. "But I remember. Do I know your family?"

"Maybe. I'm Elva, daughter of Byarmo, the Magnate of Ruuyalka. My husband was Karlavi, the Freeholder of Tervola." Suddenly she couldn't stay controlled. She grasped his arm so hard that her nails drew blood. "Do you know what became of my son? His name was Hauki. I got him away, in care of an Alfa servant. Hauki, Karlavi's son, Freeholder of Tervola. Do you know?"

He disengaged himself as gently as possible and shook his head. "I'm sorry. I've heard of both places, but only as names. I'm from the Aakinen Islands myself."

Her head drooped.

"Ivalo is my name," he said clumsily.

"I know."

"What?"

"Listen." She raised her eyes to him. They were quite dry. "I've been told you have important information."

He bridled. "If you think—"

"No. Please listen. Here." She fumbled in a pocket of her gown. At last her fingers closed on the vial. She held it out to him. "An antiseptic. But the label says it's very poisonous if taken internally. I brought it for you."

He stared at her for a long while.

"It's all I can do," she mumbled, looking away again.

He took the bottle and turned it over and over in his hands. The night grew silent around them.

Finally he asked, "Won't you suffer for this?"

"Not too much."

"Wait. . . . If you could get in here, you can surely escape completely. Our troops can't be far off. Or any farmer hereabouts will hide you."

She shook her head. "No. I'll stay with them. Maybe I can help in some other small way. What else has there been to keep me alive, but the hope of—It wouldn't be any better, living here, if we're all conquered. There's to be a final attack, three decades hence. Do you know that?"

"Yes. Our side takes prisoners too, and quizzes them. The first episode puzzled us. Many thought it had only been a raid by—what's the word?—by pirates. But now we know they really do intend to take our planet away."

"You must have developed some good linguists," she said, seeking impersonality. "To be able to talk with your prisoners. Of course, you yourself, after capture, could be educated by the hypnopede."

"The what?"

"The language-teaching machine."

"Oh, yes, the enemy do have them, don't they? But we do too. After the first raid, those who thought there was a danger the aliens might come back set about developing such machines. I knew Chertkoian weeks before my own capture."

"I wish I could help you escape," she said dully. "But I don't know how. That bottle is all I can do. Isn't it?"

"Yes." He regarded the thing with a fascination.

"My patron—Golyev himself—said his men would rip you open to get your knowledge. So I thought—"

"You're very kind." Ivalo grimaced, as if he had tasted something foul. "But your act may turn out pointless. I don't know anything useful. I wasn't even sworn to secrecy about what I do know. Why've I held out, then? Don't ask me. Stubbornness. Anger. Or just hating to admit that my people—our people, damn it!—that they could be so weak and foolish."

"What?" Her glance jerked up to him.

"They could win the war at a stroke," he said. "They won't. They'd rather die, and let their children be enslaved by the Third Expedition."

"What do you mean?" She crouched to hands and knees, bowstring-tense.

He shrugged. "I told you, a number of people on Vaynamo took the previous invasion at its word, that it was the vanguard of a conquering army. There was no official action. How could there be, with a government as feeble as ours? But some of the research biologists—"

"Not a plague!"

"Yes. Mutated from the local coryzoid virus. Incubation period, approximately one month, during which time it's contagious. Vaccination is still effective two weeks after exposure, so all our people could be safeguarded. But the Chertkoians would take the disease back with them. Estimated deaths, ninety percent of the race."

"But—"

"That's where the government did step in," he said with bitterness. "The information was suppressed. The virus cultures were destroyed. The theory was, even to save ourselves we couldn't do such a thing."

Elva felt the tautness leave her. She sagged. She had seen small children on Chertkoi too.

"They're right, of course," she said wearily.

"Perhaps. Perhaps. And yet we'll be overrun and butchered, or reduced to serfdom. Won't we? Our forests will be cut down, our mines gutted, our poor Alfavala exterminated. . . . To hell with it." Ivalo gazed at the poison vial. "I don't have any scientific data, I'm not a virologist. It can't do any military harm to tell the Chertkoians. But I've seen what they've done to us. I would give them the sickness."

"I wouldn't." Elva bit her lip.

He regarded her for a long time. "Won't you escape? Never mind being a planetary heroine. There's nothing you can do. The invaders will go home when they've wrecked all our industry. They won't come again for thirty years. You can be free most of your life."

"You forget," she said, "that if I leave with them,

and come back, the time for me will only have been one or two years." She sighed. "I can't help make ready for the next battle. I'm just a woman. Untrained. While maybe . . . oh, if nothing else, there'll be more Vaynamoan prisoners brought to Chertkoi. I have a tiny bit of influence. Maybe I can help them."

Ivalo considered the poison. "I was about to use this anyway," he muttered. "I didn't think staying alive was worth the trouble. But now—if you can—No." He gave the vial back to her. "I thank you, my lady."

"I have an idea," she said, with a hint of color in her voice. "Go ahead and tell them what you know. Pretend I talked you into it. Then I might be able to get you exchanged. It's barely possible."

"Oh, perhaps," he said, not believing. "I'll try."

She rose to go. "If you are set free," she stammered, "will you make a visit to Tervola? Will you find Hauki, Karlavi's son, and tell him you saw me? If he's alive."

569 A.C.C.:

Dirzh had changed while the ships were away. The evolution continued after their return. The city grew bigger, smokier, uglier. More people each year dropped from client status, went underground and joined the gangs. Occasionally, these days, the noise and vibration of pitched battles down in the tunnels could be detected up on patron level. The desert could no longer be seen, even from the highest towers, only the abandoned mine and the slag mountains, in process of conversion to tenements. The carcinogenic murkiness crept upward until it could be smelled on the most elite balconies. Teleshows got noisier and nakeder, to compete with live performances, which were now offering more elaborate bloodlettings than old-fashioned combats. The news from space was of a revolt suppressed on Novagal, resulting in such an acute labor shortage that workers were drafted from Imfan and shipped thither.

Only when you looked at the zenith was there no apparent change. The daylit sky was still cold purplish-blue, with an occasional yellow dustcloud. At night there were still the stars, and a skull.

And yet, thought Elva, you wouldn't need a large telescope to see the Third Expedition fleet in orbit—eleven hundred spacecraft, the unarmed ones loaded with troops and equipment, nearly the whole strength of Chertkoi marshaling to conquer Vaynamo. Campaigning across interstellar distances wasn't easy. You couldn't send home for supplies or reinforcements. You broke the enemy or he broke you. Fleet Admiral Bors Golyev did not intend to be broken.

He did not even plan to go home with news of a successful probing operation or a successful raid. The Third Expedition was to be final. And he must allow for the Vaynamoans having had a generation in which to recuperate. He'd smashed their heavy industry, but if they were really determined, they could have rebuilt. No doubt a space fleet of some kind would be waiting to oppose him.

He knew it couldn't be of comparable power. Ten million people, forced to recreate all their mines and furnaces and factories before they could lay the keel of a single boat, had no possibility of matching the concerted efforts of six and a half billion whose world had been continuously industrialized for centuries, and who could draw on the resources of two subject planets. Sheer mathematics ruled it out. But the ten million could accomplish something; and nuclear-fusion missiles were to some degree an equalizer. Therefore Bors Golyev asked for so much strength that the greatest conceivable enemy force would be swamped. And he got it.

Elva leaned on the balcony rail. A chill wind fluttered her gown around her, so that the rainbow hues rippled and ran into each other. She had to admit the fabric was lovely. Bors tried hard to please her. (Though why must he mention the price?) He was so childishly happy himself, at his accomplishments, at his new eminence, at the eight-room apartment which he now rated on the very heights of the Lebedan Tower.

"Not that we'll be here long," he had said, after they first explored its intricacies. "My son Nivko has done good work in the home office. That's how come I got this command; experience alone wasn't enough. Of course, he'll expect me to help along his sons. . . . But anyhow, the Third Expedition can go even sooner than I'd hoped. Just a few months, and we're on our way."

"We?" murmured Elva.

"You do want to come, don't you?"

"The last voyage, you weren't so eager."

"Uh, yes. I did have a deuce of a time, too, getting you aboard. But this'll be different. First, I've got so much rank I'm beyond criticism, even beyond jealousy. And second, well, you count too. You're not any picked-up native female. You're Elva! The girl who on her own hook got that fellow Ivalo to confess."

She turned her head slightly, regarding him sideways from droop-lidded blue eyes. Under the ruddy sun, her hair turned to raw gold. "I should think the news would have alarmed them, here on Chertkoi," she said. "Being told that they nearly brought their own extinction about. I wonder that they dare launch another attack."

Golyev grinned. "You should have heard the ruckus. Some Directors did vote to keep hands off Vaynamo. Others wanted to sterilize the whole planet with cobalt missiles. But I talked 'em around. Once we've beaten the fleet and occupied the planet, its whole population will be hostage for good behavior. We'll make examples of the first few goozes who give us trouble of any sort. Then they'll know we mean what we say when we announce our policy. At the first suspicion of plague among us, we'll lay waste a continent. If the suspicion is confirmed, we'll bombard the whole works. No, there won't be any bug warfare."

"I know. I've heard your line of reasoning before. About five hundred times, in fact."

"Destruction! Am I really that much of a bore?" He came up behind her and laid his hands on her shoulders. "I don't mean to be. Honest. I'm not used to talking to women, that's all."

"And I'm not used to being shut away like a prize fish, except when you want to exhibit me," she said sharply.

He kissed her neck. His whiskers tickled. "It'll be different on Vaynamo. When we're settled down. I'll be governor of the planet. The Directorate has as good as promised me. Then I can do as I want. And so can you."

"I doubt that. Why should I believe anything you say? When I told you I'd made Ivalo talk by promising you would exchange him, you wouldn't keep the promise." She tried to wriggle free, but his grip was too strong. She contented herself with going rigid. "Now, when I tell you the prisoners we brought back this time are to be treated like human beings, you whine about your damned Directorate—"

"But the Directorate makes policy!"

"You're the Fleet Admiral, as you never lose a chance to remind me. You can certainly bring pressure to bear. You can insist the Vaynamoans be taken out of those kennels and given honorable detention—"

"Awww, now." His lips nibbled along her cheek. She turned her head away and continued:

"—and you can get what you insist on. They're your own prisoners, aren't they? I've listened enough to you, and your dreary officers when you brought them home. I've read books, hundreds of books. What else have I got to do, day after day and week after week?"

"But I'm busy! I'd like to take you out, honest, but—"

"So I understand the power structure on Chertkoi just as well as you do, Bors Golyev. If not better. If you don't know how to use your influence, then slough off some of that conceit, sit down and listen while I tell you how."

"Well, uh, I never denied, sweetling, you've given me some useful advice from time to time."

"So listen to me. I say all the Vaynamoans you hold are to be given decent quarters, recreation, and respect. What did you capture them for, if not to get some use out of them? And the proper use is not to titillate yourself by kicking them around. A dog would serve that purpose better.

"Furthermore, the fleet has to carry them back to Vaynamo. All of them."

"What? You don't know what you're talking about! The logistics is tough enough without—"

"I do so know what I'm talking about. Which is more than I can say for you. You want guides, intermediaries, puppet leaders, don't you? Not by the score, a few cowards and traitors, as you have hitherto. You need hundreds. Well, there they are, right in your hands."

"And hating my guts."

"Give them reasonable living conditions and they won't. Not quite so much, anyhow. Then bring them back home—a generation after they left, all their friends aged or dead, everything altered once you've conquered the planet. And let me deal with them. You'll get helpers."

"Uh, well, uh, I'll think about it."

"You'll do something about it!" She eased her body, leaning back against the rubbery muscles of his chest. Her face turned upward, with a slow smile. "You're good at doing things, Bors."

"Oh, Elva—"

Later: "You know one thing I want to do? As soon as I'm well established in the governorship? I want to marry you. Properly and openly. Let 'em be shocked. I won't care. I want to be your husband, and the father of your kids, Elva. How's that sound? Mistress Governor General Elva Golyev of Vaynamo Planetary Province. Never thought you'd get that far in life, did you?"

583 A.C.C.:

As they neared the end of the journey, he sent her to his cabin. An escape suit—an armored cylinder with propulsors, air regenerator, food and water supplies, which she could enter in sixty seconds—occupied most of the room. "Not that I expect any trouble," he said. "But if something should happen . . . I hope you can make it down to the surface." He paused. The officers on the bridge moved quietly about their tasks; the engines droned; the distorted stars of near-light velocity framed his hard brown face. There was a thin sheen of sweat on his skin; not fear, but an effort to say something.

"I love you, you know," he finished. Quickly, he turned back to his duties. Elva went below.

Clad in a spaceman's uniform, seated on the bunk, enclosed in toning metal, she felt the inward wrench as the agoratron went off and speed was converted back to atomic mass. The cabin's private viewscreen showed stars in their proper constellations again, needle-sharp against blackness. Vaynamo was tiny and blue, still several hundred thousand kilometers remote. Elva ran fingers through her hair. The scalp beneath felt tight, and her lips were dry. A person couldn't help being afraid, she thought. Just a little afraid.

She called up the memory of Karlavi's land, where he had now lain for sixty-two years. Reeds whispered along the shores of Rovaniemi, the wind made a rippling in long grass, and it was time again for the lampflowers to blow, all down the valley. Dreamlike at the edge of vision, the snowpeaks of the High Mikkela floated in an utter blue.

I'm coming back, Karlavi, she thought.

In her screen, the nearer vessels were glinting toys, plunging through emptiness. The further ones were not visible at this low magnification. Only the senses

of radar, gravpulse, and less familiar creations, ana-
lyzed by whirling electrons in a computer bank, gave
any approach to reality. But she could listen in on the
main intercom line to the bridge if she chose, and hear
those data spoken. She flipped the switch. Nothing
yet, only routine reports. Had the planet's disc grown
a trifle?

Have I been wrong all the time? she thought. Her
heart stopped for a second.

Then: "Alert! Condition red! Alert! Condition red!
Objects detected, approaching nine-thirty o'clock, fifteen degrees high. Neutrino emissions indicate nuclear engines."

"Alert! Condition yellow! Quiescent object detected
in orbit about target planet, two-thirty o'clock, ten
degrees low, circa 75,000 kilometers distant. Extremely
massive. Repeat, quiescent. Low level of nuclear activity,
but at bolometric temperature of ambient space. Possibly an abandoned space fortress, except for being so
massive."

"Detected objects identified as space craft. Approaching with average radial velocity of 250 KPS. No
evident deceleration. Number very large, estimated at
five thousand. All units small, about the mass of our
scoutboats."

The gabble went on until Golyev's voice cut through:
"Attention! Fleet Admiral to bridge of all units. Now
hear this." Sardonically: "The opposition is making a
good try. Instead of building any real ships—they
could only have constructed a few at best—they've
turned out thousands of manned warboats. Their plan
is obviously to cut through our formation, relying on
speed, and release tracking torps in quantity. Stand by
to repel. We have enough detectors, antimissiles,
negafields, to overwhelm them in this department too.
Once past us, the boats will need hours to decelerate
and come back within decent shooting range. By that
time we should be in orbit around the planet. Be alert

for possible emergencies, of course. But I only expect
standard operations will be necessary. Good shooting!"

Elva strained close to her screen. All at once she
saw the Vaynamoan fleet, sparks, but a horde of them,
twinkling among the stars. Closer! Her fingers strained
against each other. *They* must *have some plan*, she
told herself. *If I'm blown up in five minutes — I was
hoping I'd get down to you, Karlavi. But if I don't,
goodbye, goodbye.*

The fleets neared each other: on the one side, ponderous dreadnaughts, cruisers, auxiliary warcraft,
escorting swarms of transport and engineer ships; on
the opposite side, needle-thin boats whose sole armor
was velocity. The guns of Chertkoi swung about, hoping for a lucky hit. At such speeds it was improbable.
The fleets would interpenetrate and pass in a frac-
tional second. The Vaynamoans could not be blasted
until they came to grips near their home world.
However, if a nuclear shell should find its mark now —
what a blaze in heaven!

The flagship staggered.

"Engine room to bridge. What's happened?"

"Bridge to engine room. Gimme some power there!
What in all destruction — ?"

"*Sharyats* to *Askol*. *Sharyats* to *Askol*. Am thrown
off course. Accelerating. What's going on?"

"Look out!"

"*Fodorev* to *Zuevots*! Look alive, you bloody fool!
You'll ram us!"

Cushioned by the internal field, Elva felt only the
minutest fraction of that immense velocity change.
Even so a wave of sickness went through her. She
clutched at the bunk stanchion. The desk ripped from
a loose mooring and crashed into the wall, which
buckled. The deck split open underfoot. A roar went
through the entire hull, ribs groaned as they bent,
plates screamed as they sheared. A girder snapped in
twain and spat sharp fragments among a gun turret

crew. A section broke apart, air gushed out, a hundred men died before the sealing bulkheads could close.

After a moment, the stabilizing energies regained interior control. The images on Elva's screen steadied. She drew a shaken lungful of air and watched. Out of formation, the *Askol* plunged within a kilometer of her sister ship the *Zuevots*—just when that cyclopean hull smashed into the cruiser *Fodorev*. Fire sheeted as accumulator banks were shorted. The two giants crumpled, glowed white at the point of impact, fused, and spun off in a lunatic waltz. Men and supplies pinwheeled from the cracks gaping in them. Two gun turrets wrapped their long barrels around each other like intertwining snakes. Then the whole mess struck a third vessel. Steel chunks exploded into space.

Through the noise and the human screaming, Golyev's voice blasted. "Pipe down there! Belay that! By Creation, I'll shoot the next man who whimpers! The enemy will be here in a minute. All stations, by the numbers, report."

A measure of discipline returned. These were fighting men. Instruments fingered outward, the remaining computers whirred, minds made deductive leaps, gunners returned to their posts. The Vaynamoan fleet passed through, and the universe exploded in brief pyrotechnics. Many a Chertkoian ship died then, its defenses too battered, its defenders too stunned to ward off the tracking torpedoes. But others fought back, saved themselves, and saw their enemies vanish in the distance.

Still they tumbled off course, their engines helpless to free them. Elva heard a physicist's clipped tones give the deduction from his readings. The entire fleet had been caught in a cone of gravitational force emanating from that massive object detected in orbit. Like a maelstrom of astronomical dimensions, it had snatched them from their paths. Those closest and in the most intense field strength—a fourth of the armada—had been wrecked by sheer deceleration.

Now the force was drawing them down the vortex of itself.

"But that's impossible!" wailed the *Askol*'s chief engineer. "A gravity attractor beam of that magnitude . . . Admiral, it can't be done! The power requirements would burn out any generator in a microsecond!"

"It's being done," said Golyev harshly. "Maybe they figured out a new way to feed energy into a space distorter. Now, where are those figures on intensity? And my calculator . . . Yeh. The whole fleet will soon be in a field so powerful that—Well, we won't let it happen. Stand by to hit that generator with everything we've got."

"But sir . . . we must have—I don't know how many ships—close enough to it now to be within total destruction radius."

"Tough on them. Stand by. Gunnery Control, fire when ready."

And then, whispered, even though that particular line was private and none else in the ship would hear: "Elva. Are you all right down there? Elva!"

Her hands had eased their trembling enough for her to light a cigaret. She didn't speak. Let him worry. It might reduce his efficiency.

Her screen did not happen to face the vortex source, and thus did not show its destruction by the nuclear barrage. Not that that could have registered. The instant explosion of sun-center ferocity transcended any sense, human or electronic. Down on Vaynamo surface, in broad daylight, they must have turned dazzled eyes from that brilliance. Anyone within a thousand kilometers of those warheads died, no matter how much steel and force field he had interposed. Twoscore Chertkoian ships were suddenly manned by corpses. Those further in were fused to lumps. Still further in, they ceased to exist, save as gas at millions of degrees temperature. The vessels already crashed on the giant station were turned into unstable isotopes, their very atoms dying.

But the station itself vanished. And Vaynamo had only the capacity to build one such monster. The Chertkoian ships were free again.

"Admiral to all captains!" cried Golyev. "Admiral to all captains. Let the reports wait. Clear the lines. I want every man in the fleet to hear me. Stand by for message.

"Now hear this. This is Supreme Commander Bors Golyev. We just took a rough blow, boys. The enemy had an unsuspected weapon, and cost us a lot of casualties. But we've destroyed the thing. I repeat, we blew it out of the cosmos. And I say, well done! I say also, we still have a hundred times the strength of the enemy, and he's shot his bolt. We're going on in. We're going to—"

"Alert! Condition red! Enemy boats returning. Enemy boats returning. Radial velocity circa 50 KPS, but acceleration circa 100 G."

"What?"

Elva herself saw the Vaynamoan shooting stars come back into sight.

Golyev tried hard to shout down the panic of his officers. Would they stop running around like old women? The enemy had developed something else, some method of accelerating at unheard-of rates under gravitational thrust. But not by witchcraft! It would be an internal-stress compensator developed to ultimate efficiency, plus an adaptation of whatever principle was used in the attractor vortex. Or it could be a breakthrough, a totally new principle, maybe something intermediate between the agoratron and the ordinary interplanetary drive. . . . "Never mind what, you morons! They're still only a flock of splinters! Kill them!"

But the armada was roiling about in blind confusion. The detectors had given more seconds of warning, which were lost in understanding that the warning was correct and in frantically seeking to rally men already shaken. Then the splinter fleet was in among the Chertkoians. It braked its furious relative velocity with a near-instantaneous quickness for which the Chertkoian gunners and gun computers had never been prepared. However, the Vaynamoan gunners were ready. And even a boat can carry torpedoes which will annihilate a battleship.

In a thousand fiery bursts, the armada died.

Not all of it. Unarmed craft were spared, if they would surrender. Vaynamoan boarding parties freed such of their countrymen as they found. The *Askol*, under Golyev's personal command, stood off its attackers and moved doggedly outward, toward regions where it could use the agoratron to escape. The captain of a prize revealed that over a hundred Vaynamoans were aboard the flagship. So the attempt to blow it up was abandoned. Instead, a large number of boats shot dummy missiles, which kept the defense fully occupied. Meanwhile a companion force lay alongside, cut its way through the armor, and sent men in.

The Chertkoian crew resisted. But they were grossly outnumbered and outgunned. Most died, under bullets and grenades, gas and flame-throwers. Certain holdouts, who fortified a compartment, were welded in from the outside and left to starve or capitulate, whichever they chose. Even so, the *Askol* was so big that the boarding party took several hours to gain full possession.

The door opened. Elva stood up.

At first the half-dozen men who entered seemed foreign. In a minute—she was too tired and dazed to think clearly—she understood why. They were all in blue jackets and trousers, a uniform. She had never before seen two Vaynamoans dressed exactly alike. *But of course they would be,* she thought in a vague fashion. *We had to build a navy, didn't we?*

And they remained her own people: fair skin, straight hair, high cheekbones, tilted light eyes which gleamed all the brighter through the soot of battle. And, yes, they still walked like Vaynamoans, the swinging freeman's gait and the head held high, such as she had not seen for . . . for how long? So their clothes didn't matter, nor even the guns in their hands.

Slowly, through the ringing in her ears, she realized that the combat noise had stopped.

A young man in the lead took a step in her direction. "My lady—" he began.

"Is that her for certain?" asked someone else, less gently. "Not a collaborator?"

A new man pushed his way through the squad. He was grizzled, pale from lack of sun, wearing a sleazy prisoner's coverall. But a smile touched his lips, and his bow to Elva was deep.

"This is indeed my lady of Tervola," he said. To her: "When these men released me, up in Section Fourteen, I told them we'd probably find you here. I am so glad."

She needed a while to recognize him. "Oh. Yes." Her head felt heavy. It was all she could do to nod. "Captain Ivalo. I hope you're all right."

"I am, thanks to you, my lady. Someday we'll know how many hundreds of us are alive and sane—and here!—because of you."

The squad leader made another step forward, sheathed his machine pistol and lifted both hands toward her. He was a well-knit, good-looking man, blond of hair, a little older than she: in his mid-thirties, perhaps. He tried to speak, but no words came out, and then Ivalo drew him back.

"In a moment," said the ex-captive. "Let's first take care of the unpleasant business."

The leader hesitated, then, with a grimace, agreed. Two men shoved forward Bors Golyev. The admiral dripped blood from a dozen wounds and stumbled in his weariness. But when he saw Elva, he seemed to regain himself. "You weren't hurt," he breathed, as if the words were holy. "I was so afraid . . . "

Ivalo said like steel: "I've explained the facts of this case to the squad officer here, as well as his immediate superior. I'm sure you'll join us in our wish not to be inhumane, my lady. And yet a criminal trial in the regular courts would publicize matters best forgotten and could only give him a limited punishment. So we, here and now, under the conditions of war and in view of your high services—"

The squad officer interrupted. He was white about the nostrils. "Anything you order, my lady," he said. "You pass the sentence. We'll execute it at once."

"Elva," whispered Golyev.

She stared at him, remembering fire and enslavements and a certain man dead on a barricade. But everything seemed distant, not quite real.

"There's been too much suffering already," she said. She pondered a few seconds. "Just take him out and shoot him."

The officer looked relieved. He led his men forth. Golyev started to speak, but was hustled away too fast.

Ivalo remained in the cabin. "My lady—" He began, slow and awkward.

"Yes?" As her weariness overwhelmed her, Elva sat down again on the bunk. She fumbled for a cigaret. There was no emotion in her, only a dull wish for sleep.

"I've wondered . . . Don't answer this if you don't want to. You've been through so much."

"That's all right," she said mechanically. "The trouble is over now, isn't it? I mean, we mustn't let the past obsess us."

"Of course. Uh, they tell me Vaynamo hasn't changed much. The defense effort was bound to affect society somewhat, but they've tried to minimize that, and succeeded. Our culture has a built-in stability, you know, a negative feedback. To be sure, we must still take action about the home planet of those devils. Liberate their slave worlds and make certain they can't ever try afresh. But that shouldn't be difficult.

"As for you, I inquired very carefully on your behalf.

Tervola remains in your family. The land and the people are as you remember."

She closed her eyes, feeling the first thaw within herself. "Now I can sleep," she told him.

Remembering, she looked up with a touch of startlement. "But you had a question for me, Ivalo?"

"Yes. All this time, I couldn't help wondering. Why you stayed with the enemy. You could have escaped. Did you know all the time how great a service you were going to do?"

Her own smile was astonishing to her. "Well, I knew I couldn't be much use on Vaynamo," she said. "Could I? There was a chance I could help on Chertkoi. But I wasn't being brave. The worst had already happened to me. Now I need only wait . . . a matter of months only, my time . . . and everything bad would be over. Whereas, well, if I'd escaped from the Second Expedition, I'd have lived most of my life in the shadow of the Third. Please don't make a fuss about me. I was actually an awful coward."

His jaw dropped. "You mean you knew we'd win? But you couldn't have! Everything pointed the other way!"

The nightmare was fading more rapidly than she had dared hope. She shook her head, still smiling, not triumphant but glad to speak the knowledge which had kept her alive. "You're being unfair to our people. As unfair as the Chertkoians were. They thought that because we preferred social stability and room to breathe, we must be stagnant. They forgot you can have bigger adventures in, well, in the spirit, than in all the physical universe. We really did have a very powerful science and technology. It was oriented toward life, toward beautifying and improving instead of exploiting nature. But it wasn't less virile for that. Was it?"

"But we had no industry to speak of. We don't even now."

"I wasn't counting on our factories, I said, but on

our science. When you told me about that horrible virus weapon being suppressed, you confirmed my hopes. We aren't saints. Our government wouldn't have been quite so quick to get rid of the plague—would at least have tried to bluff with it—if there weren't something better in prospect. Wouldn't they?

"I couldn't even guess what our scientists might develop, given two generations which the enemy did not have. I did think they would probably have to use physics rather than biology. And why not? You can't have an advanced chemical, medical, genetic, ecological technology without knowing all the physics there is to know. Can you? Quantum theory explains mutations. But it also explains atomic reactions, or whatever they used in those new machines.

"Oh, yes, Ivalo, I felt sure we'd win. All I had to do myself was work to get us prisoners—especially me, to be quite honest—get us there at the victory."

He looked at her with awe. Somehow that brought back the heaviness in her. *After all,* she thought ... *sixty-two years. Tervola abides. But who will know me? I am going to be so much alone.*

Boots rang on metal. The young squad leader stepped back in. "That's that," he said. His bleakness vanished and he edged closer to Elva, softly, almost timidly.

"I trust," said Ivalo with a rich, growing pleasure in his voice, "that my lady will permit me to visit her from time to time."

"I hope you will," she murmured.

"We temporal castaways are bound to be disoriented for a while," he said. "We must help each other. You, for example, may have some trouble adjusting to the fact that your son Hauki, the Freeholder of Tervola—"

"Hauki!" She sprang to her feet. The cabin blurred around her.

"—is now a vigorous elderly man who looks back on a most successful life," said Ivalo. "Which includes the begetting of Karlavi here." Her grandson's strong hands closed about her own. "Who in turn," finished Ivalo, "is the recent father of a bouncing baby boy named Hauki. And all your people are waiting to welcome you home."

HIGH TREASON

In three hours by the clock they will be here to kill me. The door will crack open. Two noncoms will step through and flank it, in parade uniform with stunners at the ready. I don't know whether their faces will wear loathing and righteousness, or that sick pity I have observed on some aboard this ship, but it is certain that they will be pathetically young, because all the enlisted ratings are. Then Erik Halvorsen will stride in between them and come to attention. So will I. "Edward Breckinridge," he will say like a machine, and proceed with the formula. Not so long ago he called me Ed, and we were messmates, and on our last leave we went on a drinking bout which must by now have become a part of the local mythology. (This was in Port Desire, but next day we flitted down to the sea, which is golden coloured on that planet, and tumbled in the surf and lay on the sand letting sunlight and thunder possess us.) I don't know what will be in his eyes either. Curious, that one's closest male friend should be so unpredictable. But since he was always a good officer, he can be counted on to play his role out.

So can I. There is no gain in breaking the ritual, and ample reason for not doing so. Perhaps I should not even have dismissed the chaplain. With so much religiosity about, as our universe goes down in wreck, I have painted myself more strongly Lucifer by not spending these last hours in prayer. Will my children hear at school, He wasn't just a traitor, he was a dirty atheist—? Never mind, I am not entitled to a great deal, but let me claim the dignity of remaining myself.

There will also be a kind of dignity in what follows: barbaric, macabre, and necessary. I will march down the corridor between the stiff bodies and stiffer faces of men I commanded; drums will drown the mutter of engines and priest. The inner airlock door will already stand wide. I will enter the chamber. The door will close. Then, for a moment, I can be alone. I shall try to hold to me the memory of Alice and the children, but perhaps my sweat will stink too harshly.

They don't pump the air out of the chamber in cases like this. That would be cruel. They simply pull the emergency switch. (No, not "they." One man's hand must do it. But whose? I don't want to know.) An engine will strain against the atmospheric pressure, one kilogram per square centimetre that we have borne with us, along with salt blood and funny little patches of hair and funny little instincts, all the way from Earth. The outer door will swing. Suddenly my coffin brims with darkness and stars. Earth's air rejects me. I fly out. The ship resumes hyperdrive.

For me, then, the universe will no longer ever have been.

But I ramble. It was well meant of them to give me this psychograph. The written word lies, the distorted molecules of a thought-recording tape do not. My apologia can be analysed for sincerity as well as logic. The worlds will be assured that I was at least an honest fool, which could make things easier for Alice, Jeanne, small Bobby who—her last letter said—has begun to look like his father. On the other hand, being no expert in the use of the machine, I will commit more of myself to the record than I like.

Well, keep trying, Ed, old chap. You can always wipe the tape. Though why you should be concerned about your privacy, when you are going to be dead—

Drusilla.

NO.

Go away. Take back your summer-scented hair, the feel of breasts and belly, the bird that sang in the garden beyond your window, take them back, Alice is my girl and I'd simply been away from her too long, and no, that isn't true either, I damn well had fun with you, Dru my puss, and I don't regret a microsecond of our nights but it would hurt Alice to know, or would she understand, Christ-Osiris-Baldr-Xipe, I can't even be sure about that.

Get your mind back to higher things. Like battle. Quite okay to kill, you know, it's love which is dangerous and must be kept on tight leash, no, now I'm knee-jerking like one of those Brotherhood types. The soldier is akin to the civil monitor, both trained in violence because violence is sometimes necessary for the purposes of society. My problem was, what do you do when those purposes become impossible of attainment?

You fight. The Morwain will not forget either, certain hours amidst the blaze of Cantrell's Cluster. Part of my defence, remember, Erik Halvorsen?—my squadron inflicted heavy damage on the enemy—but the court martial couldn't follow such logic. Why did I attack a superior force after betraying a planet . . . a species? My claim is on record, that in my considered judgment the mission on which we had been ordered would have had catastrophic results, but that something might have been accomplished by striking elsewhere. Be it said, though, here to the ultimate honesty of this machine, I hoped to be captured. I have no more death wish than you, Erik.

And *someone* will have to represent men, when the Morwain come. Why not myself?

One reason why not, among others: Hideki Iwasaki. (I mean Iwasaki Hideki, the Japanese put the surname first, we're such a richly variant life form.) "Yahhh!" he screamed when we took our direct hit. I saw the control turret flare with lightnings, I saw him penetrated, through earthquake shudder in the ship and a whistle of departing air that pierced my helmet, my phones heard him scream.

Then darkness clapped down upon us. The gee-field had gone dead too, I floated, whirling until I caromed off a bulkhead and caught a stanchion. My mouth was full of blood, which tasted like wet iron. As the dazzle cleared from my retina, I saw the master panel shine blue, emergency lighting, and Hideki outlined before it. I knew him by the number fluorescing on his armour. Air gushed from him, as fast as the tank could replace it, white with condensing moisture, mingled with blood in thick separate globules. I thought amidst my pulses, gloriously, Why, we're disabled. Totally. We haven't gone onto standby control, we're rudderless in space, the switchover circuits must be fused. We can only surrender. Plug in your jack quick, man, raise Comcentre and order the capitulation signal broadcast. No, wait. First you pass command on formally, to Feinstein aboard the *Yorktown*, so that the squadron may proceed with its battle. But then you're out of action. You'll come home with the Morwain.

Iwasaki's gauntlets moved. He had tools in them. Dying, he floated in front of the smitten superconductor brain and made a jackleg repair. It didn't take long. Just a matter of a few connections, so that the standby system could get the order to take over. I should have thought of trying it myself. That I did not, well, yes, I admit that that was my real treason. But when I saw what he was doing, I shoved myself to him, along with Mboto and Ghopal, and lent a hand.

We couldn't do much. He was the electronics officer. Besides, as for me, his blood drifted across my faceplate and fogged it. But we passed him what he needed from the tool kit. By the blue light, through the black smears, I saw his face a little, drained of everything but sweat and will. He did not permit himself to die until he had finished.

The lights came back on. So did weight. And the viewscreens. And the audio inductors. We'd have to get along on tanked air until we could shift to the other turret. I looked into space. The stars were thick here, heartlessly brilliant against black, but sharpest was a flash half a million kilometres away. And: "¡Por Dios!" cried the evaluation officer, "she was a Jango cruiser! Someone's put a missile in her!"

Turned out the *Agincourt* had done so. I hear her captain has been cited for a medal. Is he grateful to me?

At the moment, though, I knew only that Iwasaki had resurrected the *Syrtis Minor* and I must therefore continue to fight her. I called for the medics to come see if they could resurrect him too. He was a good little man, who had shyly shown me pictures of his good little children, under the cherry trees of Kyoto. But later I heard there was no chance for him. With normal hospital facilities, he could have been hooked into a machine until a new gastrointestinal tract had been grown; however, warships haven't room or mass to spare for such gadgets.

I plugged myself back into control. Reports snapped through my ears, numbers flickered before my eyes, I made my decisions and issued my orders. But chiefly I was conscious of a background whine in my phones, blood and a little vomit on my tongue. We were not going to be captured after all.

Instead, we fought free and returned to base, what was left of us.

I wonder if military men have always been intellectuals. It isn't in their legend. Rather, we think of headlong Alexander, methodical Caesar, Napoleon stumping across Europe, Malanowicz and his computers. But shouldn't we likewise remember Aristotle, the Julian calendar, the Code, the philosophical project? At any rate, when you fight across interstellar distances, for commonwealths embodying whole planetary systems, you have to understand the machines which make it possible; you have to try to understand races as sentient as man, but separated from us by three or four thousand million years of evolution; you even have to know something about man himself, lest minds fall to pieces out yonder. So the average officer today is better educated and has done a good bit more thinking than the average Brother of Love.

Oh, that Brotherhood! I wish they could have sat, dirt and self-righteousness and the whole dismal works, in Colonel Goncharov's class.

Sunlight slanted across Academy lawns, lost itself among oak leaves, emerged to glance off a cannon which had fired at Trafalgar, and struck the comets upon his shoulders. I sat and worshipped, at first, for he had won the Lunar Crescent before I was born. But then he asked me to do what was harder.

"Gentlemen," he said, in that slow, accented Esperanto which was such a joke in our barracks — and he leaned across his desk, balanced on fingertips, and the sun touched his hair also, it was still rust colour, and made shadows in the creases of his face; and, yes, a smell of green (E)arth blew in, with the sleepy noise of a mower somewhere in the middle distance — "gentlemen, you have heard a good many fine words about honour, *esprit de corps,* and service to mankind. They are true enough. But you will not live up to them unless you can see your service in its proper perspective. The Cosmocorps is not the élite of human society, its mission is not the purpose of society, it must not expect the highest material rewards or even the highest honours which society has to offer.

"We are an instrument.

"Man is not alone in this universe. Nor is he entitled to every habitable world. There are other races, with their own hopes and ambitions, their own pains and fears; they look out of other eyes and they think other thoughts, but their aims are no less legitimate to them than ours are to us. It is well when we can be friends with them.

"But that isn't forever possible. Some of you will explain it by original sin, some by Karma, some by simple mortal fallibility. The fact remains that societies do conflict. In such cases, one must try to negotiate the dispute. And true negotiation can only take place between equals. Therefore equality in the capability of inflicting harm, as well as in other and higher capabilities, is essential. I do not say this is good, I say merely that it is so. You are to become part of the instrument which gives Earth and the Union that capability.

"An instrument can be misused. A hammer can drive a nail or crush a skull. All too often, armies have been similarly misused. But the fact that you have accepted military discipline and will presently accept commissions does not absolve you from your responsibilities as citizens.

"*Read* your Clausewitz. War is not an end but a continuation of political intercourse. The most horrible disasters of horrible history occurred when that was forgotten. Your duty as officers—a duty too high and difficult to be included in the Articles—will be to remember."

I suppose that basically I am a humourless type. I like a joke as well as you do, I rather distinguished myself in my class by my fund of limericks, a poker game or a drinking bout is fun, but I do take some things with a possibly priggish seriousness.

Like this matter of racial hatred. I will no more

tolerate that word "Jango" than I would have tolerated "Nigger" or "Gook" a few centuries ago. (You see, I've read quite a lot of history. Hobby of mine, and a way to pass the long time between stars.) It was brought against me at the court martial. Tom Deare testified that I had spoken well of the Morwain. They were fair-minded men on the board, who reprimanded him and struck his words from the record, but—Tom, you were my friend. Weren't you?

Let me set straight what happened. Memory gets more total with every sweep of that minute hand. We were on Asphodel for refitting. Once this was the pet hope of every spaceman. Next to Earth herself, perhaps more so for many, Asphodel! (Yes, yes, I know it's an entire world, with ice caps and deserts and stinking swamps, but I mean the part we humans made our own, in those magnificent days when we thought we had the freedom of the galaxy, and could pick and choose our colony sites.) Mountains shouldering white into a cornflower sky, valleys one dazzle of flowers and bird wings, the little laughterful towns and the girls. . . . But this was late in the war. You hated to go out after dark, for the enemy held those stars. Most of the towns were already empty, doors creaked in the wind, echoes rang hollow from your footfall in the streets. Now and then a thunderclap rolled, another ferry taking off with another load of civilians for evacuation. Asphodel fell to the Morwain two months afterward.

We sat in a deserted tavern, Tom and I, violating regs by drinking liquor which could not be taken away. There was nothing else to do. War is mostly hurry up and wait. Sunlight came in, and the same green smell I remembered across an eon, and a dog ran by outside, abandoned, bewildered, hungry.

"Oh, God *damn* them!" Tom shouted into silence.

"Who?" I asked, pouring myself a refill. "If you mean those officious bastards in Q.M., I entirely agree, but aren't you wishing a rather large job onto the Almighty?"

"This is no time to be funny," he said.

"It's no time to be anything else," I answered. We had just heard about the destruction of the Ninth Fleet.

"The Jangos," he said. "The filthy, slimy, slithering, pervert-begotten Jangos."

"The Morwain, you mean," I said. I was rather drunk too, or I would simply have held my peace. But it buzzed in my brain. "They aren't filthy. Cleaner by instinct than we are. You don't see litter in their cities. Their perspiration is glutinous, they walk like cats, and they have three sexes, but what of it?"

"What *of* it?" He raised a fist. His features had gone white, except for two fever-spots on the cheekbones. "They're going to take over the universe and you ask what of it?"

"Who says they're going to?"

"The news, you clotbrain!"

I couldn't answer directly, so I said, with that exaggerated consciousness of each single word which comes at a certain stage of drink; "Earth-type planets are none too common. They wanted the same real estate we did. Border disputes led to war. Now their announced purpose is to draw Earth's teeth, just as ours was to draw theirs. But they haven't said anything about throwing us off the planets—most of the planets—we already hold. That'd be too costly."

"No, it wouldn't. They'll only need to massacre our colonials."

"Would we massacre—what's the figure?—about twenty thousand million in either case—would we massacre that many thinking creatures?"

"I'd like to," he got out between his teeth.

"Look," I said, "forget the propaganda. As the war dragged on, and went badly, we've lost all sense of proportion. Suppose they do occupy us?"

"Those tentacled horrors," he whispered, "under the spires of Oxford."

Well, for me it would be strangers walking the Wyoming earth where free men once whooped their cattle down the long trail; and for Iwasaki, demon shapes gaping before Buddha at Kamakura; and for Goncharov, if he was unfortunate enough to be still alive, an alien victory monument raised in the holy Kremlin; and on and on, man-history's tapestry warped into a shape our dead would never have recognized. But—"They'll set up a government, if they win," I told him, "and we'll have to learn some new ways of thinking. But you know, I've studied them, and I met some of them before the war and got pretty friendly, and you know, they admire a lot about us."

He sat altogether still for a long while, before he breathed, "You mean you don't care if they win?"

"I mean that we'll have to face facts . . . if they win," I said. "We'll have to adapt, in order to conserve as much as we can. We could be useful to them."

That was when he hit me.

Well, I didn't hit back, I walked straight out of there, into the obscenely beautiful sunlight, and left him weeping. The next day we said nothing about the incident and worked together with stiff politeness.

But he has testified that I want to be a collaborationist.

Alice, did you ever understand what the war was about? You said goodbye with a gallantry which was almost more than I could endure, and the one time in these five years that I have had Earth furlough, we had too much else CENSOR CENSOR CENSOR. But I suspect that to you these imperial questions were simply a thing, like sickness or a floater crash, which could eat your man.

It was raining when last I left. The ground was still dark with winter, here and there a bank of dirty snow melting away. The sky hung low, like some vague grey roof, and threw tendrils of mist around the house. But I could see quite a distance across this ranch of ours, over the high plateau until the buttes, where I was someday going to take my son hunting, blocked off vision. The rain was soft, it made little drops in your hair, like Hiddy's blood—No, anyhow, I heard our brook chuckle, the one we installed the first year we owned the place, and the air smelled wet too, and I was as conscious of an aching toe as I was of your body or of the stiffness in my gullet.

I hope you find yourself another man. That may not be easy. It won't be, if I know you; for you are a traitor's widow, and you have too much cleanliness to take one of those Brothers who will come sucking around. But, well, someone from the Cosmocorps, returned to cope as best he can with an Earth gone strange.

Sure, I'm jealous of him. But curiously, not of the fact that you will tell him, "I love you" in the dark. Only of his becoming father to Jeanne and Bobby. So does this justify Drusilla (and others, now and then) when I never doubted you would stay loyal to me?

But I am supposed to justify something allegedly more important. The trouble is, it's so childishly simple that I can't see why this psychograph is needed.

Look: The Morwain and the Terrestrial spheres had interpenetrated long before the war. "Border dispute" is a bad phrase; the universe is too big for borders. They have a thriving colony on the second planet of GGC 421387, which has extended its industry throughout the system. And this planet is a bare fifty light-years from Earth.

The fighting began much further away. Savamor, as we call the planet in question—human throats can't make that particular music—was then a liability to them. They had to defend it, which tied up considerable strength.

We evacuated Asphodel, didn't we? Yes, but Savamor was too valuable. Not just the industry and the strategic location, though naturally they counted too. Savamor is a myth.

I have been there. That was as a newly fledged lieutenant, aboard the old *Dan-no-ura*, in days when the Fleet made goodwill visits. Already there were disputes, there had been clashes, an ugliness was in the air. We knew, and they knew, that we orbited our ships around the planet as a warning.

Nevertheless we were understandably excited about getting leave. This was where the Dancers had gone to escape the upheavals at home, this was where they had raised those cities which remain a wonder and written the Declaration for a new chapter—oh, think of America shining before weary old Europe, but think also of Paris.

We got off at Darway port, and I shook my party in order to drift about on my own. When I was among elfin green towers, on a green-carpeted lane, and the long line of jewelposts glistened before me . . . what could I do but call it the Emerald City? After some hours I was tired and sat down on a terrace to hear the melodies. They're plangent, on no scale that men ever invented, but I liked them. Watching the beings go by, not just Morwain but beings from twenty different species, a thousand different cultures, I felt so cosmopolitan that it was like kissing my first girl.

Before long a Morwa joined me. "Sir," he said in fluent Esperanto—I won't try to remember the nuances of his accent—"may this one have the joy of your presence?"

"My pleasure," I said. And we got to talking. Of course, there was no drink, but none was required, I was quite intoxicated enough.

Tamulan was one of his names. At first we just exchanged pleasantries, then we got onto customs, then into politics. He was unfailingly courteous, even when I got a little overheated about aggressions against our colonies. He simply pointed out how the matter looked from his side—but never mind now. You will be hearing the same things in years to come.

"We must not fight," he said. "We have too much in common."

"Maybe that's why we do fight," I said, and congratulated myself on so neat an insight.

His tentacles drooped; a man would have sighed. "Perhaps so. But we are natural allies. Consider our societies, consider how the stars lie in the galaxy. Who would profit from a war between Earth and Morwai, except the Bilturs?"

In those days the Bilturs were remote from Sol. We hadn't borne their pressure, that had been Morwai's job. "They're sentient too," I said.

"They are monsters," he replied. At the time, I didn't believe what he went on to tell me. Now I have studied too much to disbelieve. I will not admit that there is any race which has forfeited its right to existence, but there are certainly cultures which have.

"Come, though," he said at length, "twilight cools inward and one hears a rustle of nest-found feathers. Will you grace our home by taking dinner?"

Our home, you note. Not his, but his and his mates' and the fuzzy little cubs'. We can learn some things from the Morwain.

And they from us, to be sure. Chiaroscuro painting; Périgordian cuisine; the Bill of Rights. However, such matters have been cheapened by noise about What We Are Fighting For. They will need time to recover.

So what have we been fighting for? Not a few planets; both sides are realistic enough to horse trade them, albeit our conflicting claims were the proximate cause of battle. Nor, in truth, any desire on either side to impose a particular set of values on the galaxy; only our commentators are sufficiently stupid to believe that's even desirable. Why, then?

Why me? Why have I fought?

Because I was a career officer. Because men of my blood were fighting. Because I do not want aliens walking our land and ordering us about. *I do not.*

I say into the psychograph, and I am going to leave this tape unwiped because I most passionately want to be believed, my wish is that Earth should win. For this I would not only give my own life; that's easy, if you don't stop to think about the implications, and it's always possible. No, I would throw Alice, and Bobby, and Jeanne who must by now have become the most enchanting awkward hybrid of child and girl, into the furnace. Not to speak of Paris, and the caves where my ancestors drew the mammoths they dared hunt, and the whole damned state of Wyoming—from which it follows that Savamor planet would occasion me simply the mildest regret. Doesn't it?

As for why my feelings run thus, we must go deeper than psycho-dynamics has yet managed. In spite of glib talk about "instinct of territoriality" and "symbol identification," I don't believe we really know

Why men were born: but surely we are
brave,
Who take the Golden Road to Samarkand.

(Will they remember Flecker, when Earth has been changed?)

I'm rambling again. My position can be put approximately, in crude terms: Somebody has to have the final say—not any dictatorship, just the tribunal power—as to what is to happen in the galaxy. I want it to be my people.

No, let's modify that. I only want my people to have the final say as to what is to happen to them.

If, for this purpose, we must destroy Tamulan who was so hospitable, and his mates and his fuzzy cubs that climbed over my knees, and the Emerald City, well, so be it. Earth should not be dominated by anyone. Nor dominate anyone else, ideally; trouble is, nobody's allowed simply to mind his own business. We get down to some kind of bedrock when we say that man must be free to settle man's destiny.

My question, then, is merely, What do you do when you see that this isn't going to be possible?

I would like to write a love letter to Earth, but I am no writer and I can only call up a jumble: a sky that burned with sunset one snow-clad evening; "We hold these truths to be self-evident, that all men are created free and equal;" the astonishing smallness of Stonehenge, so that you need some time to feel the sheer mass of it, and the astonishing mass of the Parthenon, so that you must sit a while in the spilling Athenian sunlight to grasp its beauty; moonlight on a restless ocean; Beethoven's quartets; the cadence of boots in a rain-wet street; a hand axe chipped out by some heavy-browned Neanderthal who also wondered why men were born; a kiss which becomes more than a kiss, and nine months later a red, wrinkled, indignant blob of life; the feel of a horse's muscles flowing between my thighs; caviar, champagne, and eyes meeting in the middle of elegance; outrageous puns; Mrs. Elton, my neighbour, who raised three sons to manhood after her own man was dead — no, the clock is moving. I have to compose my thoughts most carefully now.

None less than General Wang briefed me. He sat in the command room, in the depths of Hell-Won't-Have-It, with the star tank a-glitter behind his big bald head, and after I came to attention there was a silence so long that the rustle of the ventilators began to run up and down my spine. When he finally said, "At ease, Colonel. Sit down," I was shocked to hear he had grown old.

He played with a duplipen for a while longer before he raised his eyes and said, "You notice we are alone. This is a matter for absolute security. At present an 87 per cent probability of success is computed — success defined as mission accomplished with less than 50 per cent casualties — but if word should get out the operation will become hopeless."

I never really believed those rumours about Morwain agents among us. No being who would sell out his own species could make officer grade, could he? However, I nodded and said, "Understood, sir."

He swivelled around to face the tank. "This thing has a very limited value," he remarked in the same dead voice. "There are too many stars. But it can illustrate the present situation. Observe." His hands passed over the controls, some of those swimming points of light turned gold and some blood colour.

Enemy colour.

I saw how we had reeled back across the parsecs, I saw the ugly salient thrusting in among those suns which still were ours, and even then I guessed what was to come and snatched after words of protest.

"This system . . . entire sector dependent on it . . . interior lines of communication . . . depots . . . repair centre—" I scarcely heard. I was back on Savamor, in Tamulan's home.

Oh, yes, a squadron could get through. Space is too big to guard everywhere. One would meet defences at the end of the trip, which were not too heavy when attack was unexpected, and afterward one must fight back through ships which would converge like hornets from every point of the three-dimensional compass; but yes, indeed, the probability was more than 85 per cent that one could shoot a doomsday barrage into the sky of Savamor.

It wouldn't even be inhumane. Simply a concerted flash of so many megatons that the whole atmosphere was turned momentarily into an incandescent plasma. True, the firestorms would run for months afterward, and nothing would be left but desert, and if any life whatsoever survived it would need several million years to crawl back from the oceans. But Tamulan would never know what had happened. If Tamulan wasn't off with his own fleet somewhere; if he hadn't already died with a laser beam through his guts, or gasping for air that wasn't around him any longer, or vomiting in radiation sickness, as I'd seen human men do. Without a habitable planet for their economic foundation, industries on the other worlds around GGC 421387 could no longer be maintained. Without the entire system for base and supply centre, the salient must be pinched off. Without that salient, pointed like a knife at Earth—

"Sir," I said, "they haven't bombarded any of our colonies."

"Nor we any of theirs," Wang said. "Now we have no choice."

"But—"

"Be still!" He surged half out of his chair. One eyelid began to twitch. "Do you think I have not lain awake about this?"

Presently, in the monotone with which he began: "It will be a heavy setback for them. We will be able to hold this sector for an estimated year longer: which is to say, prolong the war a year."

"For the sake of that—"

"Much could happen in a year. We might develop a new weapon. They might decide Earth is too expensive a conquest. If nothing else, a year can be lived in, back home."

"Suppose they retaliate," I said.

He is a brave man; he met my gaze. "One cannot act, or even exist, without risk," he said.

I had no answer.

"If you feel grave objections, Colonel," he said, "I shall not order you into this. I shall not so much as think ill of you. There are plenty of others."

Nor could I answer that.

Be it made plain here, as it was at my eminently fair trial: no man under my command is in any way to blame for what happened. Our squadron took space with myself the only one in all those ships who knew what the mission was. My subordinate captains had been told about a raid in the Savamor environs, and took for granted that we were after some rogue planet used for a stronghold, much like our own. The missile officers must have had their suspicions, after noting what cargo was given into their care, but they stand far down the chain. And they assumed that last-minute information caused me to shift course and make for Cantrell's Cluster. There we fought our bloody, valiant, and altogether futile battle, won, and limped home again.

Thus I am responsible for much death and maiming. Why?

My official defence was that I had decided the attack on Savamor was lunacy, but knowing that the Morwain salient also depended on the Cluster, I hoped to accomplish our purpose by a surprise attack there. Nonsense. We only shook them up a little, as any second-year cadet could have predicted.

My private reason is that I had to cripple the strength which Wang would otherwise use to destroy Savamor, with a more reliable officer in charge. Facts vindicate my logic. We have already abandoned Hell-Won't-Have-It, and could now find no way past the triumphantly advancing enemy. Nor would there be any point in it; they have straightened out their front and the rest of the war must be fought along conventional lines.

My ultimate motive was the hope of being captured. They would have treated us decently, as we have thus far treated our own prisoners. In time I would have returned to Alice, with the favour of the Morwain behind me. And isn't my race going to need go-betweens?

Eventually, leaders? For they can't hold us down too long. The Bilturs are coming, the Morwain will want allies. We can set a price on our friendship, and the price can perhaps be freedom.

Once upon a time, the English fought the French, and the Americans fought the English, and those were fairly clean wars as wars go. They left no lasting hates. It was possible later for the nations to make fellowship in the face of the real enemy. But who, across the centuries, has forgiven Dachau?

Had we fired on Savamor, I don't believe the Morwain would have laid Earth waste. Tamulan's people aren't that kind. Nevertheless, would they not have felt bound to tear down every work, every institution, every dream of the race which was capable of such a thing; and rebuild in their own image? And could they ever have trusted us again?

Whereas, having fought and been defeated honourably, we may hope to save what is really ours: may even hope to have it admired and imitated, a decade or two from now.

Of course, this is predicated on the assumption that Earth will lose the war. One keeps believing a miracle will come, can we but hold out long enough. I did myself; I had to strangle the belief. And then, in my arrogance, I set my single judgment against what can only be called that of my entire people.

Was I right? Will my statue stand beside Jefferson's and Lincoln's, for Bobby to point at and say, He was my father—? Or will they spit on our name until he must change it in the silly hope of vanishing? I don't know. I never will.

So I am now going to spend what time remains in thinking about

THE END

THE ALIEN ENEMY

Winter darkness falls early on Rotterdam. When my flitter had parked, I walked to a parapet and saw light in star clusters, nebulae, comet tails, filling the spaces of the city. Windows were blinking out in the offices, where towers lifted row on row from the waterfront. But vehicles swarmed, signs danced, shops beckoned, the pavements made a luminous web as far inland as I could see — it appeared to flicker with the ground traffic that counted endless rosaries along it — and the harbor and canals interwove a softer sheen. I was too high to make out people through all that gloom and glow. They were melted into a mere humanity, and their voices came to me as the distant surf of machines.

Up here was less illumination, just some tubes around the lanes and walkways, a fluorescent door to the elevator head, and whatever spilled down from the beacon. So although the air was raw and damp in my nostrils, forcing my hands into tunic pockets, I could look past the electric star which marks this building, out to a few of the real stars. Orion was aloft and the

Charles Wain stood on its head over the Pole. I shivered
and wished the Ministry of Extraterrestrial Affairs
had picked some other place for a centrum, an island
farther south where the constellations bloom after
dark like flowers.

But even the Directorate has to make compromises.
The desirable places on Earth filled up long ago, and
then the less desirable, and then the undesirable, until
the only clear horizons left are on the mountain roofs,
the icecaps, the stone-and-sand deserts, whatever is
still worse to make a living from than the bottom of a
megalopolis. The bureaucrats I work for did not do so
badly; the Low Countries complex has much to recommend it. They control a lot of wealth and are correspondingly influential.

Anyway, I don't have to live in Rotterdam, except a
few days at a time, reporting in or getting briefed.
Otherwise I mostly spend my furloughs at one or
another resort, as expensive and exclusive as possible.
Thus I needn't observe what man has inflicted on this
planet his mother while I was gone. Spaceman's pay
accumulates wonderfully on the long hauls, years or
decades in a stretch. I can afford whatever I want on
Earth: even clean air, trees, a brook to drink from, a
deer to glimpse, unlighted nights when I take a girl
out and show her the stars I have visited.

Let me see, I thought, once this is over with here,
where should I go? Hitherto I've avoided places where
Cumae is visible. But why, really? Hm . . . catalogued
HR 6806, 33.25 light-years distant, K2 dwarf of luminosity 0.62 Sol . . . yes, I'll want a small telescope as
well as some large brags for the girl. . . .

One star detached itself and whirred toward me.
Startled, I realized that this must be Tom Brenner
coming. Suddenly I was in no more mood to brag
about what I had done at Cumae than I was on first
returning. I didn't want to confront him, especially
alone. If I hurried, I could be inside before he set
down. I could await him together with d'Indre, im-

pregnable in the apparatus of government.

But no. I had seen too much—we had both seen too much, he and I, and all those men and women and children for whom he must speak tonight—on the high plains of his planet. In our very separate ways, we had both known the terror of the alien enemy. I could never be totally an official to him. So I stayed by the parapet, waiting. The breath came out of me like smoke and the cold crept inside.

On Sibylla it was always hot. Cumae glowers half again as great in the sky of that world as Sol does on Earth, and pours down nearly twice the energy. Those wavelengths are poor in ultraviolet but rich in infrared. The sunlight is orange-tinted, not actually furnace color though it feels that way.

I asked Brenner why the colonists didn't move upward. Peaks shouldered above the horizon. Their snows were doubly bright against the purplish heaven, doubly beautiful against the gray-green bushland that stretched around us, murmurous and resinous under a dry wind. I saw that timberline, or whatever passed for it, reached almost to the tops. The dark, slightly iridescent hues suggested denser growth than here. Yonder must be a well-watered country, fertile in soil, and cool, cool.

"Not enough air," he said. He spoke English, with a faint American twang remaining after generations. They were chiefly Americans who went to Sibylla. "We're about as high on this massif as we can go."

"But . . . oh, yes," I recalled. "The pressure gradient's steeper than on Earth. Your planet's got fifty percent more diameter, a third more surface gravity."

"And less air to start with." Brenner cleared his throat. I recognized the preliminary to a speech.

"We leave the lowlands be because they're too hot, not because of too thick an atmosphere," he said. "Remember, this is a metal-poor globe, lowish density in spite of its mass. So it didn't outgas as much as it might have, in the beginning. Also, on account of the slow rotation, it don't have any magnetic field worth mentioning. Cumae may not be the liveliest star in the universe, but it does spit plenty protons and photons and stuff to thin out an atmosphere that hasn't got a magnetic field to hide behind. We get a pretty strong radiation background too, for the same reason; gives medical problems, and it'd be worse higher up. Furthermore, when you got an extra ought-point-three gee on you, and manual labor to do, you need lots of oxygen. So the long and the short of it is, we can't colonize the real heights." He cocked his head at me. "Didn't they brief you ay-tall, son?"

I looked back at him hard, feeling I rated more respect as the first officer of an exploratory ship. His leathery features crinkled in a slow grin. The President of Sibylla was no more formal than the rest of his ten thousand people.

He wore the usual archaic kilts, blouse, boots, sun helmet set rakishly on his grizzled head, machete at hip. But my uniform was less neat than his garb, ten minutes after we had left the buggy by the roadside and started climbing. The gravity didn't bother me; we use rougher accelerations on a craft like the *Bering*. I was aware of my flesh and bones dragging downward, nothing worse. The heat, though, the booming and thrusting wind, the scanted lungfuls I breathed, dryness afire in nose and throat, malignant grab of branches and slither of sandy soil, something faintly intoxicant about the plant odors, had entered me. I was sweat-drenched, dusty, a-gasp and a-tremble, and gladder than I should be of a chance to rest.

I decided not to stand on the dignity I didn't have. Besides, I thought, we were men together in the face of the not human. It had killed, it could kill again, it could smite Earth herself. I felt lonelier in that wide grim landscape than ever between the stars.

"They gave us what information was available," I said. "But it was simultaneously too ample—for one head to contain—and too little—for the totality of a world. Hard for us to guess what's significant and what's incidental. And you've been isolated from us for nearly two centuries. Nothing but a thread of laser contact, with a third of each century needed to cross the distance between. Our fleet took longer still, of course; the big ships aren't meant to go above one gee, so they need a year to approach light speed and another year to decelerate. Inboard time at minimum tau factor isn't negligible either. We experienced several months in covering those parsecs. And we were wondering the whole way if we'd arrive to find the aliens had returned—arrive to find you dead here and a trap set for us. Under the circumstances, sir, we were bound to forget some of what we'd learned."

"Well, yes, I reckon you would at that," Brenner said. "Getting back to why we've settled this Devil's Meadows district, I can tell you we haven't got any better place, and most are not as good. Sibylla is not Earth and never will be."

"But you have colonized the polar regions, haven't you? The original expedition team suggested it, and my briefing said—"

"We abandoned them a spell back. They do have higher air pressure and lower background count, at a reasonable average temperature. But that's only an average. Don't you forget, the rotation period is locked to two-thirds of the year, we being so close to the sun. Sixty-five Earthdays of light are tolerable, though it gets too hot toward evening for us to work. We can grow crops, sort of, with lamps to help through the sixty-five-day night. But at the poles, a thirty-seven-degree axial tilt, the seasons are too flinkin' extreme. What with everything else they had going against them, our poor little terrestrial plants kept dying off there. We haven't the industry or the resources to practice greenhouse agriculture on the needful scale." Brenner shrugged. "Finally we gave up and everybody moved equatorward."

I glanced down the crater slope. The road from Jimstown was dirt, a track nearly lost to sight, rutted, overgrown in places, little used since the destruction of New Washington. But traffic had never been heavy along it; no community on Sibylla was ever more than an overgrown village, and most were less. Tiny at this remove stood Brenner's buggy. The lank horse sniffed discouragedly at the brush it could not eat.

We might have taken a flitter from one of the relief ships. But that would have meant waiting until it could be unloaded and fetched down from orbit. Besides, I had wanted some feel of what Sybilla and its people were really like.

I was getting it.

High hopes, two hundred years ago. People who were going to an uncrowded unplundered world, a whole new world, and this time build things right. They understood there would be hardships, danger, strangeness, on a planet for which our kind of life is not really fitted. But there would be nothing that men had not encountered and overcome elsewhere. The explorers had made certain of that beforehand.

Economics was a stronger motive than decency for being sure. The Directorate takes a bit of political pressure off itself with each colony it establishes, but does not really solve any physical problems at home; and the cost of sending the big ships is fantastic. The aim is to make Earth's people look up through the dust and smoke and say, "Well, at least somebody's doing all right out there, and maybe we'll be picked to go in the next emigration, if we stay in favor with the authorities meanwhile." Failures would be very, very upsetting. Only the news of outright attack had justified organizing the Colonial Fleet to evacuate the Sibyllans.

The investment in them was so huge. Their ancestors came with tools, machinery, chemicals, seeds, suspense-frozen animal embryos, scientific gear . . . the basics. Of course, they brought a full stock of technical references too. As population expanded, they would build fusion power stations, they would replace the native life forms in ever larger areas with terrene species, they would at last create Paradise. To judge from their laser reports, they had been following out the plan. It was going slowly, because Sibylla was uncommonly hostile, but it was going.

Now—the reasons why they had not rebuilt were plain to see. The lean ships that appeared in the sky, sixty-eight years ago, bombing and flaming, had knocked the foundations out from under the colony. Too much plant was wrecked, too many lives were lost, too few resources were left. For a lifetime, the people could merely hang on, keep their economy stumbling along at a seventeenth- or eighteenth-century level, cling to the hope that we would answer their appeal. And all the while they knew fear.

I looked again at Tom Brenner. Before he was born, the enemy aliens had destroyed from pole to pole. In days—Earth-days—their fleet had departed back into unknownness. At any instant they might return, and not be content with blowing his toy towns off the map. I wondered how deep the weariness went that I read upon him. Yet he stood straight, and he had a squinty-eyed grin, and two of his children had survived to adulthood and one grandchild was alive and healthy.

"Come on," I said in a harshened voice. "Let's get this finished."

We didn't stop till we mounted the rim and looked down into the fused black bowl where New Washington had been. A few skeletons of buildings jutted from the edges, but only a few, their frameworks grotesquely twisted. I estimated that the blast had released fifty megatons.

The star became a taxi. It glided to a halt across the deck from me and balanced while the stocky figure climbed out. I wondered how he paid it. They had told me the Sibyllans were interned on a military reservation while the Director and his cabinet decided what to do about them. Well, when d'Indre demanded a live conference with the old man, perhaps the colonel had taken pity and slipped him some munits so he could arrive like a citizen, not a consignment.

The taxi took off. Brenner started toward the door. At home he had walked with a rolling, ursine gait. Here he flowstepped, light and easy as an Earthdweller on Mars. His cloak flapped loose, his singlet was open on the broad hairy chest. The unaccustomed cold didn't seem to bother him, rather he savored it.

I moved to intercept him. "Good evening," I said.

Shadows barred our faces. He leaned forward to peer at me. The cigar dropped from his jaws. "Holy hopping Judas—Nick Simić!" He shook his head in bewilderment. "But you, your ship, you stayed behind."

"Your settlement was out of touch with astronautics," I said. My tone was sharper than intended; I really wanted to gentle the shock for him. "The Colonial Fleet accelerates at one gee. But in an exploratory vessel like the *Bering*, we're selected professionals; and the motors have a lot less mass to act on. We load ourselves with gravanol and crank her up as high as ten gees. In five or six weeks we're close to light speed and can ease off. I've been home for a year."

"You, uh, didn't stay long on Sibylla, then."

"Long enough."

"Well." He straightened. The remembered chuckle sounded in his throat. "Quite a surprise, son, quite a surprise. But pleasant." He thrust out his hand. I took it. His clasp was firm. "And how are your shipmates?"

"Very well, thank you, the last I saw. The *Bering* has left again. Further study of the Delta Eridani System. The third planet looks promising, but its ecology is peculiar and—" I realized I was chattering to avoid speaking truth. "I stayed," I said, "since I was in charge of our investigation on the ground and drafted our report. Citizen d'Indre wanted me for a consultant when you arrived."

"I'm sorry if you missed going on account of us."

"No matter. I'm in line for a command of my own." That was true, but I said it merely to cheer him a little. "How are your people doing?"

"Okay to date." Brenner didn't seem in need of consolation, now that he had gotten over his surprise. I don't suppose anyone grew old on Sibylla who couldn't land on his feet when the floor caved in. He drew a breath and gave that straight-in-the-eye look which he had once described as Horsetrader's Honest Expression Number Three. "'Course," he said, "we wonder a wee bit why we're held incommunicado and till when."

"That has to be decided," I said. "What happens tonight could be pivotal."

"Don't the proles know we're here?"

"Nothing except rumors. Your story has to be handled like fulminate. You can't imagine how restless those billions there are." My hand swept an arc around the city. It growled and grumbled. "The original news, nonhuman vessels attacking Sibylla, was let out with infinite care, and only because it couldn't be suppressed. Considering that they seemed to have faster-than-light travel, and something like gravity control, the way you told it, the photographs you transmitted—Panic can bring riot, insurrection." I paused. "So can rage."

"Um. Yeh." The lines deepened around Brenner's mouth, but somehow he kept his tone easy. "Well, what say we get on with it? . . . Oh, almost forgot." He stooped to pick up the cigar. "Soldier gave me some o' these. Friendly taste. No tobacco on our planet, you recall. We'd everything we could do to raise enough food to keep alive."

My gullet tightened. "Put that thing away!" I exclaimed. "Over the side with it! Don't you understand who we're about to see? Jules d'Indre, Minister of Extraterrestrial Affairs. What he recommends be done about you, the Director is almost sure to decree. I warn you, Brenner, be careful!"

He regarded me a while before he obeyed. His next words were astonishing. "Did that girl who traveled with you, Laurie MacIver, did she ship out in the *Bering*?"

"Why, yes."

"Too bad." He spoke softly, and for a moment laid his hand on my shoulder. "I think you want to help us, son, according to your lights. But she had something extra. You know the word *simpático*?"

I nodded. "She is that," I agreed.

We went ranging about, she and I, after a ground-effect car had been brought down and assembled. My thought was to interview as many Sibyllans as possible before they left. None were alive who had experienced the attack, but older ones might recollect what the generation before them had said, and might have noticed significant things in the bombed-out towns before salvage and erosion blurred the clues. Laurie accompanied me for several reasons. We didn't need a computer officer here, and you don't travel alone on another planet. But primarily, she understood people, she listened, and they talked freely because they sensed that she cared.

It is not true what the alleydwellers snigger, that spacewomen are nothing but a convenience for spacemen. They hold down responsible posts. And in the black ocean between stars, among the deaths that lair on every new world, on return to an Earth grown strange, you need someone very special.

Just the same, we had thin luck. Sunset handicapped us. Cumae hung low and went lower, casting an inflamed light that was hard to see by across the plateaus. But the air had cooled sufficiently for outdoor work, and everyone on those pitiful farms toiled till he dropped in his tracks. They must complete their daylight jobs—discing and sowing at the present season, plus hay harvest, livestock roundup, and I don't know what else—largely with muscle power.

They could only illuminate a limited part of their
holdings after the moonless dark came upon them,
truck gardens and such that would fail otherwise.
Metal and manpower were too scarce to produce the
factories which could have produced the machines
and energy sources they lacked.

To be sure, this was the last round for them. They
were going to Earth. But you can't spaceload ten
thousand human beings overnight. The Fleet was barely
able to carry the rations they would need on their
journey. They must feed themselves meanwhile, and
they had no reserves. I was appalled at the wretched
yields, the scrawny animals, the stunted timber. And,
while most of the individuals I saw were whipcord
tough, they were undersized, they had few living
children, the graveyards were broad and filled.

"Terrene life is so marginal here," Laurie said as we
drove. Her voice was muted with compassion. We had
no logical need for a recital of the facts. We had
known them since before we left Earth, when we
studied the reports of communications from Sibylla.
But those were words. Here she met the reality. She
needed to put it back into words for herself, before she
could reach beyond the anguish and think about practical ways to help.

"Not simply that the native species are poisonous
to us," she said. "They poison the soil for our crops.
You have to keep weeds, bacteria, everything out of a
field for years before the rain's leached it to the point
where you can begin building a useful ecology. And
then it's apt to be attacked by something—new poi-
sons seeping in, diseases, stormwinds—and at best,
it never gets strongly established."

I nodded and listed the causes, to hold off the idea
of a personally evil cosmos. "Long nights, weird
seasons, shortage of several trace elements, ultraviolet
poverty coupled with X-ray and particle irradiation,
gravity tending to throw terrene fluid balances out of
kilter, even the geological instability. Some of their

best mines collapsed in earthquakes in the early days, did you know?—and never could be reopened. Oh, yes, it's a hard world for humans."

My fist struck the control panel and I said with a barren anger: "But so are others. There's nothing wrong here that men haven't found, and beaten. The wildlife is worse on Zion, the weight is heavier on Atlas, a full-fledged ice age is under way on Asgard, Lucifer is hotter and has a higher particle count—"

She turned in her seat to face me. Sundown light, streaming through the turret, changed her gold hair to copper against purple shadows. "But none of those were attacked," she said.

"Not yet," I said. "At least, as far as we know."

We should not have mentioned it. The thought had haunted us since we returned from our last voyage and got the news. It dwelt in the back of every mind on Earth. Perhaps it had done so since man first ventured beyond the Solar System. Our few score parsecs of exploring are no trail whatsoever into that wilderness which is the galaxy. Who can doubt that others prowl it, with longer legs and sharper fangs?

Why had they struck? How? Where else? *Who's next?*

The Sibyllans did their best to answer Laurie's questions and mine. But not only were they hard-pressed for time and dull-witted with exhaustion, their information was scant. I had now inspected the ruins, some photographs of ships in flight, eyewitness accounts, compiled histories. The basic narrative was in my brain.

The raiders could not hit everywhere at once. Josiah Brenner, Tom's father, President in his day, got most population centers evacuated before they went up in fireballs. A majority already lived on isolated farms, it took so many hectares to support one person. For the same reason, the former townsfolk scattered across the whole habitable planet afterward.

The result was that hardly anyone today knew

anything that I did not. In fact, my picture of the
catastrophe was clearer than most. The ordinary
Sibyllan had neither time nor energy for studying the
past. The educational level had plummeted; children
generally left school to work before they were twelve
Earth-years old. Folklore took the place of books.

The books themselves were vague. No real census
or scholarship was possible. "Casualties were heavy,"
said the chroniclers, and told many tales of suffering
and heroism. But the figures they gave were obvious
guesswork, often contradicting someone else's. I believed I could make a better estimate myself on the
basis of one fact. The Sibyllan population which the
original colonizing scheme had projected for this decade was some two hundred thousand. The actual
population was a twentieth of that.

After a while, Laurie and I quit. We could do more
good back in Jimstown, helping prepare for the exodus.
With facilities as primitive as they were here, that was
going to be a harrowing job. Our crew would stay
after the Fleet left and search for further clues. Besides,
I didn't fancy traveling after dark.

We had to, though. Passing near a scarp, our car
was struck by a boulder when the crust shivered and
started a landslide. The damage took hours to fix — in
that smoldering light and abominable wind. We could
have called for a flitter, but that would have meant
leaving the car till dawn. It might be totally wrecked,
and it could ill be spared. We drove on.

Cumae went under the mountains. Night thickened
as clouds lifted. Presently it was absolute, except
where our headlights speared before us, picking out
bushes that tossed in the wind and occasional three-
eyed animals that slunk between them. The air grew
louder, thrusting against the sides, making them quiver
and resonate, until the noise filled our skulls. Then
the rain came, a cloudburst such as Earth has never
seen, mixed with hail like knucklebones.

"We'd better take shelter!" I yelled. Laurie could

barely hear me through the drumbeat and the howling. "High ground—get away from flash floods—" Lightning blinded me; the whole heaven was incandescent, again and again and again, and thunder picked me up and shook me. I strained over the charts, the inertial navigator, yes, this way, a farmstead. . . .

We could not have made it on wheels. The ground effect held us above mudslides, water avalanches, flattened crops and splintered orchards. Barely, it held us, though the hurricane tried to fling us back into the rising river which had been a valley. I do not know how long it was before we found the cottage, save that it was long indeed.

The house stood. Like most dwellings on Sibylla, it was a fortress, rock walls, shuttered slit windows, ponderous doors, roof held down by cables. In thin air, driven by high temperature differentials and solar irradiations, you must expect murderous weather from time to time. The barns were smashed, there having been insufficient manpower and materials to build them as sturdily, and no doubt the cattle and crops were lost. But the house stood.

I reached its lee, threw out a couple of ground anchors, put the autopilot on standby, and opened the escape hatch. Laurie slipped, the wind caught her, she almost went downhill to her death. I grabbed her, though, got dragged into the mud but hung on somehow. Clinging together, we fought our way through a universe of storm to the house. The door was bolted from within. Our pounding was lost in the racket. I remembered about hurricane doors before the hail beat us unconscious. We found one on the south side, an airlock-type arrangement which could safely admit refugees. At that, I had hell's own time reclosing and dogging the outer door before we opened the inner.

We stumbled through, into a typical Sibyllan home. One room served for cooking, eating, sleeping, handcrafting, everything. Screens offered some pretense of privacy, but here they stood unused against the sooty, unornamented walls. A brick oven gave reasonable warmth, but the single lantern was guttering and demon-shaped shadows moved in every corner.

A man and his wife sat on a bench by a cradle that he must have made himself. She had her face against his breast, her arms around his neck, and wept, not loudly, only with a despair so complete that she had no strength left to curse God. He held her, murmuring, sometimes stroking her faded hair. With one foot he rocked the cradle.

They didn't notice us for a moment. Then he let her go and climbed erect, a burly man, his beard flecked with gray, his clothes clean but often patched. She remained seated, staring at us, trying to stop her tears and comprehend what we were.

Wind, rain, thunder invaded the stout walls. I heard the man say, slowly, "You're from Earth."

"Yes." I introduced us. He shook hands in an absentminded fashion and mumbled his own name too low for me to catch.

"You can stay here, sure," he added. "We got food in the cupboard till the storm passes. Afterward, Jimstown's walking distance."

"We can do better than that," I said, commanding a smile forth, trying to ignore our drowned-rat condition, for they needed whatever comfort was to be gotten. "We have a car."

Laurie went to the woman. "Don't cry, please, my dear," she murmured; somehow I heard her through the noise, and her head shone in the murk. "I know your farm's wiped out. But you're leaving soon anyway, and we'll see you're taken care of, you and your whole fam—Oh!" She stopped. Her teeth gleamed, catching at her lip.

The woman was not pregnant. But, craning my neck, I too saw that the cradle stood empty.

"I buried her around sundown," the man said, looking past me. His tone was flat and his face was stiff, but the scarred hands kept twisting together. "A little girl. She lived several weeks. We hoped—And now the rain must've washed her out. I did think Sibylla might have let her sleep. We wrapped her up snug, and gave her a doll I'd made, so she wouldn't be too lonesome after we were gone. But everything's scattered now, I reckon."

"I'm sorry," I groped. "Maybe . . . later—" Barely in time, I saw Laurie's furious headshake. "What a terrible thing."

Laurie sat down by the wife and whispered to her.

Once, on our way home, she told me what had been confided that night, hoping it would influence my report. This was the one child they had had, after five miscarriages. The birth was difficult and the doctor did not think any more were possible.

I told her it was no surprise. Standing by that cradle, I had recalled the few children elsewhere and the many graves. And at once, like a blow to the guts, wildly swearing to myself I must be wrong, I saw the face of the alien enemy.

Jules d'Indre sat behind his desk, a shriveled, fussily dressed man whom it was wise to respect. He nodded, quick dip of bald head, as Brenner and I came in. "Be seated, citizens," he did not invite, he ordered.

I found the edge of a chair. My pulse thuttered and my palms were wet. Brenner leaned back, meeting those eyes, faintly smiling. "How d'you do, sir?" he drawled.

"Let us not waste words," d'Indre said. "Perhaps you are not aware how uncommon a physical confrontation in line of business is on Earth. I would normally use a vidiphone three-way, and during working hours. Can you guess why I did otherwise?"

"Informality," Brenner said. "No record, no snoops, no commitments to anything. Suits me. We lived old-fashioned on Sibylla. Not that we wanted to, understand. His smile departed, his voice grew crisp, I had a sense of sparks flying. "It gave us some old-fashioned ideas, however, like about the rights of man."

D'Indre's schoolmaster accent did not alter. "Rights are forfeited when one perpetrates a felony."

"Who's done what and with which unto whom?"

"The Colonial Fleet has been tied up on a useless mission for almost seventy years. Billions of munits have been spent." D'Indre leaned forward. He tapped a pencil on the edge of the desk, *tick-tick* into an all-underlying silence. "The first thing I wish to know, Brenner, is how many were privy to the hoax."

The leather visage sought mine. "What made you report the attack was faked?" Brenner asked calmly, even amiably.

"I didn't want to," burst from me. "I tried—everything—my whole team did. We couldn't risk Earth being unprepared, if there was any chance a hostile fleet existed. And—" I noticed my hands reach toward him—"we didn't want to hurt you!"

"I know," he said, briefly serious. His tone lightened again: "But I've got a curiosity. The fake was arranged by some mighty smart men. Time must've faded the evidence. What put you on?"

"Oh . . . any number of things," I forced myself to say. "Close study of certain pictures turned up some unlikely perspectives in them. Analysis of crater material gave results that were consistent with the explosion of stationary plants, not of warheads. Any warhead we could think of needs a fission trigger, or it'd be too bulky. Analyzing the bones of supposed missile victims, we got clear indications that they'd died years earlier. Some of the diaries and correspondence, allegedly from the immediate post-attack period, contradict each other more than is reasonable, when you apply symbolic logic. I could go on, but it's in the report. No single detail conclusive, but no doubt left after the whole jigsaw puzzle was fitted together."

I wet my lips. "Sir," I said to d'Indre, "our team discussed suppressing the facts. We decided we couldn't do that to Earth. But you should know we did seriously consider it. We were that sorry for these people."

Tick-tick. "You have not answered my question, Brenner."

"Hey?" The Sibyllan coughed. "How many were in on the conspiracy? Just a few. Key men that my dad recruited. Still fewer today. The least number necessary to keep things shuffled around so nobody who wasn't in on it would suspect."

"That has to be true, sir," I blurted. "Ten thousand ordinary mortals can't keep a secret or act a role."

"Obvious." *Tick-tick.* "How did you, or rather your predecessors, avoid massacring their own populace?"

"Well, everybody thanked his luck that he'd not been in a target area or was evacuated in time," Brenner said. "He heard about casualties, but they'd always happened somewhere else, in places where nobody lived that he knew. He couldn't check up, supposing it occurred to him. Sibylla never had global electronic communications, or fast transport except for some official flitters. What did exist—like a newspaper or three—was lost when the towns went. Took quite a spell even to re-establish a mail service. Meanwhile everything was confused, and refugees were getting relocated among strangers, and—The stunt wasn't easy, Dad told me. But it did come off. Later, histories and chronicles and such were written; and who had reason to suspect them? Everybody knew our numbers were way below the original forecasts, and dwindling. But accurate pre-disaster figures were filed only in certain heads now, that kept their mouths shut. And nobody had time to sit down and think hard. So it came to be taken for granted that the loss of people was mainly, if not entirely, due to the attack and its aftermath. I assure you, sir, nearly everyone among us honestly believes in the alien enemy."

His gaze challenged d'Indre. "Do what you like to me and my partners," he said. "We were ready for this, if the truth should come out. But you can't punish ten thousand who also got foxed!"

"Presumably the Director will not wish to do so,"
d'Indre said as if stating a theorem. "Nevertheless, the
problem of assimilating them, so that they can make a
living on this overcrowded world, may well prove
insoluble. And individuals are apt to be subjected to
mob violence. And it is politically impossible to send
them to a different planet, when so many others desire that for themselves. Did the conspirators foresee
this?"

"Yes," Brenner said. He sat straight. The big fists
clenched on his knees. "But there was no mucking
choice. We had to get off Sibylla. We—my father's
group—didn't think Earth would fetch us just because we were slowly dying. We'd already gotten too
many refusals of our pleas for help, only a little help.
'Too expensive,' we were told. 'They cope with the
same problems elsewhere. Why can't you?' Unquote.

"Expensive!" The word ripped from him, together
with a detonating obscenity. I started where I sat.
D'Indre did not change expression, but he stopped
tapping that pencil. Brenner clamped lips together,
took a breath, and went doggedly on: "To be quite
frank, sir, on the basis of what knowledge I have, I
wouldn't put it past certain officials to fake incoming
messages from a colony that stopped sending."

For the first time, I saw d'Indre lose color. The
pencil broke in his fingers. Doubtless Brenner noticed
too, for he paused through several still seconds before
he finished: "Survival knows no law. My father and
his men created a false enemy so their grandchildren
could be saved from the real one."

"Which was?" d'Indre whispered.

"Sibylla, of course," Brenner said, almost as softly.
"The world where everything was wrong. Where the
sum total defeated us. Like a woman who wouldn't
miscarry *too* often in high gravity, except that she
never got enough ultraviolet or oxygen, and did get too
many hard roentgens, and had a poor diet, and was

overworked, and the very daylight wasn't the right color for easy vision. . . . An entire world, fighting us on a hundred different fronts, never letting up. That was the alien enemy. We wouldn't have lasted another century."

I said into the silence which followed: "Earth has known some analogies. Like the Vikings, around the year 1000. They made themselves rulers of England, Ireland, Normandy, Russia. They ranged unbeatable through half of Europe. They settled Iceland, they discovered America. But they could not hold Greenland. They had a colony there, and it hung on for maybe four hundred years, always more isolated, poorer, smaller, hungrier, weaker. In the end it perished. When archaeologists dug up the skeletons of the last survivors, every one was dwarfed and deformed. Greenland had beaten them."

"I've read about it," Brenner said. "Men won in the end. Eskimos, who had the right technology for the place. Europeans, later, with sheer power of machinery. We, our race, we'll lick Sibylla yet, one way or another. But it's taken the first battle. In such cases, a good general retreats."

D'Indre had recovered his poise. "I also know the history," he said. "Captain Simić's report was exhaustive. I wished, however, to add a personal encounter to my data store before deciding what disposal of this affair I should advise."

Brenner folded his arms and waited.

"As a matter of fact," d'Indre said, "Captain Simić has already proposed a solution which seems viable to me. Parts of Earth remain empty because development has been economically unfeasible. The tropical deserts, for example, the Sahara or the Rub' al-Qali. Sand, stone, drought, low water table or none, fierce heat and light, no worthwhile minerals. Converting them by machine would tie up too much capital equipment and skilled personnel that are badly needed elsewhere. Theoretically, the task could be accomplished by minimal robotic and maximal hand labor. But who among the proles combines the necessary attitude and hardihood? It will be interesting to see if the Sibyllans do."

Briefly, humanness broke through him. "I am sorry, especially for the children," he said. "But under present circumstances, this is the best that anyone can give you."

Brenner remained steady. "I sort of expected it," he said. "The captain dropped a few hints on our way down here. What about us, uh, conspirators?"

D'Indre spread his hands. "Your colony will need leadership. I daresay the Director will rule that providing such leadership is an acceptable expiation."

Brenner's own right hand crashed on the desk. Laughter roared from him. "Why, man!" he cried. "After what we've been up against, you think a nice kind Earthside desert's going to be any problem?"

Discussion dragged on. I took small part. My mind wandered and wondered. I didn't speak, lest I jeopardize the solution that was being hammered out. But take these people, I thought. A world battled them for generations. What those now alive had experienced was of no importance compared to what their germ plasm had experienced. With that natural selection in their past, what would they do with their future?

Ten thousand of them among billions—set down in the worst lands on Earth—could make a difference? Nonsense!

I got rid of the notion. I took command of my ship and went off on a voyage. I came home after eighty-five years and found that I had not thought nonsense after all.

THE PUGILIST

They hadn't risked putting me in the base hospital or any other regular medical facility. Besides, the operation was very simple. Needed beforehand: a knife, an anesthetic, and a supply of coagulant and enzyme to promote healing inside a week. Needed afterward: drugs and skillful talking to, till I got over being dangerous to myself or my surroundings. The windows of my room were barred; I was brought soft plastic utensils with my meals; my clothes were pajamas and paper slippers; and two husky men sat in the hall near my open door. Probably I was also monitored on closed-circuit TV.

There was stuff to read, especially magazines which carried stories about the regeneration center in Moscow. Those articles bore down on the work being still largely experimental. A structure as complicated as a hand, a leg, or an eye wouldn't yet grow back right, though surgery helped. However, results were excellent with the more basic tissues and organs. I saw pics of a girl whose original liver got mercury poisoned, a man who'd had most of his skin burned off in an accident, beaming from the pages as good as new, or so the text claimed.

Mannix must have gone to some trouble to find those issues. The latest was from months ago. You didn't see much now that wasn't related to the war.

Near the end of that week my male nurse gave me a letter from Bonnie. It was addressed to me right here, John Reed AFB, Willits, California 95491, in her own slanty-rounded handwriting, and according to the postmark—when I remembered to check that several hours later—had doubtless been mailed from our place, not 30 kilometers away. The envelope was stamped EXAMINED, but I didn't think the letter had been dictated. It was too her. About, how the kids and the roses were doing, and the co-op where she worked was hoping the Recreation Bureau would okay its employees vacationing at Lake Pillsbury this year, and hamburger had been available day before yesterday, and she'd spent three hours with her grandmother's old cookbook deciding how to fix it, "and if only you'd been across the table, you and your funny slow smile; oh, do finish soon, Jim-Jim, and c'mon home!"

I read slowly, the first few times. My hands shook so much. Later I crawled into bed and pulled the sheet over my face against bugeyes.

Mannix arrived next morning. He's small and chipper, always in the neatest of civies, his round red face always amiable—almost always—under a fluff of white hair. "Well, how are you, Colonel Dowling?" he exclaimed as he bounced in. The door didn't close behind him at once. My guards would watch awhile. I stand 190 cm. in my bare feet and black belt.

I didn't rise from my armchair, though. Wasn't sure I could. It was as if that scalpel had, actually, teased the bones out of me. Windows stood open to a cool breeze and a bright sky. Beyond the neat buildings and electric fence of the base I could see hills green with forest roll up and up toward the blueness of the

Sierra. It felt like painted scenery. Bonnie acts in civic theater.

Mannix settled on the edge of my bed. "Dr. Arneson tells me you can be discharged anytime, fit for any duty," he said. "Congratulations."

"Yeah," I managed to say, though I could hear how feeble the sarcasm was. "You'll send me right back to my office."

"Or to your family? You have a charming wife."

I stirred and made a noise. The guard in the entrance looked uneasy and dropped a hand to his stunner. Mannix lifted a palm. "If you please," he chirped. "I'm not baiting you. Your case presents certain difficulties. As you well know."

I'd imagined I was, not calm, but numb. I was wrong. Blackness took me in a wave that roared. "Why, why, why?" I felt rip my throat. "Why not just shoot me and be done?"

Mannix waited till I sank back. The wind whined in and out of me. Sweat plastered the pajamas to my skin. It reeked.

He offered me a cigarette. At first I ignored him, then accepted both it and the flare of his lighter, and dragged my lungs full of acridness. Mannix said mildly, "The surgical procedure was necessary, Colonel. You were told that. Diagnosis showed cancer."

"The f-f-f—the hell it did," I croaked.

"I believe the removed part is still in alcohol in the laboratory," Mannix said. "Would you like to see it?"

I touched the hot end of the cigarette to the back of my hand. "No," I answered.

"And," Mannix said, "regeneration is possible."

"In Moscow."

"True, the Lomonosov Institute has the world's only such capability to date. I daresay you've been reading about that." He nodded at the gay-colored covers on the end table. "The idea was to give you hope. Still . . . you are an intelligent, technically educated man. You realize it isn't simple to make the adult

DNA repeat what it did in the fetus, and not repeat identically, either. Not only are chemicals, catalysts, synthevirus required; the whole process must be monitored and computer-controlled. No wonder they concentrate on research and save clinical treatment for the most urgent cases." He paused. "Or the most deserving."

"I saw this coming," I mumbled.

Mannix shrugged. "Well, when you are charged with treasonable conspiracy against the People's Republic of the United States—" That was one phrase he had to roll out in full, every time.

"You haven't proved anything," I said mechanically.

"The fact of your immunity to the usual interrogation techniques is, shall we say, indicative." He grew arch again. "Consider your own self-interest. Let the war in the Soviet Union break into uncontrolled violence, and where is Moscow? Where's the Institute? The matter is quite vital, Colonel."

"What can I do?" I asked out of hollowness.

Mannix chuckled. "Depends on what you know, what you are. Tell me and we'll lay plans. Eh?" He cocked his head. Bonnie, who knew him merely as a political officer, to be invited to dinner now and then on that account, liked him. She said he ought to play the reformed Scrooge, except he'd be no good as the earlier, capitalist Scrooge, before the Spirits of the New Year visited him.

"I've been studying your file personally," he went on. "And I'm blessed if I can see why you should have gotten involved in this unsavory business. A fine young man who's galloped through his promotions at the rate you have. It's not as if your background held anything un-American. How did you ever get sucked in?"

He bore down a little on the word "sucked." That broke me.

I'd never guessed how delicious it is to let go, to admit—fully admit and take into you—the fact that you're whipped. It was like, well, like the nightly

surrender to Bonnie. I wanted to laugh and cry and
kiss the old man's hands. Instead, stupidly, all I could
say was, "I don't know."

The answer must lie deep in my past.

I was a country boy, raised in the backwoods of
Georgia, red earth, gaunt murky-green pines, cardi-
nals and mockingbirds, and a secret fishing hole. The
government had tried to modernize our area before I
was born, but it didn't lend itself to collectives. So
mostly we were allowed to keep our small farms,
stores, sawmills, and repair shops on leasehold. The
schools got taped lectures on history, ideology, and the
rest. However, this isn't the same as having trained
political educators in the flesh. Likewise, our local
scoutmaster was lax about everything except woodcraft.
And while my grandfather mumbled a little about
damn niggers everywhere like nothing since Recon-
struction, he used to play poker with black Sheriff
Jackson. Sometimes he, Granddad, that is, would take
on a bit too much moon and rant about how poor,
decent Joe Jackson was being used. My parents saw
to it that no outsiders heard him.

All in all, we lived in a pretty archaic fashion. I
understand the section has since been brought up to
date.

Now patriotism is as Southern as hominy grits.
They have trouble realizing this further north. They
harp on the Confederate Rebellion, though actually—as
our teachers explained to us—folk in those days were
resisting Yankee capitalism, and the slaveholders were
a minority who milked the common man's love for his
land. True, when the People's Republic was proclaimed,
there was some hothead talk, even some shooting. But
there was never any need for the heavy concentration
of marshals and deputies they sent down to our states.
Damn it, we still belonged.

We were the topmost rejoicers when word came:
the Treaty of Berlin was amended; the United States

could maintain armed forces well above police level and was welcomed to the solid front of peace-loving nations against the Sino-Japanese revisionists.

Grandad turned into a wild man in a stiff jacket. He'd fought for the imperialist régime once, when it tried to suppress the Mekong Revolution, though he never said a lot about that. Who would? (I suppose Dad was lucky, just ten years old at the time of the Sacred War, which thus to him was like a hurricane or some other natural spasm. Of course, the hungry years afterward stunted his growth.) "This's the first step!" Granddad cried to us. "The first step back! You hear?" He stood outdoors waving his cane, autumn sumac a shout of red behind him, and the wind shouted too, till I imagined old bugles blowing again at Valley Forge and Shiloh and Omaha Beach. Maybe that was when I first thought I might make the army a career.

A year later, units of the new service held maneuvers beneath Stone Mountain. Granddad had been tirelessly reading and watching news, writing letters, making phone calls from the village booth, keeping in touch. Hence he knew about the event well in advance, knew the public would be invited to watch from certain areas, and saved his money and his travel allowance till he could not only go himself but take me along.

And it was exciting, oh, yes, really beautiful when the troops went by in ground-effect carriers like magic boats, the dinosaur tanks rumbled past, the superjets screamed low overhead, while the Star and Stripes waved before those riders carved in the face of the mountain.

Except—the artillery opened up. Granddad and I were quite a ways off; the guns were toys in our eyes; we'd see a needle-thin flash, a puff where the shell exploded; long, long afterward, distance-shrunken thunder reached us. The monument was slow to crumble away. That night, in the tourist dorm, I heard a speech about how destroying that symbol of oppression marked the dawn of our glorious new day. I didn't pay much attention. I kept seeing Granddad, there under the Georgia sky, suddenly withered and old.

Nobody proposed I go home to Bonnie. Least of all myself. Whether or not I could have made an excuse for . . . not revealing to her what had happened . . . I couldn't have endured it. I did say, over and over, that she had no idea I was in the Stephen Decatur Society. This was true. Not that she would have betrayed me had she known, Bonnie whose heart was as bright as her hair. I was already too far in to back out when first we met, too weak and selfish to run from her; but I was never guilty of giving her guilty knowledge.

"She and your children must have had indications," Mannix murmured. "If only subliminal. They might be in need of correctional instruction."

I whimpered before him. There are camps and camps, of course, but La Pasionara is the usual one for West Coast offenders. I've met a few of the few who've been released from it. They are terribly obedient, hard-working, and close-mouthed. Most lack teeth. Rumor says conditions can make young girls go directly from puberty to menopause. I have a daughter.

Mannix smiled. "At ease. Jim. Your family's departure would tip off the Society."

I blubbered my thanks.

"And, to be sure, you may be granted a chance to win pardon, if we can find a proper way," he soothed me. "Suggestions?"

"I, I, I can tell you . . . what I know—"

"An unimaginative minimum. Let us explore you for a start. Maybe we'll hit on a unique deed you can do." Mannix drummed his desktop.

We had moved to his office, which was lush enough that the portraits of Lenin and the President looked startlingly austere. I sat snug and warm in a water chair, cigarettes, coffee, brandy to hand, nobody before me or behind me except this kindly white-haired man and his recorder. But I was still gulping, sniffing, choking, and shivering, still too dazed to think. My lips tingled and my body felt slack and heavy.

"What brought you into the gang, Jim?" he asked as if in simple curiosity.

I gaped at him. I'd told him I didn't know. But maybe I did. Slowly I groped around in my head. The roots of everything go back to before you were born.

I'd inquired about the origins of the organization, in my early days with it. Nobody knew much except that it hadn't been important before Sotomayor took the leadership—whoever, wherever he was. Until him, it was a spontaneous thing.

Probably it hadn't begun right after the Sacred War. Americans had done little except pick up pieces, those first years. They were too stunned when the Soviet missiles knocked out their second-strike capability and all at once their cities were hostages for the good behavior of their politicians and submarines. They were too relieved when no occupation followed, aside from inspectors and White House advisors who made sure the treaty limitations on armaments were observed. (Oh, several generals and the like were hanged as war criminals.) True, the Soviets had taken a beating from what U.S. nukes did get through, sufficient that they couldn't control China or, later, a China-sponsored Japanese S.S.R. The leniency shown Americans was not the less welcome for being due to a shortage of troops.

Oath-brothers had told me how they were attracted by the mutterings of friends, and presently recruited, after Moscow informed Washington that John Halpern would be an unacceptable candidate for President in the next election. Others joined in reaction against a collectivist sentiment whose growth was hothouse-forced by government, schools, and universities.

I remember how Granddad growled, on a day when we were alone in the woods and I'd asked him about that period:

"The old order was blamed for the war and war's consequences, Jimmy. Militarists, capitalists, imperialists, racists, bourgeoisie. Nobody heard any different any more. Those who'd've argued weren't gettin' published or on the air, nothin'." He drew on his pipe. Muscles bunched in the angle of his jaw. "Yeah, everybody was bein' blamed—except the liberals who'd worked to lower our guard so their snug dreams wouldn't be interrupted, the conservatives who helped 'em so's to save a few wretched tax dollars, the radicals who disrupted the country, the copouts who lifted no finger—" The bit snapped between his teeth. He stooped for the bowl and squinted at it ruefully while his heel ground out the scattered ashes. At last he sighed. "Don't forget what I've told you, Jimmy. But bury it deep, like a seed."

I can't say if he was correct. My life was not his. I wasn't born when the Constitutional Convention proclaimed the People's Republic. Nor did I ever take a strong interest in politics.

In fact, my recruitment was glacier gradual. In West Point I discovered step by step that my best friends were those who wanted us to become a first-class power again, not conquer anybody else, merely cut the Russian apron strings . . . Clandestine bitching sessions, winked at by our officers, slowly turned into clandestine meetings which hinted at eventual action. An illegal newsletter circulated . . . After graduation and assignment, I did trivial favors, covering up for this or that comrade who might otherwise be in trouble, supplying bits of classified information to fellows who said they were blocked from what they needed by stupid bureaucrats, hearing till I believed it that the proscribed and abhorred Stephen Decatur Society was not counterrevolutionary, not fascist, simply patriotic and misunderstood. . . .

The final commitment to something like that is when you make an excuse to disappear for a month—in any case, a backpacking trip with a couple of guys, though my C.O. warned me that asocial furloughs might hurt my career—and you get flitted to an unspecified place where they induct you. One of the psychotechs there explained that the treatment, drugs, sleep deprivation, shock conditioning, meant more than installing a set of reflexes. Those guarantee you can't be made to blab involuntarily, under serum or torture. But the suffering has a positive effect too: it's a rite of passage. Afterward you can't likely be bribed either.

Likely. The figures may change on a man's price tag, but he never loses it.

I don't yet know how I was detected. A Decaturist courier had cautioned my cell about microminiature listeners which can be slipped a man in his food, operate off body heat, and take days to be eliminated. With my work load, both official on account of the crisis and after hours in preparing for our coup, I must have gotten careless.

Presumably, though, I was caught by luck rather than suspicion, in a spot check. If the political police had identified any fair-sized number of conspirators, Mannix wouldn't be as anxious to use me as he was.

Jarred, I realized I hadn't responded to his last inquiry. "Sir," I begged, "honest, I'm no traitor. I wish our country had more voice in its own affairs. Nothing else."

"A Titoist." Recognizing my glance of dull surprise at the new word, he waved it off. "Never mind. I forgot they've re-improved the history text since I was young. Let's stick to practical matters, then."

"I, I can . . . identify for you—those in my cell." Jack, whose wife was pregnant; Bill who never spared everyday helpfulness; Tim . . . "B-but there must be others on the base and in the area, and, well, some of them must know *I* belong."

"Right." Mannix nodded. "We'll stay our hand as regards those you have met. Mustn't alert the organization. It does seem to be efficient. That devil Sotomayor—Well. Let's get on."

He was patient. Hours went by before I could talk coherently.

At that time he had occasion to turn harsh. Leaning across his desk he snapped: "You considered yourself a patriot. Nevertheless you plotted mutiny."

I cringed. "No, sir. Really. I mean, the idea was—was—"

"Was what?" In his apple face stood the eyes of Old Scrooge.

"Sir, when civil war breaks out in the Motherland—those Vasiliev and Kunin factions—"

"Party versus army."

"What?" I don't know why I tried to argue. "Sir, last I heard, Vasiliev's got everything west of the, uh, Yenisei . . . millions of men under arms, effective control of West Europe—"

"You do not understand how to interpret events. The essential struggle is between those who are loyal to the principles of the party, and those who would substitute military dictatorship." His finger jabbed. "Like you, Dowling."

We had told each other in our secret meetings, we Decatur folk, better government by colonels than commissioners.

"No, sir, no, sir," I protested. "Look, I'm only a soldier. But I see . . . I smell the factions here too . . . the air's rotten with plotting . . . and what about in Washington? I mean, do we *know* what orders we'll get, any day now? And what is the situation in Siberia?"

"You have repeatedly been informed, the front is stabilized and relatively quiet."

My wits weren't so shorted out that I hinted the official media might ever shade the truth. I did reply: "Sir, I'm a missileman. In the, uh, the opinion of every colleague I've talked with—most of them loyal, I'm certain—what stability the front has got is due to the fact both sides have ample rockets, lasers, the works.

If they both cut loose, there'd be mutual wipeout. Unless we Americans—We hold the balance." Breath shuddered into me. "Who's going to order our birds targeted where?"

Mannix sat for a while that grew very quiet. I sat listening to my heart stutter. Weariness filled me like water a sponge. I wanted to crawl off and curl up in darkness, alone, more than I wanted Bonnie or my children or tomorrow's sunrise or that which had been taken from me. But I had to keep answering.

At last he asked, softly, almost mildly, "Is this your honest evaluation? Is this why you were in a conspiracy to seize control of the big weapons?"

"Yes, sir." A vacuum passed through me. I shook myself free of it. "Yes, sir. I think my belief—the belief of most men involved—is, uh, if a, uh, a responsible group, led by experts, takes over the missile bases for the time being . . . those birds won't get misused. Like by, say, the wrong side in Washington pulling a coup—" I jerked my head upright.

"Your superiors in the cabal have claimed to you that the object is to keep the birds in their nests, keep America out of the war," Mannix said. "How do you know they've told you the truth?"

I thought I did. Did I? Was I? Big soft waves came rolling.

"Jim," Mannix said earnestly, "they've tricked you through your whole adult life. Nevertheless, what we've learned shows me you're important to them. You're slated for commander here at Reed, once the mutiny begins. I wouldn't be surprised but what they've been grooming you for years, and that's how come your rapid rise in the service. Clues there—But as for now, you must have ways to get in touch with higher echelons."

"Uh-huh," I said. "Uh-huh. Uh-huh."

Mannix grew genial. "Let's discuss that, shall we?"

I don't remember being conducted to bed. What

stands before me is how I woke, gasping for air, nothing in my eyes except night and nothing in the hand that grabbed at my groin.

I rolled over on my belly, clutched the pillow and crammed it into my mouth. Bonnie, Bonnie, I said, they've left me this one way back to you. I pledge allegiance to you, Bonnie, and to the Chuck and Joanlet you have mothered, and *screw* the rest of the world!

("Even for a man in his thirties," said a hundred teachers, intellectuals, officials, entertainers out of my years, "or even for an adolescent, romantic atavism is downright unpatriotic. The most important thing in man's existence is his duty to the people and the molding of their future." The echoes went on and on.)

I've been a rat, I said to my three, to risk—and lose—the few things which counted, all of which were ours. Bonnie, it's no excuse for my staying with the Decaturists, that I'd see you turn white at this restriction or that command to volunteer service or yonder midnight vanishing of a neighbor. No excuse, nothing but a rationalization. I've led us down my rathole, and now my duty is to get us out, in whatever way I am able.

("There should be little bloodshed," the liaison man told our cell; we were not shown his face. "The war is expected to remain stalemated for the several weeks we need. When the moment is right, our folk will rise, disarm and expel everybody who isn't with us, and dig in. We can hope to seize most of the rocket bases. Given the quick retargetability of every modern bird, we will then be in a position to hit any point on Earth and practically anything in orbit. However, we won't. The threat—plus the short-range weapons—should protect us from counterattack. We will sit tight and thus realize our objective: to keep the blood of possibly millions off American hands, while giving America the self-determination that once was hers.")

Turn the Decaturists over to the Communists. Let all the ists kill each other off and leave human beings in peace.

("My friend, my friend," Mannix sighed, "you cannot be naive enough to suppose the Asians have no hand in this. You yourself, I find, were involved in our rocket-scattering of munitions across the rebellious parts of India. Should they not make use of trouble in our coalition? Have they not been advising, subsidizing, equipping, infiltrating the upper leadership of your oh-so-patriotic Decatur Society? Let the Soviet Union ruin itself—which is the likeliest outcome if America doesn't intervene—let that happen, and, yes, America could probably become the boss of the Western Hemisphere. But we're not equipped to conquer the Eastern. You're aware of that. The gooks would inherit. The Russians may gripe you. You may consider our native leaders their puppets. But at least they're white; at least they share a tradition with us. Why, they helped us back on our feet, Jim, after the war. They let us rearm, they aided it, precisely so we could cover each other's backs, they in the Old World, we in the New . . . Can you prove your Society isn't a Jappochink tool?")

No, but I can prove we have rockets here so we'll draw some of the Jappochink fire in the event of a big war.—They're working on suicide regardless of what I do, Bonnie. America would already have declared for one splinter or the other, if America weren't likewise divided. Remember your Shakespeare? Well, Caesar has conquered the available world and is dead; Anthony and Octavian are disputing his loot. What paralyzes America is—has to be—a silent struggle in Washington. Maybe not altogether silent; I get word of troop movements, "military exercises" under separate commands, throughout the Atlantic states. . . . Where can we hide, Bonnie?

("We have reason to believe," said the political lecturer to us at assembly, "that the conflict was instigated, to a considerable degree at least, by *agents provacateurs* of the Asian deviationists, who spent the past twenty years or more posing as Soviet citizens and worming their way close to the top. With our whole hearts we trust the dispute can be settled peacefully. Failing that, gentlemen, your duty will be to strike as ordered by your government, to end this war before irrevocable damage has been done the Motherland.")

There is no place to hide, Bonnie Brighteyes. Nor can we bravely join the side of the angels. There are no angels either.

("Yeah, sure, I've heard the same," said Jack who belonged to my cell. "If we grab those bases and refuse to join this fight, peace'll have to be negotiated, lives and cultural treasures 'ull be spared, the balance of power 'ull be preserved, yeah, yeah. — Think, man. What do you suppose Sotomayor and the rest really want? Isn't it for the war to grow hot — incandescent? Never mind who tries the first strike. The Kuninists might, thinking they'd better take advantage of a U.S. junta fairly sympathetic to them before it's overthrown. Or the Visilievsts might, they being party types who can't well afford a compromise. Either way, no matter who comes out on top, the Soviets overnight turn themselves into the junior member of our partnership. Then *we* tell *them* what to do for a change.")

Not that I am altogether cynical, Bonnie. I don't choose to believe we've brought Chuck and Joan into a world of sheer wolves and jackals — when you've said you wish for a couple more children. No, I've simply changed my mind, simply had demonstrated to me that our best chance — mankind's best chance — lies with the legitimate government of the United States as established by the People's Constitutional Convention.

Next day Mannix turned me over to his interrogation specialists, who asked me more questions than I'd known I had answers for. A trankstim pill kept me alert but unemotional, as if I were operating myself by remote control.

Among other items, I showed them how a Decaturist

who had access to the right equipment made contact with fellows elsewhere, whom he'd probably never met, or with higher-ups whom he definitely hadn't. The method had been considered by political police technicians, but they'd failed to devise any means of coping.

Problem: How do you maintain a network of illicit communications?

In practice you mostly use the old-fashioned mail drop. It's unfeasible to read the entire mails. The authorities must settle for watching the correspondence of suspicious individuals, and these may have ways of posting and collecting letters unobserved.

Yet sometimes you need to send a message fast. The telephone's no good, of course, since computers became able to monitor every conversation continuously. However those same machines, or their cousins, can be your carriers.

Remember, we have millions of computers around these days, nationally interconnected. They do drudge work like record keeping and billing; they operate automated plants; they calculate for governmental planners and R & D workers; they integrate organizations; they keep day-by-day track of each citizen; etc., etc. Still more than in the case of the mails, the volume of data transmissions would swamp human overseers.

Give suitable codes, programmers and other technicians can send practically anything practically anywhere. The printout is just another string of numbers to those who can't read it. Once it has been read, the card is recycled and the electronic traces are wiped as per routine. That message leaves the office in a single skull.

Naturally, you save this capability for your highest priority calls. I'd used it a few times, attracting no attention, since my job on base frequently required me to prepare or receive top-secret calculations.

I couldn't give Mannix's men any code except the latest that had been given me. Every such message was re-encoded en route, according to self-changing programs buried deep down in the banks of the machines concerned. I could, though, put him in touch with somebody close to Sotomayor. Or, rather, I could put myself in touch.

What would happen thereafter was uncertain. We couldn't develop an exact plan. My directive was to do my best, and if my best was good enough, I'd be pardoned and rewarded.

I was rehearsed in my cover story till I was letter perfect, and given a few items like phone numbers to learn. Simulators and reinforcement techniques made this quick.

Perhaps my oath-brothers would cut my throat immediately, as a regrettable precaution. That didn't seem to matter. The drug left me no particular emotion except a desire to get the business done.

At a minimum, I was sure to be interrogated, strip-searched, encephalogrammed, X-rayed, checked for metal and radioactivity. Perhaps blood, saliva, urine, and spinal fluid would be sampled. Agents have used pharmaceuticals and implants for too many years.

Nevertheless Mannix's outfit had a weapon prepared for me. It was not one the army had been told about. I wondered what else the political police labs were working on. I also wondered if various prominent men, who might have been awkward to denounce, had really died of strokes or heart attacks.

"I can't tell you details," said a technician. "With your education, you can figure out the general idea for yourself. It's a micro version of the fission gun, enclosed in lead to baffle detectors. You squeeze—you'll be shown how—and the system opens; a radioactive bombards another material which releases neutrons which touch off the fissionable atoms in one of ten successive chambers."

Despite my chemical coolness, awe drew a whistle from me. Given the right isotopes, configurations, and shielding, critical mass gets down to grams, and you can direct the energy through a minilaser. I'd known that. In this system, the lower limit must be milligrams; and the efficiency must approach one hundred percent, if you could operate it right out of your own body.

Still—"You do have components that'll register if I'm checked very closely," I said.

The technician grinned. "I doubt you will be, where we have in mind. They'll load you tomorrow morning."

Because I'd need practice in the weapon, I wasn't drugged then. I'd expected to be embarrassed. But when I entered an instrument-crammed concrete room after being unable to eat breakfast, I suddenly began shaking.

Two P.P. men I hadn't met before waited for me. One wore a lab coat, one a medic's tunic. My escort said, "Dowling," closed the door and left me alone with them.

Lab Coat was thin, bald, and sourpussed. "Okay, peel down and let's get started," he snapped.

Medic, who was a fattish blond, laughed—giggled, I thought in a gust of wanting to kill him. "Short arm inspection," he said.

Bonnie, I reminded myself, and dropped my clothes on a chair. Their eyes went to my crotch. Mine couldn't. I bit jaws and fists together and stared at the wall beyond them.

Medic sat down. "Over here," he ordered. I obeyed, stood before him, felt him finger what was left. "Ah," he chuckled. "Balls but no musket, eh?"

"Shut up, funny man," Lab Coat said and handed him a pair of calipers. I felt him measure the stump.

"They should've left more," Lab Coat complained. "At least two centimeters more."

"This glue could stick it straight onto his bellybutton," Medic said.

"Yeah, but the gadgets aren't rechargeable," Lab Coat retorted. "He'll go through four or five today before the final one, and nothing but elastic collars holding 'em in place. What a clot of a time I'll have fitting *them*." He shuffled over to a workbench and got busy.

"Take a look at your new tool," Medic invited me. "Generous, eh? Be the envy of the neighborhood. And what a jolt for your wife."

The wave was red, not black, and tasted of blood. I lunged, laid fingers around his throat, and bawled—I can't remember—maybe, "Be quiet, you filthy fairy, before I kill you!"

He squealed, then gurgled. I shook him till his teeth rattled. Lab Coat came on the run. "Stop that!" he barked. "Stop or I'll call a guard!"

I let go, sank down on the floor—its chill flowed into my buttocks, up my spine, out along my rib cage—and struggled not to weep.

"You bastard," Medic chattered. "I'm gonna file charges, I am."

"You are not. Another peep and I'll report you." Lab Coat hunkered beside me, laid an arm around my shoulder, and said, "I understand, Dowling. It was heroic of you to volunteer. You'll get the real thing back when you're finished. Never forget that."

Volunteer?

Laughter exploded. I whooped, I howled, I rolled around and beat my fists on the concrete, my muscles ached from laughing when finally I won back to silence.

After that, and a short rest, I was calm—cold, even—and functioned well. My aim improved fast, till I could hole the center circle at every shot.

"You've ten charges," Lab Coat reminded me. "No more. The beam being narrow, the head's your best target. If the apparatus gets detected after all, or if you're in Dutch for some other reason and your ammo won't last, press inward from the end—like this—and it'll self-destruct. You'll be blown apart and escape a bad time. Understand? Repeat."

He didn't bother bidding me good-by at the end of the session. (Medic was too sulky for words.) No doubt he'd figured what sympathy to administer earlier. Efficiency is the P.P. ideal. Mannix, or somebody, must have ordered my gun prepared almost at the moment I was arrested, or likelier before.

My escort had waited, stolid, throughout those hours. Though I recognized it was a practical matter of security, I felt hand-lickingly grateful to Mannix that this fellow—that very few people—knew what I was.

The day after, I placed my call to the Decaturists. It was brief. I had news of supreme importance—the fact I'd vanished for almost a month made this plausible—and would stand by for transportation at such-and-such different rendezvous, such-and-such different times.

Just before the first of these, I swallowed a stim with a hint of trank, in one of those capsules which attach to the stomach wall and spend the next three hundred hours dissolving. No one expected I'd need more time before the metabolic price had to be paid. A blood test would show its presence, but if I was carrying a vital message, would I not have sneaked me a supercharger?

I was not met, and went back to my room and waited. A side effect, when every cell worked at peak, was longing for Bonnie. Nothing sentimental; I loved her, I wanted her, I had to keep thrusting away memories of eyes, lips, breasts beneath my hand till my hand traveled downward. . . . In the course of hours, I learned how to be a machine.

They came for me at the second spot on my list, a trifle past midnight. The place was a bar in a village of shops and rec centers near the base. It wasn't the sleek, state-owned New West, where I'd be recognized by officers, engineers, and party functionaries who could afford to patronize. This was a dim and dingy shack, run by a couple of workers on their own time, at the tough end of town. Music, mostly dirty songs, blared from a taper, ear-hurtingly loud, and the booze was rotgut served in glasses which seldom got washed. Nevertheless I had to push through the crowd and, practically, the smoke—pot as well as tobacco. The air smelled of sweat.

You see more of this kind of thing every year. I imagine the government only deplores the trend officially. People need some unorganized pleasure. Or, as the old joke goes, "What is the stage between socialism and communism called? Alcoholism."

A girl in a skimpy dress made me a business offer. She wasn't bad-looking, in a sleazy fashion, and last month I'd merely have said no, thanks. As it was, the drug in me didn't stop me from screaming, "Get away, you whore!" Scared, she backed off, and I drew looks from the men around. In cheap civies, I was supposed to be inconspicuous. Jim Dowling, officer, rocketeer, triple agent, boy wonder, ha! I elbowed my way onward to the bar. Two quick shots eased my shakes, and the racket around forgot me.

I'd almost decided to leave when a finger tapped my arm. A completely forgettable little man stood there. "Excuse me," he said. "Aren't you Sam Chalmers?"

"Uh, no, I'm his brother Roy." Beneath the once more cold surface, my pulse knocked harder.

"Well, well," he said. "Your father's told me a lot about you both. My name's Ralph Wagner."

"Yes, he's mentioned you. Glad to meet you, Comrade Wagner."

We shook hands and ad-libbed conversation a while. The countersigns we'd used were doubtless obsolete, but he'd allowed for my having been out of touch. Presently we left.

A car bearing Department of Security insignia was perched on the curb. Two much larger men, uniformed, waited inside. We joined them, the blowers whirred, and we were off. One man touched a button. A steel plate slid down and cut us three in the rear seat off from the driver. The windows I could see turned opaque.

I had no need to know where we were bound. I did estimate our acceleration and thus our cruising speed. About 300 K.P.H. Going some, even for a Security vehicle!

From what Granddad had told me, this would have been lunacy before the war. Automobiles were so thick then that often they could barely crawl along. Among my earliest memories is that the government was still congratulating itself on having solved that problem.

Wind hooted around the shell. A slight vibration thrummed through my bones. The overhead light was singularly bleak. The big man on my left and the small man on my right crowded me.

"Okay," said the big man, "what happened?"

"I'll handle this," said he who named himself Wagner. The bruiser snapped his mouth shut and settled back. He was probably the one who'd kill me if that was deemed needful, but he was not the boss.

"We've been alarmed about you." Wagner spoke as gently as Mannix. In an acid way I liked the fact that he didn't smile.

I attempted humor in my loneliness: "I'd be alarmed if you hadn't been."

"Well?"

"I was called in for top-secret conferences. They've flitted me in and out—to Europe and back—under maximum security."

The big man formed an oath. Wagner waited.

"They've gotten wind of our project," I said.

"I don't know of any other vanishments than yours," Wagner answered, flat-voiced.

"Would you?" I challenged.

He shrugged. "Perhaps not."

"Actually," I continued, "I wasn't told about arrests and there may have been none. What they discussed was the Society, the Asians—they have a fixed idea the Peking-Tokyo Axis has taken over the Society— and what they called 'open indications.' The legal or semilegal talk you hear about 'socialist lawfulness,'

'American socialism,' and the rest. Roger Mannix—he
turns out to be high in the P.P., by the way, and a
shrewd man; I recommend we try to knock him off—
Mannix takes these signs more seriously than I'd imagined anybody in the government did." I cleared my
throat. "Details at your convenience. The upshot is,
the authorities decided there is a definite risk of a
cabal seizing the rocket bases. Never mind whether
they have the data to make that a completely logical
conclusion. What counts is that it *is* their conclusion."

"And right, God damn it, right," muttered the big
man. He slammed a fist on his knee.

"What do they propose to do?" Wagner asked, as if
I'd revealed the government was considering a reduced egg ration.

"That was a . . . tough question." I stared at the
blank, enclosing panel. "They dare not shut down the
installations, under guard of P.P., who don't know a
mass ratio from a hole in the ground. Nor dare they
purge the personnel, hoping to be left with loyal skele-
ton crews—because they aren't yet sure who those
crews had better be loyal to. Oh, I saw generals and
commissioners scuttling around like toads in a chamber pot, believe me." Now I turned my head to confront his eyes. "And believe me," I added, "we were
lucky they happened to include one Decatur man."

Again, under the tranquilization and the stimula-
tion (how keenly I saw the wrinkles around his mouth,
heard cleft air brawl, felt the shiver of speed, snuffed
stale bodies, registered the prickle of hairs and sweat
glands, the tightened belly muscles and selfseizing
guts beneath!), fear fluttered in me, and under the
fear I was hollow. The man on whom I had turned my
back could put a gun muzzle at the base of my skull.

Wagner nodded. "Yes-s-s."

Though it was too early to allow myself relief, I saw
I'd passed the first watchdog. The Society might have
been keeping such close surveillance that Wagner would
know there had in fact been no mysterious travels of

assorted missilemen.

This wasn't plausible, Mannix had declared. The Society was limited in what it could do. Watching every nonmember's every movement was ridiculous.

"Have they reached a decision?" Wagner asked.

"Yes." No matter how level I tried to keep it, my voice seemed to shiver the bones in my head. "American personnel will be replaced by foreigners till the crisis is past. I suppose you know West Europe has a good many competent rocketeers. In civilian jobs, of course; still, they could handle a military assignment. And they'd be docile, regardless of who gave orders. The Spanish and French especially, considering how the purges went through those countries. In short, they'd not be players in the game, just parts of the machinery."

My whetted ears heard him let out a breath. "When?"

"Not certain. A move of that kind needs study and planning beforehand. A couple, three weeks? My word is that we'd better compress our own timetable."

"Indeed. Indeed." Wagner bayoneted me with his stare. "If you are correct."

"You mean if I'm telling the truth," I said on his behalf.

"You understand, Colonel Dowling, you'll have to be quizzed and examined. And we'll meet an ironic obstacle in your conditioning against involuntary betrayal of secrets."

"Eventually you'd better go ahead and trust me . . . after all these years."

"I think that will be decided on the top level."

They took me to a well-equipped room somewhere and put me through the works. They were no more unkind than necessary, but extremely thorough. Never mind details of those ten or fifteen hours. The thoroughness was not quite sufficient. My immunity and my story held up. The physical checks showed nothing suspicious. Mannix had said, "I expect an inhibition too deep for consciousness will prevent the idea from occurring to them." I'd agreed. The reality was what had overrun me.

Afterward I was given a meal and—since I'd freely admitted being full of stim—some hours under a sleep inducer. It didn't prevent dreams which I still shiver to recall. But when I was allowed to wake, I felt rested and ready for action.

Whether I'd get any was an interesting question. Mannix's hope was that I'd be taken to see persons high in the outfit, from whom I might obtain information on plans and membership. But maybe I'd be sent straight home. My yarn declared that, after the bout of talks was over, I'd requested a few days' leave, hinting to my superiors that I had a girlfriend out of town.

My guards, two young men now grown affable, couldn't guess what the outcome would be. We started a poker game but eventually found ourselves talking. These were full-time undergrounders. I asked what made them abandon their original identities. The first said, "Oh, I got caught strewing pamphlets and had to run. What brought me into the Society to start with was . . . well, one damn thing after another, like when I was a miner and they boosted our quota too high for us to maintain safety structures and a cave-in killed a buddy of mine."

The second, more bookish, said thoughtfully, "I believe in God."

I raised my brows. "Really? Well, you're not forbidden to go to church. You might not get a good job, positively never a clearance, but—"

"That's not the point. I've heard a lot of preachers in a lot of different places. They're all windup toys of the state. The Social Gospel, you know—no, I guess you don't."

Wagner arrived soon afterward. His surface calm was like dacron crackling in a wind. "Word's come, Dowling," he announced. "They want to interview you, ask your opinions, your impressions, you having been our sole man on the spot."

I rose. "They?"

"The main leadership. Sotomayor himself, and his chief administrators. Here." Wagner handed me a wallet. "Your new ID card, travel permit, ration tab, the works, including a couple of family snapshots. Learn it. We leave in an hour,"

I scarcely heard the latter part. Alfredo Sotomayor! The half-legendary president of the whole Society!

I'd wondered plenty about him. Little was known. His face was a fixture on post office walls, wanted for a variety of capital crimes, armed and dangerous. The text barely hinted at his political significance. Evidently the government didn't wish to arouse curiosity. The story told me, while I was in the long process of joining, was that he'd been a firebrand in his youth, an icily brilliant organizer in middle life, and in his old age was a scholar and philosopher, at work on a proposal for establishing a "free country," whatever that meant. Interested, I'd asked for some of his writings. They were denied me. Possession was dangerous. Why risk a useful man unnecessarily?

I was to meet rebellious Lucifer, whom I would be serving yet had not the political police laid hand on me and mine.

Not that those fingers had closed on Bonnie or the kids. They would if I didn't undo my own rebelliousness. Camp La Pasionara. . . . What was Sotomayor to me?

How could I believe a spig bandit had any real interest in America, except to plunder her? I had *not* been shown those writings.

"You feel well, Jim?" asked the man who believed in God. "You look kind of pale."

"Yeah, I'm okay," I mumbled. "Better sit down, though, and learn my new name."

A fake Security car, windows blanked, could bring me to an expendable hidey-hole like this, off in a lonely section of hills. The method was too showy for a meeting which included brains, heart, and maybe

spinal cord of Decatur. Wagner and I would use public transportation.

We walked to the nearest depot, a few kilometers
off. I'd have enjoyed the sunlight, woods, peace asparkle
with bird song, if Bonnie had been my companion
(and I whole, I whole). As was, neither of us spoke.
At the newsstand I bought a magazine and read about
official plans for my future while the train was an
hour late. It lost another hour, for some unexplained
reason, en route. About par for the course. Several
times the coach rattled to the sonic booms of military
jets. Again, nothing unusual, especially in time of
crisis. The People's Republic keeps abundant warcraft.

Our destination was Oakland. We arrived at 2000,
when the factories were letting out, and joined the
pedestrian swarm. I don't like city dwellers. They
smell sour and look grubby. Well, that's not their
fault; if soap and hot water are in short supply, people
crowded together will not be clean. But their grayness
goes deeper than their skins—except in ethnic districts,
of course, which hold more life but which you'd better
visit in armed groups.

Wagner and I found a restaurant and made the
conversation of two petty production managers on a
business trip. I flatter myself that I gave a good
performance. Concentrating on it took my mind off
the food and service.

Afterward we saw a movie, an insipidity about boy
on vacation volunteer meets girl on collective. When it
and the political reel had been endured, meeting time
was upon us. We hadn't been stopped to show our
papers, and surely any plain-clothes man running a
random surveillance had lost interest in us. A street
car groaned us to a surprisingly swank part of town,
and the house to which we walked was a big old mansion in big old grounds full of the night breath of roses.

"Isn't this too conspicuous?" I wondered.

"Ever tried being inconspicuous in a tenement?"
Wagner responded. "The poor may hate the civil police,

but the prospect of reward money makes them eyes and ears for the P.P."

He hesitated. "Since you could check it out later anyway," he said, "I may as well tell you we're at the home of Lorenzo Berg, commissioner of electric power for northern California. He's been one of us since his national service days."

I barely maintained my steady pace. This fact alone would buy me back my life.

A prominent man is a watched man. Berg's task in the Society had been to build, over the years, the image of a competent bureaucrat, who had no further ambitions and therefore was no potential menace to anybody, but who amused himself by throwing little parties where skewball intellectuals would gather to discuss the theory of chess or the origin of *Australopithecus*. Most of these affairs were genuine. For the few that weren't, he had the craft to nullify the bugs in his house and later play tapes for them which had been supplied him. Of course, a mobile tapper could have registered what was actually said—he dared not screen the place—but the P.P. had more to do than make anything but spot checks on a harmless eccentric.

Thus Berg could provide a scene for occasional important Society meetings. He could temporarily shelter fugitives. He could maintain for this area that vastly underrated tool, a reference library; who'd look past the covers of his many books and microreels? Doubtless his services went further, but never into foolish flamboyancies.

I don't recall him except as a blur. He played his role that well, even that night among those men. Or was he his role? You needn't be a burning-eyed visionary to live by a cause.

A couple like that were on hand. They must have been able in their fields. But one spoke of his specialty, massive sabotage, too lovingly for me. My missiles were counterforce weapons, not botulin mists released

among women and children. Another, who was a
black, dwelt on Russian racism. I'm sure his citations
were accurate, of how the composition of the Polit-
buro has never since the beginning reflected the na-
tionalities in the Soviet Union. Yet what had that to do
with us and why did his eyes dwell so broodingly on
the whites in the room?

The remaining half dozen were entirely business-
like in their various ways, except Sotomayor, who gave
me a courteous greeting and then sat quietly and
listened. They were ordinary Americans, which is to
say a mixed lot, a second black man, a Jew to judge by
the nose (it flitted across my mind how our schools
keep teaching that the People's Republic has abolished
the prejudices of the imperialist era, which are described in detail), a Japanese-descended woman, the
rest of them like me . . . except, again, Sotomayor, who
I think was almost pure Indio. His features were
rather long and lean for that, but he had the cheekbones,
the enduringly healthy brown skin, dark eyes altogether alive under straight white hair, flared nostrils
and sensitive mouth. He dressed elegantly, and sat
and stood as erect as a candle.

I repeated my story, was asked intelligent questions,
and carried everything off well. Maybe I was helped
by Bonnie having told me a lot about theater and
persuading me to take occasional bit parts. The hours
ticked by. Finally, around 0100, Sotomayor stirred and
said in his soft but youthful voice: "Gentlemen, I
think perhaps we have done enough for the present,
and it might arouse curiosity if the living room lights
shone very late on a midweek night. Please think
about this matter as carefully as it deserves. You
will be notified as to time and place of our next
meeting."

All but one being from out of town, they would
sleep here. Berg led them off to their cots. Sotomayor
said he would guide me. Smiling, as we started up a
grand staircase the Socialist Functionalist critics would

never allow to be built today, he took my arm and
suggested a nightcap.

He rated not a shakedown but a suite cleared for
his use.

Although a widower, Berg maintained a large house-
hold. Four grown sons pleaded the apartment shortage
as a reason for living here with their families and so pre-
venting the mansion's conversion to an ordinary tenement. They and the wives the Society had chosen for
them had long since been instructed to stay completely
passive, except for keeping their kids from overhearing
anything, and to know nothing of Society affairs.

Given that population under this roof, plus a habit
of inviting visiting colleagues to bunk with him, plus
always offering overnight accommodations when parties got wet, Berg found that guests of his drew no
undue notice.

All in all, I'd entered quite a nest. And the king
hornet was bowing me through his door.

The room around me was softly lit, well furnished,
dominated by books and a picture window. The latter
overlooked a sweep of city—lanes of street lamps cut
through humpbacked darknesses of buildings—and
the Bay and a deeper spark-speckled shadow which
was San Francisco. A nearly full moon bridged the
waters with frailty. I wondered if men would ever get
back yonder. The requirements of defense against the
revisionists—

Why in the name of madness was I thinking about
that?

Sotomayor closed the door and went to a table
whereon stood a bottle, a carafe of water, and an ice
bucket which must be an heirloom. "Please be seated,
Colonel Dowling," he said. "I have only this to offer
you, but it is genuinely from Scotland. You need a
drink, I'm sure, tense as you are."

"D-does it show that much?" Hearing the idiocy of
the question, I hauled myself to full awareness. Tomor-

row morning, when the group dispersed, Wagner would conduct me home and I would report to Mannix. My job was to stay alive until then.

"No surprise." He busied himself. "In fact, your conduct has been remarkable throughout. I'm grateful for more than your service, tremendous though that may turn out to be. I'm joyful to know we have a man like you. The kind is rare and precious."

I sat down and told myself over and over that he was my enemy. "You, uh, you overrate me, sir."

"No. I have been in this business too long to cherish illusions. Men are limited creatures at best. This may perhaps make their striving correspondingly more noble, but the limitations remain. When a strong, sharp tool comes to hand, we cherish it."

He handed me my drink, took a chair opposite me, and sipped at his own. I could barely meet those eyes, however gentle they seemed. Mine stung. I took a long gulp and blurted the first words that it occurred to me might stave off silence: "Why, being in the Society is such a risk, sir, would anybody join who's not, well, unusual?"

"Yes, in certain cases, through force of circumstance. We have taken in criminals—murderers, thieves—when they looked potentially useful."

After a moment of stillness, he added slowly: "In fact, revolutionaries, be they Decaturists or members of other outfits or isolated in their private angers— revolutionaries have always had motivations as various as their humanity. Some are idealists; yet let us admit that some of the ideals are nasty, like racism. Some want revenge for harm done them or theirs by officials who may have been sadistic or corrupt but often were merely incompetent or overzealous, in a system which allows the citizen no appeal. Some hope for money or power or fame under a new dispensation. Some are oldfashioned patriots who want us out of the empire. Am I right that you fall in that category, Colonel Dowling?"

"Yes," I said, you were.

Sotomayor's gaze went into me and beyond me. "One reason I want to know you better," he said, "is that I think you can be educated to a higher ideal."

I discovered, with a sort of happiness, that I was interested enough to take my mind off the fact I was drinking the liquor of a man who believed I was his friend and a man. "To your own purposes, sir?" I asked. "You know, I never have been told what you yourself are after."

"On as motley a collection as our members are, the effect of an official doctrine would be disruptive. Nor is any required. The history of Communist movements in the last century gives ample proof. I've dug into history, you realize. The franker material is hard to find, after periodic purges of the libraries. But it's difficult to eliminate a book totally. The printing press is a more powerful weapon than any gun—for us or for our masters." Sotomayor smiled and sighed. "I ramble. Getting old. Still, I have spent these last years of mine trying to understand what we are doing, in the hope we can do what is right."

"And what are your conclusions, sir?"

"Let us imagine our takeover plan succeeds," he answered. "We hold the rocket bases. Given those, I assure you there are enough members and sympathizers in the rest of the armed services and in civilian life that, while there will doubtless be some shooting, the government will topple and we will take over the nation."

The drink slopped in my hand. Sweat prickled forth on my skin and ran down my ribs.

Sotomayor nodded. "Yes, we are that far along," he said. "After many years and many human sacrifices, we are finally prepared. The war has given us the opportunity to use what we built."

Surely, I thought wildly, the P.P., military intelligence, high party officials, surely they knew something of the sort was in the wind. You can't altogether conceal a trend of such magnitude.

Evidently they did not suspect how far along it was.

Or . . . wait . . . you didn't need an enormous number of would-be rebels in the officer corps. You really only needed access to the dossiers and psychographs kept on everybody. Then in-depth studies would give you a good notion of how the different key men would react.

"Let us assume, then, a junta," Sotomayor was saying. "It cannot, must not be for more than the duration of the emergency. Civilian government must be restored and made firm. But *what* government? That is the problem I have been working on."

"And?" I responded in my daze.

"Have you ever read the original Constitution of the United States? The one drawn in Philadelphia in 1786?"

"Why . . . well, no. What for?"

"It may be found in scholarly works. A document so widely disseminated cannot be gotten rid of in 30 or 40 years. Though if the present system endures, I do not give the old Constitution another 50." Sotomayor leaned forward. Beneath his softness, intensity mounted. "What were you taught about it in school?"

"Oh . . . well, uh, let me think . . . Codification of the law for the bourgeoisie of the cities and the slaveowners of the South . . . Modified as capitalism evolved into imperialism . . . "

"Read it sometime." A thin finger pointed at a shelf. "Take it to bed with you. It's quite brief."

After a moment: "Its history is long, though, Colonel Dowling, and complicated, and not always pleasant — especially toward the end, when the original concept had largely been lost sight of. Yet it was the most profoundly revolutionary thing set down on paper since the New Testament."

"Huh?"

He smiled again. "Read it, I say, and compare today's version, and look up certain thinkers who are mentioned in footnotes if at all—Hobbes, Locke, Hamilton, Burke, and the rest. Then do your own thinking. That won't be easy. Some of the finest minds which ever existed spent centuries groping toward the idea—that law should be a contract the people make among each other, and that every man has absolute rights, which protect him in making his private destiny and may never be taken from him."

His smile had dissolved. I have seldom heard a bleaker tone: "Think how radical that is. Too radical, perhaps. The world found it easier to bring back overlords, compulsory belief, and neolithic god-kings."

"W-would you . . . revive the old government?"

"Not precisely. The country and its people are too changed from what they were. I think, however, we could bring back Jefferson's original idea. We could write a basic law which does not compromise with the state, and hope that in time the people will again understand."

He had spoken as if at a sacrament. Abruptly he shook himself, laughed a little, and raised his glass. "Well!" he said. "You didn't come here for a lecture. *A vuestra salud.*"

My hand still shook when I drank with him.

"We'd better discuss your personal plans," he suggested. "I know you've had a hatful of business lately, but none of us dare stay longer than overnight here. Where might you like to go?"

"Sir?" I didn't grasp his meaning at once. Drug or no, my brain was turning slowly under its burdens. "Why . . . home. Back to base. Where else?"

"Oh, no. Can't be. I said you have proved you are not a man we want to risk."

"Bu-but . . . if I don't go back, it's a giveaway!"

"No fears. We have experts at this sort of thing. You will be provided unquestionable reasons why your leave should be extended. A nervous collapse, maybe, plausible in view of the recent strains on you, and fakeable to fool any military medic into prescribing a

rest cure. Why, your family can probably join you at
some pleasant spot." Sotomayor chuckled. "Oh, you'll
work hard. We want you in consultation, and between
times I want to educate you. We'll try to arrange a
suitable replacement at Reed. But one missile base is
actually less important than the duties I have in mind
for you."

I dropped my glass. The room whirled. Through a
blur I saw Sotomayor jump up and bend over me,
heard his voice: "What's the matter? Are you sick?"

Yes, I was. From a blow to the . . . the belly.

I rallied, and knew I might argue for being returned
home, and knew it would be no use. Fending off his
anxious hands, I got to my feet. "Exhaustion, I guess,"
I slurred. "Be okay in a minute. Which way's uh
bathroom?"

"Here." He took my arm again.

When the door had closed on him, I stood in tiled
sterility and confronted my face. But adrenalin pumped
through me, and Mannix's chemicals were still there.
Everything Mannix had done was still there.

If I stalled until too late . . . the Lomonosov Institute might or might not survive. If it did, I might or
might not be admitted. If it didn't, something equivalent might or might not be built elsewhere in some
latter year. I might or might not get the benefit thereof,
before I was too old.

Meanwhile Bonnie—and my duty was not, not to
anybody's vague dream—and I had barely a minute to
decide—and it would take longer than that to change
my most recent programming—

Act! yelled the chemicals.

I zipped down my pants, took my gun in my right
hand, and opened the door.

Sotomayor had waited outside. At his back I saw
the main room, water, moon, stars. Astonishment
smashed his dignity. "Dowling, *¿esta usted loco?* What
the flaming hell—?"

Each word I spoke made me more sure, more

efficient? "This is a weapon. Stand back."

Instead, he approached. I remembered he had been in single combats and remained vigorous and leathery. I aimed past him and squeezed as I had been taught. The flash of light burned a hole through carpet and floorboards at his feet. Smoke spurted from the pockmark. It smelled harsh.

Sotomayor halted, knees bent, hands cocked. Once, hunting in the piny woods of my boyhood, we'd cornered a bobcat. It had stood the way he did, teeth peeled but body crouched moveless, watching every instant for a chance to break free.

I nodded. "Yeah," I said. "A zap gun. Sorry, I've changed teams."

He didn't stir, didn't speak, until he forced me to add: "Back. To yonder phone I see. I've got a call to make." My lips twitched sideways. "I can't very well do otherwise, can I?"

"Has that thing—" he whispered, "has that thing been substituted for the original?"

"Yes," I said. "Forget your *machismo*. I've got the glands."

"Pugilist," he breathed, almost wonderingly.

Faintly through the blood-filled stiffness of me, I felt surprise. "What?"

"The ancient Romans often did the same to their pugilists," he said in monotone. "Slaves who boxed in the arenas, iron on their fists. The man kept his physical strength, you see, but his bitterness made him fight without fear or pity. . . . Yes. Pavlov and those who used Pavlov's discoveries frequently got good reconditioning results from castration. Such a fundamental shock. This is more efficient. Yes."

Fury leaped in me. "Shut your mouth! They'll grow me back what I've lost. I love my wife."

Sotomayor shook his head. "Love is a convenient instrument for the almighty state, no?"

He had no right to look that scornful, like some aristocrat. History had dismissed them, the damned feudal oppressors; and when the men in this house were seized, and the information, his own castle would crash down.

He made a move. I leveled my weapon. His right hand simply gestured, touching brow, lips, breast, left and right shoulders. "Move!" I ordered.

He did—straight at me, shouting loud enough to wake the dead in Philadelphia.

I fired into his mouth. His head disintegrated. A cooked eyeball rolled out. But he had such speed that his corpse knocked me over.

I tore free of the embrace of those arms, spat out his blood, and leaped to lock the hall door. Knocking began a minute afterward, and the cry, "What's wrong? Let me in!"

"Everything's all right," I told the panel. "Comrade Sotomayor slipped and nearly fell. I caught him."

"Why's he silent? Let us in!"

I'd expected nothing different and was already dragging furniture in front of the door. Blows and kicks, clamor and curses waxed beyond. I scuttled to the telephone—sure, they provided this headquarters well—and punched the number Mannix had given me. An impulse would go directly to a computer which would trace the line and dispatch an emergency squad here. Five minutes?

They threw themselves at the door, thud, thud, thud. That isn't as easy as the shows pretend. It would go down before long, though. I used bed, chairs, and tables to barricade the bathroom door. I chinked my fortress with books and placed myself behind, leaving a loophole.

When they burst through, I shot and I shot and I shot. I grew hoarse from yelling. The air grew sharp with ozone and thick with cooked meat.

Two dead, several wounded, the attackers retreated. It had dawned on them that I must have summoned help and they'd better get out.

The choppers descended as they reached the street.

My rescuers of the civil police hadn't been told anything, merely given a Condition A order to raid a place. So I must be held with the other survivors to wait for higher authority. Since the matter was obviously important, this house was the jail which would preserve the most discretion.

But they had no reason to doubt my statement that I was a political agent. I'd better be confined respectfully. The captain offered me my pick of rooms and was surprised when I asked for Sotomayor's if the mess there had been cleaned up.

Among other features, it was the farthest away from everybody else, the farthest above the land.

Also, it had that bottle. I could drink if not sleep. When that didn't lift my postcombat sadness, I started thumbing through books. There was nothing else to do in the night silence.

I read: We hold these Truths to be self-evident, that all Men are created equal, that they are endowed by their Creator with certain unalienable Rights, that among these are Life, Liberty, and the Pursuit of Happiness—That to secure these Rights, Governments are instituted among Men, deriving their just Powers from the Consent of the Governed, that whenever any Form of Government becomes destructive of those Ends, it is the Right of the People to alter or to abolish it, and to institute new Government, laying its Foundation on such Principles, and organizing its Powers in such Form, as to them shall seem most likely to effect their Safety and Happiness.

I read: We the People of the United States . . . secure the Blessings of Liberty to ourselves and our Posterity . . .

I read: Congress shall make no law respecting an establishment of religion, or prohibiting the free exercise thereof; or abridging the freedom of speech, or of the press; or the right of the people peacefully to assemble, and to petition the Government for a redress of grievances.

I read: The powers not delegated to the United States by the Constitution, nor prohibited by it to the States, are reserved to the States respectively, or to the people.

I read: "I have sworn upon the altar of God eternal hostility toward every form of tyranny over the mind of man."

I read: "In giving freedom to the slave, we assure freedom to the free,—honourable alike in what we give and what we preserve."

I read: But they shall sit every man under his vine and under his fig tree; and none shall make them afraid. . . .

When Mannix arrived—in person—he blamed my sobbing on sheer weariness. He may have been right.

Oh, yes, he kept his promise. My part in this affair could not be completely shielded from suspicion among what rebels escaped the roundup. A marked man, I had my best chance in transferring to the technical branch of the political police. They reward good service.

So, after our internal crisis was over and the threat of our rockets made the Kunin faction quit, with gratifyingly little damage done the Motherland, I went to Moscow and returned whole.

Only it's no good with Bonnie, I'm no good at all.

I TELL YOU, IT'S TRUE

The mansion stood on the edge of Ban Pua town, hard by the Nan River. Through a door open to its shady-side verandah, you saw slow brown waters and intensely green trees beyond that flickered in furnace sunlight. Somewhere monkeys chattered. A couple of men in shabby uniforms stoically kept watch. Their rifles looked too big for them. George Rainsdon wondered if they had personally been in combat against his countrymen.

He brought his attention back to the interior. *Now,* he thought. The sweat that plastered his shirt to him felt suddenly cold. Yet this room, stripped of the luxuries that the landlord owner had kept, was almost serene in its austerity. The four Thais across the table were much more at ease than the five Americans.

Rainsdon knew what implacability underlay those slight, polite smiles. Behind Chukkri hung portraits of Lenin and Ho Chi Minh.

Attendants brought tea and small cakes.

Rainsdon made a sitting bow. "Again I thank Your

128

Excellency for agreeing to receive our delegation," he said with the fluency that years as a diplomat in Bangkok had given him. "Believe me, sir, the last thing my government wishes is a repetition of the Vietnam tragedy. We desire no involvement in the conflict here except to act as peacemakers." He laid on the table the box he was carrying. "In token, we beg that you accept this emblem of friendship."

"I thank you," the leader of the Sacred Liberation Movement answered. "The solution of your difficulty is quite simple. You need merely withdraw your military personnel. But let us see the gift you graciously bring."

He opened the package and took forth a handsome bronze statuette in an abstract native-derived style. Its plaque held soft words. One of his generals frowned. Chukkri flashed him a sardonic glance that might as well have said aloud, *Not even the Americans are stupid enough to imagine that assassinating us will halt the advance of our heroic troops.* "Please thank your President on my behalf," he uttered.

The warmth of his touch completed the activation of a circuit.

Rainsdon leaned forward. *Go for broke!* His slight giddiness passed into a feeling that resembled his emotions when he had led infantry charges in Korea in his long passed youth. The rehearsed but wholly sincere words torrented from him:

"Your Excellency. Gentlemen. Let me deliver, at this private and informal conference, the plain words of the United States Government. The United States has no aggressive intentions toward the people of Thailand or any other country. Our sole desire is to help Thailand end the civil war on terms satisfactory to everyone. The first and most essential prerequisite for peace is that your organization accept a cease-fire and negotiate in good faith with the legitimate government to arrange a plebiscite. Your ideology is alien to the Thai people and must not be forced on them. However, you will be free to advocate it, to persuade by precept and example, to offer candidates for office. If defeated, they must accept with grace; if victorious, they must work within the existing system. But we do not want you to renounce your principles publicly. If nothing else, you can be valuable intermediaries between us and capitals like Hanoi and Peking. Thereby you will truly serve the cause of peace and the liberation of the people."

They sat still, the short, neat Asian men, for a time that grew and grew. Rainsdon's back ached from tension. Would it work? Could it? *How* could it? He had said nothing they hadn't heard a thousand times before and scorned as mendacious where it was not meaningless. They had fought, they had lost friends dear to them, they were ready to be slain themselves or to fight on for a weary lifetime; their cause was as holy to them as that of Godfrey of Bouillon had been to him—though it was no mere Jerusalem they would rescue from the infidel, it was mankind.

Finally, frowning, a fist clenched beside his untasted cup of tea, Chukkri said, very low and slow: "I had not considered the matter in just those terms before. Would you explain in more detail?"

Rainsdon heard a gasp from his aides. They had not expected their journey would prove anything except a barren gesture. Glory mounted in him. *It does work! By God, it works!*

He got busy. The circuitry in the statuette would fuse itself into slag after three hours. That ought to be ample time. The CIA had planned this operation with ultimate care.

The laboratories stood on the peninsula south of San Francisco, commanding a magnificent view of ocean if it were possible to overlook the freeway, the motels, and the human clutter on the beach. The sanctum where Edward Sigerist and Manuel Duarte had brought their guests made it easy to ignore such encroachments. The room, though big, was windowless;

the single noise was a murmur of ventilators blowing air which carried a faint tinge of ozone; fluorescent panels threw cold light on the clutter of gadgetry burying the workbenches around the walls, and on the solitary table in the center where six men sat and regarded a thing.

Fenner from MIT spoke: "Pretty big for that level of output, isn't it?" His tone was awed; he was merely breaking a lengthy silence.

"Breadboard circuit," Sigerist answered, equally unnecessarily considering what a jumble of wires and electronic components the thing was. "Any engineer could miniaturize it to the size of your thumb, for short-range work, in a few months. Or scale it up for power, till three of them in synchronous satellites could blanket the Earth. If he couldn't do that, from the cookbook, he'd better go back to chipping flints." He was a large, shaggy, rumpled man. His voice was calm but his eyes were haunted.

"Of course, he'd need the specs," said his collaborator, lean, intense, dark-complexioned Duarte. His glance ranged over the visitors. Fenner, physicist, sharp-featured beneath a cupola of forehead; Mottice, bio-chemist from London, plump and placid except for the sweat that now glistened on his cheeks; tiny Yuang of the Harvard psychology department; and Ginsberg of Cal Tech, who resembled any grocer or bookkeeper till you remembered his Nobel Prizes for quantum field theory and molecular biology. "That's why we brought you gentlemen here."

"Why the secrecy?" Yuang asked. "Our work has all been reported in the open literature. Others can build on it, as you have done. Others doubtless will."

"N-n-not inevitably," Sigerist replied. "Kind of a fluke, our success. This isn't a big outfit, you know. Mostly we contract to do R and D on biomedical instrumentation. I'm alone in having a completely free hand, which is how come I get away with studying dowsing. I was carrying on Rocard's investigations, which were published back in the mid-'60s and never got the attention they deserved."

Receiving blank stares: "Essentially, he gave good theoretical and experimental grounds for supposing that dowsing results from the nervous system's response to variations in terrestrial magnetism. I was using your data too, Dr. Mottice, Dr. Ginsberg. Then at the Triple-A-S meeting three years ago, I happened to meet Manuel at an afterhours beer party. He was with General Electric . . . He called to my notice the papers by Dr. Yuang and Dr. Fenner. We both took fire; I arranged for him to transfer here; we worked together. Kept our mouths shut, at first because we weren't sure where we were going, later because we made a breakthrough and suddenly realized what it meant to the world." He shrugged. "An unlikely set of coincidences, no?"

"Well," Ginsberg inquired, "what effects do you anticipate?"

"For openers," Duarte told him, "we can stop the war in Thailand. Soon after, we can stop all war everywhere."

The room was long, mirrored, ornate in the red plush fashion of Franz Josef's day. The handful of men who sat there were drab by contrast, like beetles.

Not a bad comparison, thought the President of the United States. *For Party Secretary Tupilov, at least. Premier Grigorovitch seems a bit more human.*

He made the slight, prearranged hand signal. His interpreter responded by nervously tugging his necktie. It energized a circuit in what appeared to be a cigarette case.

"First," said the President, "I want to express my appreciation of your cooperativeness. I hope the considerable concessions made by the United States, especially with regard to the Southeast Asia question, seemed more than a bribe to win your presence here. I hope they indicated that my government genuinely desires a permanent settlement of the conflicts that rack the world — a settlement such that armed strife can never occur again."

While his interpreter put it into Russian, he watched the two overlords. His heart thumped when Grigorovitch beamed and nodded. Tupilov's dourness faded to puzzlement; he shook his big bald head as if to clear away an interior haze.

His political years had taught the President how to assume sternness at will, however more common geniality was. "I shall be blunt," he continued. "I shall tell you certain home truths in unvarnished language. We can have no peace until every nation is secure. This requires general nuclear disarmament, enforced by adequate inspection. It requires that the great powers join to guarantee every country safety, not against overt invasion alone, but also against subversion and insurrection. Undeniably, every nation that we Americans label 'free' is not. Many of their governments are tyrannical and corrupt. But liberation is not to be accomplished through violent revolution on the part of fanatics who, if successful, would upset the world balance of power and so bring us to the verge of the final war.

"Instead, peace requires that the leading nations cooperate to make available to the people of every country the means for orderly replacement of their governments through genuinely free elections. This presupposes that they be granted freedom of speech, assembly, petition, travel, and worship, in fact as well as in name.

"Gentlemen, we have talked too long and done too little about democracy. We must begin by putting our own houses in order. You will not resent my stating that your house is in the most urgent need of this."

For the only time on record, Igor Tupilov wept.

"I find it hard to believe," Mottice whispered. "That fundamental a change . . . from a few radio quanta?"

"We found it hard to believe, too," Sigerist admitted, grimly rather than excitedly. "However, your work on synergistics had suggested that the right combination of impulses might trigger autocatalytic transformations in the synapeses. It doesn't take a lot, you see. These events happen on the molecular level. What's needed is not quantity but quality: the exact frequencies, amplitudes, phases, and sequences."

"Our initial evidence came from rats," Duarte said. "When we could alter their training at will, we proceeded to monkeys, finally man. The human pattern turned out to be a good deal more complex, as you'd expect. Finding it was largely a matter of cut-and-try . . . and, again, sheer luck."

Yuang scowled. "You still don't know precisely what the chemistry and neurology are?"

"How could we, two of us in this short a time? Our inducer ought to make quite a research tool!"

"I am wondering about possible harm to the subject."

"We haven't found any," Sigerist stated, "and we didn't just use volunteers for experimentation, we took part ourselves. Nothing happens except that the subject believes absolutely what he's told or what he reads while he's in the inducer field. There doesn't seem to be decay of the new patterns afterward. Why should there be? What we have is nothing but an instant re-educator."

"Instant brainwasher," Ginsberg muttered.

"Well, it's subject to abuse, like all tools," Fenner said. They could see enthusiasm rising in him. "Imagine, though, the potentialities for good. A scalpel can kill a man or save his life. Maybe the inducer can save his soul."

The agent of the Human Relations Board smiled across his desk. "I think our meeting has a symbolic value beyond even what we hope to accomplish," he said.

Hatred smoldered back at him from dark eyes under a bush of hair. One brown fist thumped a chair arm. The bearded lips spat: "Get with it, mother! I promised you an hour o' my time for your donation to the Black Squadron, and sixty minutes by that clock is what you're gonna get, mother."

The local head of Citizens for Law and Order turned mushroom pallid. His dull-blue eyes popped behind their rimless glasses. "What?" he exclaimed. "You . . . gave government funds . . . to that gang of . . . of nihilists — ?"

"You will recall, sir," the Human Relations agent replied, mildly, "that you agreed to come after I promised that the investigation of the assault on Reverend Washington would be dropped."

He pressed a button on his desk. "Ringing for coffee," he said, repeating his smile. "I suspect we'll be here longer than an hour."

He leaned forward. As he spoke, passion transfigured his homely features. "Sirs," he declared, "you are both men whose influence goes well beyond this community. Your power for good is potentially still greater than your power for evil. A moderate solution to the problems which called forth your respective organizations must be found . . . before the country we share is torn apart. It can be found! If not perfect satisfaction, then equal and endurable dissatisfaction. If not utopia, then human decency. The white man must lay aside his superiority complex, his greed, his indifference to the suffering around him. The black man must lay aside his hatred, his impatience, his unrealistic separatism. We must work and sacrifice together. We must individually strive to give more than we get, in order that our children may inherit what is rightfully theirs: freedom, equality, and well-being under the law. For we are in fact all equals, all Americans, all brothers in our common humanity."

He spoke on, and his visitors looked from him to each other with a widening gaze, and at last, slowly, their hands reached forth to clasp.

"And if a mistake is made," Duarte answered Fenner in a sarcastic tone, "why, you give the patient a jolt of inducer and straighten him out again." He grinned. "Sig and I actually got to playing with that. He made me a Baptist. I retaliated by making him a vegetarian."

"How'd it feel?" Yuang inquired, sharp-voiced.

"M-m-m . . . hard to describe." Sigerist rubbed his chin and leaned back in his chair till he looked at the ceiling. "We knew what was going on, you see, which our test subjects didn't. Nevertheless, vegetarianism seemed utterly right. No, let me rephrase that: it *was* right. I'd think of what I've read about slaughter-houses and — We foresaw this, naturally. We stuck by our promises to return next day and be, uh, disillusioned, told we'd been forced into a channel, that our prior beliefs and preferences were normal for us. I thought I could make the comparison later, having then experienced both attitudes, and decide objectively which was better. But right away, when Manuel spoke to me, after the slight initial fogginess of mind had cleared, right away I decided what the hell, I do like steak."

Duarte sobered. "For my part," he said, "frankly, I miss God. I've considered going back to religion. Might have done so by now, except I realize certain faiths are . . . well, easier to hold, and I'd be sensible to investigate first."

Penny twisted a strand of blond hair nervously between her fingers. Her bare foot kicked an old copy of the *Tribe* against a catbox ammoniacally overdue for changing, with a dry rustle and a small puff of flug. Sunlight straggled through the window grime to glisten off bacon grease on the dishes which filled the sink in one corner of her pad.

"Like, talk," she invited. "Do your thing."

"I hope you don't consider me a busybody," said the social worker in the enormous hat. She sighed. "You probably do. But with your unemployment compensation expiring—"

Penny sat down on the mattress which served for a bed, lit a cigarette, and wished it were a joint. "I'll get along."

The social worker raised a plump arm to point at Billy, playing contentedly with himself in his playpen. At eighteen months, his face had acquired enough individuality that Penny had felt sure Big Dick was the father. She often wondered where Big Dick had gone.

"I'm concerned about him," the social worker proceeded. "Don't you realize you're creating a misfit?"

"This is a world he ought to fit into?" Penny drawled. "Come off it." The smoke was pleasantly acrid in her nostrils.

"Do listen, darling." The social worker gripped her big purse, almost convulsively, squeezing together the brass knobs on its clasp. "You're throwing away his life as well as your own."

For a moment the peace emblem drawn on the wall wobbled. *Damn tobacco,* Penny thought. *Cancer.* She stubbed out the cigarette on the floor. It occurred to her that she really must unplug the bathtub drain, or anyway wash her feet in the sink . . . Oddly hard to concentrate. The woman in the enormous hat droned on:

"—you'll move in with yet another man, or he'll move in with you. Don't you realize that a kiss can transmit syphilis? You could infect your little boy."

Oh, no! Horror struck. *I never thought about that!*

"—You say you are protesting the evil and corruption of society. What evil? What corruption? Look around you. Look at the Thailand Peace, the Vienna Détente, the Treaty of Peking. What about the steady decline of interracial violence, the steady growth of interracial cooperation? What about the new penological program, hundreds of prisoners let out of jail every day, going straight and staying straight?"

"Well," Penny stammered, "well, uh, yeah, I guess that's true, like I seen it in the papers, I guess, only can you trust the kept press?"

"Of course you can! Not that the press is kept. This is a free country. You have your own newspapers of dissent, don't you?"

"Well, we got a lot to dissent about," Penny said. The way the visitor talked and acted, she had to be a person who'd understand. "I don't work on one myself, though. Like, that's not my bag. I'm not the kind that wants to kill pigs or throw rocks, either. I mean, a pig's human too, you know? Only when my friends keep getting busted or clubbed, like that, I can't blame they get mad. See what I mean? If we could all love each other, the problems would go away. Only most people are so uptight they can't love, they don't know how, and the problems get worse and worse." Penny shook her head, trying to clear out the haze. *But things* are *getting better like she said!* "Maybe they've finally begun to learn how in the establishment?"

"They have always known, my dear," the social worker answered. "What they have found at last is practical ways to cure troubles. We have a wonderful future before us. And violence, dropping out, unfair criticism is not what's bringing it. What we need is cooperation within the system.

"You're not with it, Penny. I'll tell you where it's at. Law is where it's at; the police aren't your enemies, they're your friends, your protectors. Cleanliness is where it's at, health, leaving dope alone, regular habits, regular work; that's how you contribute your share to the commune. And marriage. You simply don't know what love is till you're making it with one cat, the two of you sharing your whole lives, raising fine clean bright children in a country you are proud of—"

I . . . I never saw . . . never understood. . . .

Finally Penny cried on the large bosom, in the comforting circle of the plump arms. The social worker soothed her, murmured to her, breathed in her ear, "You don't have to give up your friends, you know. On the contrary. Help them. Help me call them together for a rally where we can tell them—"

"What happens to the person who operates the inducer, hands out the propaganda?" Fenner wondered.

"Oh, the impulses can be screened off," Sigerist replied. "You can easily imagine how. We used a grounded metal-mesh booth. Manuel's since designed a screen in the form of a net over the head, which could be disguised by a wig or a hat. For weak short-range projections, anyhow. Powerful ones, meant to cover a large area, would doubtless continue to require a special room for the speaker." He hesitated. "We haven't established whether psychoinduction occurs with more than one type of radio input. If it does, perhaps a shield against a given type can be bypassed by another."

"I tried to lie, experimentally, while under the field myself," Duarte said. "And I couldn't. I'd try to convince a volunteer that, oh, that two and two equals five. Right off, I'd get appalled and think, 'You can't do that to him! It isn't a fact!' Of course, fiction or poetry or something like that was okay to read aloud, except I got some odd looks from our subjects when I kept explaining at length that what they were hearing was untrue."

"So we'd either speak our lies from the booth," Sigerist put in, "or we'd tell them things we knew . . . believed . . . were real. That's another funny experience. Reinforcement in the brain, I suppose. At any rate, you grow quite vehement, about everything from Maxwell's equations on up. We confined ourselves to that sort of thing with the volunteers, understand. First, we'd no right to tamper with their minds. Second, we didn't want to give the game away. They were always told this was a study of how the tracings on a new kind of three-dimensional EEG correlate with verbal stimuli. Our falsehoods were neutral items. 'Have you heard Doc Malanowicz is trying to use the Hilsch tube in respiratory function measurements?' Next day we'd disabuse them, always in such a fashion that they didn't suspect. We hope. The spectacular

lies we saved for each other." His chuckle was not too
happy a sound. "I'm a Republican and Manuel's a
Democrat. When we were experimenting, both of us
under the inducer field—the temptation to make a
convert grew almighty strong."

"Ladies and gentlemen, the President of the United
States."

"My fellow Americans. Tonight I wish to discuss
with you the state of the nation and of the world. Our
problems are many and grave. You know them both
by name and by experience—international turmoil;
cruel ideologies; subversion; outright treason; lawless-
ness; domestic discord, worsened by the unfair criticism of certain so-called intellectuals—a small minority,
I hasten to add, since by and large the intellectual
community is firmly loyal to the American ideal.

"What is that ideal? Let me tell you the eternal
truths on which this country is founded, for which it
stands. We believe in God. We believe in country; we
stand ready to fight and die if need be, in the convic-
tion that America's cause is always just. We believe in
the democratic process, and therefore in the leaders
which that process has given us—"

Ginsberg whistled. "If this gadget fell into the wrong
hands—Help!"

"Would it necessarily?" Fenner asked. His glance
flickered around the table. "I know what you're thinking," he said in a hurried voice. " 'The H-bomb's not
in a class with this.' Right? Well, let me remind you
that thermonuclear fusion is on the point of giving us
unlimited power . . . clean power, that doesn't poison
air or soil. Let me remind you of lives saved and
knowledge gained through abundant radionuclides.
And the big birds haven't flown yet, have they?" He
drew breath. "If this, uh, inducer is as advertised, and
I see no reason to doubt that, why, can't you see what
it'll mean? Research. Therapy. Yes, and securing the

world. I don't mind admitting I'd turn it on some of those characters who're destroying the ecology that keeps us all alive. Why not? Why can't the inducer be used judiciously?"

"One problem is, when you have the specs, this is an easy thing to build, at least on a small scale," Sigerist replied. "Now when in history was perfect security achieved? You can't reach the entire human race, you know. You may broadcast 'Love thy neighbor' while flooding the planet with inducer waves. But what of the guy who doesn't tune you in? Suppose he happens to be reading *Mein Kampf* instead? Or is down in a mine or driving through a tunnel? Or simply asleep?

"Is everyone who's to be given any knowledge of the inducer's existence . . . will everybody be dragooned first into a mental Janissary corps? I don't see how that can be practical. Their very presence and behavior would tip off shrewd men. And then there are ways . . . burglary, assassination, duplication of research. . . . And once the fact is loose—"

Pidge had to stand a minute and fight his nerves after he stepped out of the car. What if something went wrong?

The suburban street (trees, hedges, lawns, flowers, big well-built houses, under afternoon sunlight that brought forth an odor of growth and a chorus of birdsong) pressed him with its alienness. He was from the inner city, tenements, dark little stores, bars and poolhalls that smelled of urine, smog and blowing trash and thundering trucks and gray crowds. This place was too goddamn quiet. Nobody around except a couple of kids playing in a yard, a starchy nurse pushing a stroller down the sidewalk, a dog or two.

Pidge squared his narrow shoulders. *Don't crawfish now! After the casing you've done, the money you've laid out*—He rallied resentment. *You're not doing a thing except claiming your share. The rich bitches have pushed you around too goddamn long.*

And he wasn't drawing any attention here. He was sure he wasn't. White, and small, not like those bastards who'd shoved him out of their way through his whole life, oh, he'd show them how brains counted. . . . Shave, haircut, good suit, conservative tie, shined shoes, Homburg hat (the wires and transistors beneath his wig enclosed his scalp like claws), briefcase from the Goodwill and car borrowed but you couldn't tell that by looking. And he'd spent many hours in this neighborhood, watched, eased into conversation with servants; everything was known, everything planned, he'd only to go through with his program.

And They wouldn't appreciate his backing out. He'd had a tough time as was, wheedling till They let him in on the operation—the set of operations—he'd gotten wind of. Buying in had cost him all he could scrape together and a third of the haul when he was finished. And it had demanded he do his own legwork and prove he had a good plan.

Well, sure, they'd had plenty of trouble, expense, and risk beforehand, to make these jobs possible. Finding out what was being done in the jails that turned so many guys into squares, hell, into stoolies; finding guards who could be bought; arranging for an apparatus to be smuggled out and stuff to be left behind so the fuzz would think it'd simply been busted; getting those scientific guys to copy the apparatus. And of course it couldn't be used more than for maybe a week, on the scale that they intended. Though people were awful stodgy, unalert, these days—those that watched the speeches on TV or read the papers; don't ever do that, Pidge—the cops wouldn't be too dumb to understand what had happened. Then the apparatus wouldn't be good for anything but hit-and-run stuff.

If Pidge screwed up now, They would be mad. Probably They'd make an example of him.

He shivered. His shoes clacked on the sidewalk.

The doorbell of his target sounded faintly in his

ears. He tried to wet his lips, but his tongue was too
dry. The door swung noiselessly open. A maid said,
"Yes, can I help you?"

Pidge pressed the clasp of his briefcase the way
he'd been taught. "I have an appointment with Mr.
Ames," he said.

For an instant she hesitated. His heart stumbled.
He knew the reason for her surprise; he'd studied this
layout plenty close. The industrialist always spent
Wednesdays at home, seeing no one except people he
liked. He could afford to.

The maid's brow cleared. "Please come in, sir."

After that, it was a piece of cake. Ames got on the
phone and managed to arrange the withdrawal of
almost two million in bills, certified checks, and bearer
bonds without causing suspicion. He thought Pidge
was giving him a chance to make a killing. His wife
and staff made no fuss about waiting in an offside
room, when Pidge whispered to them that national
security was involved.

Naturally, the Brink's truck took a couple of hours
to arrive. Pidge had himself a bonus meanwhile. Ames'
daughter came back from high school, and she was a
looker. Not expert in bed, you couldn't expect that of a
virgin, but he sure made her anxious to please him.
Pidge had never had a looker before. He was tempted
to bring her along. But no, too risky. With his kind of
money he'd be able to have whatever he wanted. He
would.

After the armored truck was gone and the haul had
been transferred in suitcases to Pidge's car, he told the
people of the house that life was worthless and an
hour from now they should let Ames shoot them.
Then the man should do himself in. Pidge drove off to
his rendezvous with Their representative, who held
his ticket and passport.

"Oh, you can raise assorted horrors," Fenner argued,
"but to be alive is to take chances, and I don't see any

risks here that can't be handled. I mean, the United States Government isn't a bloc, it's composed of people, mostly intelligent and well-meaning. Their viewpoints vary. They're quite able to anticipate a possible monolith and take precautions."

"Tell me, what is a monolith?" Sigerist retorted. "Where does rehabilitation leave off and brainwashing begin? What are the constitutional rights of Birchers and militants? Of criminals, for that matter?"

"You're right," Mottice said. The sweat was running heavily down his face; they caught the reek of it. "This must never be used on humans without their prior consent and full understanding."

"Not even on those who're killing American boys and Thai peasants?" Sigerist asked. "Not even to head off nuclear war? Given such an opportunity to help, can you do nothing and live with yourself afterward? And once you've started, where do you stop?"

"You can't keep the secret forever," Duarte said. "Believe me, we've tried to think of ways. Every plausible consequence of the inducer's existence that we've talked about involves the destruction of democracy. And none of the safety measures can work for the rest of eternity. The world has more governments, more societies than ours. Maybe you can convert their present leaders. But the fact of conversion will be noticed, the leaders will have successors, the successors could take precautions of their own and quietly instigate research."

In his last years George Rainsdon always had a headache. He was old when the mesh was planted beneath his scalp, and the technique was new. The results were therefore none too good in his case; and the doctors said that doing the job over would likely cause further nerve damage. As a rule the pain was no worse than a background, never completely outside his awareness. Today it was bad, and he knew it would increase till he lay blind and vomiting.

"I'm going home early," he told his secretary, and

rose from the desk.

Penelope Gorman's impeccable façade opened to reveal sympathy. "Another sick spell?" she murmured.

Rainsdon nodded, and wished he hadn't when the pain sloshed around his skull. "I'll recover. The pills really do help." He attempted to smile. "The cause is good, remember."

Her lips tightened. "Good? Only in a way, sir. Only because of the Asians, the radicals, the criminals. Without them, we wouldn't need protection."

"Certainly not," Rainsdon agreed. The indoctrination lecture, required of every citizen before implantation was performed, had made that clear. (A beautiful ceremony had evolved, too, for the younger generation: the eighteen-year-old candidates solemn in their new clothes, families and friends present, wreaths of flowers on the inducer, religious and patriotic exhortations that stirred the soul.) To be sure, crime and political deviancy were virtually extinct. Yet they could rise again. Without preventive measures, they would, and this time the inducer would let them wreck America. Eternal vigilance is the price of liberty.

Tragic, that indoctrination of the whole world had not been possible. But in the chaos that followed the Treaty of Peking, the breakup of the Communist empires after Communism was renounced . . . a Turkoman adventurer somehow welding together a kingdom in Central Asia, somehow obtaining the inducer, probably from a criminal . . . the United States too preoccupied with Latin America, with inculcating those necessary bourgeois virtues that the pseudointellectuals used to sneer at . . . and suddenly the Asians had produced nuclear weapons, insulating the helmets for everybody, their domain expanded with nightmare speed, soon they too were in space and could cover the Western Hemisphere with inducer signals, turning all men into robots unless defenses were erected, civilian as well as military—Rainsdon forced his mind out of that channel. Truth was truth; still, people did tend to get obsessed with their righteous indignation.

"You knock off too, Mrs. Gorman," he said. "I've no chores for you till I recover." The small advisory service —international investments—that he had founded after leaving a diplomatic corps that no longer needed many personnel used public data and computer lines. His office was thus essentially a one-man show.

"Thank you, sir. I appreciate your kindness. I'm snowed under by work in the Edcorps."

"The what?" he asked, having scarcely heard through a fresh surge of migraine.

"Educational Corps. You know. Volunteers, helping poor children. The regular schools teach them to honor their country and obey the law, of course. But schooling can't overcome the harm from generations of neglect, can't teach them skills to make them useful and productive citizens, without extra coaching." Mrs. Gorman rattled her speech off so fast that it must be one she often gave. Repetition didn't seem to lessen her earnestness. *Sexual sublimation?* Rainsdon wondered. He'd had occasion to visit her apartment. Aside from photographs of her late husband, it might almost have been a cell in a convent.

They left together. She matched her pace to his shuffle. The elevator took them down and they emerged on Fifth Avenue. Sunlight spilled through the crisp autumn air that could blow nowhere but in New York. Pedestrians strode briskly along the sidewalks. How wise the government had been to phase out private automobiles! How wise the government was!

"Shall I see you home, Mr. Rainsdon? You look quite ill."

"No, thank you, Mrs. Gorman. I'll catch a bus here and—"

The words thundered forth.

PEOPLE OF AMERICA! CLAIM YOUR FREEDOM! YOUR DIABOLICAL RULERS HAVE ENSLAVED YOU WITH LIES AND SHUT YOU AWAY FROM THE TRUTH BY WIRES IN YOUR VERY

BODIES. EVERYTHING YOU HAVE BEEN FORCED TO BELIEVE IS FALSE. BUT THE HOUR OF YOUR DELIVERANCE IS AT HAND. THE SCIENTISTS OF THE ASIAN UNION HAVE FOUND THE MEANS TO BREAK OPEN YOUR MENTAL PRISON. NOW HEAR THE TRUTH, AND THE TRUTH SHALL MAKE YOU FREE! HELP YOUR FRIENDS, YOUR LIBERATORS, THE FREE PEOPLE OF THE ASIAN UNION, TO DESTROY YOUR OPPRESSORS AND EXPLOITERS! RISE AGAINST THE AMERICAN DICTATORSHIP. DESTROY ITS FACTORIES, OFFICES, MILITARY FACILITIES, DESTROY THE BASIS OF ITS POWER. KILL THOSE WHO RESIST. DIE IF YOU MUST, THAT YOUR CHILDREN MAY BE FREE!

Down and down the skyscraper walls, from building after building, from end to end of the megalopolis, the voices roared. Rainsdon knew an instant when there flashed through him, *Megaphone-taper units, radio triggered, my God, they must've planted them over the whole country, a million in New York alone, but they're small and cheap, and somewhere beyond that bright blue sky a spacecraft is beaming —* Then he knew how he had been betrayed, chained, vampirized by monsters of cynicism whose single concern was to grind down forever the aspirations of mankind, until the Great Khan had been forced to draw his flaming sword of justice.

Penny ripped apart her careful hairdo. Graying blond tresses spilled, Medusa locks, over her breasts while she discarded gown, shoes, stockings, corset, the stifling convict uniform put on her by a gaoler civilization. Her shriek cut through the howl of the crowd in the only words of protest she knew, remembered from distant childhood. *"Fuck the establishment! Freedom now!"*

Rainsdon grabbed her arm. "Follow me," he said into her ear. His headache was nearly gone in a glandular rush of excitement, his thoughts leaped, it was like being young again and leading a charge in Korea, save that today his cause was holy. "Come on." He dragged her back inside.

She struggled. "What you at, man? Lemme go! I got pigs to kill."

"Listen." He gestured at the human mass which seethed and bawled outside. "You'd be trampled. That's no army, that's a mob. Think. If the Asians can develop an inducer pattern that gets past our mesh, be sure the kept American technicians have imagined the possibility. Maybe they've developed a shield against it. They'd have sat on that, hoping to keep secret— Anyway, they'll have made preparations against our learning the truth. They'll send in police, the Guard, tanks, helicopters, the works. And these buildings, they probably screen out radiation, they must be full of persons who haven't had the slave conditioning broken. Penelope, our best service is to find that voice machine and guard it with our lives. Give more people a chance to come out where the truth can reach them."

They located the device in an office and waited, deafened, tormented, stunned by its magnitude of sound. Hand in hand, they stood their prideful watch.

But no one disturbed them for the hour or two that remained, and they never felt the blast that killed them.

The Asians knew that American missile sites were insulated against any radio impulses that might be directed at the controllers. They counted on those missiles staying put. For what would be the point of an American launch, when Washington could no longer govern its own subjects? At the agreed-upon moment, their special envoy was offering the President the help of the Great Khan in restoring order; at a price to be sure.

The Great Khan's advisors were wily men. However, being themselves conditioned, they did not realize they were fanatics; and being fanatics, they did not have the empathy to see that their opponents would necessarily resemble them.

In strike and counterstrike, the big birds flew.

"Well, that's certainly a hairy bunch of scenarios," Fenner admitted after a long discussion. "Are you sure things would turn out so bad?"

"The point is," Sigerist replied, "do we dare assume they wouldn't?"

"What do you propose, then?" Mottice asked.

"That's what we've invited you here to help decide," Duarte said.

Ginsberg shifted his bulky body. "I suspect you mean you want us to ratify a decision you've already made," he said, "and its nature is obvious."

"Suppression—No, damn it!" Fenner protested. "I admit we need to exercise caution, but suppressing data—"

"Worse than that," Sigerist said most softly. "As the recognized authorities in your different fields, you'll have to steer your colleagues away from this area altogether."

"How will we do that?" Yuang demanded. "Suppose I cook an experiment. Somebody is bound to repeat it."

"We're big game, you know," Mottice put in. "A new-made Ph.D. who found us out would make a name for himself. Which would reinforce him in pursuing that line of work."

"The ways needn't be crude," Sigerist said. "If you simply, without any fuss, drop various projects as 'unpromising,' well, you're able men who'll get results elsewhere; you're leaders, who set the fashion. If you scoff a bit at the concept of neuroinduction, raise an eyebrow when Rocard is mentioned . . . it can be done."

He paused. Drawing a breath, rising to his feet, he said, "It must be done."

Ginsberg realized what was intended and scrabbled frantically across the table at the device. Sigerist pinioned his arms. Duarte pulled an automatic from his pocket. "Stand back!" the younger man shouted.

"I'm a good target shooter. Back!"

They stumbled into a corner. Ginsberg panted, Fenner cursed; Mottice glared; Yuang, after a moment, nodded. Duarte held the gun steady. Sigerist began crying. "This was our work too, you know," he said through the tears. He pressed a button. A vacuum tube glowed and words come out of a tape recorder.

Five years afterward, Sigerist and his family tuned in a program. Most educated persons did, around the world. The Premier of the Chinese People's Republic had announced a major speech on policy, using and celebrating the three synchronous relay satellites which his country had lately put into orbit. Simultaneous translation into many languages would be provided.

Considering the belligerence of previous statements, Sigerist joined the rest of the human race in worrying about what would be said. He, his wife, the children who were the purpose of their lives, gathered in a solemn little group before the screen. The hour in Peking was well before dawn, which assured that India was the sole major foreign country where live listening would be inconvenient. Well, the eastern Soviet Union too, not to mention China itself; but there would be rebroadcasts, printed texts, commentaries for weeks to come.

When the talk was over, Sigerist's wife sought his arms and gasped with relief. He held her close and grinned shakily across her shoulder at the kids. The Premier's words had been so reasonable, so unarguably right. They had opened his eyes to any number of things which had not occurred to him before. For a moment during those revelations he'd wondered, been afraid . . . and then, actually quite early in the speech, the Premier had smiled with his unmatched kindliness and said: "The enemies of progress have accused us of brainwashing, including by electronic methods. I tell you, and you will believe me, nothing of the sort has ever happened."

KINGS WHO DIE

Luckily, Diaz was facing the other way when the missile exploded. It was too far off to blind him permanently, but the retinal burns would have taken a week or more to heal. He saw the glare reflected in his view lenses. As a ground soldier he would have hit the rock and tried to claw himself a hole. But there was no ground here, no up or down, concealment or shelter, on a fragment of spaceship orbiting through the darkness beyond Mars. Diaz went loose in his armor. Countdown: brow, jaw, neck, shoulders, back, chest, belly. . . . No blast came, to slam him against the end of his lifeline and break any bones whose muscles were not relaxed. So it had not been a shaped charge shell, firing a cone of atomic-powered concussion through space. Or if it was, he had not been caught in the danger zone. As for radiation, he needn't worry much about that. Whatever particles and gamma photons he got at this distance should not be too big a dose for the anti-X in his body to handle the effects.

He drew a breath which was a good deal shakier

than the Academy satorist would have approved of. ("If your nerves twitch, cadet-san, then you know yourself alive and they need not twitch. Correct?" To hell with that, except as a technique.) Slowly, he hauled himself in until his boots made magnetic contact and he stood, so to speak, upon his raft. Then he turned about for a look.

"Nombre de Dios," he murmured, a hollow noise in the helmet. Forgotten habit came back, with a moment's recollection of his mother's face. He crossed himself.

Against blackness and a million wintry stars, a gas cloud expanded. It glowed in many soft hues, the center still bright, edges fading into vacuum. Shaped explosions did not behave like that, thought the calculator part of Diaz; this had been a standard fireball type. But the cloud was nonspherical. Hence a ship had been hit, a big ship, but whose?

Most of him stood in wonder. A few years ago he'd spent a furlough at Antarctic Lodge. He and some girl had taken a snowcat out to watch the aurora, thinking it would make a romantic background. But when they saw the sky, they forgot about each other for a long time. There was only the aurora.

The same awesome silence was here, as that incandescence which had been a ship and her crew swelled and vanished into space.

The calculator in his head proceeded with its business. Of those American vessels near the *Argonne* when first contact was made with the enemy, only the *Washington* was sufficiently massive to go out in a blast of yonder size and shape. If that was the case Captain Martin Diaz of the United States Astromilitary Corps was a dead man. The other ships of the line were too distant, traveling on vectors too unlike his own, for their scoutboats to come anywhere close. On the other hand, it might well have been a Unasian battlewagon. Diaz had small information on the dispositions of the enemy fleet. He'd had his brain full just directing the torp launchers under his immediate command. If that had indeed been a hostile dread-naught that got clobbered, surely none but the *Washington* could have delivered the blow, and its boats would be near—

There!

For half a second Diaz was too stiffened by the sight to react. The boat ran black across waning clouds, accelerating on a streak of its own fire. The wings and sharp shape that were needed in atmosphere made him think of a marlin he had once hooked off Florida, blue lightning under the sun. . . . Then a flare was in his hand, he squeezed the igniter and radiance blossomed.

Just an attention-getting device, he thought, and laughed unevenly as he and Bernie Sternthal had done, acting out the standard irreverences of high school students toward the psych course. But Bernie had left his bones on Ganymede, three years ago, and in this hour Diaz's throat was constricted and his nostrils full of his own stench. He skyhooked the flare and hunkered in its harsh illumination by his radio transmitter. Clumsy in their gauntlets, his fingers adjusted controls, set the revolving beams on SOS. If he had been noticed, and if it was physically possible to make the velocity changes required, a boat would come for him. The Corps looked after its own.

Presently the flare guttered out. The pyre cloud faded to nothing. The raft deck was between Diaz and the shrunken sun. But the stars that crowded on every side gave ample soft light. He allowed his gullet, which felt like sandpaper, a suck from his one water flask. Otherwise he had several air bottles, an oxygen reclaim unit, and a ridiculously large box of Q rations. His raft was a section of inner plating, torn off when the *Argonne* encountered the ball storm. She was only a pursuit cruiser, unarmored against such weapons. At thirty miles per second, relative, the little steel spheres tossed in her path by some Unasian gun had not left much but junk and corpses. Diaz had found no other survivors. He'd lashed what he could salvage onto this raft, including a shaped torp charge that rocketed him clear of the ruins. This far spaceward, he didn't need screen fields against solar particle radiation. So he had had a small hope of rescue. Maybe bigger than small, now.

Unless an enemy craft spotted him first. His scalp crawled with that thought. His right arm, where the thing he might use in the event of capture lay buried, began to itch. But no, he told himself, don't be sillier than regulations require. That scoutboat was positively American. The probability of a hostile vessel being in detection range of his flare and radio—or able to change vectors fast enough—or giving a damn about him in any event—approached so close to zero as made no difference.

"Wish I'd found our bottle in the wreckage," he said aloud. He was talking to Carl Bailey, who'd helped him smuggle the Scotch aboard at Shepard Field when the fleet was alerted for departure. The steel balls had chewed Carl to pieces, some of which Diaz had seen. "It gripes me not to empty that bottle. On behalf of us both, I mean. Maybe," his voice wandered on, "a million years hence, it'll drift into another planetary system and owl-eyed critters will pick it up in boneless fingers, eh, Carl, and put it in a museum." He realized what he was doing and snapped his mouth shut. But his mind continued. *The trouble is, those critters won't know about Carl Bailey, who collected antique jazz tapes, and played a rough game of poker, and had a D.S.M. and a gimpy leg from rescuing three boys whose patroller crashed on Venus, and went on the town with Martin Diaz one evening not so long ago when— What did happen that evening, anyhow?*

There was a joint down in the Mexican section of San Diego which Diaz remembered was fun. So they caught a giro outside the Hotel Kennedy, where the spacemen were staying—they could afford swank, and felt they owed it to the Corps—and where they had bought their girls dinner. Diaz punched the cantina's name. The autopilot searched its directory and swung the cab onto the Embarcadero-Balboa skyrail.

Sharon sighed and snuggled into the curve of his arm. "How beautiful," she said. "How nice of you to show me this." He felt she meant a little more than polite banality. The view through the bubble really was great tonight. The city winked and blazed, a god's hoard of jewels, from horizon to horizon. Only in one direction was there anything but light: westward, where the ocean lay aglow. A nearly full moon stood high in the sky. He pointed out a tiny glitter on its dark edge.

"Vladimir Base."

"Ugh," said Sharon. "Unasians." She stiffened a trifle.

"Oh, they're decent fellows," Bailey said from the rear seat.

"How do you know?" asked his own date, Naomi, a serious-looking girl and quick on the uptake.

"I've visited them a time or two," he shrugged.

"What?" Sharon exclaimed. "When we're at *war*?"

"Why not?" Diaz said. "The ambassador of United Asia gave a party for our President just yesterday. I watched on the newscreen. Big social event."

"But that's different," Sharon protested. "The war goes on in space, not on Earth, and—"

"We don't blow up each other's Lunar bases, either," Bailey said. "Too close to home. So once in a while we have occasion to, uh, parley is the official word. Actually, the last time I went over—couple years ago now—it was to return a crater-bug we'd borrowed and bring some alga-blight antibiotic they needed. They poured me full of excellent vodka."

"I'm surprised you admit this so openly," said Naomi.

"No secret, my dear," purred Diaz in his best grandee manner, twirling an imaginary mustache. "The newscreens simply don't mention it. Wouldn't be popular, I suppose."

"Oh, people wouldn't care, seeing it was the Corps," Sharon said.

"That's right," Naomi smiled. "The Corps can do no wrong."

"Why, thankee kindly." Diaz grinned at Sharon, chucked her under the chin and kissed her. She held back an instant, having met him only this afternoon. But of course she knew what a date with a Corpsman usually meant, and he knew she knew, and she knew he knew she knew, so before long she relaxed and enjoyed it.

The giro stopped those proceedings by descending to the street and rolling three blocks to the cantina. They entered a low, noisy room hung with bullfight posters and dense with smoke. Diaz threw a glance around and wrinkled his nose. "*Sanamabiche!*" he muttered. "The tourists have discovered it."

"Uh-huh," Bailey answered in the same disappointed *sotto voce*. "Loud tunics, lard faces, 3V, and a juke wall. But let's have a couple drinks, at least, seeing we're here."

"That's the trouble with being in space two or three years at a time," Diaz said. "You lose track. Well . . ." They found a booth.

The waiter recognized him, even after so long a lapse, and called the proprietor. The old man bowed nearly to the floor and begged they accept tequila from his private stock. "*No, no, Señor Capitán, conserva el dinero, por favor.*" The girls were delighted — picturesqueness seemed harder to come by each time Diaz made Earthfall — and the evening was off to a good start in spite of everything.

But then someone paid the juke. The wall came awake with a scrawny blonde fourteen-year-old, the latest fashion in sex queens, wearing a grass skirt and three times life size.

Bingle-jingle-jungle-bang-POW!
Bingle-jingle-jangle-bang-UGH!

Uh'm uh redhot Congo gal an' Uh'm lookin'
*   fuh a pal*
Tuh share muh bingle-jingle-bangle-jungle-
*   ugh-YOW!*

"What did you say?" Sharon called through the saxophones.

"Never mind," Diaz grunted. "They wouldn't've included it in your school Spanish anyway."

"Those things make me almost wish World War Four would start," Naomi said bitterly.

Bailey's mouth tightened. "Don't talk like that," he said. "Wasn't Number Three a close enough call for the race? Without even accomplishing its aims, for either side. I've seen—Any war is too big."

Lest they become serious, Diaz said thoughtfully above the racket: "You know, it should be possible to do something about those Kallikak walls. Like, maybe, an oscillator. They've got oscillators these days which'll even goof a solid-state apparatus at close range."

"The FCC wouldn't allow that," Bailey said. "Especially since it'd interfere with local 3V reception."

"That's bad? Besides, you could miniaturize the oscillator so it'd be hard to find. Make it small enough to carry in your pocket. Or in your body, if you could locate a doctor who'd, uh, perform an illegal operation. I've seen uplousing units no bigger than—"

"You could strew 'em around town," Bailey said, getting interested. "Hide 'em in obscure corners and—"

Ugga-wugga-wugga, hugga-hugga me, do!

"I *wish* it would stop," Naomi said. "I came here to get to know you, Carl, not that thing."

Bailey sat straight. One hand, lying on the table, shaped a fist. "Why not?" he said.

"Eh?" Diaz asked.

Bailey rose. "Excuse me a minute." He bowed to the girls and made his way through the dancers to the wall control. There he switched the record off.

Silence fell like a meteor. For a moment, voices were
stilled, too. Then a large tourist came barreling off his
bar stool and yelled, "Hey, wha'd'you think you're—"

"I'll refund your money, sir," Bailey said mildly.
"But the noise bothers the lady I'm with."

"Huh? Hey, who d'yuh think yuh are, you—"

The proprietor came from around the bar. "If the
lady weeshes it off," he declared, "off it stays."

"What kinda discrimination is this?" roared the
tourist. Several other people growled with him.

Diaz prepared to go help, in case things got rough.
But his companion pulled up the sleeve of his mufti
tunic. The ID bracelet gleamed into view. "First Lieutenant Carl H. Bailey, United States Astromilitary Corps,
at your service," he said; and a circular wave of
quietness expanded around him. "Please forgive my
action. I'll gladly stand the house a round if—"

But that wasn't necessary. The tourist fell all over
himself apologizing and begged to buy the drinks.
Someone else bought them next, and someone after
him. Nobody ventured near the booth, where the
spacemen obviously wanted privacy. But from time to
time, when Diaz glanced out, he got many smiles and
a few shy waves. It was almost embarrassing.

"I was afraid for a minute we'd have a fight," he
said.

"N-no," Bailey answered. "I've watched our prestige develop exponentially, being Stateside while my
leg healed. I doubt if there's an American alive who'd
lift a finger against a Corpsman these days. But I
admit I was afraid of a scene. That wouldn't've done
the name of the Corps any good. As things worked
out, though . . ."

"We came off too bloody well," Diaz finished. "Now
there's not even any pseudolife in this place. Let's
haul mass. We can catch the transpolar shuttle to
Paris if we hurry."

But at that moment the proprietor's friends-and-relations, who also remembered him, began to arrive. They must have been phoned the great news. Pablo was there, Manuel, Carmen with her castanets, Juan with his guitar, Tio Rico waving a bottle in each enormous fist; and they welcomed Diaz back with embraces, and soon there was song and dancing, and the fiesta ended in the rear courtyard watching the moon set before dawn, and everything was like the old days, for Señor Capitán Diaz's sake. That had been a hell of a good furlough.

Another jet splashed fire across the Milky Way. Closer this time, and obviously reducing relative speed. Diaz croaked out a cheer. He had spent weary hours waiting. The hugeness and aloneness had eaten farther into his defenses than he wished to realize. He had begun to understand why some people were disturbed to see the stars on a clear mountain night. (Where wind went soughing through Jeffrey pines whose bark smelled like vanilla if you laid your head close, and a river flowed cold and loud over stones—oh, Christ, how beautiful Earth was!) He shoved such matters aside and reactivated his transmitter.

The streak winked out and the stars crowded back into his eyes. But that was all right, it meant the boat had decelerated as much as necessary, and soon a scooter would be homing on his beam, and water and food and sleep, and a new ship and eventually certain letters to write. That would be the worst part—but not for months or years yet, not till one side or the other conceded the present phase of the war. Diaz found himself wishing most for a cigarette.

He hadn't seen the boat's hull this time, of course; no rosy cloud had existed to silhouette its blackness. Nor did he see the scooter until it was almost upon him. That jet was very thin, since it need only drive a few hundred pounds of mass on which two spacesuited men sat. They were little more than a highlight and a shadow. Diaz's pulse filled the silence. "Hallo!" he called in his helmet mike. "Hallo, yonder!"

They didn't reply. The scooter matched velocities a few yards off. One man tossed a line with a luminous bulb at the end. Diaz caught it and made fast. The line was drawn taut. Scooter and raft bumped together and began gently rotating.

Diaz recognized those helmets.

He snatched for a sidearm he didn't have. A Unasian sprang to one side, lifeline unreeling. His companion stayed mounted, a chucker gun cradled in his arms. The sun rose blindingly over the raft edge.

There was nothing to be done. Yet. Diaz fought down a physical nausea of defeat, "raised" his hands and let them hang free. The other man came behind him and deftly wired his wrists together. Both Unasians spent a few minutes inspecting the raft. The man with the gun tuned in on the American band. "You make very clever salvage, sir," he said.

"Thank you," Diaz whispered.

"Come, please." He was lashed to the carrier rack. Weight tugged at him as the scooter accelerated.

They took an hour or more to rendezvous. Diaz had time to adjust his emotions. The first horror passed into numbness; then he identified a sneaking relief, that he would get a reasonably comfortable vacation from war until the next prisoner exchange; and then he remembered the new doctrine, which applied to all commissioned officers on whom there had been time to operate.

I may never get the chance, he thought frantically. *They told me not to waste myself on anything less than a cruiser; my chromosomes and several million dollars spent in training me make me that valuable to the country, at least. I may go straight to Pallas, or wherever their handiest prison base is, in a lousy scoutboat or cargo ship.*

But I may get a chance to strike a blow that'll hurt. Have I got the guts? I hope so. No, I don't even know if I hope it. This is a cold place to die.

The feeling passed. Emotional control, drilled into him at the Academy and practiced at every refresher course, took over. It was essentially psychosomatic, a matter of using conditioned reflexes to bring muscles and nerves and glands back toward normal. If the fear symptoms, tension, tachycardia, sweat, decreased salivation, and the rest, were alleviated, then fear itself was. Far down under the surface, a four-year-old named Martin woke from nightmare and screamed for his mother, who did not come; but Diaz grew able to ignore him.

The boat became visible, black across star clouds. No, not a boat. A small ship . . . abnormally large jets and light guns, a modified Panyushkin . . . what had the enemy been up to in his asteroid shipyards? Some kind of courier vessel, maybe. Recognition signals must be flashing back and forth. The scooter passed smoothly through a lock that closed again behind it. Air was pumped in, and Diaz went blind as frost condensed on his helmet. Several men assisted him out of the armor. They hadn't quite finished when an alarm rang, engines droned, and weight came back. The ship was starting off at about half a gee.

Short bodies in green uniforms surrounded Diaz. Their immaculate appearance reminded him of his own unshaven filthiness, how much he ached, and how sandy his brain felt. "Well," he mumbled, "where's your interrogation officer?"

"You go more high, Captain," answered a man with colonel's insignia. "Forgive us we do not attend your needs at once, but he says very important."

Diaz bowed to the courtesy, remembering what had been planted in his arm and feeling rather a bastard. Though it looked as if he wouldn't have occasion to use the thing. Dazed by relief and weariness, he let himself be escorted along corridors and tubes until he stood before a door marked with great black Cyrillic warnings and guarded by two soldiers. Which was almost unheard of aboard a spaceship, he thought joltingly.

There was a teleye above the door. Diaz barely glanced at it. Whoever sat within the cabin must be staring through it, at him. He tried to straighten his shoulders. "Martin Diaz," he croaked, "Captain, USAC, serial number—"

Someone yelled from the loudspeaker beside the pickup. Diaz half understood. He whirled about. His will gathered itself and surged. He began to think the impulses that would destroy the ship. A guard tackled him. A rifle butt came down on his head. And that was that.

They told him forty-eight hours passed while he was in sickbay. "I wouldn't know," he said dully. "Nor care." But he was again in good physical shape. Only a bandage sheathing his lower right arm, beneath the insigneless uniform given him, revealed that surgeons had been at work. His mind was sharply aware of its environment—muscle play beneath his skin, pastel bulkheads and cold fluorescence, faint machine-quiver underfoot, gusts from ventilator grilles, odors of foreign cooking, and always the men, with alien faces and carefully expressionless voices, who had caught him.

At least he suffered no abuse. They might have been justified in resenting his attempt to kill them. Some would call it treacherous. But they gave him the treatment due an officer and, except for supplying his needs, left him alone in his tiny bunk cubicle. Which was worse, in some respects, than punishment. Diaz was actually glad when he was at last summoned for an interview.

They brought him to the guarded door and gestured him through. It closed behind him.

For a moment Diaz noticed only the suite itself. Even a fleet commander didn't get such space and comfort. The ship had long ceased accelerating, but spin provided a reasonable weight. The suite was constructed within a rotatable shell, so that the same deck was "down" as when the jets were in operation. Diaz stood on a Persian carpet, looking past low-legged furniture to a pair of arched doorways. One revealed a bedroom, lined with microspools—ye gods, there must be ten thousand volumes! The other showed part of an office, a desk, and a great enigmatic control panel and—

The man seated beneath the Monet reproduction got up and made a slight bow. He was tall for a Unasian, with a lean mobile face whose eyes were startlingly blue against a skin as white as a Swedish girl's. His undress uniform was neat but carelessly worn. No rank insignia were visible, for a gray hood, almost a coif, covered his head and fell over the shoulders.

"Good day, Captain Diaz," he said, speaking English with little accent. "Permit me to introduce myself: General Leo Ilyitch Rostock, Cosmonautical Service of the People of United Asia."

Diaz went through the rituals automatically. Most of him was preoccupied with how quiet this place was, how vastly quiet. . . . But the layout was serene. Rostock must be fantastically important if his comfort rated this much mass. Diaz's gaze flickered to the other man's waist. Rostock bore a sidearm. More to the point, though, one loud holler would doubtless be picked up by the teleye mike and bring in the guards from outside.

Diaz tried to relax. *If they haven't kicked my teeth in so far, they don't plan to. I'm going to live.* But he couldn't believe that. Not here, in the presence of this hooded man. Still more so, in this drawing room. Its existence beyond Mars was too eerie. "No, sir, I have no complaints," he heard himself saying. "You run a good ship. My compliments."

"Thank you." Rostock had a charming, almost boyish smile. "Although this is not my ship, actually. Colonel Sumoro commands the *Ho Chi Minh*. I shall convey your appreciation to him."

"You may not be called the captain," Diaz said
bluntly, "but the vessel is obviously your instrument."

Rostock shrugged. "Will you not sit down?" he
invited, and resumed his own place on the couch.
Diaz took a chair across the table from him, feeling
knobby and awkward. Rostock pushed a box forward.
"Cigarette?"

"Thank you." Diaz struck and inhaled hungrily.

"I hope your arm does not bother you."

Diaz's belly muscles tightened. "No. It's all right."

"The surgeons left the metal ulnar bone in place, as
well as its nervous and muscular connections. Complete replacement would have required more hospital
equipment than a spaceship can readily carry. We did
not want to cripple you by removing the bone. After
all, we were only interested in the cartridge."

Diaz gathered courage and snapped: "The more I
see of you, General, the sorrier I am that it didn't
work. You're big game."

Rostock chuckled. "Perhaps. I wonder, though, if
you are as sorry as you would like to feel you are. You
would have died too, you realize."

"Uh-huh."

"Do you know what the weapon embedded in you
was?"

"Yes. *We* tell our people such things. A charge of
isotopic explosive, with a trigger activated by a particular series of motor nerve pulses. Equivalent to
about ten tons of TNT." Diaz gripped the chair arms,
leaned forward and said harshly: "I'm not blabbing
anything you don't now know. I daresay you consider
it a violation of the customs of war. Not me! I gave no
parole—"

"Certainly, certainly." Rostock waved a deprecating
hand. "We hold . . . what is your idiom? . . . no hard
feelings. The device was ingenious. We have already
dispatched a warning to our Central, whence the word
can go out through the fleet, so your effort, the entire

project, has gone for nothing. But it was a rather gallant attempt."

He leaned back, crossed one long leg over the other, and regarded the American candidly. "Of course, as you implied, we would have proceeded somewhat differently," he said. "Our men would not have known what they carried, and the explosion would have been triggered posthypnotically, by some given class of situations, rather than consciously. In that way, there would be less chance of betrayal."

"How did you know, anyway?" Diaz sighed.

Rostock gave him an impish grin. "As the villain of this particular little drama, I shall only say that I have my methods." Suddenly he was grave. "One reason we made so great an effort to pick you up before your own rescue party arrived, was to gather data on what you have been doing, you people. You know how comparatively rare it is to get a prisoner in space warfare; and how hard to get spies into an organization of high morale which maintains its own laboratories and factories off Earth. Divergent developments can go far these days, before the other side is aware of them. The miniaturization involved in your own weapon, for example, astonished our engineers."

"I can't tell you anything else," Diaz said.

"Oh, you could," Rostock answered gently. "You know as well as I what can be done with a shot of babble juice. Not to mention other techniques — nothing melodramatic, nothing painful or disabling, merely applied neurology — in which I believe Unasia is ahead of the Western countries. But don't worry, Captain. I shall not permit any such breach of military custom.

"However, I do want you to understand how much trouble we went to, to get you. When combat began, I reasoned that the ships auxiliary to a dreadnaught would be the likeliest to suffer destruction of the type which leaves a few survivors. From the pattern of action in the first day, I deduced the approximate orbits and positions of several American capital ships.

Unasian tactics throughout the second day were developed with two purposes: to inflict damage, of course, but also to get the *Ho* so placed that we would be likely to detect any distress signals. This cost us the *Genghis*—a calculated risk that did not pay off—I am not omniscient. But we did hear your call.

"You are quite right about the importance of this ship here. My superiors will be horrified at my action. But of necessity, they have given me carte blanche. And since the *Ho* itself takes no direct part in any engagement if we can avoid it, the probability of our being detected and attacked was small."

Rostock's eyes held Diaz's. He tapped the table, softly and repeatedly, with one fingernail. "Do you appreciate what all this means, Captain?" he asked. "Do you see how badly you were wanted?"

Diaz could only wet his lips and nod.

"Partly," Rostock said, smiling again, "there was the desire I have mentioned, to . . . er . . . check up on American activities during the last cease-fire period. But partly, too, there was a wish to bring you up to date on what we have been doing."

"Huh?" Diaz half scrambled from his chair, sagged back and gaped.

"The choice is yours, Captain," Rostock said. "You can be transferred to a cargo ship when we can arrange it, and so to an asteroid camp, and in general receive the normal treatment of a war prisoner. Or you may elect to hear what I would like to discuss with you. In the latter event, I can guarantee nothing. Obviously I can't let you go home in a routine prisoner exchange with a prime military secret of ours. You will have to wait until it is no longer a secret—until American intelligence has learned the truth, and we know that they have. That may take years. It may take forever, because I have some hope that the knowledge will change certain of your own attitudes.

"No, no, don't answer now. Think it over. I will see you again tomorrow. In twenty-four hours, that is to say."

Rostock's eyes shifted past Diaz, as if to look through the bulkheads. His tone dropped to a whisper. "Have you ever wondered, like me, why we carry Earth's rotation period to space with us? Habit; practicality; but is there not also an element of magical thinking? A hope that somehow we can create our own sunrises? The sky is very black out there. We need all the magic we can invent. Do we not?"

Several hours later, alarms sounded, voices barked over the intercoms, spin was halted but weight came quickly back as the ship accelerated. Diaz knew just enough Mandarin to understand from what he overheard that radar contact had been made with American units and combat would soon resume. The guard who brought him dinner in his cubicle confirmed it, with many a bow and hissing smile. Diaz had gained enormous face by his audience with the man in the suite.

He couldn't sleep, though the racket soon settled down to a purposeful murmur with few loud interruptions. Restless in his bunk harness, he tried to reconstruct a total picture from the clues he had. The primary American objective was the asteroid base system of the enemy. But astromilitary tactics were too complicated for one brain to grasp. A battle might go on for months, flaring up whenever hostile units came near enough in their enormous orbitings to exchange fire. Eventually, Diaz knew, if everything went well—that is, didn't go too badly haywire—Americans would land on the Unasian worldlets. That would be the rough part. He remembered ground operations on Mars and Ganymede far too well.

As for the immediate situation, though, he could only make an educated guess. The leisurely pace at which the engagement was developing indicated that ships of dreadnaught mass were involved. Therefore no mere squadron was out there, but an important segment of the American fleet, perhaps the task force headed by the *Alaska*. But if this was true, then the *Ho Chi Minh* must be directing a flotilla of comparable size.

Which wasn't possible! Flotillas and subfleets were bossed from dreadnaughts. A combat computer and its human staff were too big and delicate to be housed in anything less. And the *Ho* was not even as large as the *Argonne* had been.

Yet what the hell was this but a command ship? Rostock had hinted as much. The activity aboard was characteristic: the repeated sound of courier boats coming and going, intercom calls, technicians hurrying along the corridors, but no shooting.

Nevertheless . . .

Voices jabbered beyond the cell door. Their note was triumphant. Probably they related a hit on an American vessel. Diaz recalled brushing aside chunks of space-frozen meat that had been his Corps brothers. Sammy Yoshida was in the *Utah Beach*, which was with the *Alaska*—Sammy who'd covered for him back at the Academy when he crawled in dead drunk hours after taps, and some years later had dragged him from a shell-struck foxhole on Mars and shared oxygen till a rescue squad happened by. Had the *Utah Beach* been hit? Was that what they were giggling about out there?

Prisoner exchange, in a year or two or three, will get me back for the next round of the war, Diaz thought in darkness. *But I'm only one man. And I've goofed somehow, spilled a scheme which might've cost the Unies several ships before they tumbled. It's hardly conceivable I could smuggle out whatever information Rostock wants to give me. But there'd be some tiny probability that I could, somehow, sometime. Wouldn't there?*

I don't want to. Dios mio, *how I don't want to! Let me rest a while, and then be swapped, and go back for a long furlough on Earth, where anything I ask for is*

*mine and mainly I ask for sunlight and ocean and
flowering trees. But Carl liked those things too, didn't
he?*

A lull came in the battle. The fleets had passed
each other, decelerating as they fired. They would take
many hours to turn around and get back within combat range. A great quietness descended on the *Ho*.
Walking down the passageways, which thrummed with
rocketblast, Diaz saw how the technicians slumped at
their posts. The demands on them were as hard as
those on a pilot or gunner or missile chief. Evolution
designed men to fight with their hands, not with
computations and pushbuttons. Maybe ground combat wasn't the worst kind at that.

The sentries admitted Diaz through the door of the
warning. Rostock sat at the table again. His coifed
features looked equally drained, and his smile was
automatic. A samovar and two teacups stood before
him.

"Be seated, Captain," he said tonelessly. "Pardon
me if I do not rise. This has been an exhausting time."

Diaz accepted a chair and a cup. Rostock drank
noisily, eyes closed and forehead puckered. There might
have been an extra stimulant in his tea, for before long
he appeared more human. He refilled the cups, passed
out cigarettes, and leaned back on his couch with a
sigh.

"You may be pleased to know," he said, "that the
third pass will be the final one. We shall refuse further combat and proceed instead to join forces with
another flotilla near Pallas."

"Because that suits your purposes better," Diaz
said.

"Well, naturally. I compute a higher likelihood of
ultimate success if we followed a strategy of . . . no
matter now."

Diaz leaned forward. His heart slammed. "So this
is a command ship," he exclaimed. "I thought so."

The blue eyes weighed him with care. "If I give you any further information," Rostock said—softly, but the muscles tightened along his jaw—"you must accept the conditions I set forth."

"I do," Diaz got out.

"I realize that you do so in the hope of passing on the secret to your countrymen," Rostock said. "You may as well forget about that. You won't get the chance."

"Then why do you want to tell me? You won't make a Unie out of me, General." The words sounded too stuck up, Diaz decided. "That is, I respect your people and so forth, but . . . uh . . . my loyalties lie elsewhere."

"Agreed. I don't hope or plan to change them. At least, not in an easterly direction." Rostock drew hard on his cigarette, let smoke stream from his nostrils, and squinted through it. "The microphone is turned down," he remarked. "We cannot be overheard unless we shout. I must warn you, if you make any attempt to reveal what I am about to say to you to any of my own people, I shall not merely deny it but order you sent out the airlock. It is that important."

Diaz rubbed his hands on his trousers. The palms were wet. "Okay," he said.

"Not that I mean to browbeat you, Captain," said Rostock hastily. "What I offer is friendship. In the end, maybe, peace." He sat a while longer, looking at the wall, before his glance shifted back to Diaz. "Suppose you begin the discussion. Ask me what you like."

"Uh . . . " Diaz floundered about, as if he'd been leaning on a door that was thrown open. "Uh . . . well, was I right? Is this a command ship?"

"Yes. It performs every function of a flag dreadnaught, except that it seldom engages in direct combat. The tactical advantages are obvious. A smaller, lighter vessel can get about much more readily, hence be a correspondingly more effective directrix. Furthermore, if due caution is exercised, we are not likely to be detected and fired at. The massive armament of a dreadnaught is chiefly to stave off the missiles that can annihilate the command post within. Ships of this class avoid that whole problem by avoiding attack in the first place."

"But your computer! You, you must have developed a combat computer as . . . small and rugged as an autopilot. . . . I thought miniaturization was our specialty."

Rostock laughed.

"And you'd still need a large human staff," Diaz protested. "Bigger than the whole crew of this ship!

"Wouldn't you?" he finished weakly.

Rostock shook his head. "No." His smile faded. "Not under this new system. I am the computer."

"What?"

"Look." Rostock pulled off his hood.

The head beneath was hairless, not shaved but depilated. A dozen silvery plates were set into it, flush with the scalp; in them were plug outlets. Rostock pointed toward the office. "The rest of me is in there," he said. "I need only set the jacks into the appropriate points of myself, and I become . . . no, not part of the computer. It becomes part of me."

He fell silent again, gazing now at the floor. Diaz hardly dared move, until his cigarette burned his fingers and he had to stub it out. The ship pulsed around them. Monet's picture of sunlight caught in young leaves was like something seen at the far end of a tunnel.

"Consider the problem," Rostock said at last, low. "In spite of much loose talk about giant brains, computers do not think, except perhaps on an idiot level. They simply perform logical operations, symbol-shuffling, according to instructions given them. It was shown long ago that there are infinite classes of problems that no computer can solve: the classes dealt with in Gödel's theorem, that can only be solved by the nonlogical process of creating a metalanguage. Creativity is not logical and computers do not create.

"In addition, as you know, the larger a computer becomes, the more staff it requires, to perform such operations as data coding, programming, retranslation of the solutions into practical terms, and adjustment of the artificial answer to the actual problems. Yet your own brain does this sort of thing constantly . . . because it is creative. Moreover, the advanced computers are heavy, bulky, fragile things. They use cryogenics and all the other tricks, but that involves elaborate ancillary apparatus. Your brain weighs a kilogram or so, is quite adequately protected in the skull, and needs less than a hundred kilos of outside equipment—your body.

"I am not being mystical. There is no reason why creativity cannot someday be duplicated in an artificial structure. But I think that structure will look very much like a living organism; will, indeed, be one. Life has had a billion years to develop these techniques.

"Now if the brain has so many advantages, why use a computer at all? Obviously, to do the uncreative work, for which the brain is not specifically designed. The brain visualizes a problem of, say, orbits, masses, and tactics, and formulates it as a set of matrix equations; then the computer goes swiftly through the millions of idiot counting operations needed to produce a numerical solution. What we have developed here, we Unasians, is nothing but a direct approach. We eliminate the middle man, as you Americans would say.

"In yonder office is a highly specialized computer. It is built from solid-state units, analogous to neurons, but in spite of being able to treat astromilitary problems, it is a comparatively small, simple, and sturdy device. Why? Because it is used in connection with my brain, which directs it. The normal computer must have its operational patterns built in. Mine develops synapse pathways as needed, just as a man's lower brain can develop skills under the direction of the cerebral cortex. And these pathways are modifiable by experience; the system is continually restructuring itself. The normal computer must have elaborate failure detection systems and arrangements for rerouting. I in the hookup here sense any trouble directly, and am no more disturbed by the temporary disability of some region than you are disturbed by the fact that most of your brain cells at any given time are resting.

"The human staff becomes superfluous here. My technicians bring me the data, which need not be reduced to standardized format. I link myself to the machine and . . . think about it . . . there are no words. The answer is worked out in no more time than any other computer would require. But it comes to my consciousness not as a set of figures, but in practical terms, decisions about what to do. Furthermore, the solution is modified by my human awareness of those factors too complex to go into mathematical form — like the physical condition of men and equipment, morale, long-range questions of logistics and strategy and ultimate goals. You might say this is a computer system with common sense. Do you understand, Captain?"

Diaz sat still for a long time before he said, "Yes. I think I do."

Rostock had gotten a little hoarse. He poured himself a fresh cup of tea and drank half, struck another cigarette and said earnestly: "The military value is obvious. Were that all, I would never have revealed this to you. But something else developed as I practiced and increased my command of the system. Something quite unforeseen. I wonder if you will comprehend." He finished his cup. "The repeated experience has . . . changed me. I am no longer human. Not really."

The ship whispered, driving through darkness.

"I suppose a hookup like that would affect the emotions," Diaz ventured. "How does it feel?"

"There are no words," Rostock repeated, "except those I have made for myself." He rose and walked restlessly across the subdued rainbows in the carpet, hands behind his back, eyes focused on nothing Diaz could see. "As a matter of fact, the emotional effect may be a simple intensification. Although . . . there are myths about mortals who became gods. How did it feel to them? I think they hardly noticed the palaces and music and feasting on Olympus. What mattered was how, piece by piece, as he mastered his new capacities, the new god won a god's understanding. His perception, involvement, detachment, totalness . . . there *are* no words."

Back and forth he paced, feet noiseless but metal and energies humming beneath his low and somehow troubled voice. "My cerebrum directs the computer," he said, "and the relationship becomes reciprocal. True, the computer part has no creativity of its own; but it endows mine with a speed and sureness you cannot imagine. After all, a great part of original thought consists merely in proposing trial solutions— the scientist hypothesizes, the artist draws a charcoal line, the poet scribbles a phrase—and testing them to see if they work. By now, to me, this mechanical aspect of imagination is back down on the subconscious level where it belongs. What my awareness senses is the final answer, springing to life almost simultaneously with the question, and yet with a felt reality to it such as comes only from having pondered and tested the issue thousands of times.

"Also, the amount of sense data I can handle is fantastic. Oh, I am blind and deaf and numb away from my machine half! So you will realize that over the months I have tended to spend more and more time in the linked state. When there was no immediate command problem to solve, I would sit and savor total awareness. Or I would think."

In a practical tone: "That is how I perceived that you were about to sabotage us, Captain. Your posture alone betrayed you. I guessed the means at once and ordered the guards to knock you unconscious. I think, also, that I detected in you the potential I need. But that demands closer examination. Which is easily given. When I am linked, you cannot lie to me. The least insincerity is written across your whole organism."

He paused, to stand a little slumped, looking at the bulkhead. For a moment Diaz's legs tensed. *Three jumps and I can be there and get his gun!* But no, Rostock wasn't any brainheavy dwarf. The body in that green uniform was young and trained. Diaz took another cigarette. "Okay," he said. "What do you propose?"

"First," Rostock said, turning about—and his eyes kindled—"I want you to understand what you and I are. What the spacemen of both factions are."

"Professional soldiers," Diaz grunted uneasily. Rostock waited. Diaz puffed hard and plowed on, since he was plainly expected to, "The last soldiers left. You can't count those ornamental regiments on Earth, nor the guys sitting by the big missiles. Those missiles will never be fired. World War Three was a large enough dose of nucleonics. Civilization was lucky to survive. Terrestrial life would be lucky to survive, next time around. So war has moved into space. Uh . . . professionalism . . . the old traditions of mutual respect and so forth have naturally revived." He made himself look up. "What more clichés need I repeat?"

"Suppose your side completely annihilated our ships," Rostock said. "What would happen?"

"Why . . . that's been discussed theoretically . . . by damn near every political scientist, hasn't it? The total command of space would not mean total command of Earth. We could destroy the whole Eastern Hemisphere without being touched. But we wouldn't, because Unasia would fire its cobalt weapons while dying, and we'd have no Western Hemisphere to come home to, either. Not that that situation will ever arise. Space is too big; there are too many ships and fortresses scattered around; combat is too slow a process. Neither fleet can wipe out the other."

"Since we have this perpetual stalemate, then," Rostock pursued, "why do we have perpetual war?"

"Um . . . well, not really. Cease-fires—"

"Breathing spells! Come now, Captain, you are too intelligent to believe that rigmarole. If victory cannot be achieved, why fight?"

"Well, uh, partial victories are possible. Like our capture of Mars, or your destruction of three dreadnaughts in one month, on different occasions. The balance of power shifts. Rather than let its strength continue being whittled down, the side which is losing asks for a parley. Negotiations follow, which end to the relative advantage of the stronger side. Meanwhile the arms race continues. Pretty soon a new dispute arises, the cease-fire ends, and maybe the other side is lucky that time."

"Is this situation expected to be eternal?"

"No!" Diaz stopped, thought a minute, and grinned with one corner of his mouth. "That is, they keep talking about an effective international organization. Trouble is, the two cultures are too far apart by now. They can't live together."

"I used to believe that myself," Rostock said. "Lately I have not been sure. A world federalism could be devised which would let both civilizations keep their identities. Many such proposals have in fact been made, as you know. None has gotten beyond the talking stage. None ever will. Because you see, what maintains the war is not the difference between our two cultures, but their similarity."

"Whoa, there!" Diaz bristled. "I resent that."

"Please," Rostock said. "I pass no moral judgments. For the sake of argument, at least, I can concede you the moral superiority, remarking only in parenthesis that Earth holds billions of people who not only fail to comprehend what you mean by freedom but would not like it if you gave it to them. The similarity I am talking about is technological. Both civilizations are based on the machine, with all the high organization and dynamism which this implies."

"So?"

"So war is a necessity—Wait! I am not talking about 'merchants of death,' or 'dictators needing an outside enemy,' or whatever the current propaganda lines are. I mean that conflict is built into the culture. There *must* be an outlet for the destructive emotions generated in the mass of the people by the type of life they lead. A type of life for which evolution never designed them.

"Have you ever heard about L. F. Richardson? No? He was an Englishman in the last century, a Quaker, who hated war but, being a scientist, realized the phenomenon must be understood clinically before it can be eliminated. He performed some brilliant theoretical and statistical analyses which showed, for example, that the rate of deadly quarrels was nearly constant over the decades. There could be many small clashes or a few major ones, but the result was the same. Why were the United States and the Chinese Empire so peaceful during the nineteenth century? The answer is that they were not; they had their Civil War and Taiping Rebellion, which devastated them as much as required. I need not multiply examples. We can discuss this later in detail. I have carried Richardson's work a good deal further and more rigorously. I say to you now only that civilized societies must have a certain rate of immolations."

Diaz listened to silence for a minute before he said: "Well, I've sometimes thought the same. I suppose you mean we spacemen are the goats these days?"

"Exactly. War fought out here does not menace the planet. By our deaths we keep Earth alive."

Rostock sighed. His mouth drooped. "Magic works, you know," he said, "works on the emotions of the people who practice it. If a primitive witch doctor told a storm to go away, the storm did not hear, but the tribe did and took heart. The ancient analogy to us, though, is the sacrificial king in the early agricultural societies; a god in mortal form, who was regularly slain so that the fields might bear fruit. This was not mere superstition. You must realize that. It worked—on the people. The rite was essential to the operation of their culture, to their sanity and hence to their survival.

"Today the machine age has developed its own sacrificial kings. We are the chosen of the race, the best it can offer. None gainsays us. We may have what we choose, pleasure, luxury, women, adulation—only not the simple pleasures of wife and child and hope, for we must die that the people may live."

Again silence, until: "Do you seriously mean that's why the war goes on?" Diaz breathed.

Rostock nodded.

"But nobody . . . I mean, people wouldn't—"

"They do not reason these things out, of course. Traditions develop blindly. The ancient peasant did not elaborate logical reasons why the king must die. He merely knew this was so, and left the syllogism for modern anthropologists to expound. I did not see the process going on today until I had had the chance to . . . to become more perceptive than I had been," Rostock said humbly.

Diaz couldn't endure sitting any longer. He jumped to his feet. "Assuming you're right," he snapped, "and you may be, what of it? What can be done?"

"Much," Rostock said. Calm descended on his face like a mask. "I am not being mystical about this, either. The sacrificial king has reappeared as the end product of a long chain of cause and effect. There is no reason inherent in natural law why this must be. Richardson was right in his basic hope, that when war becomes understood, as a phenomenon, it can be eliminated. This would naturally involve restructuring the entire terrestrial culture—gradually, subtly. Remember—" His hand shot out, seized Diaz's shoulder and gripped painfully hard. "There is a new element in history today. Us. The kings. We are not like those who spend their lives under Earth's sky. In some ways we are more, in other ways less, but always we are different. You and I are more akin to each other than to our planet-dwelling countrymen. Are we not?

"In the time and loneliness granted me, I have used all my new powers to think about this. Not only think; this is so much more than cold reason. I have tried to feel. To love what is, as the Buddhists say. I believe a nucleus of spacemen like us, slowly and secretly gathered, wishing the good of everyone on Earth and the harm of none, gifted with powers and insights they cannot really imagine at home—I believe we may accomplish something. If not us, then our sons. Men ought not to kill each other, when the stars are waiting."

He let go, turned away and looked at the deck. "Of course," he mumbled, "I, in my peculiar situation, must first destroy a number of your brothers."

They had given Diaz a whole pack of cigarettes, an enormous treasure out here, before they locked him into his cubicle for the duration of the second engagement. He lay in harness, hearing clang and shout and engine roar through the vibrating bulkheads, stared at blackness, and smoked until his tongue was foul. Sometimes the *Ho* accelerated, mostly it ran free and he floated. Once a tremor went through the entire hull, near miss by a shaped charge. Doubtless gamma rays, ignoring the magnetic force screens, sleeted through the men and knocked another several months off their life expectancies. Not that that mattered; spacemen rarely lived long enough to worry about degenerative diseases. Diaz hardly noticed.

Rostock's not lying. Why should he? What could he gain? He may be a nut, of course. But he doesn't act like a nut either. He wants me to study his statistics and equations, satisfy myself that he's right. And he must be damn sure I will be convinced, to tell me what he has.

How many are there like him? Few, I'm sure. The man-machine symbiosis is obviously new, or we'd've

*had some inkling ourselves. This is the first field trial
of the system. I wonder if the others have reached the
same conclusions as Rostock. No, he said he doubts
that; their minds impressed him as being more deeply
channeled than his. He's a lucky accident.*

*Lucky? Now how can I tell? I'm only a man. I've
never experienced an IQ of a thousand, or whatever
the figure may be. A god's purposes aren't necessarily
what a man would elect.*

An eventual end to war? Well, other institutions
had been ended, at least in the Western countries:
judicial torture, chattel slavery, human sacrifice—no,
wait, according to Rostock human sacrifice had been
revived.

"But is our casualty rate high enough to fit your
equations?" Diaz had argued. "Space forces aren't as
big as old-time armies. No country could afford that."

"Other elements than death must be taken into
account," Rostock answered. "The enormous expense
is one factor. Taxpaying is a form of symbolic self-
mutilation. It also tends to direct civilian resentments
and aggressions against their own governments, thus
taking some pressure off international relations.

"Chiefly, though, there is the matter of emotional
intensity. A spaceman does not simply die, he usually
dies horribly; and that moment is the culmination of a
long period under grisly conditions. His groundling
brothers, administrative and service personnel, suffer
vicariously: 'sweat it out,' as your idiom so well
expresses the feeling. His kinfolk, friends, women, are
likewise racked. When Adonis dies—or Osiris, Tammuz,
Baldur, Christ, Tlaloc, whichever of his hundred names
you choose—the people must in some degree share
his agony. That is part of the sacrifice."

Diaz had never thought about it in quite that way.
Like most Corpsmen, he had held the average civilian
in thinly disguised contempt. But . . . from time to
time, he remembered, he'd been glad his mother died
before he enlisted. And why did his sister hit the

bottle so hard? Then there had been Lois, she of the fire-colored hair and violet eyes, who wept as if she would never stop weeping when he left for duty. He'd promised to get in touch with her on his return, but of course he knew better.

Which did not erase memories of men whose breath and blood came exploding from burst helmets; who shuddered and vomited and defecated in the last stages of radiation sickness; who stared without immediate comprehension at a red spurt which a second ago had been an arm or a leg; who went insane and must be gassed because psychoneurosis is catching on a six months' orbit beyond Saturn; who—Yeah, Carl had been lucky.

You could talk as much as you wished about Corps brotherhood, honor, tradition, and gallantry. It remained sentimental guff. . . . No, that was unjust. The Corps had saved the people, their lives and liberties. There could be no higher achievement—for the Corps. But knighthood had once been a noble thing, too; then, lingering after its day, it became a yoke and eventually a farce. The warrior virtues were not ends in themselves. If the warrior could be made obsolete. . . .

Could he? How much could one man, even powered by a machine, hope to do? How much could he even hope to understand?

The moment came upon Diaz. He lay as if blinded by shellburst radiance.

As consciousness returned, he knew first, irrelevantly, what it meant to get religion.

"By God," he told the universe, "we're going to try!"

The battle would resume shortly. At any moment, in fact, some scoutship leading the American force might fire a missile. But when Diaz told his guard he wanted to speak with General Rostock, he was taken there within minutes.

The door closed behind him. The living room lay empty, altogether still except for the machine throb, which was not loud since the *Ho* was running free. Because acceleration might be needful on short notice, there was no spin. Diaz hung weightless as fog. And the Monet flung into his eyes all Earth's sunlight and summer forests.

"Rostock?" he called uncertainly.

"Come," said a voice, almost too low to hear. Diaz gave a shove with his foot and flew toward the office.

He stopped himself by grasping the doorjamb. A semicircular room lay before him, the entire side taken up by controls and meters. Lights blinked, needles wavered on dials, buttons and switches and knobs reached across black paneling. But none of that was important. Only the man at the desk mattered, who free-sat with wires running from his head to the wall.

Rostock seemed to have lost weight. Or was that an illusion? The skin was drawn taut across his high cheekbones and gone a dead, glistening white. His nostrils were flared and the colorless lips held tense. Diaz looked into his eyes, once, and away again. He could not meet them. He could not even think about them. He drew a shaken breath and waited.

"You made your decision quickly," Rostock whispered. "I had not awaited you until after the engagement."

"I . . . I didn't think you would see me till then."

"This is more important." Diaz felt as if he were being probed with knives. He could not altogether believe it was his imagination. He stared desperately at paneled instruments. Their nonhumanness was like a comforting hand. *They must be for the benefit of maintenance techs*, he thought in a distant part of himself. *The brain doesn't need them.* "You are convinced," Rostock said in frank surprise.

"Yes," Diaz answered.

"I had not expected that. I hoped for little more than your reluctant agreement to study my work." Rostock regarded him for a still century. "You were ripe for a new faith," he decided. "I had not taken you for the type. But then, the mind can only use what data are given it, and I have hitherto had small opportunity to meet Americans. Never since I became what I am. You have another psyche from ours."

"I need to understand your findings, sir," Diaz said. "Right now I can only believe. That isn't enough, is it?"

Slowly, Rostock's mouth drew into a smile of quite human warmth. "Correct. But given the faith, intellectual comprehension should be swift."

"I . . . I shouldn't be taking your time . . . now, sir," Diaz stammered. "How should I begin? Should I take some books back with me?"

"No." Acceptance had been reached; Rostock spoke resonantly, a master to his trusted servant. "I need your help here. Strap into yonder harness. Our first necessity is to survive the battle upon us. You realize that this means sacrificing many of your comrades. I know how that will hurt you. Afterward we shall spend our lives repaying our people . . . both our peoples. But today I shall ask you questions about your fleet. Any information is valuable, especially details of construction and armament which our intelligence has not been able to learn."

Doña mía. Diaz let go the door, covered his face and fell free, endlessly. *Help me.*

"It is not betrayal," said the superman. "It is the ultimate loyalty you can offer."

Diaz made himself look at the cabin again. He shoved against the bulkhead and stopped by the harness near the desk.

"You cannot lie to me," said Rostock. "Do not deny the pain I am giving you." Diaz glimpsed his fists clamping together. "Each time I look at you, I share what you feel."

Diaz clung to his harness. There went an explosion through him.

NO, BY GOD!

Rostock screamed.

"Don't," Diaz sobbed. "I don't want—" But wave after wave ripped outward. Rostock flopped about in his harness and shrieked. The scene came back, ramming home like a bayonet.

"We like to put an extra string on our bow," the psych officer said. Lunar sunlight, scarcely softened by the dome, blazed off his bronze eagles, wings and beaks. "You know that your right ulna will be replaced with a metal section which contains a nerve-triggered nuclear cartridge. But that may not be all, gentlemen."

He bridged his fingers. The young men seated on the other side of his desk stirred uneasily. "In this country," the psych officer said, "we don't believe humans should be turned into puppets. Therefore you will have voluntary control of your bombs; no post-hypnosis, Pavlov reflex, or any such insult. However, those of you who are willing will receive a rather special extra treatment, and that fact will be buried from the consciousness of every one of you.

"Our reasoning is that if and when the Unasians learn about the prisoner weapon, they'll remove the cartridge by surgery but leave the prosthetic bone in place. And they will, we hope, not examine it in microscopic detail. Therefore they won't know that it holds an oscillator, integrated with the crystal structure. Nor will you; because what you don't know, you can't babble under anesthesia.

"The opportunity may come, if you are captured and lose your bomb, to inflict damage by this reserve means. You may find yourself near a crucial electronic device, for example a spaceship's autopilot. At short range, the oscillator will do an excellent job of bollixing it. Which will at least discomfit the enemy, and may give you a chance to escape.

"The posthypnotic command will be such that you'll remember about this oscillator when conditions seem right for using it. Not before. Of course, the human mind is a damned queer thing; it twists and turns and bites its own tail. In order to make an opportunity to strike this blow, your subconscious may lead you down strange paths—may even have you seriously contemplating treason, if treason seems the only way of getting access to what you can wreck. Don't let that bother you afterward, gentlemen. Your superiors will know what happened.

"Nevertheless, the experience may be painful. And posthypnosis is, at best, humiliating to a free man. So this aspect of the program is strictly volunteer. Does anybody want to go for broke?"

The door flung open. The guards burst in. Diaz was already behind the desk, next to Rostock. He yanked out the general's sidearm and fired at the soldiers. Free-fall recoil sent him back against the computer panel. He braced himself, fired again, and used his left elbow to smash the nearest meter face.

Rostock clawed at the wires in his head. For a moment Diaz guessed what it must be like to have random oscillations in your brain, amplified by an electronic engine that was part of you. He laid the pistol to the screaming man's temple and fired once more.

Now to get out! He shoved hard, arrowing past the sentries, who rolled through the air in a crimson galaxy of blood globules. Confusion boiled in the corridor beyond. Someone snatched at him. He knocked the fellow aside and dove along a tubeway. Somewhere hereabouts should be a scooter locker—there, and nobody around!

He didn't have time to get on a spacesuit, even if a Unasian one would have fitted, but he slipped an air dome over the scooter. That, with the heater unit and oxy reclaim, would serve. He didn't want to get off anywhere en route; not before he'd steered the machine through an American hatch.

With luck, he'd do that. Their command computer gone, the enemy were going to get smeared. American ships would close in as the slaughter progressed. Eventually one should come within range of the scooter's little radio.

He set the minilock controls, mounted the saddle, dogged the air dome, and waited for ejection. It came none too soon. Three soldiers had just appeared down the passageway. Diaz applied full thrust and jetted away from the *Ho*. Its blackness was soon lost among the star clouds.

Battle commenced. The first Unasian ship to be destroyed must have been less than fifty miles distant. Luckily, Diaz was facing the other way when the missile exploded.

A MAN TO MY WOUNDING

> I have slain a man to my wounding, and a
> young man to my hurt.
>
> — *Genesis*, iv, 23

His names were legion and his face was anybody's.
Because a Senator was being hunted, I stood on a
corner and waited for him.

The arm gun was a slight, annoying drag under my
tunic. Lord knew the thing should be almost a part of
me after so many years, but today I had the jaggers.
It's always harder on the nerves to defend than to
stalk. A vending machine was close by, and I might
have bought a reefer, or even a cigaret, to calm me
down; but I can't smoke. I got a whiff of chlorine
several years ago, during an assassination in Morocco,
and the regenerated lung tissue I now use is a bit

cranky. Nor did my philosophical tricks work: meditation on the koans of Zen, recital of elementary derivatives and integrals.

I was alone at my post. In some towns, where private autos haven't yet been banned from congested areas, my assignment would have given me trouble. Here, though, only pedestrians and an occasional electroshuttle got between me and my view, kitty-corner across the intersection of Grant and Jefferson to The Sword Called Precious Pearl. I stood as if waiting for a particular ride. A public minivid was on the wall behind me, and after a while I decided it wouldn't hurt to see if anything had happened. Not that I expected it yet. The Senator's escorted plane was still airborne. I hardly thought the enemy would have gotten a bomb aboard. However—

I dropped a coin in the box and turned the dials in search of a newscast.

" . . . development was inevitable, toward greater and greater ferocity. For example, we think of the era between the Peace of Westphalia and the French Revolution as one of limited conflicts. But Heidelberg and Poltava suffice to remind us how easily they got out of hand. Likewise, the relative chivalry of the post-Napoleonic nineteenth century evolved into the trench combat of the First World War, the indiscriminate aerial bombings of the Second, and the atomic horrors of the Third."

Interested, I leaned closer to the little screen. I only needed one eye to watch that bar. The other could study this speaker. He was a fortyish man with sharp, intelligent features. I liked his delivery, vivid without being sentimental. I couldn't quite place him, though, so I thumbed the info switch. He disappeared for a moment while a sign in the screen told me this was a filmed broadcast of an address by Juan Morales, the new president of the University of California, on the topic: "Clausewitz's Analysis Reconsidered."

It was refreshing to hear a college president voice

something besides noises about education in the Cybernetic Age. I recalled now that Morales was an historian of note, and moderately active in the Libertarian Party. Doubtless the latter experience had taught him to speak with vigor. The fact that the Enterprise Party had won the last election seemed only to have honed him more fine-edged.

"The Third World War, short and inconclusive as it was, made painfully clear that mass destruction had become ridiculous," he went on. "War was traditionally an instrument of national policy, a means of getting acquiescence to something from another state when less drastic measures had failed. But a threat to instigate mutual suicide has no such meaning. At the same time, force remains the *ultima ratio*. It is no use to preach that killing is wrong, that human life is infinitely valuable, and so on. I'm afraid that in point of blunt, regrettable fact, human life has always been a rather cheap commodity. From a man defending his wife against a homicidal maniac, on to the most complex international problems, issues are bound to arise occasionally which cannot be resolved. If these issues are too important to ignore, men will then fight.

"The need of the world today is, therefore, not to plan grandiose renunciations of violence. I know that many distinguished thinkers regard our present system of killing—not whole populations, but the leaders of those populations—as a step forward. Certainly it is more efficient, even more humane, than war. But it does not lead logically to a next step of killing no one at all. Rather, it has merely shifted the means of enforcing the national will.

"Our task is to understand this process. That will not be easy. Assassination evolved slowly, almost unconsciously, like every other viable institution. Like old-fashioned war, it has its own reaction upon the political purposes for which it is used. Also like war, it has its own evolutionary tendencies. Once we thought we had contained war, made it a safely limited duel between gentlemen. We learned better. Let us not make the same complacent mistake about our new system of assassination. Let us—"

"Shine, mister?"

I looked down into a round face and black almond eyes. The boy was perhaps ten years old, small, quick, brilliant in the mandarin tunic affected by most Chinatown youngsters these days. (A kind of defiance, an appeal: Look, we're Americans too, with a special and proud heritage; our ancestors left the old country before the Kung She rose up to make humans into machinery.) He carried a box under his arm.

"What time machine did you get off of?" I asked him.

"A shoe blaster's no good," he said with a grin. "I give you a hand shine, just like the Nineties. The Gay Nineties, I mean, not the Nasty Nineties." As I hesitated: "You could ride in my cable car, too, only I'm still saving money to get one built. Have a shoe shine and help make San Francisco picturesque again!"

I laughed. "Sure thing, bucko. I may have to take off in a hurry, though, so let me pay you in advance."

He made a sparrow's estimate of me. "Five dollars."

The cost of a slug of bourbon didn't seem excessive for a good excuse to loiter here. Besides, I like kids. Once I hoped to have a few of my own. Most people in the Bureau of National Protection (good old Anglo-Saxon hypocrisy!) do; they keep regular hours, like any other office workers. However, the field agent—or trigger man, if you don't want euphemisms—has no business getting married. I tried, but shouldn't have. A few years later, when the memory wasn't hurting quite so much, I saw how justified she had been.

I flipped the boy a coin. He speared it in midair and broke out his apparatus. Morales was still talking. The boy cocked an eye at the screen. "What's he so thermal about, mister? The assassination that's on?"

"The whole system." I switched the program off hastily, not wanting to draw even this much attention to my real purpose.

But the kid was too bright. Smearing wax on a shoe, he said, "Gee, I don't get it. How long we been fighting those old Chinese, anyhow? Seven months? And nothing's happened. I bet pretty soon they'll call the whole show off and talk some more. It don't make sense. Why not *do* something first?"

"The two countries might agree on an armistice," I said with care. "But that won't be for lack of trying to do each other dirt. A lot of wars in early days got called off too, when neither side found it could make any headway. Do you think it's easy to pot the President, or Chairman Kao-Tsung?"

"I guess not. But Secretive Operative Dan Steelman on the vid—"

"Yeah," I grunted. "Him."

If I'd been one of those granite-jawed microcephalics with beautiful female assistants, whom you see represented as agents of the BNP, everything would have looked clear-cut. The United States of America and the Grand Society of China were in a formally declared state of assassination, weren't they? Our men were gunning for their leaders, and vice versa, right?

Specifically, Senator Greenstein was to address an open meeting in San Francisco tonight, rallying a somewhat reluctant public opinion behind the Administration's firm stand on the Cambodian question. He could do it, too. He was not only floor leader of the Senate Enterprisers, but a brilliant speaker and much admired personally, a major engine of our foreign policy. At any time the Chinese would be happy to bag him. The Washington branch of my corps had already parried several attempts. Here on the West Coast he'd be more vulnerable.

So Secretive Operative Dan Steelman would have arrested the man for whom I stood waiting the minute he walked into the bar where I'd first spotted him. After a fist fight which tore apart the whole saloon, we'd get the secret papers that showed the Chinese consulate was the local HQ of their organization, we'd raid the joint, fade-out to happy ending and long spiel about Jolt, the New Way to Take LSD.

Haw. To settle a single one of those clichés, how stupid is an assassination corps supposed to be? A consulate or embassy is the last place to work out of. Quite apart from its being watched as a matter of routine, diplomatic relations are too valuable to risk by such a breach of international law.

Furthermore, I didn't want to give the Chinese the slightest tip-off that we knew The Sword Called Precious Pearl was a rendezvous of theirs. Johnny Wang had taken months to get himself contacted by their agents, months more to get sucked into their outfit, a couple of years to work up high enough that he could pass on an occasional bit of useful information to us, like the truth about that bar. If they found out that we'd learned this, they'd simply find another spot.

They might also trace back the leak and find Johnny, whom we could ill afford to lose. He was one of our best. In fact, he'd bagged Semyanov by himself, during the Russo-American assassination a decade ago. (He passed as a Buryat Mongol, got a bellhop job in the swank new hotel at Kosygingrad, and smuggled in his equipment piece by piece; when the Soviet Minister of Production finally visited that Siberian town on one of his inspection trips, Johnny Wang was all set to inject the air conditioning of the official suite with hydrogen cyanide.)

My sarcasm surprised the boy. "Well, gee," he said, "I hadn't thought much about it. But I guess it is tough to get a big government man. Real tough. Why do they even try?"

"Oh, they have ways," I said, not elaborating. The ways can be too unpleasant. Synergic poison, for example. Slip your victim the first component, harmless in itself, weeks ahead of time; then, at your leisure, give him the other dose, mixed in his food or sprayed as an aerosol in his office.

Though nowadays, with the art of guarding a man twenty-four hours a day so highly developed, the trend is back again toward more colorful brute force. If he is not to become a mere figurehead, an important man has to move around, appear publicly, attend conferences; and that sometimes lays him open to his hunters.

"Like what?" the boy persisted.

"Well," I said, "if the quarry makes a speech behind a shield of safety plastic, your assassin might wear an artificial arm with a gun inside. He might shoot a thermite slug through the plastic and the speaker, then use a minijato pack to get over the police cordon and across the rooftops."

Actually, such a method is hopelessly outdated now. And it isn't as horrible as some of the things the laboratories are working on—like remote-control devices to burn out a brain or stop a heart. I went on quickly:

"A state of assassination is similar to a football game, son. A contest, not between individual oafs such as you see on the vid, but between whole organizations. The guy who makes the touchdown depends on line backs, blocking, a long pass. The organizations might probe for months before finding a chink in the enemy armor. But if we knock off enough of their leaders, one after the next, eventually men will come to power who're so scared, or otherwise ready to compromise, that negotiations can recommence to our advantage."

I didn't add that two can play at that game.

As a matter of fact, we and the Chinese had been quietly nibbling at each other. Their biggest prize so far was the Undersecretary of State; not being anxious to admit failure, our corps let the coroner's verdict of accidental death stand, though we had ample evidence to the contrary. Our best trophy was the Commissar of Internal Waterways for Hopeh Province. That doesn't sound like much till you realize what a lot of traffic still goes by water in China, and that his

replacement, correspondingly influential, favored con-
ciliating the Americans.

To date there hadn't been any really big, really
decisive coups on either side. But Johnny Wang had
learned that four top agents of the Chinese corps were
due in town—at the same time as Senator Greenstein.

More than that he had not discovered. The cell type
of organization limits the scope of even the most
gifted spy. We did not know exactly where, when, or
how those agents were to arrive: submarine, false
bottom of a truck, stratochute, or what. We did not
know their assignments, though the general idea seemed
obvious.

Naturally, our outfit was alerted to protect Greenstein
and the other bigwigs who were to greet him. Every
inch of his route, before and after the speech, had
been preplanned in secret and was guarded one way
or another. Since the Chinese presumably expected us
to be so careful, we were all the more worried that
they should slip in their crack hunters at this exact
nexus. Why waste personnel on a hopeless task? Or
was it hopeless?

Very few men could be spared from guard duty. I
was one. They had staked me out in front of The
Sword Called Precious Pearl and told me to play by
ear.

The shoeshine rag snapped around my feet. The
boy's mind had jumped to my example, football, which
was a relief. I told him I didn't think we'd make the
Rose Bowl this year, but he insisted otherwise. It was
a lot of fun arguing with him. I wished I could keep
on.

"Well." He picked up his kit. "How's that, mister?
Pretty good, huh? I gotta go now. If I was you, I
wouldn't wait any longer for some old girl."

His small form vanished in the crowd as I looked at
my watch and realized I'd been here almost an hour.
What was going on in that building I was supposed to
have under surveillance?

What did I already know?

For the thousandth time I ran through the list. We knew the joint was a meeting place of the enemy, that only the owner and a single bartender were Chinese agents, that the rest of the help were innocent and unaware. Bit by bit, we'd studied them and the layout. We'd gotten a girl of our own in, as a waitress. We knew about a storeroom upstairs, always kept locked and burglar-alarmed; we hadn't risked making a sneak entry, but doubtless it was a combination office, file room, and cache for tools and weapons.

Posting myself today at the dragon-shaped bar, I had seen a little man enter. He was altogether ordinary, not to be distinguished from the rest of the Saturday afternoon crowd. His Caucasian face might be real or surgical; the Kung She does have a lot of whites in its pay, just as we have friends of Oriental race. Nothing had differentiated this man except that he spoke softly for a while with that bartender who was a traitor, and then went upstairs. I'd faded back outside. The building had no secret passages or any such nonsense. My man could emerge from the front door onto Grant Street, or out a rear door and a blind alley to Jefferson. My eyes covered both possibilities.

But I'd been waiting an hour now.

He might simply be waiting too. However, the whole thing smelled wrong.

I reached my decision and slipped into the grocery store behind me. A phone booth stood between the bok choy counter and the candied ginger shelf. I dialed local HQ, slipped a scrambler on the mouthpiece, and told the recorder at the other end what I'd observed and what I planned. There wasn't much the corps could do to help or even to stop me, nailed down as they were by the necessity of protecting the Senator and his colleagues. But if I never reported back, it might be useful for them to know what I'd been about.

I pushed through the crowd, hardly conscious of

them. Not that I needed to be. I knew them by heart. The Chinatown citizens, selling their Asian wares, keeping alive their Cantonese language after a century or more over here. Other San Franciscans, looking for amusement. The tourists from Alaska, Massachusetts, Iowa, cratered Los Angeles. The foreigners: Canadians, self-conscious about belonging to the world's wealthiest nation, leaning backward to be good fellows; Europeans, gushing over our old buildings and quaint little shops; Russians, bustling earnestly about with cameras and guidebooks; an Israeli milord, immaculate, reserved, veddy veddy Imperial; a South African or Indonesian in search of a white clerk to order around; and a few Chinese proper— consular officials or commercial representatives—stiff in their drab uniforms but retaining a hint of old Confucian politeness.

Possibly, face remodeled, speech and gait and tastes reconditioned, a Chinese assassin, stalking me. But I couldn't linger to worry about that. I had one of my own to hunt.

Crossing the street, I bent my attention to a koan I'd found helpful before—"What face did you wear before your mother and father conceived you?"—and reentered The Sword Called Precious Pearl in a more relaxed and efficient state. I stood by the entrance a moment, letting my pupils adjust to cool, smoky dimness.

A waitress passed near. Not ours, unfortunately; Joan didn't come on duty till twenty hundred. But I'd read the dossiers on everyone working here. The girl I saw was a petite blonde. Surgery had slanted her blue eyes, which made for a startling effect; the slit-skirt rig she wore on the job added to that. Our inquiries, Joan's reports, everything tagged her as being impulsive, credulous, and rather greedy.

My scheme was chancy, but an instinctive sense of desperation was growing on me. I tapped her arm and donned a sort of smile. "Excuse me, miss."

"Yes?" She stopped. "Can I bring you something, sir?"

"Just a little information. I'm trying to locate a friend." I slipped her a two-hundred-dollar bill. She nodded very brightly, tucked the bill in her belt pouch, and led me into a cavernous rear booth. I seated myself opposite her and closed the curtains, which I recognized as being of sound-absorbent material.

"Yes, sir?" she invited.

I studied her through the twilight. Muffled, the talk and laughter and footsteps in the barroom seemed far away, not quite real. "Don't get excited, sis," I said. "I'm only looking for a guy. You probably saw him. He came in an hour or so ago, talked to Slim at the bar, then went upstairs. A short baldish fellow. Do you remember?"

Her sudden start took me by surprise. I hadn't expected her to attach any significance to this. "No," she whispered. "I can't—you'd better—"

My pulse flipflopped, but I achieved a chuckle. "He's a bit shy, but I am too. I just want a chance to talk with him privately, without Slim knowing. It's a business deal, see, and I want him to hear my offer. All I'm asking you to do is tell me if he's still in that storeroom." As her eyes grew round: "Yes, I know that's the only possible place for him to have gone. Nothing else up there but an office and such, and those're much too public."

"I don't know," she said jaggedly.

"Well, can you find out?" I took my wallet forth, extracted ten kilobuck notes, and shuffled them before her. "This is yours for the information, and nobody has to be told. In fact, nobody had better be told. Ever."

Fine beads of sweat glittered on her forehead, catching the wan light. She was scared. Not of me. I don't look tough, and anyhow she was used to petty gangsters. But she had seen something lately that disconcerted her, and when I showed up and touched on the same nerve, it was a shock.

"You under contract here?" I asked, keeping my voice mild.

Her golden head shook.

"Then I'd quit if I were you," I said. "Today. Go work somewhere else—the other end of town or a different city altogether."

I decided to take a further risk, and pulled my right sleeve back far enough for her to glimpse the gun barrel strapped to my forearm.

"This is not a healthy spot," I went on. "Slim's got himself mixed up with something."

I observed her closely. My next line could go flat on its face, it was so straight from the tall corn country. Or it could be a look at hell. She was so rattled by now that I decided she might fall for it.

"Zombie racket," I said.

"Oh no!" She had shrunk away from me when I showed the gun. At my last words she sagged against the booth wall, and her oblique blue eyes went blank.

I had her hooked. Finding someone who'd believe that story on so little evidence was my first break today. And I needed one for damn sure.

Not that the racket doesn't still exist, here and there. And where it does, it's the ghastliest form of enslavement man has yet invented. But mostly it's been wiped out. Not even legitimate doctors do much psychosurgery any more, and certainly not for zombie merchants. (I refer to the civilized world; totalitarian governments continue to find the procedures useful.)

"You needn't tell Slim, or anyone, why you're quitting," I said, placing the bills on the table. "That's jet fare to any other spot in the world, and a stake till you get another job. I understand there are lots of openings around von Braunsville these days, what with the spaceport being expanded."

She nodded, stiff in the neck muscles.

"Okay, sis," I finished. "Believe me, you needn't get involved in this at all. I just want to know whatever you noticed about that little guy."

"I saw him talk to Slim and then go upstairs by himself." She spoke so low I could barely hear. "That was kind of funny—unusual, I mean. A couple of us girls talked about it. Then I saw him come down again maybe fifteen minutes ago. You know, in this business you got to keep watching everywhere, see if the customers are happy and so on."

"Uh-huh," I said. The hope of finding someone this observant was what had brought me back here.

"Well, he came down again," she said. "He must have been the same man, because nobody else goes upstairs this time of day. And like you said, he must have gone in the storeroom. They don't ever allow anybody else in there, I guess you know. Well, when he came back, he didn't look like himself. He wore different clothes—red tunic, green pants—and he had thick black hair and walked different, and he carried a little bag or satchel. . . . "

Her voice trailed off. I tried to imagine how a man might strangle himself. Of course that private room would have disguise materials! Not that a skilled agent needs much; it's fantastic what a simple change of posture will do.

My man had altered his looks, collected whatever tools he needed, and sauntered out the front door under my eye like any departing patron.

For a moment I debated coldly whether the enemy knew this place was known to us. Probably not. They had merely been taking a sensible extra precaution. The fault was ours—no, mine—for underestimating their thoroughness.

I looked hard at the girl. Well, I consoled myself, they in their turn had underestimated her and her companions. That's a characteristic failing of the present-day Chinese: to forget that the unregimented common man is able to see and think about things he hasn't been conditioned to see and think about. Nonetheless, they were now ahead on points: because I had no idea where my mouse-turned-cat was bound.

"What's the matter?" The girl's tones became shrill. "I told you everything I know. It scared me some—wasn't the first funny goings-on I'd noticed here—but I figured it was Slim's business. Then you came along and—Go on! Get out of here!"

"I don't suppose you observed which way he turned as he went out the door?" I asked.

She shook her head. The rest of her was shaking too.

I sighed. "Makes no difference. Well, thanks, sis. If you don't want to attract attention to yourself, you better take a happypill before going back to work."

She agreed by fumbling in her pouch. So as not to be noticed either, I remained slumped for another few minutes. By then the girl was in orbit. She looked at me rosily, giggled, and said, "Care to offer me a job yourself? You bought quite a few hours of my time already, you know."

"I bought your plane fare," I told her sharply, and left. Sometimes I think a temporary zombie is as gruesome as a permanent one, and more dangerous to civilization.

I had been racing around in my own skull while I waited, like any trapped rat, getting nowhere. A full-dress attempt on Senator Greenstein—even with the hope of also bagging the Governor, the state chairman of the Enterprise Party, and various other jupiters—didn't seem plausible. The only way I could see to get them at once would be by, say, a light super-fast rocket bomber, descending from the stratosphere with ground guidance. But such weapons were banned by the World Disarmament Convention. If the Chinese were about to break *that*. . . . Impossible! What use is it to be the chief corpse in a radioactive desert?

Had the enemy research labs come up with a new technique: the virus gun, the invisibility screen, or any of those dream gadgets? Conceivable, but doubtful. One of our own major triumphs had been a raid on their central R & D plant in Shanghai. We hadn't gotten Grandfather Scientist Feng as hoped, but our agents had machine-gunned a number of valuable lesser men and blown up the main building. There was every reason to believe we were ahead of them in armaments development. The Chinese had nothing we didn't have more of, except perhaps imagination.

And yet they wouldn't slip four of their best killers into this country merely for a lark. The trigger man of real life bears no resemblance to the one on your living-room screen. He has to have the potentialities to start with, and such genes are rare. Then a lot of expensive talent goes into training him, peeling off ordinary humanness and installing the needful reflexes. I say this quite without modesty, sometimes wishing to hell I'd flunked out. But at any rate, a top-grade field agent is not expended lightly.

So where was my boy?

I slouched down Grant Street, under the dragon lamps and the peaked tile roofs, thinking that I might already know the answer. The prominent men in this area didn't total so very many. If the agent murdered cleverly enough, as he was trained to do, the result would pass for an accident—though naturally, when-ever a big name dies during a state of assassination, the presumption is that it was engineered. The corps can't investigate every case of home electrocution, iodine swallowed by mistake for cough syrup, drowning, suicide. . . . However, no operative kills obscure folk. He has no rational motive for it, and we aren't sadists; we are the kings who die for the people so that little boys with shoeshine kits may not again be fried on molten streets. . . .

I don't know what put the answer in my head. Hunch, subconscious ratiocination, ESP, lucky guess—I just don't know. But I have said that a trigger man is a special and lonely creature. I stood unmoving for an instant. The crowd milled around me, frantic in search of something to fill the rest of the thirty-hour week; I was a million light-years elsewhere, and it was cold.

Then I started running.

I slowed down after a while, which was more efficient under these conditions. I told myself that dsin y equals cos y dy and dcos y equals minus sin y dy, I asked myself how high is green, and presently I arrived in front of New Old St. Mary's church, where the taxis patrol. Somebody's mother was hailing one. As it drew up I pushed her aside, hopped into the bubble, closed it on her gray hairs, and said, "Berkeley!"

No use urging speed on the pilot. I had to sit and fume. The knowledge that it followed the guide cables faster and more safely than any human chauffeur was scant consolation. I could have browbeaten a man.

The Bay looked silver, down a swooping length of street. The far side was a gleam of towers and delicate colors; they rebuilt well over there, though of course it so happened the bomb had left them a clearer field than in San Francisco. The air was bright and swift, and I could see the giant whale shape of a transpolar merchant submarine standing in past Alcatraz Peace Memorial. Looking at that white spire, I wondered if the old German idea about a human race mind might not be correct; and if so, how grisly a sense of humor does it have?

But I had business on hand. As the taxi swooped into the Bay tunnel I took the city index off its shelf by the phone and leafed through. The address I wanted . . . yes, here. . . . "Twenty-eight seventy-eight Buena Vista," I told the pilot.

I had no idea if the resident was at home; but neither did my opponent, I supposed. I should call ahead, warn. . . . No. If my antagonist was there already, he mustn't be tipped off that I knew.

We came out onto the freeway and hummed along at an even 150 KPH, another drop in a river of machines. The land climbed rapidly on this side too. We skirted the city within a city which is the UC campus, dropped off the freeway at Euclid, and followed that avenue between canyonlike apartment house walls to Buena Vista. This street was old and narrow and dignified. We had to slow, while I groaned.

"Twenty-eight seventy-eight Buena Vista," my voice played back to me. The change from my money jingled down. I scooped it up and threw back a coin.

"Drive on past," I said "Let me off around the next bend."

I heard a clicking. The pilot didn't quite understand, bucked my taped words on to a human dispatcher across the Bay, got its coded orders, and obeyed.

I walked back, the street on my right and a high hedge on my left. Roofs and walls swept away below me, falling to the glitter of great waters. San Francisco and Marin County lifted their somehow unreal hills on the farther side. A fresh wind touched my skin. My footfalls came loudly, and the arm gun weighed a million kilograms.

At the private driveway I turned and walked in. Landscaped grounds enclosed a pleasant modernistic mansion; the University does well by its president. An old gardener was puttering with some roses. I began to realize just how thin my hunch was.

He straightened and peered at me. His face was wizened, his clothes fifty years out of date, his language quaint. "What's the drag, man?"

"Looking for a chap," I said. "Important message. Any strangers been around?"

"Well, I dunno. Like, we get a lot of assorted cats."

I flipped a ten-dollar coin up and down in a cold hand. "Medium height, thin," I said. "Black hair, smallish nose, red tunic, green slacks, carrying a bag."

"Dunno," repeated the gardener. "I mean, like hard to remember."

"Have a beer on me," I said, my heartbeat accelerating. I slipped him the coin.

"Cat went in about fifteen minutes ago. Said he was doing the Sonaclean repair bit, like."

That was a good gimmick. Having your things cleaned with supersonics is expensive, but once you've bought the apparatus it's so damned automatic it diagnoses its own troubles and calls for its own service men. I took the porch steps fast and leaned on the chimes. A voice from the scanner cooed, "How do you do, sir. Your business, please."

"I'm from Sonaclean," I snapped. "Something appears to be wrong with your set."

"We have a repairman here now, sir."

"The continuator doesn't mesh with the hypostat. We got an alarm. You'd better let me talk to him."

"Very good, sir. One moment, please."

I waited for about sixty geological epochs till the door was opened manually, by the same house-maintenance technician who'd quizzed me. I'd know that pigeon voice in hell, where as a matter of fact I was.

"This way, please, sir." She led me down a hall, past a library loaded with books and microspools, and opened a panel on a downward stair. "Straight that way."

I looked into fluorescent brightness. Perhaps, I thought in a remote volume of myself, death is not black; perhaps death is just this featureless luminosity, forever. I went down the stairs.

The brains as well as the guts and sinews of the house were down here. A monitor board blinked many red eyes at me; a dust precipitator buzzed within an air shaft. I looked across the glazed plastic floor and saw my man beside an open Sonaclean. His tools were spread out in front of him, and he stood in a posture that looked easy but wasn't. If need be, he could lift his arm and shoot in the same motion that dropped him on the floor and bounced him sideways. And yet his face was kindly, the eyes tired, the skin sagging a bit with surgical middle age.

"Hello," he said. "What brings you here?"

He wasn't expecting anyone from the company, of course. He'd disconnected the Sonaclean the moment he arrived. I didn't believe he meant to plant a bomb, or any such elaborate deal. He'd fiddle around awhile,

put the machine back together, go upstairs. Maybe
this was simply a reconnoitering expedition, or maybe
he knew where Morales was and would slay him this
same day. Yes, probably the latter.

He'd slip to Juan Morales' study, kill him with a
single karate chop, arrange a rug or stool to make the
death look accidental, come back to the head of this
stairway, and take his leave. Quite likely no one would
ever check with the Sonaclean people. Even if somebody did, my man would have vanished long ago; and
he was unmemorable. Even here, now, a few meters
from him, realizing he must have a gun beneath his
tunic sleeve, I found it hard to fix him in my mind. His
mediocrity was the work of a great artist.

Was he even the one I sought? His costume combination was being worn this instant by a million harmless citizens; his face was anyone's; the sole deadliness
might be housed in my own sick brain.

I grunted. "Air-filter inspection."

He turned back to his dojiggling with the machine.
And I knew that he was my man.

He took seconds to comprehend what I had said.
An American would have protested at once, "Hey, this
is Saturday—" As he whipped about on his heel, my
right arm lifted.

Our guns hissed together, but mine was aimed. He
lurched back from sheer impact. The needle stood full
in his neck. For an instant he sagged against the wall,
then blindness seized his eyes. I crouched, waiting for
him to lose consciousness.

Instead, the lips peeled from his teeth, his spine
arched, and he left the wall in a stiff rigadoon. While
he screamed I cursed and ran up the stairs, three at a
time.

The housie came into the library from the opposite
side. "What's the matter?" she cried. "Wait! Wait, you
can't—"

I was already at the phone. I fended her off with an
elbow while I dialed local HQ, emergency extension.

That's one line that is always open, with human monitors, during a state of assassination. I rattled off my identification number and: "I'm at Twenty-eight seventy-eight Buena Vista, Berkeley. Get a revival squad here. Regular police, if our own medics aren't handy. I plugged one of the opposition with a sleepydart, but they seem to have found some means of sensitizing. He went straight into tetany. . . . Twenty-eight seventy-eight Buena Vista, yes. Snap to it, and we may still get some use out of him!"

The woman wailed behind me as I pounded back down the stairs. My man was dead, hideously rigid on the floor. I picked him up. A corpse isn't really heavier than an organic, but it feels that way.

"The deep freeze!" I roared. "Where the obscenity is your freezer? If we can keep the process from — Don't stand there and gawp! Every second at room temperature, more of his brain cells are disintegrating! Do you want them to revive an idiot?"

If he could be resurrected at all. I wasn't sure what had been done to his biochemistry to make him react so to plain old neurocaine. For his sake I could almost hope he wouldn't be viable. I could have done worse in life than be a trigger man, I guess: might have ended on an interrogation team. Not that prisoners undergo torture, nothing that crude, but — Oh, well.

The housie squealed, nearly fainted, but finally led me to a chest behind the kitchen. After which she ran off again. I dumped out several hundred dollars' worth of food to make room for my burden.

As I closed the lid Dr. Juan Morales arrived. He was quite pale, but he asked me steadily, "What happened to that man?"

"I think he had a heart attack." I mopped my face and sat down on the coldbox; my knees were like rubber.

Morales stood awhile, regarding me. Some of his color returned, but a bleakness was also gathering in him. "Miss Thomas said something about your using a needle gun," he told me, very low.

"Miss Thomas babbles," I replied.

I saw his fists clench till the knuckles stood white. "I have a family to think of," he said. "Doesn't that give me a right to know the truth?"

I sighed. "Could be. Come on, let's talk privately. Afterward you can persuade Miss Thomas she misheard me on the phone. Best to keep this off the newscasts, you realize."

He led me to his study, seated me, and poured some welcome brandy. Having refilled the glasses and offered cigars, he sat down too. The room was comfortable and masculine, lined with books, a window opening on the bayview grandeur. We smoked in a brief and somehow friendly silence.

At last he said, "I take it you're from the Bureau of National Protection."

I nodded. "Been chasing that fellow. He gave me the slip. I didn't know where he was headed, but I got a hunch that turned out to be correct."

"But why me?" he breathed—the question that every man must ask at least once in this life.

I chose to interpret it literally. "They weren't after Senator Greenstein or the other big politicos, not really," I said. "They simply picked this time to strike because they knew most of our manpower would be occupied, giving them a clear field everywhere else. I was wrestling with the problem of what they actually planned to do, and a bit from your lecture came back to me."

"My lecture?" His laugh was nervous, but it meant much that he could laugh in any fashion. "Which one?"

"On the vid earlier today. About the evolution of war. You were remarking on how it started as a way to break the enemy's will, and finished trying to destroy the enemy himself—not only armies, but factories, fields, cities, women, children. You were speculating if assassination might not develop along similar lines. Evidently it has."

"But me . . . I am no one! A university president, a minor local figure in a party that lost the last election—"

"It's still a major party," I said. "Its turn will come again one of these years. You're among its best thinkers, and young as politicians go. Wilson and Eisenhower were once university presidents too."

I saw a horror in his eyes, and it was less for himself, who must now live under guard and fear, than for all of us. But that, I suppose, is one of the reasons he was a target.

"Sure," I said, "they're gunning for the current President, for Senator Greenstein, for the other Americans who stand in their way in this crisis. Maybe they'll succeed, maybe they won't. In either case, it won't be the last such conflict. They're looking ahead— twenty years, thirty years. As long as we have a state of assassination anyway, they figure they might as well weaken us for the future by killing off our most promising leaders of the next generation."

I heard a siren. That must be the revival squad. I rose. "You might try to guess who else they'll hunt," I told him. "Three other operatives are loose that I know of, and we may not extract enough information from the one I got."

He shook his head in a blind, dazed way. "I'm thinking of more than that," he said. "It's like being one of the old atomic scientists on Hiroshima Day. Suddenly an academic proposition has become real."

I paused at the door. He went on, not looking at me, talking only to his nightmare:

"It's more than the coming necessity of guarding every man who could possibly interest them—though God knows that will be a heavy burden, and when we have to start guarding every gifted child. . . . It's more, even, than our own retaliation in kind; more than the targets spreading from potential leaders to potential scientists to potential teachers and artists and I dare not guess what else. It's that the bounds have been broken.

"I see the rules laid aside once more, in the future. Sneak-attack assassinations. Undeclared assassinations. Assassination with massive weapons that take a thousand bystanders. Permanent states of assassination, dragging on for decade after decade, and no reason for them except the gnawing down of the others because they are the others.

"Whole populations mobilized against the hidden enemy, with each man watching his neighbor like a shark, with privacy, decency, freedom gone. Where is it going to end?" he asked the sky and the broad waters. "Where is it going to end?"

AMONG THIEVES

His Excellency M'Katze Unduma, Ambassador of the Terrestrial Federation to the Double Kingdom, was not accustomed to being kept waiting. But as the minutes dragged into an hour, anger faded before a chill deduction.

In this bleakly clock-bound society a short delay was bad manners, even if it were unintentional. But if you kept a man of rank cooling his heels for an entire sixty minutes, you offered him an unforgivable insult. Rusch was a barbarian, but he was too canny to humiliate Earth's representative without reason.

Which bore out everything that Terrestrial Intelligence had discovered. From a drunken junior officer, weeping in his cups because Old Earth, Civilization, was going to be attacked and the campus where he had once learned and loved would be scorched to ruin by *his* fire guns—to the battle plans and annotations thereon, which six men had died to smuggle out of the Royal War College—and now, this degradation of the ambassador himself—everything fitted.

The Margrave of Drakenstane had sold out Civilization.

Unduma shuddered, beneath the iridescent cloak, embroidered robe, and ostrich-plume headdress of his rank. He swept the antechamber with the eyes of a trapped animal.

This castle was ancient, dating back some eight hundred years to the first settlement of Norstad. The grim square massiveness of it, fused stone piled into a turreted mountain, was not much relieved by modern fittings. Tableservs, loungers, drapes, jewel mosaics, and biomurals only clashed with those fortress walls and ringing flagstones; fluorosheets did not light up all the dark corners, there was perpetual dusk up among the rafters where the old battle banners hung.

A dozen guards were posted around the room, in breastplate and plumed helmet but with very modern blast rifles. They were identical seven-foot blonds, and none of them moved at all, you couldn't even see them breathe. It was an unnerving sight for a Civilized man.

Unduma snubbed out his cigar, swore miserably to himself, and wished he had at least brought along a book.

The inner door opened on noiseless hinges and a shavepate officer emerged. He clicked his heels and bowed at Unduma. "His Lordship will be honored to receive you now, excellency."

The ambassador throttled his anger, nodded, and stood up. He was a tall thin man, the relatively light skin and sharp features of Bantu stock predominant in him. Earth's emissaries were normally chosen to approximate a local ideal of beauty—hard to do for some of those weird little cultures scattered through the galaxy—and Norstad-Ostarik had been settled by a rather extreme Caucasoid type which had almost entirely emigrated from the home planet.

The aide showed him through the door and disappeared. Hans von Thoma Rusch, Margrave of Draken-

stane, Lawman of the Western Folkmote, Hereditary
Guardian of the White River Gates, et cetera, et cetera,
et cetera, sat waiting behind a desk at the end of an
enormous black-and-red tile floor. He had a book in
his hands, and didn't close it till Unduma, sandals
whispering on the great chessboard squares, had come
near. Then he stood up and made a short ironic bow.

"How do you do, your excellency," he said. "I am
sorry to be so late. Please sit." Such curtness was no
apology at all, and both of them knew it.

Unduma lowered himself to a chair in front of the
desk. He would *not* show temper, he thought, he was
here for a greater purpose. His teeth clamped together.

"Thank you, your lordship," he said tonelessly. "I
hope you will have time to talk with me in some detail.
I have come on a matter of grave importance."

Rusch's right eyebrow tilted up, so that the archaic
monocle he affected beneath it seemed in danger of
falling out. He was a big man, stiffly and solidly built,
yellow hair cropped to a wiry brush around the long
skull, a scar puckering his left cheek. He wore Army
uniform, the gray high-collared tunic and old-fashioned
breeches and shiny boots of his planet; the trident
and suns of a primary general; a sidearm, its handle
worn smooth from much use. If ever the iron barbarian with the iron brain had an epitome, thought
Unduma, here he sat!

"Well, your excellency," murmured Rusch—though
the harsh Norron language did not lend itself to
murmurs—"of course I'll be glad to hear you out. But
after all, I've no standing in the Ministry, except as
unofficial advisor, and—"

"Please." Unduma lifted a hand. "Must we keep up
the fable? You not only speak for all the landed
warloads— and the Nor-Samurai are still the most
powerful single class in the Double Kingdom—but
you have the General Staff in your pouch and, ah, you
are well thought of by the royal family. I think I can
talk directly to you."

Rusch did not smile, but neither did he trouble to deny what everyone knew, that he was the leader of the fighting aristocracy, friend of the widowed Queen Regent, virtual step-father of her eight-year-old son King Hjalmar—in a word, that he was the dictator. If he preferred to keep a small title and not have his name unnecessarily before the public, what difference did that make?

"I'll be glad to pass on whatever you wish to say to the proper authorities," he answered slowly. "Pipe." That was an order to his chair, which produced a lit briar for him.

Unduma felt appalled. This series of—informalities—was like one savage blow after another. Till now, in the three hundred-year history of relations between Earth and the Double Kingdom, the Terrestrial ambassador had ranked everyone but God and the royal family.

No human planet, no matter how long sundered from the main stream, no matter what strange ways it had wandered, failed to remember that Earth was Earth, the home of man and the heart of Civilization. No *human* planet—had Norstad-Ostarik, then, gone the way of Kolresh?

Biologically, no, thought Unduma with an inward shudder. Nor culturally—yet. But it shrieked at him, from every insolent movement and twist of words, that Rusch had made a political deal.

"Well?" said the Margrave.

Unduma cleared his throat, desperately, and leaned forward. "Your lordship," he said, "my embassy cannot help taking notice of certain public statements, as well as certain military preparations and other matters of common knowledge—"

"And items your spies have dug up," drawled Rusch.

Unduma started. "My lord!"

"My good ambassador," grinned Rusch, "it was you who suggested a straightforward talk. I know Earth has spies here. In any event, it's impossible to hide so large a business as the mobilization of two planets for war."

Unduma felt sweat trickle down his ribs.

"There is . . . you . . . your Ministry has only announced it is a . . . a defense measure," he stammered.
"I had hoped . . . frankly, yes, till the last minute I
hoped you . . . your people might see fit to join us
against Kolresh."

There was a moment's quiet. *So* quiet, thought
Unduma. A redness crept up Rusch's cheeks, the scar
stood livid and his pale eyes were the coldest thing
Unduma had ever seen.

Then, slowly, the Margrave got it out through his
teeth: "For a number of centuries, your excellency, our
people hoped Earth might join them."

"What do you mean?" Unduma forgot all polished
inanities. Rusch didn't seem to notice. He stood up
and went to the window.

"Come here," he said. "Let me show you something."

The window was a modern inset of clear, invisible
plastic, a broad sheet high in the castle's infamous
Witch Tower. It looked out on a black sky, the sun was
down and the glacial forty-hour darkness of northern
Norstad was crawling toward midnight.

Stars glittered mercilessly keen in an emptiness
which seemed like crystal, which seemed about to
ring thinly in contracting anguish under the cold.
Ostarik, the companion planet, stood low to the south,
a gibbous moon of steely blue; it never moved in that
sky, the two worlds forever faced each other, the windy
white peaks of one glaring at the warm lazy seas of
the other. Northward, a great curtain of aurora flapped
halfway around the cragged horizon.

From this dizzy height, Unduma could see little of
the town Drakenstane: a few high-peaked roofs and
small glowing windows, lamps lonesome above frozen
streets. There wasn't much to see anyhow—no big
cities on either planet, only the small towns which
had grown from scattered thorps, each clustered

humbly about the manor of its lord. Beyond lay winter fields, climbing up the valley walls to the hard green blink of glaciers. It must be blowing out there, he saw snowdevils chase ghostly across the blue-tinged desolation.

Rusch spoke roughly: "Not much of a planet we've got here, is it? Out on the far end of nowhere, a thousand light-years from your precious Earth, and right in the middle of a glacial epoch. Have you ever wondered why we don't set up weather-control stations and give this world a decent climate?"

"Well," began Unduma, "of course, the exigencies of—"

"Of war." Rusch sent his hand upward in a chopping motion, to sweep around the alien constellations. Among them burned Polaris, less than thirty parsecs away, huge and cruelly bright. "We never had a chance. Every time we thought we could begin, there would be war, usually with Kolresh, and the labor and materials would have to go for that. Once, about two centuries back, we did actually get stations established, it was even beginning to warm up a little. Kolresh blasted them off the map.

"Norstad was settled eight hundred years ago. For seven of those centuries, we've had Kolresh at our throats. Do you wonder if we've grown tired?"

"My lord, I . . . I can sympathize," said Unduma awkwardly. "I am not ignorant of your heroic history. But it would seem to me . . . after all, Earth has also fought—"

"At a range of a thousand light-years!" jeered Rusch. "The forgotten war. A few underpaid patrolmen in obsolete rustbucket ships to defend unimportant outposts from sporadic Kolreshite raids. We live on their borders!"

"It would certainly appear, your lordship, that Kolresh is your natural enemy," said Unduma. "As indeed it is of all Civilization, of Homo sapiens himself. What I cannot credit are the, ah, the rumors of an, er, alliance—"

"And why shouldn't we?" snarled Rusch. "For seven hundred years we've held them at bay, while your precious so-called Civilization grew fat behind a wall of our dead young men. The temptation to recoup some of our losses by helping Kolresh conquer Earth is very strong!"

"You don't mean it!" The breath rushed from Unduma's lungs.

The other man's face was like carved bone. "Don't jump to conclusions," he answered. "I merely point out that from our side there's a good deal to be said for such a policy. Now if Earth is prepared to make a different policy worth our while—do you understand? Nothing is going to happen in the immediate future. You have time to think about it."

"I would have to . . . communicate with my government," whispered Unduma.

"Of course," said Rusch. His bootheels clacked on the floor as he went back to his desk. "I've had a memorandum prepared for you, an unofficial informal sort of protocol, points which his majesty's government would like to make the basis of negotiations with the Terrestrial Federation. Ah, here!" He picked up a bulky folio. "I suggest you take a leave of absence, your excellency, go home and show your superiors this, ah—"

"Ultimatum," said Unduma in a sick voice.

Rusch shrugged. "Call it what you will." His tone was empty and remote, as if he had already cut himself and his people out of Civilization.

As he accepted the folio, Unduma noticed the book beside it, the one Rusch had been reading: a local edition of Schakspier, badly printed on sleazy paper, but in the original Old Anglic. Odd thing for a barbarian dictator to read. But then, Rusch was a bit of an historical scholar, as well as an enthusiastic kayak racer, meteor polo player, chess champion, mountain climber, and . . . and all-around scoundrel!

Norstad lay in the grip of a ten-thousand-year winter, while Ostarik was a heaven of blue seas breaking on warm island sands. Nevertheless, because Ostarik harbored a peculiarly nasty plague virus, it remained an unattainable paradise in the sky till a bare two hundred fifty years ago. Then a research team from Earth got to work, found an effective vaccine, and saw a mountain carved into their likeness by the Norron folk.

It was through such means—and the sheer weight of example, the liberty and wealth and happiness of its people—that the Civilization centered on Earth had been propagating itself among colonies isolated for centuries. There were none which lacked reverence for Earth the Mother, Earth the Wise, Earth the Kindly: none but Kolresh, which had long ceased to be human.

Rusch's private speedster whipped him from the icicle walls of Festning Drakenstane to the rose gardens of Sorgenlos in an hour of hell-bat haste across vacuum. But it was several hours more until he and the queen could get away from their courtiers and be alone.

They walked through geometric beds of smoldering blooms, under songbirds and fronded trees, while the copper spires of the little palace reached up to the evening star and the hours-long sunset of Ostarik blazed gold across great quiet waters. The island was no more than a royal retreat, but lately it had known agonies.

Queen Ingra stooped over a mutant rose, tiger striped and a foot across; she plucked the petals from it and said close to weeping: "But I liked Unduma. I don't want him to hate us."

"He's not a bad sort," agreed Rusch. He stood behind her in a black dress uniform with silver insignia, like a formal version of death.

"He's more than that, Hans. He stands for decency—Norstad froze our souls, and Ostarik hasn't thawed them. I thought Earth might—" Her voice trailed off.

She was slender and dark, still young, and her folk came from the rainy dales of Norstad's equator, a farm race with gentler ways than the miners and fishermen and hunters of the red-haired ice ape who had bred Rusch. In her throat, the Norron language softened to a burring music; the Drakenstane men spat their words out rough-edged.

"Earth might what?" Rusch turned a moody gaze to the west. "Lavish more gifts on us? We were always proud of paying our own way."

"Oh, no," said Ingra wearily. "After all, we could trade with them, furs and minerals and so on, if ninety per cent of our production didn't have to go into defense. I only thought they might teach us how to be human."

"I had assumed we were still classified Homo sapiens," said Rusch in a parched tone.

"Oh, you know what I mean!" She turned on him, violet eyes suddenly aflare. "Sometimes I wonder if *you're* human, Margrave Hans von Thoma Rusch. I mean free, free to be something more than a robot, free to raise children knowing they won't have their lungs shoved out their mouths when a Kolreshite cruiser hulls one of our spaceships. What is our whole culture, Hans? A layer of brutalized farmhands and factory workers—serfs! A top crust of heel-clattering aristocrats who live for nothing but war. A little folk art, folk music, folk saga, full of blood and treachery. Where are our symphonies, novels, cathedrals, research laboratories . . . where are people who can say what they wish and make what they will of their lives and be happy?"

Rusch didn't answer for a moment. He looked at her, unblinking behind his monocle, till she dropped her gaze and twisted her hands together. Then he said only: "You exaggerate."

"Perhaps. It's still the basic truth." Rebellion rode in her voice. "It's what all the other worlds think of us."

"Even if the democratic assumption—that the eternal verities can be discovered by counting enough noses—were true," said Rusch, "you cannot repeal eight hundred years of history by decree."

"No. But you could work toward it," she said. "I think you're wrong in despising the common man, Hans . . . when was he ever given a chance, in this kingdom? We could make a beginning now, and Earth could send psychotechnic advisors, and in two or three generations—"

"What would Kolresh be doing while we experimented with forms of government?" he laughed.

"Always Kolresh." Her shoulders, slim behind the burning-red cloak, slumped. "Kolresh turned a hundred hopeful towns into radioactive craters and left the gnawed bones of children in the fields. Kolresh killed my husband, like a score of kings before him. Kolresh blasted your family to ash, Hans, and scarred your face and your soul—" She whirled back on him, fists aloft, and almost screamed: "Do you want to make an ally of Kolresh?"

The Margrave took out his pipe and began filling it. The saffron sundown, reflected off the ocean to his face, gave him a metal look.

"Well," he said, "we've been at peace with them for all of ten years now. Almost a record."

"Can't we find allies? Real ones? I'm sick of being a figurehead! I'd befriend Ahuramazda, New Mars, Lagrange—We could raise a crusade against Kolresh, wipe every last filthy one of them out of the universe!"

"Now who's a heel-clattering aristocrat?" grinned Rusch.

He lit his pipe and strolled toward the beach. She stood for an angry moment, then sighed and followed him.

"Do you think it hasn't been tried?" he said patiently. "For generations we've tried to build up a permanent alliance directed at Kolresh. What temporary ones we achieved have always fallen apart. Nobody loves us enough—and, since we've always taken the heaviest blows, nobody hates Kolresh enough."

He found a bench on the glistening edge of the strand, and sat down and looked across a steady march of surf, turned to molten gold by the low sun and the incandescent western clouds. Ingra joined him.

"I can't really blame the others for not liking us," she said in a small voice. "We are overmechanized and undercultured, arrogant, tactless, undemocratic, hardboiled . . . oh, yes. But their own self-interest—"

"They don't imagine it can happen to them," replied Rusch contemptuously. "And there are even pro-Kolresh elements, here and there." He raised his voice an octave: "Oh, my dear sir, my dear Margrave, what are you *saying*? Why, of *course* Kolresh would never attack us! They made a *treaty* never to attack us!"

Ingra sighed, forlornly. Rusch laid an arm across her shoulders. They sat for a while without speaking.

"Anyway," said the man finally, "Kolresh is too strong for any combination of powers in this part of the galaxy. We and they are the only ones with a military strength worth mentioning. Even Earth would have a hard time defeating them, and Earth, of course, will lean backward before undertaking a major war. She has too much to lose; it's so much more comfortable to regard the Kolreshite raids as mere piracies, the skirmishes as 'police actions.' She just plain will not pay the stiff price of an army and a navy able to whip Kolresh and occupy the Kolreshite planets."

"And so it is to be war again." Ingra looked out in desolation across the sea.

"Maybe not," said Rusch. "Maybe a different kind of war, at least—no more black ships coming out of *our* sky."

He blew smoke for a while, as if gathering courage, then spoke in a quick, impersonal manner: "Look

here. We Norrons are not a naval power. It's not in our
tradition. Our navy has always been inadequate and
always will be. But we can breed the toughest soldiers
in the known galaxy, in unlimited numbers; we can
condition them into fighting machines, and equip them
with the most lethal weapons living flesh can wield.

"Kolresh, of course, is just the opposite. Space
nomads, small population, able to destroy anything
their guns can reach but not able to dig in and hold it
against us. For seven hundred years, we and they have
been the elephant and the whale. Neither could ever
win a real victory over the other; war became the
normal state of affairs, peace a breathing spell. Because of the mutation, there will always be war, as
long as one single Kolreshite lives. We can't kill them,
we can't befriend them—all we can do is to be bled
white to stop them."

A wind sighed over the slow thunder on the beach.
A line of sea birds crossed the sky, thin and black
against glowing bronze.

"I know," said Ingra. "I know the history, and I
know what you're leading up to. Kolresh will furnish
transportation and naval escort; Norstad-Ostarik will
furnish men. Between us, we may be able to take
Earth."

"We will," said Rusch flatly. "Earth has grown
plump and lazy. She can't possibly rearm enough in a
few months to stop such a combination."

"And all the galaxy will spit on our name."

"All the galaxy will lie open to conquest, once Earth
has fallen."

"How long do you think we would last, riding the
Kolresh tiger?"

"I have no illusions about them, my dear. But neither can I see any way to break this eternal deadlock.
In a fluid situation, such as the collapse of Earth
would produce, we might be able to create a navy as
good as theirs. They've never yet given us a chance to
build one, but perhaps—"

"Perhaps not! I doubt very much it was a meteor which wrecked my husband's ship, five years ago. I think Kolresh knew of his hopes, of the shipyard he wanted to start, and murdered him."

"It's probable," said Rusch.

"And you would league us with them." Ingra turned a colorless face on him. "I'm still the queen. I forbid any further consideration of this . . . this obscene alliance!"

Rusch sighed. "I was afraid of that, your highness." For a moment he looked gray, tired. "You have a veto power, of course. But I don't think the Ministry would continue in office a regent who used it against the best interests of —"

She leaped to her feet. "You wouldn't!"

"Oh, you'd not be harmed," said Rusch with a crooked smile. "Not even deposed. You'd be in protective custody, shall we say. Of course, his majesty, your son, would have to be educated elsewhere, but if you wish —"

Her palm cracked on his face. He made no motion.

"I . . . won't veto —" Ingra shook her head. Then her back grew stiff. "Your ship will be ready to take you home, my lord. I do not think we shall require your presence here again."

"As you will, your highness," mumbled the dictator of the Double Kingdom.

Though he returned with a bitter word in his mouth, Unduma felt the joy, the biological rightness of being home, rise warm within him. He sat on a terrace under the mild sky of Earth, with the dear bright flow of the Zambezi River at his feet and the slim towers of Capital City rearing as far as he could see, each gracious, in its own green park. The people on the clean quiet streets wore airy blouses and colorful kilts — not the trousers for men, ankle-length skirts for women, which muffled the sad folk of Norstad. And there was educated conversation in the gentle Tierrans language, music from an open window, laughter on the verandas and children playing in the parks: freedom, law, and leisure.

The thought that this might be rubbed out of history, that the robots of Norstad and the snake-souled monsters of Kolresh might tramp between broken spires where starved Earthmen hid, was a tearing in Unduma.

He managed to lift his drink and lean back with the proper casual elegance. "No, sir," he said, "they are not bluffing."

Ngu Chilongo, Premier of the Federation Parliament, blinked unhappy eyes. He was a small grizzled man, and a wise man, but this lay beyond everything he had known in a long lifetime and he was slow to grasp it.

"But surely—" he began. "Surely this . . . this Rusch person is not insane. He cannot think that his two planets, with a population of, what is it, perhaps one billion, can overcome four billion Terrestrials!"

"There would also be several million Kolreshites to help," reminded Unduma. "However, they would handle the naval end of it entirely—and their navy *is* considerably stronger than ours. The Norron forces would be the ones which actually landed, to fight the air and ground battles. And out of those paltry one billion, Rusch can raise approximately one hundred million soldiers."

Chilongo's glass crashed to the terrace. "What!"

"It's true, sir." The third man present, Mustafa Lefarge, Minister of Defense, spoke in a miserable tone. "It's a question of every able-bodied citizen, male and female, being a trained member of the armed forces. In time of war, virtually everyone not in actual combat is directly contributing to some phase of the effort—a civilian economy virtually ceases to exist. They're used to getting along for years at a stretch with no comforts and a bare minimum of necessities." His voice grew sardonic. "By necessities, they mean things like food and ammunition—not, say, entertainment or cultural activity, as we assume."

"A hundred million," whispered Chilongo. He stared at his hands. "Why, that's ten times our *total* forces!"

"Which are ill-trained, ill-equipped, and ill-regarded by our own civilians," pointed out Lefarge bitterly.

"In short, sir," said Unduma, "while we could defeat either Kolresh or Norstad-Ostarik in an all-out war—though with considerable difficulty—between them they can defeat us."

Chilongo shivered. Unduma felt a certain pity for him. You had to get used to it in small doses, this fact which Civilization screened from Earth: that the depths of hell are found in the human soul. That no law of nature guards the upright innocent from malice.

"But they wouldn't dare!" protested the Premier. "Our friends . . . everywhere—"

"All the human-colonized galaxy will wring its hands and send stiff notes of protest," said Lefarge. "Then they'll pull the blankets back over their heads and assure themselves that now the big bad aggressor has been sated."

"This note—of Rusch's." Chilongo seemed to be grabbing out after support while the world dropped from beneath his feet. Sweat glistened on his wrinkled brown forehead. "Their terms . . . surely we can make some agreement?"

"Their terms are impossible, as you'll see for yourself when you read," said Unduma flatly. "They want us to declare war on Kolresh, accept a joint command under Norron leadership, foot the bill and—No!"

"But if we have to fight anyway," began Chilongo, "it would seem better to have at least one ally—"

"Has Earth changed that much since I was gone?" asked Unduma in astonishment. "Would our people really consent to this . . . this extortion . . . letting those hairy barbarians write our foreign policy for us—Why, jumping into war, making the first declaration ourselves, it's unconstitutional! It's *un-Civilized*!"

Chilongo seemed to shrink a little. "No," he said.

"No, I don't mean that. Of course it's impossible; better to be honestly defeated in battle. I only thought, perhaps we could bargain—"

"We can try," said Unduma skeptically, "but I never heard of Hans Rusch yielding an angstrom without a pistol at his head."

Lefarge struck a cigar, inhaled deeply, and took another sip from his glass. "I hardly imagine an alliance with Kolresh would please his own people," he mused.

"Scarcely!" said Unduma. "But they'll accept it if they must."

"Oh? No chance for us to get him overthrown—assassinated, even?"

"Not to speak of. Let me explain. He's only a petty aristocrat by birth, but during the last war with Kolresh he gained high rank and a personal following of fanatically loyal young officers. For the past few years, since the king died, he's been the dictator. He's filled the key posts with his men: hard, able, and unquestioning. Everyone else is either admiring or cowed. Give him credit, he's no megalomaniac—he shuns publicity—but that simply divorces his power all the more from responsibility. You can measure it by pointing out that everyone knows he will probably ally with Kolresh, and everyone has a nearly physical loathing of the idea—but there is not a word of criticism for Rusch himself, and when he orders it they will embark on Kolreshite ships to ruin the Earth they love."

"It could almost make you believe in the old myths," whispered Chilongo. "About the Devil incarnate."

"Well," said Unduma, "this sort of thing has happened before, you know."

"Hm-m-m?" Lefarge sat up.

Unduma smiled sadly. "Historical examples," he said. "They're of no practical value today, except for giving the cold consolation that we're not uniquely betrayed."

"What do you mean?" asked Chilongo.

"Well," said Unduma, "consider the astropolitics of the situation. Around Polaris and beyond lies Kolresh territory, where for a long time they sharpened their teeth preying on backward autochthones. At last they started expanding toward the richer human-settled planets. Norstad happened to lie directly on their path, so Norstad took the first blow—and stopped them.

"Since then, it's been seven hundred years of stalemated war. Oh, naturally Kolresh outflanks Norstad from time to time, seizes this planet in the galactic west and raids that one to the north, fights a war with one to the south and makes an alliance with one to the east. But it has never amounted to anything important. It can't, with Norstad astride the most direct line between the heart of Kolresh and the heart of Civilization. If Kolresh made a serious effort to by-pass Norstad, the Norrons could—and would—disrupt everything with an attack in the rear.

"In short, despite the fact that interstellar space is three-dimensional and enormous, Norstad guards the northern marches of Civilization."

He paused for another sip. It was cool and subtle on his tongue, a benediction after the outworld rotgut.

"Hm-m-m, I never thought of it just that way," said Lefarge. "I assumed it was just a matter of barbarians fighting each other for the usual barbarian reasons."

"Oh, it is, I imagine," said Unduma, "but the result is that Norstad acts as the shield of Earth.

"Now if you examine early Terrestrial history—and Rusch, who has a remarkable knowledge of it, stimulated me to do so—you'll find that this is a common thing. A small semicivilized state, out on the marches, holds off the enemy while the true civilization prospers behind it. Assyria warded Mesopotamia, Rome defended Greece, the Welsh border lords kept England safe, the Transoxanian Tartars were the shield of Persia, Prussia blocked the approaches to western Europe . . . oh, I could add a good many examples. In every instance, a somewhat backward people on the distant frontier of a civilization, receive the worst hammer-blows of the really alien races beyond, the wild men who would leave nothing standing if they could get at the protected cities of the inner society."

He paused for breath. "And so?" asked Chilongo.

"Well, of course suffering isn't good for people," shrugged Unduma. "It tends to make them rather nasty. The marchmen react to incessant war by becoming a warrior race, uncouth peasants with an absolute government of ruthless militarists. Nobody loves them, neither the outer savages nor the inner polite nations.

"And in the end, they're all too apt to turn inward. Their military skill and vigor need a more promising outlet than this grim business of always fighting off an enemy who always comes back and who has even less to steal than the sentry culture.

"So Assyria sacks Babylon; Rome conquers Greece; Percy rises against King Henry; Tamerlane overthrows Bajazet; Prussia clanks into France—"

"And Norstad-Ostarik falls on Earth," finished Lefarge.

"Exactly," said Unduma. "It's not even unprecedented for the border state to join hands with the very tribes it fought so long. Percy and Owen Glendower, for instance . . . though in that case, I imagine both parties were considerably more attractive than Hans Rusch or Klerak Belug."

"What are we going to do?" Chilongo whispered it toward the blue sky of Earth, from which no bombs had fallen for a thousand years.

Then he shook himself, jumped to his feet, and faced the other two. "I'm sorry, gentlemen. This has taken me rather by surprise, and I'll naturally require time to look at this Norron protocol and evaluate the other data. But if it turns out you're right"—he bowed urbanely—"as I'm sure it will—"

"Yes?" said Unduma in a tautening voice.

"Why, then, we appear to have some months, at

least, before anything drastic happens. We can try to gain more time by negotiation. We do have the largest industrial complex in the known universe, and four billion people who have surely not had courage bred out of them. We'll build up our armed forces, and if those barbarians attack we'll whip them back into their own kennels and kick them through the rear walls thereof!"

"I hoped you'd say that," breathed Unduma.

"*I* hope we'll be granted time," Lefarge scowled. "I assume Rusch is not a fool. We cannot rearm in anything less than a glare of publicity. When he learns of it, what's to prevent him from cementing the Kolresh alliance and attacking at once, before we're ready?"

"Their mutual suspiciousness ought to help," said Unduma. "I'll go back there, of course, and do what I can to stir up trouble between them."

He sat still for a moment, then added as if to himself: "Till we do finish preparing, we have no resources but hope."

The Kolreshite mutation was a subtle thing. It did not show on the surface: physically, they were a handsome people, running to white skin and orange hair. Over the centuries, thousands of Norron spies had infiltrated them, and frequently gotten back alive; what made such work unusually difficult was not the normal hazards of impersonation, but an ingrained reluctance to practice cannibalism and worse.

The mutation was a psychic twist, probably originating in some obscure gene related to the endocrine system. It was extraordinarily hard to describe—every categorical statement about it had the usual quota of exceptions and qualifications. But one might, to a first approximation, call it extreme xenophobia. It is normal for Homo sapiens to be somewhat wary of outsiders till he has established their bona fides; it was normal for Homo Kolreshi to *hate* all outsiders, from first glimpse to final destruction.

Naturally, such an instinct produced a tendency to inbreeding, which lowered fertility, but systematic execution of the unfit had so far kept the stock vigorous. The instinct also led to strongarm rule within the nation; to nomadism, where a planet was only a base like the oasis of the ancient Bedouin, essential to life but rarely seen; to a cult of secrecy and cruelty, a religion of abominations; to an ultimate goal of conquering the accessible universe and wiping out all other races.

Of course, it was not so simple, nor so blatant. Among themselves, the Kolreshites doubtless found a degree of tenderness and fidelity. Visiting on neutral planets—i.e., planets which it was not yet expedient to attack—they were very courteous and had an account of defending themselves against one unprovoked aggression after another, which some found plausible. Even their enemies stood in awe of their personal heroism.

Nevertheless, few in the galaxy would have wept if the Kolreshites all died one rainy night.

Hans von Thoma Rusch brought his speedster to the great whaleback of the battleship. It lay a light-year from his sun, hidden by cold emptiness; the co-ordinates had been given him secretly, together with an invitation which was more like a summons.

He glided into the landing cradle, under the turrets of guns that could pound a moon apart, and let the mechanism suck him down below decks. When he stepped out into the high, coldly lit debarkation chamber, an honor guard in red presented arms and pipes twittered for him.

He walked slowly forward, a big man in black and silver, to meet his counterpart, Klerak Belug, the Overman of Kolresh, who waited rigid in a blood-colored tunic. The cabin bristled around him with secret police and guns.

Rusch clicked heels. "Good day, your dominance," he said. A faint echo followed his voice. For some unknown reason, this folk liked echoes and always built walls to resonate.

Belug, an aging giant who topped him by a head, raised shaggy brows. "Are you alone, your lordship?" he asked in atrociously accented Norron. "It was understood that you could bring a personal bodyguard."

Rusch shrugged. "I would have needed a personal dreadnought to be quite safe," he replied in fluent Kolra, "so I decided to trust your safe conduct. I assume you realize that any harm done to me means instant war with my kingdom."

The broad, winkled lion-face before him split into a grin. "My representatives did not misjudge you, your lordship. I think we can indeed do business. Come."

The Overman turned and led the way down a ramp toward the guts of the ship. Rusch followed, enclosed by guards and bayonets. He kept a hand on his own sidearm—not that it would do him much good, if matters came to that.

Events were approaching their climax, he thought in a cold layer of his brain. For more than a year now, negotiations had dragged on, hemmed in by the requirement of secrecy, weighted down by mutual suspicion. There were only two points of disagreement remaining, but discussion had been so thoroughly snagged on those that the two absolute rulers must meet to settle it personally. It was Belug who had issued the contemptuous invitation.

And he, Rusch, had come. Tonight the old kings of Norstad wept worms in their graves.

The party entered a small, luxuriously chaired room. There were the usual robots, for transcription and reference purposes, and there were guards, but Overman and Margrave were essentially alone.

Belug wheezed his bulk into a seat. "Smoke? Drink?"

"I have my own, thank you." Rusch took out his pipe and a hip flask.

"That is scarcely diplomatic," rumbled Belug.

Rusch laughed. "I'd always understood that your

dominance had no use for the mannerisms of Civilization. I daresay we'd both like to finish our business as quickly as possible."

The Overman snapped his fingers. Someone glided up with wine in a glass. He sipped for a while before answering: "Yes. By all means. Let us reach an executive agreement now and wait for our hirelings to draw up a formal treaty. But it seems odd, sir, that after all these months of delay, you are suddenly so eager to complete the work."

"Not odd," said Rusch. "Earth is rearming at a considerable rate. She's had almost a year now. We can still whip her, but in another six months we'll no longer be able to; give her automated factories half a year beyond *that*, and she'll destroy us!"

"It must have been clear to you, sir, that after the Earth Ambassador—what's his name, Unduma—after he returned to your planets last year, he was doing all he could to gain time."

"Oh, yes," said Rusch. "Making offers to me, and then haggling over them—brewing trouble elsewhere to divert our attention—a gallant effort. But it didn't work. Frankly, your dominance, you've only yourself to blame for the delays. For example, your insisting that Earth be administered as Kolreshite territory—"

"My dear sir!" exploded Belug. "It was a talking point. Only a talking point. Any diplomatist would have understood. But you took six weeks to study it, then offered that preposterous counter-proposal that everything should revert to *you*, loot and territory both—Why, if you had been truly willing to co-operate, we could have settled the terms in a month!"

"As you like, your dominance," said Rusch carelessly. "It's all past now. There are only these questions of troop transport and prisoners, then we're in total agreement."

Klerak Belug narrowed his eyes and rubbed his chin with one outsize hand. "I do not comprehend," he said, "and neither do my naval officers. We have regular transports for your men, nothing extraordinary in the way of comfort, to be sure, but infinitely more suitable for so long a voyage than . . . than the naval units you insist we use. Don't you understand? A transport is for carrying men or cargo; a ship of the line is to fight or convoy. You do *not* mix the functions!"

"I do, your dominance," said Rusch. "As many of my soldiers as possible are going to travel on regular warships furnished by Kolresh, and there are going to be Double Kingdom naval personnel with them for liaison."

"But—" Belug's fist closed on his wineglass as if to splinter it. "Why?" he roared.

"My representatives have explained it a hundred times," said Rusch wearily. "In blunt language, I don't trust you. If . . . oh, let us say there should be disagreement between us while the armada is en route . . . well, a transport ship is easily replaced, after its convoy vessels have blown it up. The fighting craft of Kolresh are a better hostage for your good behavior." He struck a light to his pipe. "Naturally, you can't take our whole fifty-million-man expeditionary force on your battle wagons; but I want soldiers on every warship as well as in the transports."

Belug shook his ginger head. "No."

"Come now," said Rusch. "Your spies have been active enough on Norstad and Ostarik. Have you found any reason to doubt my intentions? Bearing in mind that an army the size of ours cannot be alerted for a given operation without a great many people knowing the fact—"

"Yes, yes," grumbled Belug. "Granted." He smiled, a sharp flash of teeth. "But the upper hand is mine, your lordship. I can wait indefinitely to attack Earth. You can't."

"Eh?" Rusch drew hard on his pipe.

"In the last analysis, even dictators rely on popular support. My Intelligence tells me you are rapidly losing yours. The queen has not spoken to you for a year, has she? And there are many Norrons whose first loyalty is to the Crown. As the thought of war with Earth seeps in, as men have time to comprehend how little they like the idea, time to see through your present anti-Terrestrial propaganda—they grow angry. Already they mutter about you in the beer halls and the officers' clubs, they whisper in ministry cloakrooms. My agents have heard.

"Your personal cadre of young key officers are the only ones left with unquestioning loyalty to you. Let discontent grow just a little more, let open revolt break out, and your followers will be hanged from the lamp posts.

"You can't delay much longer."

Rusch made no reply for a while. Then he sat up, his monocle glittering like a cold round window on winter.

"I can always call off this plan and resume the normal state of affairs," he snapped.

Belug flushed red. "War with Kolresh again? It would take you too long to shift gears—to reorganize."

"It would not. Our war college, like any other, has prepared military plans for all foreseeable combinations of circumstances. If I cannot come to terms with you, Plan No. So-and-So goes into effect. And obviously *it* will have popular enthusiasm behind it!"

He nailed the Overman with a fish-pale eye and continued in frozen tones: "After all, your dominance, I would prefer to fight you. The only thing I would enjoy more would be to hunt you with hounds. Seven hundred years have shown this to be impossible. I opened negotiations to make the best of an evil bargain—since you cannot be conquered, it will pay better to join with you on a course of mutually profitable imperialism.

"But if your stubbornness prevents an agreement, I can declare war on you in the usual manner and be no worse off than I was. The choice is, therefore, yours."

Belug swallowed. Even his guards lost some of

their blankness. One does not speak in that fashion across the negotiators' table.

Finally, only his lips stirring, he said: "Your frankness is appreciated, my lord. Some day I would like to discuss that aspect further. As for now, though . . . yes, I can see your point. I am prepared to admit some of your troops to our ships of the line." After another moment, still sitting like a stone idol: "But this question of returning prisoners of war. We have never done it. I do not propose to begin."

"*I* do not propose to let poor devils of Norrons rot any longer in your camps," said Rusch. "I have a pretty good idea of what goes on there. If we're to be allies, I'll want back such of my countrymen as are still alive."

"Not many are still sane," Belug told him deliberately.

Rusch puffed smoke and made no reply.

"If I give in on the one item," said Belug, "I have a right to test your sincerity by the other. We keep our prisoners."

Rusch's own face had gone quite pale and still. It grew altogether silent in the room.

"Very well," he said after a long time. "Let it be so."

Without a word, Major Othkar Graaborg led his company into the black cruiser. The words came from the spaceport, where police held off a hooting, hissing, rock-throwing mob. It was the first time in history that Norron folk had stoned their own soldiers.

His men tramped stolidly behind him, up the gangway and through the corridors. Among the helmets and packs and weapons, racketing boots and clashing body armor, their faces were lost, they were an army without faces.

Graaborg followed a Kolreshite ensign, who kept looking back nervously at these hereditary foes, till they reached the bunkroom. It had been hastily converted from a storage hold, and was scant cramped comfort for a thousand men.

"All right, boys," he said when the door had closed on his guide. "Make yourselves at home."

They got busy, opening packs, spreading bedrolls on bunks. Immediately thereafter, they started to assemble heavy machine guns, howitzers, even a nuclear blaster.

"You, there!" The accented voice squawked indignantly from a loudspeaker in the wall. "I see that. I got video. You not put guns together here."

Graaborg looked up from his inspection of a live fission shell. "Obscenity you," he said pleasantly. "Who are you, anyway?"

"I executive officer. I tell captain."

"Go right ahead. My orders say that according to treaty, as long as we stay in our assigned part of the ship, we're under our own discipline. If your captain doesn't like it, let him come down here and talk to us." Graaborg ran a thumb along the edge of his bayonet. A wolfish chorus from his men underlined the invitation.

No one pressed the point. The cruiser lumbered into space, rendezvoused with her task force, and went into nonspatial drive. For several days, the Norron army contingent remained in its den, more patient with such stinking quarters than the Kolreshites could imagine anyone being. Nevertheless, no spaceman ventured in there; meals were fetched at the galley by Norron squads.

Graaborg alone wandered freely about the ship. He was joined by Commander von Brecca of Ostarik, the head of the Double Kingdom's naval liaison on this ship: a small band of officers and ratings, housed elsewhere. They conferred with the Kolreshite officers as the necessity arose, on routine problems, rehearsal of various operations to be performed when Earth was reached a month hence—but they did not mingle socially. This suited their hosts.

The fact is, the Kolreshites were rather frightened of them. A spaceman does not lack courage, but he is a gentleman among warriors. His ship either functions well, keeping him clean and comfortable, or it does not function at all and he dies quickly and mercifully. He fights with machines, at enormous ranges.

The ground soldier, muscle in mud, whose ultimate weapon is whetted steel in bare hands, has a different kind of toughness.

Two weeks after departure, Graaborg's wrist chronometer showed a certain hour. He was drilling his men in full combat rig, as he had been doing every "day" in spite of the narrow quarters.

"Ten-SHUN!" The order flowed through captains, lieutenants, and sergeants; the bulky mass of men crashed to stillness.

Major Graaborg put a small pocket amplifier to his lips. "All right, lads," he said casually, "assume gas masks, radiation shields, all gun squads to weapons. Now let's clean up this ship."

He himself blew down the wall with a grenade.

Being perhaps the most thoroughly trained soldiers in the universe, the Norron men paused for only one amazed second. Then they cheered, with death and hell in their voices, and crowded at his heels.

Little resistance was met until Graaborg had picked up von Brecca's naval command, the crucial ones, who could sail and fight the ship. The Kolreshites were too dumfounded. Thereafter the nomads rallied and fought gamely. Graaborg was handicapped by not having been able to give his men a battle plan. He split up his forces and trusted to the intelligence of the noncoms.

His faith was not misplaced, though the ship was in poor condition by the time the last Kolreshite had been machine-gunned.

Graaborg himself had used a bayonet, with vast satisfaction.

M'Katze Unduma entered the office in the Witch Tower. "You sent for me, your lordship?" he asked. His voice was as cold and bitter as the gale outside.

"Yes. Please be seated." Margrave Hans von Thoma Rusch looked tired. "I have some news for you."

"What news? You declared war on Earth two weeks ago. Your army can't have reached her yet." Unduma leaned over the desk. "Is it that you've found transportation to send me home?"

"Somewhat better news, your excellency." Rusch leaned over and tuned a telescreen. A background of clattering robots and frantically busy junior officers came into view.

Then a face entered the screen, young, and with more life in it than Unduma had ever before seen on this sullen planet. "Central Data headquarters—Oh, yes, your lordship." Boyishly, against all rules: "We've got her! The *Bheoka* just called in . . . she's ours!"

"Hm-m-m. Good." Rusch glanced at Unduma. "The *Bhoeka* is the superdreadnought accompanying Task Force Two. Carry on with the news."

"Yes, sir. She's already reducing the units we failed to capture. Admiral Sorrens estimates he'll control Force Two entirely in another hour. Bulletin just came in from Force Three. Admiral Gundrup killed in fighting, but Vice Admiral Smitt has assumed command and reports three-fourths of the ships in our hands. He's delaying fire until he sees how it goes aboard the rest. Also—"

"Never mind," said Rusch. "I'll get the comprehensive report later. Remind Staff that for the next few hours all command decisions had better be made by officers on the spot. After that, when we see what we've got, broader tactics can be prepared. If some extreme emergency doesn't arise, it'll be a few hours before I can get over to HQ."

"Yes, sir. Sir, I . . . may I say—" So might the young Norron have addressed a god.

"All right, son, you've said it." Rusch turned off the screen and looked at Unduma. "Do you realize what's happening?"

The ambassador sat down; his knees seemed all at

once to have melted. "What have you done?" It was like a stranger speaking.

"What I planned quite a few years ago," said the Margrave.

He reached into his desk and brought forth a bottle. "Here, your excellency. I think we could both use a swig. Authentic Terrestrial Scotch. I've saved it for this day."

But there was no glory leaping in him. It is often thus, you reach a dream and you only feel how tired you are.

Unduma let the liquid fire slide down his throat.

"You understand, don't you?" said Rusch. "For seven centuries, the Elephant and the Whale fought, without being able to get at each other's vitals. I made this alliance against Earth solely to get our men aboard their ships. But a really large operation like that can't be faked. It has to be genuine—the agreements, the preparations, the propaganda, everything. Only a handful of officers, men who could be trusted to . . . to infinity"—his voice cracked over, and Unduma thought of war prisoners sacrificed, hideous casualties in the steel corridors of spaceships, Norron gunners destroying Kolreshite vessels and the survivors of Norron detachments which failed to capture them—"only a few could be told, and then only at the last instant. For the rest, I relied on the quality of our troops. They're good lads, every one of them, and therefore adaptable. They're especially adaptable when suddenly told to fall on the men they'd most like to kill."

He tilted the bottle afresh. "It's proving expensive," he said in a slurred, hurried tone. "It will cost us as many casualties, no doubt, as ten years of ordinary war. But if I hadn't done this, there could easily have been another seven hundred years of war. Couldn't there? Couldn't there have been? As it is, we've already broken the spine of the Kolreshite fleet. She has plenty of ships yet, to be sure, still a menace, but crippled. I hope Earth will see fit to join us. Between them, Earth and Norstad-Ostarik can finish off Kolresh in a hurry. And after all, Kolresh *did* declare war on you, had every intention of destroying you. If you won't help, well, we can end it by ourselves, now that the fleet is broken. But I hope you'll join us."

"I don't know," said Unduma. He was still wobbling in a new cosmos. "We're not a . . . a hard people."

"You ought to be," said Rusch. "Hard enough, anyway, to win a voice for yourselves in what's going to happen around Polaris. Important frontier, Polaris."

"Yes," said Unduma slowly. "There is that. It won't cause any hosannahs in our streets, but . . . yes, I think we will continue the war, as your allies, if only to prevent you from massacring the Kolreshites. They can be rehabilitated, you know."

"I doubt that," grunted Rusch. "But it's a detail. At the very least, they'll never be allowed weapons again." He raised a sardonic brow. "I suppose we, too, can be rehabilitated, once you get your peace groups and psychotechs out here. No doubt you'll manage to demilitarize us and turn us into good plump democrats. All right, Unduma, send your Civilizing missionaries. But permit me to give thanks that I won't live to see their work completed!"

The Earthman nodded, rather coldly. You couldn't blame Rusch for treachery, callousness, and arrogance —he was what his history had made him—but he remained unpleasant company for a Civilized man. "I shall communicate with my government at once, your lordship, and recommend a provisional alliance, the terms to be settled later," he said. "I will report back to you as soon as . . . ah, where will you be?"

"How should I know?" Rusch got out of his chair. The winter night howled at his back. "I have to convene the Ministry, and make a public telecast, and get over to Staff, and—No. The devil with it! If you need me inside the next few hours, I'll be at Sorgenlos on Ostarik. But the matter had better be urgent!"

DETAILS

The most austerely egalitarian societies—and the League is a mature culture which has put such games behind it—soon learn they must cater to the whims of their leaders. This is true for the simple reason that a mind on whose decisions all fate may turn has to function efficiently, which it can only do when the total personality is satisfied and unjarred. For Rasnagarth Kri the League had rebuilt a mile-high skyscraper. His office took up the whole roof, beneath a dome of clear plastic, so that from his post he could brood by day over the city towers and by night under the cold radiance of the Sagittarian star-clouds. It was a very long walk from the gravshaft door to the big bare desk.

Harban Randos made the walk quickly, almost jauntily. They had warned him that the High Commissioner was driven by a sense of undying haste and that it was worth a man's future to spill time on a single formality. Randos fairly radiated briskness. He was young, only a thousand years old, plumpish and sandy-haired, dressed in the latest mode of his people, the Shandakites of Garris. His tunic glittered with starry points of light and his cloak blew like a flame behind him.

He reached the desk and remained standing. Kri had not looked up. The harsh blue face was intent over a bit of paper. Around him the sky was sunny, aircraft flittered in dragonfly grace, the lesser spires glowed and burned, the city pulsed. For the blue man in the plain gray robe, none of it existed, not while he was looking at that one sheet.

After all, its few lines of text and paramathematical symbology concerned eight billion human lives. In another lifetime or so—say 10,000 years—the consequences might well concern the entire League, with a population estimated at ten to the fifteenth power souls.

After an interminable minute, Kri scribbled his decision and dropped the report down the outgoing chute. Another popped automatically from the incoming slot. He half reached for it, saw Randos waiting, and withdrew his hand. That was a gaunt hand, knobby and ropy and speckled with age.

"Harban Randos, sir, by appointment," rattled off his visitor. "Proposed agent-in-chief for new planet in Section two-three-nine-seven-six-two."

"I remember now. Sit down." Kri nodded curtly. "Coordinator Zantell and Representative Chuing urged your qualifications. What are they?"

"Graduated in seventy-five from Nimë Psychotechnic Institute in the second rank. Apprenticeship under Vor Valdran on Galeen V, rated as satisfactory." Damn the old spider! What did he think the Service was . . . the Patrol?

"Galeen was a simple operation," said Kri. "It was only a matter of guiding them along the last step to full status. The planet for which you have been recommended is a barbarous one, therefore a more difficult and complex problem."

Randos opened his mouth to protest that backward planets were, mathematically, an elementary proposition . . . Great Designer, only a single world to worry about, while the Galeenians had reached a dozen stars at the time he went there! Wisely, he closed it again.

Kri sighed. "How much do you know of the situation on this one?—No, never mind answering, it would take you all day. Frankly, you're only getting the job for two reasons. One, you are a Shandakite of Garris, which means you are physiologically identical with the race currently dominant on the planet in question. We have no other fully trained Shandakite available, and indeed no qualified man who could be surgically disguised. Everyone I would like to appoint is tied up elsewhere with more important tasks. Two, you have the strong recommendation of Zantell and Chuing.

"Very well, the post is yours. The courier boat will take you there, and supply you en route with hypnotic instruction as to the details. You already know the Service rules and the penalties for violating them.

"I wanted to see you for just one reason . . . to tell you personally what your job means. You're a young man, and think of it as a stepping stone to higher things. That's an attitude which you'll have to rub off. It's an insignificant planet of an undistinguished star, out on the far end of the galaxy, with a minimum thousand years of guidance ahead of it before it can even be considered for full status. I know that. But I also know it holds more than a billion human creatures, each one fully as valuable as you and I, each one the center of his own particular universe. If you forget that, may the Great Designer have mercy on them and on you.

"Dismissed."

Randos walked out, carefully energetic. He had been prepared for this, but it had still been pretty raw. Nobody had a right to treat a free citizen of a full-status planet like . . . like a not very trustworthy child.

Damn it, he was a man, on the mightiest enterprise men had ever undertaken, and—

And someday *he* might sit behind that desk.

Kri allowed himself a minute's reflection as Randos departed. It was so tinged with sadness that he wondered if he weren't getting too old, if he hadn't better resign for the good of the Service.

So many planets, spinning through night and cold, so many souls huddled on them . . . a half-million full-status worlds, near galactic center, members of interstellar civilization by virtue of knowing that such a civilization existed . . . and how many millions more who did not know? It seemed that every day a scoutship brought back word of yet another inhabited planet.

Each of them had its human races—red, black, white, yellow, blue, green, brown, tall or short, thin or fat, hairy or bald, tailed or tailless, but fully human, biologically human, and the scientists had never discovered why evolution should work thus on every terrestroid world. The churches said it was the will of the Designer, and perhaps they were right. Certainly they were right in a pragmatic sense, for the knowledge had brought the concept of brotherhood and duty. The duty of true civilization was to guide its brothers in darkness—secretly, gently, keeping from them the devastating knowledge that a million-year-old society already existed, until they had matured enough to take that bitter pill and join smoothly the League of the older planets. Without such guidance . . . In his younger days, Kri had seen the dead worlds, where men had once lived. War, exhaustion of resources, accumulation of lethal genes, mutant disease . . . it was so hideously simple for Genus Homo to wipe a planet bare of himself.

The old blue man sighed, and a smile tugged at his mouth. You didn't work many centuries in the Service without becoming an idealist and a cynic. An idealist who lived for the mission, and a cynic who knew when to compromise for the sake of that mission.

Theoretically, Kri was above political pressures. In fact, when there was no obvious disqualification, he often had to give somebody's favorite nephew a plum. After all, his funds and his lower echelons were politically controlled. . . .

He started, realizing how much time had passed and how many decisions had yet to be made before he could quit for the day. His wife would give him Chaos if he stayed overtime tonight. Some damned card party. He bent over the report and dismissed from his mind the planet called Earth.

The doorman was shocked.

He was used to many people going in and out of the gray stone building, not only toffs and tradesmen but foreigners and Orientals and even plain tenant farmers, come down from Yorkshire with hayseeds in their hair. Benson & McMurtrie, Import Brokers, were a big firm and had to talk to every sort. He'd served in India as a young fellow and considered himself broad-minded. But there are limits.

"'Ere, now! An' just where d'yer think you're going?"

The stocky, sunburned man with the tattered clothes and the small brass earrings paused. He had curly black hair and snapping blue eyes, and was fuming away on an old clay pipe. A common tinker, walking into Benson & McMurtrie cool as dammit! "In there, ould one, in there," he said with an Irish lilt. "Ye wouldn' be denyin' me a sight of the most beautiful colleen in London, would ye?"

"That I would," said the doorman. A passing car stirred up enough breeze to flutter the tinker's rags, flamboyant against the grimed respectability of Regent Street. "On yer wye before I calls a constable."

"Sure an' it's no way to be addressin' a craftsman, me bhoy," said the tinker. "But since ye seem to be sharin' of the Sassenach mania for the written word, then feast your eyes on this." Out of his patched garments he produced a letter of admittance, dated two years ago and signed by McMurtrie himself.

The doorman scanned it carefully, the more so as McMurtrie was eight months dead, the nice white-haired old gentleman, struck down by one of these new-fangled autos as he crossed this very street. But it gave a clear description of Sean O'Meara, occupation tinker, and set no time limit.

He handed it back. "In yer goes, then," he conceded, "though why they—Nev' mind! Behyve yerself is all I got ter sye."

Sean O'Meara nodded gaily and disappeared into the building. The doorman scratched his head. You never knew, you didn't, and those Irish were an uppity lot, a bad lot. Here Mr. Asquith was trying to give them Home Rule and the Ulstermen were up in arms about it!

Sabor Tombak had no trouble getting past the private secretary, who was a Galactic himself, but he sadly puzzled the lesser employees. Most of them concluded, after several days of speculation, that the tinker was a secret agent. It was well known that Benson & McMurtrie had sufficient financial power to be hand in glove with the Cabinet itself. They weren't so far off the mark at that.

The inner office was a ponderosity of furniture and sepia. Tombak shuddered and knocked out his pipe. Usrek Arken, alias Sir John Benson—grandson of the founder, who had actually been himself—started. "Do you have to bring that thing in here?" he complained. "The London air is foul already without you polluting it."

"Anything would be welcome as a counterirritant to this stuff," answered Tombak. His gesture included the entire office. "Why the Evil don't you guidance boys get on orbit and guide the English into decent taste? An Irish peasant without a farthing in his pocket has better-looking quarters than this kennel."

"Details, details." The sarcastic note in Arken's voice did not escape Tombak. The word had somehow become a proverb in his absence.

"Better get hold of the boss and let me report," he said. "I've an earful to give him."

"An eyeful, you mean," replied Arken. "Written up in proper form with quantitative data tabulated, if you please."

"Oh, sure, sure. Gimme time. But this won't wait for—"

"Maybe you don't know we have a new boss," said Arken slowly.

"Huh? What happened to Kalmagens?"

"Killed. Run over by a bloody Designer-damned petroleum burner eight months ago."

Tombak sat down, heavily. He had had a great regard for Kalmagens, both professionally—the Franco-Prussian business had been handled with sheer artistry—and as a friend. He dropped into fluent Gaelic for a while, cursing the luck.

At last he shook himself and asked: "What's the new man like?"

"Harban Randos of Garris. Arrived six weeks back. Young fellow, fresh out of his apprenticeship. A good psychotechnician, but seems to think the psychotechnic laws will cover every situation." Arken scowled. "And the situation right now is nasty."

"It is that," agreed Tombak. "I haven't seen many newspapers where I've been, but it's past time Kaiser Wilhelm was put across somebody's knee." He jumped back to his feet with the restless energy of two years tramping the Irish roads. "Where's Randos now? Damn it, I want to see him."

Arken lifted his brows. "All right, old chap. If you really insist, I'll call him for you, and then I'll crawl under the desk and wait for the lightning to subside."

He buzzed for the secretary and told him in English: "Send Mr. Harrison to me, please." That was for the benefit of the non-Galactic employees. When the door had closed, he remarked to Tombak:

"You know how complicated the secrecy requirement can make things. Bad enough to always have to look your Earthage, and officially die every fifty years or so, and provide a synthetic corpse, and assume a new face and a new personality. But when you're at the top, and the leading autochthons know you as an important man — Chaos! We have to fob Randos off as a senior clerk, freshly hired for nepotistic reasons."

Tombak grinned and tamped his pipe. He himself was in the lowest echelon of the five thousand Galactics serving on Earth, and refused to study for promotion. He liked the planet and its folk, he liked being soldier and sailor and cowboy and mechanic and tramp, to gather knowledge of how the Plan was progressing on the level of common humanity. He did not hanker for the symbological sweatshop work and the identity problem of the upper brackets.

A plump, undistinguished form, in somber clothes that looked highly uncomfortable, entered. "You sent for me, sir?" The door closed behind Harban Randos. "What's the meaning of this? I was engaged in an evaluation of the political dynamics, and you interrupted me precisely as I was getting the matrix set up. How many times do I have to tell you the situation is crucial? What the Chaos do you want now?"

"Sir Randos . . . Sabor Tombak, one of our field agents, returned from a survey of Ireland," murmured Arken. "He has important new information for you."

Randos did not bow, as urbanity demanded. He looked tired and harried. "Then file it and mark it urgent, for Designer's sake!"

"Trouble is," said Tombak imperturbably, "this is not stuff that can be fitted into a mass-action equation. This concerns individual people . . . angry people."

"Look here —" Randos drew a ragged breath. "I'll take time to explain to you." His tone grew elaborately satirical. "Forgive me if I repeat what you already know.

"This planet wasn't discovered till seventeen ninety-eight, and three years went by before a mission could be sent. The situation was plainly critical, so much so that our men couldn't take a century to establish themselves. They had to cut corners and work fast. By introducing technological innovations themselves and serving with uncanny distinction in several countries' armed forces and governments, they barely managed to be influential at the Congress of Vienna. Not very influential, but just sufficiently to get a stopgap balance-of-power system adopted. They couldn't prevent the antidemocratic reaction and the subsequent revolutions . . . but they did stave off a major catastrophe, and settled down to building a decent set of governments. Now their whole work is in danger.

"We're too damned few, Tombak, and have to contend with too many centuries of nationalism and vested interest. My predecessor here did manage to get high-ranking agents into the German leadership. They failed to prevent war with Denmark, Austria, and France, but a fairly humane peace treaty was managed after eighteen seventy. Not as humane as it should have been, it left the French smarting, but a good job under the circumstances."

Tombak nodded. He had seen that for himself. He had been a simple krauthead officer then, moderating the savagery of his troops . . . less for immediate mercy than for the future, a smaller legacy of hatred. But rumors had filtered down, which he later gleefully confirmed: British pressure secretly put on Bismarck to control his appetite, and the pressure had originated with the Prime Minister's good friend "Sir Colin McMurtrie." And the Boer War had been unavoidable, but the quick gestures of friendship toward the conquered had not—The Plan called for a peaceful, democratic British Commonwealth to dominate and stabilize the world.

"Kalmagens' death threw everything into confusion," went on Randos. "I suppose you know that. You fellows carried on as best you could, but the mass is not identical with the sum of the individuals concerned.

There are factors of tradition, inertia, the cumbersome social machinery . . . it takes a trained man to see the forest for the trees. Things have rapidly gone toward maximum entropy. An unstable system of checks and balances between rival imperialisms is breaking down. We have less than a year to avert a general war which will exacerbate nationalism to the point of insanity. I have to develop a program of action and get it into effect. I have *no* time to waste on details!"

"The Turkish-Italian war was a detail, of course," said Tombak blandly.

"Yes," snapped Randos. "Unfortunate, but unimportant. The Ottomans have had their day. Likewise this Balkan business."

"Saw a paper on the way here. Sun Yat-sen's government is having its troubles. Are all those Chinese another detail?"

"No, of course not. But they can wait. The main line of development toward full status is here in Western Europe. It happened by chance, but the fact is there. It's European civilization which has got to be saved from itself. Do you realize that Earth is only a century or so from atomic energy?" Randos took an angry turn around the office. "All right. I'm trying to work out a new balance, an international power alignment that will hold German ambition in check until such time as their Social Democrats can win an unmistakable majority and oust the Prussian clique. After that we can start nudging Europe toward limited federalism. That's the objective, sir, the absolute necessity, and your report had better have some relevance to it!"

Tombak nodded. "It does, Chief, I assure you. I've talked with thousands of Irish, both in Ulster and the south. Those two sections hate each other's intestinal flora. The southerners want the present Home Rule bill and the Ulstermen don't. They're being whipped up by the Carson gang, ready to fight . . . and if they do, the Irish-Irish are going to revolt on their own account."

Randos' lunar face reddened. "And you called me in to tell me this?"

"I did. Is civil war a detail?"

"In this case, Sir Tombak, yes." Randos was holding back his temper with an effort that made him sweat. "A single English division could put it down in a month, if it broke out. But it would take all Britain's and France's manhood to stop Germany, and we'd have to drag in a dozen other countries to boot. The United States might get involved. And the USA is the main line after Europe, Sir Tombak. They have to be kept out of this mad-dog nationalism, to lead the world toward reason when their day comes." He actually managed to show his teeth. "I'll forgive you this time on grounds of ignorance. But hereafter submit your reports in properly written form. The next time you disturb me with a piddling detail like Ireland, you'll go back to Sagittarius. Good day!"

He remembered to assume a meek look as he was opening the door.

There was a silence.

"Whoof!" said Tombak.

"Second the motion," said Arken. "But I warned you."

"Where's the nearest pub? I need one." Tombak prowled over to the window and looked gloomily down at the traffic. "Kalmagens was an artist," he said, "and artists don't worry about what is detail and what isn't. They just naturally see the whole picture. This chap is a cookbook psychotechnician."

"He's probably right, as far as he goes," said Arken.

"Maybe. I dunno." Tombak shrugged. "Got a suit of clothes here I can borrow? I told the doorman I was coming in to make a date with a beautiful girl, and I noticed a most nice little wench with a sort of round-heeled look at a typewriter out there. Don't want to disappoint the old fellow."

Peter Mortensen was born north of the Danevirke,

but after 1864 his people were reckoned German, and he was called up in 1914 like anyone else. Men died so fast on the eastern front that promotion was rapid, and by 1917 he was a captain. This did not happen without some investigation of his background—many Schleswig Danes were not overly glad of their new nationality—but Graf von Schlangengrab had checked personally on him and assured his superiors of his unquestionable loyalty. Indeed, the count took quite a fancy to this young man, got him transferred to Intelligence, and often used him on missions of the utmost importance.

Thus the official record, and in the twentieth century Anno Domini the record was more than the man—it *was* the man. A few rebellious souls considered this an invention of that supreme parodist, the Devil, for now the Flesh had become Word. To Galactics such as Vyndhom Vargess and Sabor Tombak, it was convenient; records are more easily altered than memories, if you have the right gadgets. So Vargess became von Schlangengrab and Tombak called himself Peter Mortensen.

A thin, bitter rain blew across muddy fields, and the Prussian pines mumbled of spring. Out in the trenches to the west, it meant little more than fresh lice and fresh assaults, human meat going upright into the gape of machine guns. To the east, where Russia lay sundered, the spring of 1917 meant some kind of new birth. Tombak wondered what sort it would be.

He sat with a dozen men in a boxcar near the head of the sealed train. The thing was damp and chilly; they huddled around a stove. Their gray uniforms steamed. Beneath them, the wheels clicked on rain-slippery rails. Now and again the train whistled, shrill and lonesome noise across the graves of a thousand years of war.

Captain Mortensen was well liked by his men: none of this Junker stiffness for him. They held numbed hands toward the stove, rolled cigarettes, and talked among themselves. "Cold, it's been a long time cold, and fuel so short. Sometimes I wonder what it ever felt like to be warm and dry."

"Be colder than this in Russia, lad. I've been there, I know."

"But no fighting this time, thank God. Only taking that funny little man toward St. Petersburg. . . . Why the devil's he so important, anyway? Hauled him clear from Switzerland in his own special train, on orders of General Ludendorff, no less, one runty Russian crank."

"What say, Captain?" asked someone. "Are you allowed, now, to tell us why?"

Tombak shrugged, and the faces of peasants and laborers and students turned to him, lost between military caps and shoddy uniforms but briefly human again with simple curiosity. "Why, sir? Is he a secret agent of ours?"

"No, I'd not say that." Tombak rolled himself a cigarette, and a corporal struck a match for him. "But the matter's quite simple. Kerensky has overthrown the Czar, you see, but wants to keep on fighting. This Ulyanov fellow has a good deal of influence, in spite of having been an exile for so long. Maybe he can come to power. If he does, he'll make peace on any terms . . . which is to say, on German terms. Then we'll no longer have an eastern front to worry about." Tombak's leathery face crinkled. "It seems worth trying, anyhow."

"I see, I see . . . thank you, Captain . . . very clever . . . "

"My own chief, Graf von Schlangengrab, urged this policy on the General Staff," confided Tombak. "The idea was his, and he talked them into it." He always had to remember that he was Peter Mortensen, doubly anxious to prove his Germanness because it had once been in doubt, and would therefore brag about the nobleman with whom he was so intimate.

What he did not add was that von Schlangengrab had been given the idea and told to execute it by a senior clerk in an English brokerage house, over an undetectable sub-radio hookup. This clerk, Mr. Harrison, had checked Galactic records on Ulyanov—whom Kalmagens had once met and investigated in London—and run a psychotechnic evaluation which gave the little revolutionary a surprising probability of success.

"Maybe then we can finish the war," muttered a sergeant. "Dear God, it's like it's gone on forever, not so?"

"I can't even remember too well what began it," confessed a private.

"Well, boys—" Tombak inhaled the harsh wartime tobacco and leaned back in a confidential mood. "I'll tell you my theory. The Irish began it."

"Ach, you joke, Captain," said the sergeant.

"Not at all. I have studied these things. In nineteen fourteen there was a great deal of international tension, if you remember. That same year the Home Rule bill was so badly handled that it alienated the Ulstermen, who were egged on by a group anxious to seize power. This caused the Catholic Irish to prepare for revolt. Fighting broke out in Dublin in July, and it seemed as if the British Isles were on the verge of civil war. Accordingly, our General Staff decided they need not be reckoned with for a while, and—"

—And the Sarajevo affair touched off the powder. Germany moved in accordance with long-laid plans because she did not expect Britain to be able to fulfill her treaty obligations to Belgium. But Britain wangled a temporary Irish settlement and declared war. If the English had looked more formidable that year, the Germans would have been more conciliatory, and war could have been postponed and the Galactic plans for establishing a firm peace could have gone on toward their fruition."

"Captain!" The sergeant was shocked.

Tombak laughed. "I didn't mean it subversively. Of course we had to fight against the Iron Ring. And we will conquer."

Like Chaos we will. The war was dragging into a stalemate. Neither side could break the other, not when Russia had gone under.

If Russia did make peace, Randos had calculated, then the stalemate would be complete. Peace could be negotiated on a basis of exhaustion in another year, and America kept out of the mess.

Privately, Tombak doubted it. On paper the scheme looked fine: the quantities representing political tensions balanced out nicely. But he had lived in America some twenty years ago, and knew her for a country which would always follow an evangelist. Like Wilson — whose original nomination and election had hinged on an unusual chance. Randos assured him that the personality of the leader meant little . . . was a detail . . . but . . .

At any rate, the main immediate objective was to get Russia out of the war, so that she might evolve a reasonably civilized government for herself. Exactly how the surrender was to be achieved was another detail, not important. This queer, bearded Ulyanov with the bookish diction and the Tartar face was the handiest tool for the job, a tool which could later be discarded in favor of the democrats.

The train hooted, clicking eastward with Ulyanov aboard.

His Party name was Lenin.

Tombak had not been in New York for three decades. The town had changed a lot; everywhere he saw the signs of a feverish prosperity.

On other planets, in other centuries, he had watched the flowering and decay of a mercantile system, big business replacing free enterprise. For certain civilizations it was a necessary step in development, but he always thought of it as a retrogression, enthroned vulgarity grinding out the remnants of genuine culture, the Folk became the People.

This was a brisk fall day, and he stepped merrily

along through the crowds, a short, sunburned, broad-shouldered young man, outwardly distinguished only by a cheerful serenity. Nor was he essentially different inside. He was a fully human creature with human genes, who simply happened to have been born on another planet. His environment had affected him, balancing anabolism and catabolism so well that he had already lived two thousand years, training mind and body. But that didn't show.

He turned off onto Wall Street and found the sky-scraper he was looking for and went up to the sacro-sanct top floor. The receptionist was female this time, and pretty. Woman suffrage had eased the team's problems by allowing them to use their wives and girl friends more openly. For a moment he didn't recognize her; the face had been changed. Then he nodded. "Hello, Yarra. Haven't seen you since . . . good Designer, since the Paris Exposition!"

"We had fun," she smiled dreamily. "Care to try it again?"

"Hmmm . . . yes, if you'll get rid of that godawful bobbed hair and cylindrical silhouette."

"Aren't they terrible? Usrek ran a computation for me, and the Americans won't return to a girl who looks like a girl for years."

"I'll get myself assigned back to Asia. Bali, for choice." Tombak sighed reminiscently. "Just worked my way back from there—deckhand on a tramp steamer to San Francisco, followed a harvesting crew across the plains, did a hitch in a garage. Lots and lots of data, but I hope the boss doesn't want it tabulated."

"He will, Sabor, he will. Want to talk to him? He's in the office now."

"Might as well get it over with."

"He's not a bad sort, really. A basically decent fellow, and a whiz at psychomath. He tries hard."

"Someday, though, he'll have to learn that—Oh, all right."

Tombak went through the door into the office of the

president. It was Usrek Arken again, alias the financier Wolfe . . . a name chosen with malice aforethought, for wolf he was on Wall Street. But what chance did brokers and corporations, operating mostly by God and by guess, have against a million-year-old science of economics? Once Randos had decided England was declining as a world power, and become an American, Wolfe's dazzling rise was a matter of a few years' routine.

Arken was in conference with Randos, but both rose and bowed. The chief showed strain, his plumpness was being whittled away and the best total-organismic training could not suppress an occasional nervous jerk. But today he seemed genial. "Ah, Sir Tombak! I'm glad to see you back. I was afraid you'd run afoul of some Chinese war lord."

"Damn near did. I was a foreign devil. If it hadn't been for our Mongoloid agent in Sinkiang—well, that's past." Tombak got out his pipe. "Had a most enjoyable trip around the world, and got friendly with thousands of people, but of course out of touch with the big events. What's been happening?"

"Business boom here in the States. That's the main thing, so I'm concentrating on it. Tricky."

Tombak frowned. "Pardon me, but why should the exact condition of business in one country be crucial?"

"Too many factors to explain in words," said Randos. "I'd need psychodynamic tensors to convince you. But look at it this way . . .

"Let's admit we bungled badly in 'fourteen and again in 'seventeen. We let the war break out, we let America get into it, and we underestimated Lenin. Instead of a republic, Russia has a dictatorship as ruthless as any in history, and paranoid to boot; nor can we change that fact, even if the rules allowed us to assassinate Stalin. We hoped to salvage a kind of world order out of the mess: once American intervention was plainly unavoidable, we started the 'War to end war' slogan and the League of Nations idea.

Somehow, though, the USA was kept out of the League, which means it's a farce unless we can get her into it."

Thanks for the "we," thought Tombak grimly. With the benefit of hindsight, he knew as well as Randos why the Russian revolution and the Versailles peace had gone awry. Lenin and Senator Lodge had been more capable than they had any right to be, and Wilson less so. That poor man had been no match for practical politicians, and had compounded the folly with his anachronistic dream of "self-determination." (Clemenceau had passed the rational judgment on that idea: *"Mon Dieu!* Must every little language have a country of its own?") But individual personalities had been brushed aside by Randos as "fluctuations, details, meaningless eddies on the current of great historical trends."

The man wasn't too stupid to see his own mistakes; but subconsciously, at least, he didn't seem able to profit by them.

"We still have an excellent chance, though," went on Randos. "I don't quite like the methods we must use, but they're the only available ones. Wall Street is rapidly becoming the financial capital of Earth, a trend which I have been strengthening. If finance can be maintained as the decisive power, within twenty years America will be the leader of the world. No one else will be able to move without her okay. Then the time will be psychologically ripe for Americans to get the idea of a new League, one with armed force to maintain the peace. The Soviets won't stand a chance."

Tombak scowled more deeply. "I can't argue with your math, Sir Randos," he answered slowly, "but I got a hunch . . ."

"Yes? Go on. You were sent around the world precisely so you could gather facts. If those facts contradict my theories, why, of course I'm wrong and we'll have to look for a new approach." Randos spoke magnanimously.

"Okay, buster, you asked for it," said Tombak in

English. He returned to Galactic: "The trouble is, these aren't facts you can fit into mass-action equations. They're a matter of, well, *feel*.

"Nationalism is rising in Asia. I talked with a Japanese officer in Shanghai . . . we'd gotten drunk together, and he was a fine fellow, and we loved each other like brothers, but he actually cried at the thought that someday he'd have to take potshots at me."

"The Japanese have talked about war with the United States for fifty years," snorted Randos. "They can't win one."

"But do they know that? To continue, though — people, Western people, don't like the present form of society either. They can't always say why, but you can tell they feel uprooted, uneasy . . . there's nothing about an interlocking directorate to inspire loyalty, you know. The trade unions are growing. If capitalism goes bust, they're going to grow almighty fast."

"To be sure," nodded Randos, unperturbed. "A healthy development, in the right time and place. But I'm here to see that capitalism does not, ah, go bust. Mass unemployment — You know yourself how unstable the Weimar Republic is. If depression is added to its other troubles, dictatorship will come to Germany within five years."

"If you ask me," snapped Tombak, "we've got too bloody damn much confidence around. Too many people are playing the stock market. It has a hectic feel, somehow. They'd do better to save their money for an emergency."

Randos smiled. "To be sure. I'll admit the market is at a dangerous peak. In this month, it's already shown some bad fluctuations. That's why Wolfe is selling right now, heavily, to bring it down."

Usrek Arken stirred. "And I continue to think, Sir Randos," he muttered, "that it'll cause a panic."

"No, it won't. I have proved, with the help of games theory, that —"

"Games theory presupposes that the players are

rational," murmured Tombak. "I have a nasty suspicion that nobody is."

"Come, now," chided Randos. "Of course nonrational elements enter in. But this civilization is in a highly cerebral stage."

"What you ought to do," snapped Tombak, "is get away from that computer of yours and go out and meet some Earthfolk."

Frost congealed on Randos' words: "That is your task, Sir Tombak. Please report your findings and stand by for further assignment. Now, if you'll pardon me, I'm busy."

Tombak swapped a glance with Arken and went out. He chatted for a while with Yarra and, silhouette or no, made a date for the next evening: Thursday, October 24, 1929.

> Now play the fife lowly and beat the drums
> slowly,
> And play the dead march as you carry my
> pall.
> Bring me white roses to lay on my coffin,
> Roses to deaden the clods as they fall.

The flames jumped up, lighting their faces: grimy, unshaven, gaunted by wind and hunger, but American faces. Tombak thought he had fallen in love with America. A Galactic had no business playing favorites, and it was perfectly obvious that in another hundred years Earth's power center would have shifted to Asia, but something in this country suited him. It still had elbow room, for both body and soul.

He finished the song and laid his guitar down as Bob Robinson gave the can of mulligan another stir. Far off, but coming along the rails near the hobo jungle, a train whistled. Tombak wondered how many times, how many places, he had heard that noise, and always it meant more lonesomeness.

"I looked at the schedule in the station." A thin man with glasses jerked his thumb at the town, a mile away. "Be a freight stopping at midnight, we can hop that one."

"If the dick don't see us," mumbled Robinson. "They got a mean dick in this place."

"I'll handle him, if it comes to that." Tombak flexed stumpy strong fingers. Maybe a Galactic shouldn't take sides, but there were some people whose faces he enjoyed altering. That storm trooper in Berlin two years ago, for instance, the lout who was kicking an inoffensive Jew around. Getting out of Germany had been like getting out of jail, and even riding the rods in the States was a welcome change.

"Be careful, Jim," murmured Rose McGraw. She leaned against Tombak with a pathetic possessiveness.

In a better age, he thought, she would have been somebody's contented housewife, minding the kids in suburbia, not tramping over a continent in a ragged print dress, rain in her hair, looking for work . . . any kind of work. Too late now, of course, at least till the war with Japan made jobs. But Randos had predicted Japan would not attack till early 1942, give or take six months, and he was usually right about such things. Almost six years to go. True, initially he had thought the Japanese would never fight, but contrary evidence piled up . . .

"Don't worry about me," said Tombak gruffly. He felt again the tugging sadness of the quasi-immortal. How many years on Earth, how many women, and with none of them could he stay more than a few months. They must not be taken off the road and fed, they must not be told the truth and comforted, Rose McGraw had to become a fading memory fast bound in misery and iron for the sake of her descendants a thousand years hence.

At least he had warned her. *"I'm not a marryin' man, I won't ever settle down."*—Not till his tour of duty on Earth ended, another seventy-five years of it and then a hundred-year vacation and then another planet circling one of those stars blinking dimly overhead. . . . Why had he ever gone into the Service?

"Think Roosevelt's gonna win?" asked Robinson. He mispronounced the name.

"Sure, Landon hasn't got a prayer." The man with glasses spoke dogmatically; he had had some education once.

"I dunno, now. Old man Roosevelt, he's for us, but how many of us stay in one place long enough to vote?"

"Enough," said Tombak. He had no doubt of the election's outcome. The New Deal under one name or another was foregone, once the Depression struck. Hoover himself had proposed essentially the same reforms. Randos had not even had to juggle the country —through propaganda, through carefully planted trains of events—to get FDR elected the first time. Tombak would be able to return from this trip and report that the changes were popular and that there was no immediate danger of American fascism or communism.

The main line of history, always the main line. Since the Rhineland debacle this year, war in Europe was not to be avoided, nor was war in the Pacific. Japanese pride and hunger had not been so small a factor after all. Tombak's mind slipped to the Washington office where Randos was manipulating senators and brain trusters.

"The important thing will be to keep the two wars separate. Russia will be neutral, because she has Japan to worry about, and Germany alone cannot conquer Britain. The United States, with British help, can defeat Japan in about five years while the European stalemate is established. Then and only then must Germany and Russia be goaded into war with each other . . . two totalitarianisms in a death struggle, weakening as they fight, with America armed from the Japanese war and ready to step in and break both of them. After that we can finally start building an

Earth fit to live on."

An Earth which had so far gone from bad to worse, reflected Tombak. He didn't deny the bitter logic of Randos' equations; but he wondered if it was going to develop that way in practice. Roosevelt, who would surely run for a third term, had strong emotional ties—he *could* not see England fight alone, and he could make the country agree with him. And Hitler, now . . . Tombak had seen Hitler speak, and met a lot of Nazis. A streak of nihilistic lunacy ran through that bunch. Against every sound military principle, they were entirely capable of attacking Russia; which would mean the emergence of the Soviet Union, necessarily aided by America, as a victorious world power.

Well . . .

"Wonder if we're someday gonna find a steady job," said someone in the night.

"Ought to have a guy like Hitler," said another man. "No nonsense about him. He'd arrange things."

"Arrange 'em with a firing squad," said Tombak sharply. "Drive men like Einstein out of the country. At that," he added thoughtfully, "Hitler and his brown-shirted, brown-nosed bastards are doing us a favor. If this goes on, we'll have more talent in this country, refugees, than anybody ever had before."

And if somebody had the idea of gathering it into one place, what would all that embittered genius do to Randos' plans?

Bob Robinson shrugged, indifference clothed in faded denim. "To hell with it. I think the stew's about done."

Harban Randos' eyes looked ready to leap out of their sockets. "No," he whispered.

"Yes." Usrek Arken slapped the papers down on the desk with a cannon-crack noise. "Winnis knows his physics, and Tombak and the others have gathered the essential facts for him to work on. They're making an atomic bomb!"

Randos turned blindly away. Outside, Washington

shimmered in the heat of midsummer, 1943. It was hard to believe that a war was being fought . . . the wrong war, with the issues irretrievably messed up, the Soviets fighting as allies of the democracies, Japan half shunted aside to make way for a Nazi defeat that would plant Russian troops in the middle of Europe . . . and meanwhile gnawing away at Nationalist China, weakening the nation for Communists who had made a truce which they weren't respecting.

"They're able to," said Randos huskily.

Tombak nodded. "They're going to," he said.

"But they don't *need—*"

"What has that got to do with anything? And after the uranium bomb comes the thermonuclear bomb and— Write your own ticket." Tombak spoke flatly, for he had come to like the people of Earth.

Randos passed a shaking hand over his face. "All right, all right. Any chance of sabotaging the project?"

"Not without tipping our hand. They've got this one watched, I tell you; we've not been able to get a single Galactic into the Manhattan District. We could blow up the works, of course . . . fake a German operation . . . but after the war, when they go through German records . . . "

"Vargess can handle the records."

"He can't handle the memories. Not the memories of thousands of people, intrinsically just as smart as you and I." Tombak bit his pipestem and heard it crack. "Okay, Randos, you're the boss. What do we do next?"

The chief sat down. For a moment he shuddered with the effort of self-control, then his body was again disciplined.

"It will be necessary to deal firmly with the Russians, force them to agree to a stronger United Nations Organization," he said. "Churchill already understands that, and Roosevelt can be persuaded. Between them, they can prepare their countries so that it'll be politically feasible. The West is going to have a monopoly of nuclear weapons at the war's end, which will be helpful . . . yes . . . "

"Roosevelt is not a well man," declared Tombak, "and I was in England only a month ago and can tell you the people aren't satisfied. They admire Churchill, love him, but they're going to want to experiment with another party. . . . "

"Calculated risk," said Randos. His confidence was returning. "Not too great."

"Nevertheless," said Tombak, "you'd better start right away to handpick those men's successors and see they get exposed to the facts of life."

"For Designer's sake, leave me alone!" yelled Randos. "I can't handle every miserable little detail!"

Rasnagarth Kri did not want to spend time interviewing a failure. It seemed as if each day brought a higher pile of work to him, more decisions to be made, a million new planets struggling toward an unperceived goal, and he had had to promise his wife he would stop working nights.

Nevertheless, a favorite nephew is a favorite nephew.

He hooded his eyes until a glittering blankness looked across the desk at Harban Randos.

"We are fortunate," he said, "that an experienced man of your race was available to take charge. For a while I actually considered breaking the rules and letting Earth know the facts immediately. But at this stage of their society, that would only be a slower damnation for them; extinction is more merciful. Whether or not the new man can rescue the planet remains to be seen. If he fails, the whole world is lost. At best, progress has been retarded two centuries, and millions of people are needlessly dead."

Randos stiffened his lips, which had been vibrating, and answered tonelessly:

"Sir, you were getting my annual reports. If I was unsatisfactory, you should have recalled me years ago."

"Every agent is allowed some mistakes," Kri told

him. "Psychodynamics is not an exact science. Furthermore, your reports, while quantitatively accurate, were qualitatively . . . lifeless. They conveyed nothing of the feel. Until the fact leaped out that nationalism and atomic energy had become contemporaneous, how could I judge?"

Feel! Randos thought of Sabor Tombak. The smug, pipe-sucking pig! He hoped Tombak would be killed; plenty of chance for that, in the next fifty or a hundred years of Earth's troubles.

No—he was doing the man an injustice. Tombak had simply been right. But Randos still couldn't like him.

"I used the standard methods, sir," he protested. "You have seen my computations. What else could I do?"

"Well—" Kri looked down at his desk. "That's hard to answer. Let me just say that human nature is so complicated that we'll never have a complete science of it. All we'll ever be able to do mathematically is predict and guide the broad trends. But those trends are made up of millions of individual people and incidents. To pervert an old saying, in government we must be able to see the trees for the forest. It takes an artist to know how and when to use the equations, and how to supplement them with his own intuitive common sense. It takes not only a technician, but a poet to write a report that will really let me know what is really going on."

He raised his eyes again and said mildly: "You can't be blamed for being neither an artist nor a poet. I gather you wish to remain in the Service?"

"Yes, sir." Randos was not a quitter.

"Very well. I'm assigning you to a chief technicianship in my own evaluation center. Consider it a promotion, a reward for honest effort. At least, you'll have higher rank and salary. You may go."

Kri thought he heard a gasp of relief, but returned to his papers.

One might as well face truth. You can't kick a favorite nephew anywhere but upstairs. The fellow might even make a good technical boss.

As for this planet called Earth, maybe the new man could salvage it. If not, well, it was only one planet.

TURNING POINT

"Please, mister, could I have a cracker for my oonta-therium?"

Not exactly the words you would expect at an instant when history changes course and the universe can never again be what it was. *The die is cast; In this sign conquer; It is not fit that you should sit here any longer; We hold these truths to be self-evident; The Italian navigator has landed in the New World; Dear God, the thing works!*—no man with any imagination can recall those, or others like them, and not have a coldness run along his spine. But as for what little Mierna first said to us, on that island half a thousand light-years from home . . .

The star is catalogued AGC 4256836, a K_2 dwarf in Cassiopeia. Our ship was making a standard preliminary survey of that region, and had come upon mystery enough—how easily Earthsiders forget that every planet is a complete world!—but nothing extraordinary in this fantastic cosmos. The Traders had noted places that seemed worth further investigation; so had the Federals; the lists were not quite identical.

After a year, vessel and men were equally jaded. We needed a set-down, to spend a few weeks refitting and recuperating before the long swing homeward. There is an art to finding such a spot. You visit whatever nearby suns look suitable. If you come on a planet whose gross physical characteristics are terrestroid, you check the biological details — very, very carefully, but since the operation is largely automated it goes pretty fast — and make contact with the autochthones, if any. Primitives are preferred. That's not because of military danger, as some think. The Federals insist that the natives have no objection to strangers camping on their land, while the Traders don't see how anyone, civilized or not, that hasn't discovered atomic energy can be a menace. It's only that primitives are less apt to ask complicated questions and otherwise make a nuisance of themselves. Spacemen rejoice that worlds with machine civilizations are rare.

Well, Joril looked ideal. The second planet of that sun, with more water than Earth, it offered a mild climate everywhere. The biochemistry was so like our own that we could eat native foods, and there didn't seem to be any germs that $UX=2$ couldn't handle. Seas, forests, meadows made us feel right at home, yet the countless differences from Earth lent a fairy-land glamour. The indigenes were savages, that is, they depended on hunting, fishing, and gathering for their whole food supply. So we assumed there were thousands of little cultures and picked the one that appeared most advanced: not that aerial observation indicated much difference.

Those people lived in neat, exquisitely decorated villages along the western seaboard of the largest continent, with woods and hills behind them. Contact went smoothly. Our semanticians had a good deal of trouble with the language, but the villagers started picking up English right away. Their hospitality was lavish whenever we called on them, but they stayed

out of our camp except for the conducted tours we
gave and other such invitations. With one vast, happy
sigh, we settled down.

But from the first there were certain disturbing
symptoms. Granted they had humanlike throats and
palates, we hadn't expected the autochthones to speak
flawless English within a couple of weeks. Every one
of them. Obviously they could have learned still faster
if we'd taught them systematically. We followed the
usual practice and christened the planet "Joril" after
what we thought was the local word for "earth"—and
then found that "Joril" meant "Earth," capitalized,
and the people had an excellent heliocentric astronomy.
Though they were too polite to press themselves on
us, they weren't merely accepting us as something
inexplicable; curiosity was afire in them, and given
half a chance they *did* ask the most complicated
questions.

Once the initial rush of establishing ourselves was
over and we had time to think, it became plain that
we'd stumbled on something worth much further study.
First we needed to check on some other areas and
make sure this Dannicar culture wasn't a freak. After
all, the neolithic Mayas had been good astronomers;
the ferro-agricultural Greeks had developed a high
and sophisticated philosophy. Looking over the maps
we'd made from orbit, Captain Barlow chose a large
island about 700 kilometers due west. A gravboat was
outfitted and five men went aboard.

Pilot: Jacques Lejeune. Engineer: me. Federal mili-
technic representative: Commander Ernest Baldinger,
Space Force of the Solar Peace Authority. Federal civil
government representative: Walter Vaughan. Trader
agent: Don Haraszthy. He and Vaughan were the
principals, but the rest of us were skilled in the mul-
tiple jobs of planetography. You have to be, on a
foreign world months from home or help.

We made the aerial crossing soon after sunrise, so
we'd have a full eighteen hours of daylight. I remem-

ber how beautiful the ocean looked below us, like one great bowl of metal, silver where the sun struck, cobalt and green copper beyond. Then the island came over the world's edge, darkly forested, crimson-splashed by stands of gigantic red blossoms. Lejeune picked out an open spot in the woods, about two kilometers from a village that stood on a wide bay, and landed us with a whoop and a holler. He's a fireball pilot.

"Well—" Haraszthy rose to his sheer two meters and stretched till his joints cracked. He was burly to match that height, and his hook-nosed face carried the marks of old battles. Most Traders are tough, pragmatic extroverts; they have to be, just as Federal civils have to be the opposite. It makes for conflict, though. "Let's hike."

"Not so fast," Vaughan said: a thin young man with an intense gaze. "That tribe has never seen or heard of our kind. If they noticed us land, they may be in a panic."

"So we go jolly them out of it," Haraszthy shrugged.

"Our whole party? Are you serious?" Commander Baldinger asked. He reflected a bit. "Yes, I suppose you are. But I'm responsible now. Lejeune and Cathcart, stand by here. We others will proceed to the village."

"Just like that?" Vaughan protested.

"You know a better way?" Haraszthy answered.

"As a matter of fact—" But nobody listened. The government operates on some elaborate theories, and Vaughan was still too new in Survey to understand how often theory has to give way. We were impatient to go outside, and I regretted not being sent along to town. Of course, someone had to stay, ready to pull out our emissaries if serious trouble developed.

We emerged into long grass and a breeze that smelled of nothing so much as cinnamon. Trees rustled overhead, against a deep blue sky; the reddish sunlight spilled across purple wildflowers and bronze-colored insect wings. I drew a savoring breath before going around with Lejeune to make sure our landing gear was properly set. We were all lightly clad; Baldinger carried a blast rifle and Haraszthy a radiocom big enough to contact Dannicar, but both seemed ludicrously inappropriate.

"I envy the Jorillians," I remarked.

"In a way," Lejeune said. "Though perhaps their environment is too good. What stimulus have they to advance further?"

"Why should they want to?"

"They don't consciously, my old. But every intelligent race is descended from animals that once had a hard struggle to survive, so hard they were forced to evolve brains. There is an instinct for adventure, even in the gentlest herbivorous beings, and sooner or later it must find expression—"

"Holy jumping Judas!"

Haraszthy's yell brought Lejeune and me bounding back to that side of the ship. For a moment my reason wobbled. Then I decided the sight wasn't really so strange . . . here.

A girl was emerging from the woods. She was about the equivalent of a Terrestrial five-year-old, I estimated. Less than a meter tall (the Jorillians average more short and slender than we), she had the big head of her species to make her look still more elfin. Long blondish hair, round ears, delicate features that were quite humanoid except for the high forehead and huge violet eyes added to the charm. Her brown-skinned body was clad only in a white loincloth. One four-fingered hand waved cheerily at us. The other carried a leash. And at the opposite end of that leash was a grasshopper the size of a hippopotamus.

No, not a grasshopper, I saw as she danced toward us. The head looked similar, but the four walking legs were short and stout, the several others were boneless appendages. The gaudy hide was skin, not chitin. I saw that the creature breathed with lungs, too. Nonetheless it was a startling monster; and it drooled.

"Insular genus," Vaughan said. "Undoubtedly harmless, or she wouldn't — But a child, coming so casually — !"

Baldinger grinned and lowered his rifle. "What the hell," he said, "to a kid everything's equally wonderful. This is a break for our side. She'll give us a good recommendation to her elders."

The little girl (damn it, I will call her that) walked to within a meter of Haraszthy, turned those big eyes up and up till they met his piratical face, and trilled with an irresistible smile:

"Please, mister, could I have a cracker for my oontatherium?"

I don't quite remember the next few minutes. They were confused. Eventually we found ourselves, the whole five, walking down a sun-speckled woodland path. The girl skipped beside us, chattering like a xylophone. The monster lumbered behind, chewing messily on what we had given it. When the light struck those compound eyes I thought of a jewel chest.

"My name is Mierna," the girl said, "and my father makes things out of wood, I don't know what that's called in English, please tell me, oh, carpentry, thank you, you're a nice man. My father thinks a lot. My mother makes songs. They are very pretty songs. She sent me out to get some sweet grass for a borning couch, because her assistant wife is going to born a baby soon, but when I saw you come down just the way Pengwil told, I knew I should say hello instead and take you to Taori. That's our village. We have *twenty-five houses*. And sheds and a Thinking Hall that's bigger than the one in Riru. Pengwil said crackers are awful tasty. Could I have one too?"

Haraszthy obliged in a numb fashion. Vaughan shook himself and fairly snapped, "How do you know our language?"

"Why, everybody does in Taori. Since Pengwil came and taught us. That was three days ago. We've been hoping and hoping you would come. They'll be so jealous in Riru! But we'll let them visit if they ask us nicely."

"Pengwil . . . a Dannicarian name, all right," Baldinger muttered. "But they never heard of this island till I showed them our map. And they couldn't cross the ocean in those dugouts of theirs! It's against the prevailing winds, and square sails—"

"Oh, Pengwil's boat can sail right into the wind," Mierna laughed. "I saw him myself, he took everybody for rides, and now my father's making a boat like that too, only better."

"Why did Pengwil come here?" Vaughan asked.

"To see what there was. He's from a place called Folat. They have such funny names in Dannicar, and they dress funny too, don't they, mister?"

"Folat . . . yes, I remember, a community a ways north of our camp," Baldinger said.

"But savages don't strike off into an unknown ocean for, for curiosity," I stammered.

"These do," Haraszthy grunted. I could almost see the relays clicking in his blocky head. There were tremendous commercial possibilities here, foods and textiles and especially the dazzling artwork. In exchange—

"No!" Vaughan exclaimed. "I know what you're thinking, Trader Haraszthy, and you are not going to bring machines here."

The big man bridled. "Says who?"

"Says me, by virtue of the authority vested in me. And I'm sure the Council will confirm my decision." In that soft air Vaughan was sweating. "We don't dare!"

"What's a Council?" Mierna asked. A shade of trouble crossed her face. She edged close to the bulk of her animal.

In spite of everything, I had to pat her head and murmur, "Nothing you need worry about, sweetheart." To get her mind, and my own, off vague fears: "Why do you call this fellow an oontatherium? That can't be his real name."

"Oh, no." She forgot her worries at once. "He's a *yao* and his real name is, well, it means Big-Feet-Buggy-Eyes-Top-Man-Underneath-And-Over. That's what I named him. He's mine and he's lovely." She tugged at an antenna. The monster actually purred. "But Pengwil told us about something called an *oont* you have at your home, that's hairy and scary and carries things and drools like a *yao*, so I thought that would be a nice English name. Isn't it?"

"Very," I said weakly.

"What is this *oont* business?" Vaughan demanded.

Haraszthy ran a hand through his hair. "Well," he said, "you know I like Kipling, and I read some of his poems to some natives one night at a party. The one about the *oont*, the camel, yeah, I guess that must have been among 'em. They sure enjoyed Kipling."

"And had the poem letter-perfect after one hearing, and passed it unchanged up and down the coast, and now it's crossed the sea and taken hold," Vaughan choked.

"Who explained that *therium* is a root meaning 'mammal'?" I asked. Nobody knew, but doubtless one of our naturalists had casually mentioned it. So five-year-old Mierna had gotten the term from a wandering sailor and applied it with absolute correctness: never mind feelers and insectoidal eyes, the *yao* was a true mammal.

After a while we emerged in a cleared strip fronting on the bay. Against its glitter stood the village, peak-roofed houses of wood and thatch, a different style from Dannicar's but every bit as pleasant and well-kept. Outrigger canoes were drawn up on the beach, where fishnets hung to dry. Anchored some way beyond was another boat. The curved, gaily painted hull, twin steering oars, mat sails and leather tackle were like nothing on our poor overmechanized Earth; but she was sloop-rigged, and evidently a deep keel made it impossible to run her ashore.

"I thought so," Baldinger said in an uneven voice. "Pengwil went ahead and invented tacking. That's an efficient design. He could cross the water in a week or less."

"He invented navigation too," Lejeune pointed out.

The villagers, who had not seen us descend, now dropped their occupations—cooking, cleaning, weaving, potting, the numberless jobs of the primitive—to come on the run. All were dressed as simply as Mierna. Despite large heads, which were not grotesquely big, odd hands and ears, slightly different body proportions, the women were good to look on: too good, after a year's celibacy. The beardless, long-haired men were likewise handsome, and both sexes were graceful as cats.

They didn't shout or crowd. Only one exuberant horn sounded, down on the beach. Mierna ran to a grizzled male, seized him by the hand, and tugged him forward. "This is my father," she crowed. "Isn't he wonderful? And he thinks a lot. The name he's using right now, that's Sarato. I liked his last name better."

"One wearies of the same word," Sarato laughed. "Welcome, Earthfolk. You do us great . . . *lula* . . . pardon, I lack the term. You raise us high by this visit." His handshake—Pengwil must have told him about that custom—was hard, and his eyes met ours respectfully but unawed.

The Dannicarian communities turned what little government they needed over to specialists, chosen on the basis of some tests we hadn't yet comprehended. But these people didn't seem to draw even that much class distinction. We were introduced to everybody by occupation: hunter, fisher, musician, prophet (I think that is what *nonalo* means), and so on. There was the same absence of taboo here as we had noticed in Dannicar, but an equally elaborate code of manners— which they realized we could not be expected to observe.

Pengwil, a strongly built youth in the tunic of his own culture, greeted us. It was no coincidence that he'd arrived at the same spot as we. Taori lay almost exactly west of his home area, and had the best anchorage on these shores. He was bursting with desire to show off his boat. I obliged him, swimming out and climbing aboard. "A fine job," I said with entire honesty. "I have a suggestion, though. For sailing along coasts, you don't need a fixed keel." I described a centerboard. "Then you can ground her."

"Yes, Sarato thought of that after he had seen my work. He has started one of such pattern already. He wants to do away with the steering oars also, and have a flat piece of wood turn at the back end. Is that right?"

"Yes," I said after a strangled moment.

"It seemed so to me." Pengwil smiled. "The push of water can be split in two parts like the push of air. Your Mister Ishihara told me about splitting and rejoining forces. That was what gave me the idea for a boat like this."

We swam back and put our clothes on again. The village was abustle, preparing a feast for us. Pengwil joined them. I stayed behind, walking the beach, too restless to sit. Staring out across the waters and breathing an ocean smell that was almost like Earth's, I thought strange thoughts. They were broken off by Mierna. She skipped toward me, dragging a small wagon.

"Hello, Mister Cathcart!" she cried. "I have to gather seaweed for flavor. Do you want to help me?"

"Sure," I said.

She made a face. "I'm glad to be here. Father and Kuaya and a lot of the others, they're asking Mister Lejeune about ma-the-*matics*. I'm not old enough to like functions. I'd like to hear Mister Haraszthy tell about Earth, but he's talking alone in a house with his friends. Will you tell me about Earth? Can I go there someday?"

I mumbled something. She began to bundle leafy strands that had washed ashore. "I didn't used to like this job," she said. "I had to go back and forth so many times. They wouldn't let me use my oontatherium because he gets buckety when his feet are wet. I told them I could make him shoes, but they said no. Now it's fun anyway, with this, this, what do you call it?"

"A wagon. You haven't had such a thing before?"

"No, never, just drags with runners. Pengwil told us about wheels. He saw the Earthfolk use them. Carpenter Huanna started putting wheels on the drags right away. We only have a few so far."

I looked at the device, carved in wood and bone, a frieze of processional figures around the sides. The wheels weren't simply attached to axles. With permission, I took the cover off one and saw a ring of hard-shelled spherical nuts. As far as I knew, nobody had explained ball bearings to Pengwil.

"I've been thinking and thinking," Mierna said. "If we made a great big wagon, then an oontatherium could pull it, couldn't he? Only we have to have a good way for tying the oontatherium on, so he doesn't get hurt and you can guide him. I've thinked . . . thought of a real nice way." She stooped and drew lines in the sand. The harness ought to work.

With a full load, we went back among the houses. I lost myself in admiration of the carved pillars and panels. Sarato emerged from Lejeune's discussion of group theory (the natives had already developed that, so the talk was a mere comparison of approaches) to show me his obsidian-edged tools. He said the coast dwellers traded inland for the material, and spoke of getting steel from us. Or might we be so incredibly kind as to explain how metal was taken from the earth?

The banquet, music, dances, pantomimes, conversation, all was as gorgeous as expected, or more so. I trust the happypills we humans took kept us from making too grim an impression. But we disappointed our hosts by declining an offer to spend the night. They guided us back by torch-glow, singing the whole distance, on a twelve-tone scale with some of the damnedest harmony I have ever come across. When we reached the boat they turned homeward again. Mierna was at the tail of the parade. She stood a long time in the coppery light of the single great moon, waving to us.

Baldinger set out glasses and a bottle of Irish. "Okay," he said. "Those pills have worn off by now, but we need an equivalent."

"Hoo, yes!" Haraszthy grabbed the bottle.

"I wonder what their wine will be like, when they invent that?" Lejeune mused.

"Be still!" Vaughan said. "They aren't going to."

We stared at him. He sat shivering with tension, under the cold fluoroluminance in that bleak little cabin.

"What the devil do you mean?" Haraszthy demanded at last. "If they can make wine half as well as they do everything else, it'll go for ten credits a liter on Earth."

"Don't you understand?" Vaughan cried. "We can't deal with them. We have to get off this planet and—Oh, God, why did we have to find the damned thing?" He groped for a glass.

"Well," I sighed, "we always knew, those of us who bothered to think about the question, that someday we were bound to meet a race like this. Man . . . what is man that Thou art mindful of him?"

"This is probably an older star than Sol," Baldinger nodded. "Less massive, so it stays longer on the main sequence."

"There needn't be much difference in planetary age," I said. "A million years, half a million, whatever the figure is, hell, that doesn't mean a thing in astronomy or geology. In the development of an intelligent race, though—"

"But they're savages!" Haraszthy protested.

"Most of the races we've found are," I reminded him. "Man was too, for most of his existence. Civilization is a freak. It doesn't come natural. Started on Earth, I'm told, because the Middle East dried out as the glaciers receded and something had to be done for a living when the game got scarce. And scientific, machine civilization, that's a still more unusual accident. Why should the Jorillians have gone beyond an Upper Paleolithic technology? They never needed to."

"Why do they have the brains they do, if they're in the stone age?" Haraszthy argued.

"Why did we, in our own stone age?" I countered. "It wasn't necessary for survival. Java man, Peking man, and the low-browed rest, they'd been doing all right. But evidently evolution, intraspecies competition, sexual selection . . . whatever increases intelligence in the first place continues to force it upward, if some new factor like machinery doesn't interfere. A bright Jorillian has more prestige, rises higher in life, gets more mates and children, and so it goes. But this is an easy environment, at least in the present geological epoch. The natives don't even seem to have wars, which would stimulate technology. Thus far they've had little occasion to use those tremendous minds for anything but art, philosophy, and social experimentation."

"What is their average IQ?" Lejeune whispered.

"Meaningless," Vaughan said dully. "Beyond 180 or so, the scale breaks down. How can you measure an intelligence so much greater than your own?"

There was a stillness. I heard the forest sough in the night around us.

"Yes," Baldinger ruminated, "I always realized that our betters must exist. Didn't expect we'd run into them in my own lifetime, however. Not in this microscopic sliver of the galaxy that we've explored. And . . . well, I always imagined the Elders having machines, science, space travel."

"They will," I said.

"If we go away—" Lejeune began.

"Too late," I said. "We've already given them this shiny new toy, science. If we abandon them, they'll come looking for us in a couple of hundred years. At most."

Haraszthy's fist crashed on the table. "Why leave?" he roared. "What the hell are you scared of? I doubt the population of this whole planet is ten million. There are fifteen billion humans in the Solar System and the colonies! So a Jorillian can outthink me. So what? Plenty of guys can do that already, and it don't bother me as long as we can do business."

Baldinger shook his head. His face might have been cast in iron. "Matters aren't that simple. The question is what race is going to dominate this arm of the galaxy."

"Is it so horrible if the Jorillians do?" Lejeune asked softly.

"Perhaps not. They seem pretty decent. But—" Baldinger straightened in his chair. "I'm not going to be anybody's domestic animal. I want my planet to decide her own destiny."

That was the unalterable fact. We sat weighing it for a long and wordless time.

The hypothetical superbeings had always seemed comfortably far off. We hadn't encountered them, or they us. Therefore they couldn't live anywhere near. Therefore they probably never would interfere in the affairs of this remote galactic fringe where we dwell. But a planet only months distant from Earth; a species whose average member was a genius and whose geniuses were not understandable by us: bursting from their world, swarming through space, vigorous, eager, jumping in a decade to accomplishments that would take us a century—if we ever succeeded—how could they help but destroy our painfully built civilization? We'd scrap it ourselves, as the primitives of our old days had scrapped their own rich cultures in the overwhelming face of Western society. Our sons would laugh at our shoddy triumphs, go forth to join the high Jorillian adventure, and come back spirit-broken by failure, to build some feeble imitation of an alien way of life and fester in their hopelessness. And so would every other thinking species, unless the Jorillians were merciful enough to leave them alone.

Which the Jorillians probably would be. But who wants that kind of mercy?

I looked upon horror. Only Vaughan had the courage to voice the thing:

"There are planets under technological blockade, you know. Cultures too dangerous to allow modern weapons, let alone spaceships. Joril can be interdicted."

"They'll invent the stuff for themselves, now they've gotten the idea," Baldinger said.

Vaughan's mouth twitched downward. "Not if the only two regions that have seen us are destroyed."

"Good God!" Haraszthy leaped to his feet.

"Sit down!" Baldinger rapped.

Haraszthy spoke an obscenity. His face was ablaze. The rest of us sat in a chill sweat.

"You've called *me* unscrupulous," the Trader snarled. "Take that suggestion back to the hell it came from, Vaughan, or I'll kick out your brains."

I thought of nuclear fire vomiting skyward, and a wisp of gas that had been Mierna, and said, "No."

"The alternative," Vaughan said, staring at the bulkhead across from him, "is to do nothing until the sterilization of the entire planet has become necessary."

Lejeune shook his head in anguish. "Wrong, wrong, wrong. There can be too great a price for survival."

"But for our children's survival? Their liberty? Their pride and—"

"What sort of pride can they take in themselves, once they know the truth?" Haraszthy interrupted. He reached down, grabbed Vaughan's shirt front, and hauled the man up by sheer strength. His broken features glared three centimeters from the Federal's. "I'll tell you what we're going to do," he said. "We're going to trade, and teach, and xenologize, and fraternize, the same as with any other people whose salt we've eaten. And take our chances like men!"

"Let him go," Baldinger commanded. Haraszthy knotted a fist. "If you strike him, I'll brig you and prefer charges at home. Let him go, I said!"

Haraszthy opened his grasp. Vaughan tumbled to the deck. Haraszthy sat down, buried his head in his hands, and struggled not to sob.

Baldinger refilled our glasses. "Well, gentlemen," he said, "it looks like an impasse. We're damned if we do and damned if we don't, and I lay odds no Jorillian talks in such tired clichés."

"They could give us so much," Lejeune pleaded.

"Give!" Vaughan climbed erect and stood trembling before us. "That's p-p-precisely the trouble. They'd give it! If they could, even. It wouldn't be ours. We probably couldn't understand their work, or use it, or . . . It wouldn't be ours, I say!"

Haraszthy stiffened. He sat like stone for an entire minute before he raised his face and whooped aloud. *"Why not?"*

Blessed be whisky. I actually slept a few hours before dawn. But the light, stealing in through the ports, woke me then and I couldn't get back to sleep. At last I rose, took the dropshaft down, and went outside.

The land lay still. Stars were paling, but the east held as yet only a rush of ruddiness. Through the cool air I heard the first bird-flutings from the dark forest mass around me. I kicked off my shoes and went barefoot in wet grass.

Somehow it was not surprising that Mierna should come at that moment, leading her oontatherium. She let go the leash and ran to me. "Hi, Mister Cathcart! I hoped a lot somebody would be up. I haven't had any breakfast."

"We'll have to see about that." I swung her in the air till she squealed. "And then maybe take a little flyaround in this boat. Would you like that?"

"Oooh!" Her eyes grew round. I set her down. She needed a while longer before she dared ask, "Clear to Earth?"

"No, not that far, I'm afraid. Earth is quite a ways off."

"Maybe someday? Please?"

"Someday, I'm quite sure, my dear. And not so terribly long until then, either."

"I'm going to Earth, I'm going to Earth, I'm going to Earth." She hugged the oontatherium. "Will you miss me awfully, Big-Feet-Buggy-Eyes-Top-Man-Underneath-And-Over? Don't drool so sad. Maybe you can come too. Can he, Mister Cathcart? He's a very nice oontatherium, honest he is, and he does so love crackers."

"Well, perhaps, perhaps not," I said. "But you'll go, if you wish. I promise you. Anybody on this whole planet who wants to will go to Earth."

As most of them will. I'm certain our idea will be accepted by the Council. The only possible one. If you can't lick 'em . . . get 'em to jine you.

I rumpled Mierna's hair. *In a way, sweetheart, what a dirty trick to play on you! Take you straight from the wilderness to a huge and complicated civilization. Dazzle you with all the tricks and gadgets and ideas we have, not because we're better but simply because we've been at it a little longer than you. Scatter your ten million among our fifteen billion. Of course you'll fall for it. You can't help yourselves. When you realize what's happening, you won't be able to stop, you'll be hooked. I don't think you'll even be able to resent it.*

You'll be assimilated, Mierna. You'll become an Earth girl. Naturally, you'll grow up to be one of our leaders. You'll contribute tremendous things to our civilization, and be rewarded accordingly. But the whole point is, it will be our civilization. Mine . . . and yours.

I wonder if you'll ever miss the forest, though, and the little houses by the bay, and the boats and songs

*and old, old stories, yes, and your darling oontatherium.
I know the empty planet will miss you, Mierna. So
will I.*

"Come on," I said. "Let's go build us that breakfast."

Poul Anderson

Five-time Hugo Winner
Three-time Nebula Winner

DAVID DRAKE

●●●●●●●●●●●●●●●●●●●●●●●●●●

C.M. Kornbluth

Best-Selling Science Fiction from TOR